"TO CUT SUCH BEAUTIFUL HAIR WOULD BE A PITY."

Jorge's tone was sardonic, but the curve of his lips deepened as he said, "Come here."

Tara shivered as she obeyed him. She was alone with this man on a deserted island. "Well, I'll have to cut it if these tangles get much worse," she replied breathlessly.

Without another word Jorge sat her down and with lean brown fingers started combing out her waist-length ebony tresses.

The feeling was heavenly. As Tara relaxed a languorous warmth stole through her body. She hadn't realized Jorge could be so gentle! It was almost as if he were making love to her....

Her eyes flew open, to meet the dark glowing look in his. Tension crackled between them, then his mouth covered hers in a burning kiss.

AND NOW...

SUPERROMANCES

Worldwide Library is proud to present a
sensational new series of modern love stories—
SUPERROMANCES

Written by masters of the genre, these longer,
sensuous and dramatic novels are truly in keeping
with today's changing life-styles. Full of intriguing
conflicts, the heartaches and delights of true love,
SUPERROMANCES are absorbing stories—
satisfying and sophisticated reading that lovers
of romance fiction have long been waiting for.

SUPERROMANCES
Contemporary love stories for the woman of today!

CHRISTINE HELLA COTT

MIDNIGHT MAGIC

A SUPERROMANCE FROM

WORLDWIDE

TORONTO · LONDON · NEW YORK · SYDNEY

Published, July 1982

First printing May 1982

ISBN 0-373-70022-9

CHAPTER ONE

TARA SAT IN THE WINDOW SEAT listening to her mother and watching her fidget with the lacy curtains. Her mother fussed with the bedspread, too, and with the cushions. She picked up a necklace from the vanity and dropped it; she rearranged the perfume bottles. And all the while Tara just sat and watched, and listened with only half a mind to her mother's busy remonstrations. The velour of Tara's blue gray dress was tucked around her feet. Her long black hair fell in a shining cascade over one slender shoulder and down past the seductive curve of a round breast; her hands, long and delicate, were curled passively in her lap.

Mrs. Lownes's own hands were fluttering up to pat agitatedly at her coiffure. Tara knew that gesture by heart; it meant that her mother was steaming herself for a major fuss. If possible, that had to be avoided. For a fleeting moment the young woman looked down at her own calm fingers and realized it was true—she wasn't excited about getting married. All the dither about a woman's wedding day being the most important day of her life was nonsense, nonsense invented by hysterical old ladies. Many people believed it, however, and her mother was one of them. But then her mother believed in love at first sight, too, whereas Tara knew it happened only in fairy tales. Real love was more a companionship than the hectic, passionate, starry-eyed thing most people expected. It was no wonder there were so many disappointed people around, Tara decided. She sighed, and in one lithe fluid movement swung her feet off the window seat.

"Mom, there are still five weeks to go!" she said placatingly. "How long does it take to see the minister, arrange a rehearsal and choose a few dresses?"

"Choose a few dresses!" Her mother was aghast. "It's going to take weeks for Madame Deperé to make your wedding gown! You *do* want Venetian lace, don't you? This is important!"

"Of course it is." Tara did her best to sound soothing. "I just have this feeling in my bones that today isn't the right day—"

"How can you talk of bones at a time like this! You *are* in love with Dennis, aren't you?" Mrs. Lownes was once again pulling nervously at the perfection of waves lying against her flushed cheek.

Tara put a comforting arm around her mother's shoulders, evading the question with a smile. "Mom, don't worry! I'll talk to Yvonna today about her bridesmaid's dress. She should be home from the hairdresser's by now...."

Usually quick to recover, Mrs. Lownes released a long nervous sigh and then smiled weakly. All was right with her world again. "I have to go to my art gallery opening at three," she said. "Do you want a lift to Yvonna's?"

Her hands were now resting calmly in the pockets of her Dior day dress, the colors of which were a perfect match for her ash-brown hair and blue eyes. She didn't look a day over thirty, a study in soft browns and blues and pinks. Tara, looking at her guiltily, felt suddenly moody and restive, unfulfilled—things she knew her mother never felt. Life for Mrs. Lownes was a smooth path of contentment, interrupted only by short bursts of concern induced by her husband, her daughter or the art gallery committee.

"Uh, no." Tara hurried to end the pause that had stretched out too long. "I want to pick up a few things, so I'll take my own car...."

But when Mrs. Lownes left the house shortly afterward, Tara was curled up again on the window seat in her room, her dark smoky eyes shadowed as they gazed out at the gray, misty afternoon. The London fog was heavy for spring, but Tara watched with gloomy satisfaction as it shrouded the immense oaks that lined the street, house after elegant house fading from view. She didn't want to see Hampstead. She didn't want to see their street. And most of all she didn't want to see one particular house—Brackenhill. But as she stared out the window, as if on cue the fog parted, and Brackenhill's pointed green roof and two chimney pots came starkly into view.

Brackenhill.... It fit right into the row of imposing residences. Everyone loved it. Her mother called it a honeymoon house. Janette Moreston, Dennis's mother, said it was the "sweetest thing in four walls." Dennis said it would give him the right image. And in a few short weeks she would be living there. With Dennis.

Shivering suddenly, Tara punched the plump red velvet cushion she'd been leaning against. She willed the fog to enclose Brackenhill. *Mrs. Dennis Moreston. Tara Moreston.* Her mind flew backward in time....

Dennis had been the proverbial boy next door. If someone had told Tara when she was ten that one day she would marry Dennis Moreston, she would have denounced that person as a traitor and made him suffer the consequences. And Tara had always fought her own battles, often with such vigor that even her father was dismayed. Mrs. Moreston had on more than one occasion called her a little demon. With her father's adventuresome spirit and an audacity inherited from her grandmother, Tara had always been in some scrape or other. Once, pretending to be a chimney sweep, she even got stuck in the flue. It had taken the Hampstead fire department to get her out, and when she'd finally arrived, black as a coal sack, on her mother's peacock hearth rug, the visiting neighbor had shrieked, "Send her away to boarding school; they'll tame her there! Thank goodness my *Dennis* knows how to behave!"

Tara could have told Mrs. Moreston a string of nasty stories about her precious Dennis. But she prided herself on not being a snitch, and so had kept her sooty lips shut over Dennis's most recent bad behavior. The day before he had forcibly tied her to a branch overhanging a small stream in which, he said, he had let loose sixty-three piranha. Tara had believed him, for the prank was in keeping with his character, and his weekly allowance was large enough to back up his claim. She had hung there precariously for ages before her best friend, Yvonna, had rescued her. In retaliation Tara had exercised blackmail, and had extracted most of Dennis's next week's allowance, with plans for annexing the following week's, as well.

Of course, both Mrs. Moreston and Mrs. Lownes now maintained that she and Dennis had been childhood sweethearts, but that was a figment of their imaginations. Tara had despised him heartily, and hadn't liked him much better years later when he left to go to Oxford. By the time he graduated from university, Tara had graduated from her private elite girls' school. But when Dennis returned home Tara had already gone abroad with her father....

Then had come two years of bliss, Tara thought dreamily, sighing as memories wrapped around her. As often happened, the wild and lonely *serras* of southern Portugal were vivid in her mind. She could still see the vibrant colors: the ochers and the brilliant lemon yellows, the towering rusty-red cliffs. She could almost smell the dusty spicy aroma of sagebrush and juniper. She had felt so alive then, so invigorated.

So what was the matter with her now, she wondered restlessly. Why did all her days melt into monotony, one after the other ad infinitum? She shrugged her shoulders.

Professor Matthew Lownes, her much adored father, had required firsthand information for a set of history novels he was planning to write. That was why he and Tara had traveled through Europe together. His wife, Lillian, who couldn't bear the thought of extensive travel, had preferred to stay at home with her council meetings, her art gallery functions and charity drives.

The research finally complete, the travelers had returned to Hampstead in time to celebrate Tara's twentieth birthday. That was when she'd met Dennis Moreston again.

His father had died a few months earlier, and the family resort/real estate business now rested solely on the young man's shoulders. Although Tara wondered how Dennis managed to fit any work into his busy social schedule, his business seemed to be doing very well. His mother never stopped talking about his wizardry and his financial acumen. And he had changed, Tara found. He was charming and sophisticated—actually handsome. His broad athletic shoulders and his cool knowing smile had all the girls aflutter. Dennis was considered an excellent catch by the mothers in the neighborhood, her own mother included.

It seemed natural for Tara and Dennis to strike up a casual friendship, for they went to the same round of balls, parties, race meetings and charity fetes. One thing led to another, and barely three months after arriving home from abroad, Tara found herself engaged.

Almost everyone thought they made a perfect couple. Dennis decided on a long engagement, a vague "couple of years," and Tara never thought to question why. She had actually been pleased with the nebulous, far-off date, although she never stopped to question that, either. So for the past two years her life had been filled with parties and more parties, one high-flying social whirl.

Tara bit her lip in a stab of frustration. Her two years of grace were almost over. In one week it would be her twenty-second birthday, and she would receive the inheritance left her by Grandmother Lownes. A month later she would be married.

June bride. Pure inexplicable panic flared up in her at the thought. Her ebony-lashed eyes, slightly tilted at the corners, filled with dark shadows as she stared out at Brackenhill.

Several months earlier a slight feeling of doubt had crept beneath the blasé manner she had learned from her friends. That feeling had grown daily, until now it was too large to rationalize away. The time of reckoning had come at long last. She had to think things through; had to face her inner disquiet instead of shying away from it.

She sighed and jumped off the window seat, then began pacing around her room like an animal in the confines of a cage. It was all so incredibly complicated! What should she do—delay the wedding? Her mother would have one of her anxiety attacks, and her friends would all snigger at her. Wasn't Dennis *the* catch, after all?

Her eyes fell on the bright cover of a book that lay on her desk in the alcove. In her present turmoil the cover seemed to laugh at her. It was one of her own books, *Toodles, the Bear with a Bad Case of Big*

Nose. During the past year and a half she'd begun writing children's stories out of sheer boredom. She enjoyed the work, even though her friends lifted their eyebrows when she told them about it. Her third effort, the *Toodles* book, had actually been published, and now royalties were trickling in. Two others had since been accepted.

Her publishing success was the most exciting thing that had happened to Tara during the past two years, but Dennis, like the others, didn't seem interested. As far as she knew he hadn't bothered to read her first book in print, although he could have done so in half an hour.

Tara shook her head in despair and growing panic. Her thick, coal-black hair fell forward on either side of her face like a heavy silk curtain. She had only five weeks left. Why did this massive doubt have to rear up now like some ludicrous jack-in-the-box? Ignoring it didn't make it go away, she knew. But even when she faced it squarely she couldn't make it vanish! And Dennis—her stomach rolled over as she remembered—was coming home today.

THAT EVENING when Dennis came to dinner, Mrs. Lownes was so pleased to have him back from Edinburgh that she forgot to ask about Yvonna's bridesmaid's dress. Tara, silently grateful, made no mention of her distressing afternoon. She did grow anxious when the conversation turned to Mrs. Lownes's gallery opening and her father asked if she'd attended. For a moment Tara felt trapped. If she said no, her father would naturally ask what she had done instead.

She would have to tell him the truth, for he always knew when she was lying. But if she explained that she'd done nothing all afternoon but sit in her window seat, her mother would have a nervous attack right there at the table. Then Tara would have to explain why she hadn't gone to see Yvonna; and how could she possibly do that in front of everyone, right in the middle of dinner?

She was feeling incredibly guilty and tongue-tied when her eyes lighted upon their butler, Arthur. He answered her beseeching look with a barely perceptible wink, then very convincingly remembered a message for Professor Lownes from a member of the university board of directors. His timely intrusion changed the subject effectively, and Tara breathed a sigh of relief as she gave Arthur a casual but grateful smile. The butler's only acknowledgment was an expression even more bland than usual as he ladled out the lobster bisque.

During the rest of the dinner Tara watched Dennis covertly, searching for answers to the questions that hammered in her mind. Her fiancé was his usual suave and debonair self. But she eventually noticed that her father was also watching Dennis, and that he seemed to be puzzled by what he saw.

Tara's doubt, far from abating as she had hoped, expanded instead. It even persisted into the evening, as she and Dennis seated themselves at a table in his favorite nightclub. La Valbonne, situated between Piccadilly and Carnaby Street, was a popular spot. She had wanted to go someplace where it would be easier to talk, but when she suggested a change of plans Dennis vetoed it. What would their friends think if they didn't show up, he had asked her cheerfully.

He was in exceptionally high spirits that night. As Tara listened to him gossiping with Yvonna she decided his business trip to Edinburgh must have been very successful. He had been up north for three weeks. But never before had business caused him to be so elated... and something else, she mused. Could it be *nervous*? Dennis was never nervous! He had what she considered an overdose of self-confidence. Other girls admired it, although it sometimes irritated Tara. As it had when he had decorated their house, Brackenhill.

He had made all the decisions himself, to the point of telling her what the color schemes would be once he had chosen them. When she protested, he said he knew what was right for them; he knew the best interior decorator; he knew what sort of image he wanted to convey. To confer with his future wife never occurred to him. Of course she would like the results....

At the time Tara had shrugged off her irritation as unimportant. Her world-weary attitude had blinded her. But now that she was thinking for herself his high-handedness triggered a fresh stab of outrage.

Perhaps she should suggest postponing the wedding for another month, Tara thought, tracing a pattern on the nightclub table with one manicured fingernail. She needed more time to think things out. Perhaps they should just forget the whole idea! Now that it was only five weeks away, marriage didn't seem wonderful anymore. She just didn't feel certain about anything....

When their friends were finally out of earshot on the dance floor, Dennis turned to her. He seldom danced himself, so he didn't ask her to now. Colored lights played over the bodies gyrating to the jungle beat, the music reverberating off the walls and through Tara's head. She kept her eyes trained on the elaborate water fountain at the head of the dance floor, knowing that soon, and as if out of nowhere, a girl in a silver-sequined bikini would appear, to dance voluptuously amid the colored sprays of water. Dennis bent farther across the table to catch her attention.

"Soon, Tara, darling, very soon your family won't be the richest on the block any longer!"

At Tara's taken-aback expression and slightly raised eyebrows he chortled, "Once the government passes that rezoning bill my latest venture will be complete! And greasing one well-placed pocket should hurry that along nicely! A perfect bit of business if I do say so myself! I'll be something of a King Midas!"

He meant to make his words amusing, Tara saw, but the gloating look on his face dispelled all humor. She recoiled inwardly. His glittering eyes made her feel even more doubtful than she had all day. Determined not to show her distaste, she leaned forward to speak over the thumping music.

"What do you mean, greasing a pocket? Dennis, isn't that bribery? Isn't that illegal?"

"Oh, heavens—" he shrugged a negligent shoulder

"—it's just a minor rezoning law! And that's all I'm going to tell you. You're to keep your pretty nose out of it!" He laughed, sounding satisfied. His pale brown eyes gleamed knowingly in the dim light as they traveled slowly down her slender neck to the firm rounded outline of her breasts. Tara tried to ignore his obvious look.

"I don't want you involved in my work," he continued. "In fact, darling, I forbid you to meddle. I want that understood right now! That goes for the traveling end of it, too. You won't be coming on any business trips; you'll stay home where you belong. Women and business don't mix." He flicked the ashes off his cigarette, and most of them missed the ashtray to spatter onto the varnished tabletop.

For a few fleeting seconds Tara stared at the scattered ashes. Dennis was usually so fastidious. It was as though the ashes were a key in her mind, opening the door to something she'd sensed all evening but hadn't actually realized until now. Her fiancé was different somehow. His charm wasn't quite in place. And he'd never said such things before, even though his slightly supercilious tone was certainly familiar. Did he have to be so...so pompous, she wondered. She swung her head around to face him, sending silky strands of black hair over her shoulder.

"But Dennis, you can't be serious!"

"No, buts, my lovely," was his astounding rejoinder. "A wife abides by her husband's wishes." His voice grated on her ears as he went on. "And that reminds me of those books of yours. I don't want all of London thinking that you write for money. Consider my image, darling!''

For a moment Tara couldn't believe her ears. This was definitely not the man she was accustomed to—or was it? "But Dennis!" she cried, unaware that several people were looking their way, attracted by her distraught voice. "I don't write for the money! I love doing it, I—"

"You're supposed to be loving *me*." His tone was offhand, as though they were discussing nothing more important than the weather.

"But what am I going to do? If I'm not allowed to travel with you and not allowed to write, am I to spend all my time with housework?" Angry sarcasm tinged her voice.

"Housework? Honestly, what would people think? I've already engaged a cook and a maid. They're a nice couple, and they'll do until—"

"Then just what are your plans for me?" Tara interrupted in a rather grim quiet tone. Her dark eyes flashed warning signals that were scarcely veiled by her thick black lashes. His remark about her writing had hurt. She bit viciously into the fullness of her bottom lip to stem the bubble of angry words, to stop the sudden bewilderment that swamped her. Was this the real Dennis, the man she'd glimpsed from time to time but had never really got to know?

"Why, darling, you'll have plenty to do! Parties, balls, charity fetes, functions. You'll have to entertain my friends and clients, and frankly, I want them to be envious of both my home and my wife. It helps. Then, of course," he continued in a lighter tone, "you'll have to make my martinis when I come home—and don't forget there's the marriage bed for you to keep warm!" Dennis gave her a grin.

Tara flinched. The marriage bed to warm, as though it were one of her duties! This new revealing side of her fiancé she didn't even like, much less love. . . .

Dennis eventually noticed her lack of response. He disliked silences and hurried to fill this one. He ordered more drinks from a waitress in a white leather loin cloth and halter top, smiling at her provocatively. Then he switched the smile to Tara, caught her hand and kissed all fingers one by one.

"Darling, where's your gorgeous smile? Why all the gloom? Thinking about the marriage bed?" He grinned again. "You're such an innocent, darling, and it's so out-of-date! Never mind—" his voice dropped to a murmur "—I'll enjoy making you respond with more than your usual rather, er, frosty ardor. And what fun it will be to melt all that ice!" His eyes burned, and yet to Tara his look felt cold as it slid down her slight but feminine shape, dwelling overlong and hungrily on the plunging neckline of her silk blouse.

The waitress returned, saving her from having to formulate an answer. Her whole body felt flushed, and she leaned forward so that her waist-length hair hid her mortification. She took a few sips of cognac, needing time to steady her nerves. *Being in love means sharing, not "making you respond"!* a voice inside her cried. Even Dennis's lovemaking was part of the facade, his "image." But why, if he didn't care for her, did he want to marry her? And was he aware that he wasn't being his usual self?

What a fool she'd been to become engaged to him—a complete fool not to realize sooner that a match between them would never work out. Make martinis and warm the marriage bed.... That was no basis for a successful relationship! She stared at his hands, which were resting on the table, and shuddered at the thought of them holding her. All her doubts *were* real; it wasn't just a case of cold feet. She and Dennis Moreston had nothing in common, especially not after what he had just said. She now had a clearer insight into his character. In his world there wasn't room for two. There was only room for Dennis—for his wishes, his desires, his money, his *image*. How sick she was of hearing that word!

Because of her own stupidity she had almost married a man she might come to loathe, Tara thought, berating herself. She'd been floating along on a cloud where nothing was serious or important, and he was part of that cloud. Tara stared distractedly at his hands. They were very much like her present existence—pampered and colorless. She was so used to being bored, as her friends were, that it had become second nature. She realized then with sharp clarity that she'd stopped thinking for herself and had drifted along with the crowd, with Dennis's suggestions. No wonder life was dull! If she had stopped to consider only for a moment, she would have realized long before this how wrong her engagement was. To think she might have gone on, might actually have married the man! Beads of perspiration broke out on her brow at her narrow escape.

"Just a week till your birthday—right, darling?" Dennis grinned, watching the dancers around them. "You'll be a rich girl then. Not everyone gets two hundred and fifty thousand pounds, eighteen shillings and tuppence on their twenty-second birthday! I'm surprised the old dear didn't leave her fortune to an occult society!" He broke into an amused chuckle. "Why do you suppose she picked your twenty-second birthday. Why not the twenty-first? She *was* an odd bird, wasn't she?"

Tara looked at him levelly, feeling as though he were an insect she was about to dissect. She had adored her grandmother, and Dennis was heaping insult onto injury. He didn't know when to stop! She opened her mouth, but after a second of reflection closed it again. If this conversation went any further she was going to throw her cognac in his face!

For the first time that evening Dennis did notice something was amiss. His eyes narrowed as he took in Tara's pale set face. The tension that already existed between them flared up, a hard tangible force. Time stood still for Tara as his eyes met hers in a silent clash of wills. At that moment their friends returned in a rush from the dance floor, and Dennis rapidly embroiled himself in the high-spirited conversation around them.

Tara settled back in her chair and returned to her own thoughts. So he'd even remembered the tuppence! That surprised her, for they never talked

about the money. The only other time it had been
mentioned between them was at their engagement,
and then, too, he had been the one to bring it up...
and he had been the one to decide not to marry until
the inheritance was hers. Was that why he wanted
her? For her wealth?

It couldn't be, she realized at once. His mother
was always boasting about how well he did finan-
cially. He boasted, too. And he never seemed to suffer any shortage of funds. He drove the latest
Jaguar sports model, bought only the finest and
most expensive clothes. Often he picked up the entire tab when they went out with a group, no matter
how many friends were with them.... She glanced
over and noticed that Dennis was twisting his
diamond-studded signet ring round and round on
his finger. He really *was* nervous, then, although no
sign of worry showed on his smooth urbane face.
The reason must have to do with his land transac-
tion deal in Edinburgh, Tara reflected. Money was
the only thing important enough to cause him anxiety. Was he worried about that rezoning law being
passed? Was he counting his chickens before they
hatched? The matter of the bribe preyed uncomfortably on her mind.

Could that be why he'd been showing her another
face? In his anxiety had he momentarily forgotten to
be charming? She watched him joking with Yvonna,
his good humor once again firmly intact. Perhaps she
was the only one of their friends who'd seen his other
side, Tara decided—the cold calculating side that reduced her to a...a mere possession, a chattel that

made martinis, impressed his friends and warmed the marriage bed!

And a chattel that just happened to come with two hundred fifty thousand pounds! Perhaps her inheritance wasn't the sole reason for his wanting to marry her, but she was sure now that it was a major consideration. If he was having problems in Edinburgh.... She remembered the way his eyes had glittered when he'd joked about being King Midas, the way he'd all but licked his lips when mentioning her inheritance. She should have realized long before this evening how much wealth meant to him.

The evening wore on and on. Her friends were positively bent on being cheerful, Tara thought, watching them with sober eyes. To her the endless jokes and teasing were meaningless, a rerun from the last party. Didn't anyone ever think of anything new to talk about?

An attractive man a few tables away caught her eye and smiled invitingly. It was obvious to him she couldn't wait to leave the nightclub, so why wasn't it obvious to Dennis? She glanced for the umpteenth time at the expensive digital watch on her wrist; it had been Dennis's last birthday present to her. With relief she finally heard Yvonna saying she was tired and wanted to go home. Out of the corner of her eye she saw the scantily clad waitress approaching with their bill.

It was at that exact moment that Dennis pulled Tara to her feet, insisting on a dance. A quick glance over her shoulder showed their friends staring after them in surprise.

DENNIS LEFT EARLY the next morning for Edinburgh. When he'd brought her home after their evening out he had promised to meet her the following day to talk. But instead he left town with no word and no message.

A day went by and Tara tried to get in touch with him. She telephoned his hotel and his office, but continually got the same prim answer: Mr. Moreston was unavailable at the moment, but would be informed of her call. He was terribly busy, she reasoned, trying to be fair, but when the second day passed and he still hadn't returned her call she knew he was avoiding her.

Each day that passed meant another delay in calling off the wedding. Now, finally, her crowd would have something new to talk about, Tara thought as she hung up the receiver in frustration one more time.

When Dennis's secretary telephoned two days later to say that he would be home the following day, Friday, and that he was looking forward to seeing his "darling fiancée" again, Tara could have choked with indignation.

She was also beginning to feel apprehensive about the effect her change of plans would have. First Dennis, then her parents, then Janette Moreston would have to be faced. And Dennis, she knew now, would be furious—if only because she was going against his wishes.

The secretary telephoned again on Friday to say that Mr. Moreston would be delayed. And, the prim voice continued, since Tara's cousin, Penny, was coming down to London for Tara's birthday party, she and Mr. Moreston would be traveling together. They should arrive late Saturday afternoon.

Tara had been so preoccupied with her own worries that she'd completely forgotten about Penny Reed, or Penelope, as her cousin preferred to be called. Penny had been invited to Tara's birthday party months before.

Tara sighed, resignedly hanging up the phone. Although Penny was only a year younger, they had never been close friends. They shared few interests and had nothing in common. There wasn't even a family resemblance, except for one small thing: their voices were very similar. Over the phone no one was able to tell them apart. This quirk of nature had aided them in childhood pranks, but Tara was often glad that many miles separated London and Edinburgh, where her relatives lived. Whenever Aunt Dorothy and her mother came together the tension in the air quickly became unbearable, and Penny didn't help matters.

All Saturday Tara prepared for Dennis's arrival, rehearsing what she would say to him. The day passed in an agony of slowness, and the afternoon came and went, showing no sign of the two travelers.

It was past midnight when Penny came giggling up the front stairs. Dennis didn't stop in, but drove his car straight home, and Tara saw the garage lights next door wink on and then off again. When she dutifully pecked her cousin on the cheek she couldn't help but notice the strong smell of liquor on the younger girl's breath, and after watching her wriggle out of her white mink jacket and walk unsteadily into the living room, she realized Penny was not just tipsy, she was drunk. Obviously she and Dennis had stopped for refreshment, and Penny, at least, had had more than her share.

Tara knew Dennis never turned down a drink, and for what she had to say she wanted him sober. She would have to wait until tomorrow after her party— or worse, the following day—before talking to him. It seemed that once she made up her mind, everything managed to conspire against her.

CHAPTER TWO

AT SUNDAY MORNING BRUNCH Tara noticed her mother's manner toward Penny was very stiff. Mrs. Lownes was incensed at the hour Penny and Dennis had arrived, and thought her daughter's lack of appetite was due to jealousy. Tara knew her mother would gladly send Penny packing, and at that thought a bit of her sense of humor returned. In consequence she felt more charitable toward her cousin when, after brunch, Penny followed her up to her bedroom, chattering incessantly.

"Isn't it funny that our birthdays are only two weeks apart—although, you know, I'd hate to share a birthday with anyone." Penny arched her back and surveyed the effect in the mirror with an approving smile. "Now that I'm going to be twenty-one in only two weeks I hope people will take me seriously when I tell them I want to be called Penelope. It sounds more grown-up, don't you think?"

She giggled and turned to view herself from another angle. "Everyone is always telling me what a smashing figure I have, but I want to be taken *seriously*! And when you look like I do, well, the boys don't want to be serious at all— Oh, did you know my mother's asked your mother if I can have my birthday party here?'' she rushed on. "I want a polo party, I think.... Won't that be just fab? And you'll never believe what mom and dad are giving me for my birthday! You'll go green! A month's cruise on the *Adventure Star*!'' Penny paused dramatically. "You know, *the* cruise ship? The one all the celebrities go on? It took just months to get my reservation, and do you know who's going to be on board...?''

Penny talked all the way through Tara's shower, and although Tara couldn't make out every word over the noise of the spray, she said "yes" and "uh-huh" whenever there was a pregnant pause.

For the first of May the weather was exceptionally warm and sunny. At the last minute, therefore, Mrs. Lownes arranged for the caterers to serve the light afternoon refreshments out in the large garden, much to Arthur's consternation. He liked to keep an eye on everything, but couldn't do so when the party was spread out all over the house and grounds. The older guests weren't expected until shortly before dinner, which would, of course, be served in the very large and elegant dining room under the butler's approving eye.

Tara crossed to her bedroom window to look down over the garden, then grinned. Given the change of plans, her mother had outdone herself. Delicate wrought-iron tables groaned under masses of flowers and delectable-looking food. Silver goblets stood like toy soldiers in neat rows, glinting in the noon sun. The goblets had been passed down from Grandmother Lownes and were invariably used outdoors, since

Lillian Lownes never allowed one of her crystal glasses to roam more than ten feet or so from its velvet-lined rosewood cabinet.

Potted palms and roses climbing on elaborate arched trellises made canopies for the tables, and Tara wondered how much such a bountiful display had set her mother back, her mind boggling at the thought. The gazebo looked equally festive, with garlands of flowers hanging from the eaves. It was furnished with bridge tables, and a small bar stood in the center.

The ordinarily beautiful garden was transformed into a fairy-tale dream, and Tara all but expected Dennis to arrive on a white charger. The only thing missing from the party was a real Prince Charming.... Tara shook her head to dispel such wishful notions. Now that she was through with Dennis it would be a long time before she showed any interest in the opposite sex!

The first of her friends arrived as Tara finished dressing. She heard the doorbell as she gave a last spray of cologne to her wrists. She was about to go downstairs when her mother hurried into her room.

"Oh, dear, you'll make such a beautiful bride!" The older woman's blue eyes filled with tears as she gazed proudly at her daughter. "And tomorrow we really must choose your wedding dress! That's what I came up to tell you. I know I'll be so lonely! It's a good thing you're only moving down the street." She dabbed at her eyes with a lacy perfumed handkerchief, kissed Tara on both cheeks, then held her at arm's length. "You have excellent taste for a girl who

doesn't care much about clothes! Now I must run! I
have to see about the punch. You know how caterers
are, and Arthur isn't getting along with them.'' She
was gone before her daughter could reply.

Tara gazed doubtfully at her reflection in the mirror. A beautiful bride? Her poor mother would be
heartbroken when she found out there wasn't going
to be a wedding, after all.

And she didn't look like a bride anyway, Tara decided. Brides were supposed to be blond with blue
eyes and luscious figures, like Penny. Her own pitch-
black, straight, waist-length hair hardly suited Venetian lace. Her dark eyes, large and wide spaced,
resembled her father's, with the same heavy fringe of
spiky lashes. No hint of blue there. Tara had his
creamy olive skin, too, which tanned rapidly; a small
straight nose; soft rounded lips; and an oval face.
Thank goodness she inherited her mother's pointed
chin instead of her father's square clefted one. But
she was glad she had his upright carriage, and that
her long legs made her tall, taller than her mother, in
fact. All in all, despite its slim curving lines, her
figure wasn't half as eye-catching as Penny's. But the
deep red silk sheath she wore did flatter her, Tara
had to admit. Its wide shoulder straps and two side
slits made her look better than usual.... Or maybe it
was the fact that she would soon be free that made
her feel so good.

When Tara strolled out onto the wide expanse of
garden lawn a number of her friends were already
gathered there, and the party was in full swing. Some
of the young men had gathered to play croquet, and

in the gazebo girls were immersed in a game of bridge. From the squeals Tara deduced that Barbie had been caught cheating again. Those who weren't involved in the games were lounging in the comfortable chaises, sipping tea, punch or champagne and gossiping as usual. Over to one side Penny was charming more than her share of young males, giggling and wriggling and getting malicious stares from hard female eyes for her efforts. Laughter, an animated argument from the croquet players and continuing squeals from the gazebo mingled with the clink of silver goblets and tea cups as Arthur fussily directed the caterers' men here and there among the guests. Tara stopped to pop a grape into her mouth before joining the throng. She had had no idea she had so many friends. How her mother had found all these people was beyond her.

"Darling!" Dennis swooped down on her from the crowd in the gazebo. His arm went possessively around her shoulders, and he stooped to plant a deliberate kiss on her mouth. The next thing she knew he was fastening a chunky, solid-silver bracelet around her wrist and murmuring, "Happy birthday" in her ear. "You're more lovely every day!" he added.

"I hated every minute away from you, darling! Did you miss me?" he demanded loudly, as if for the benefit of those who were watching. Tara noticed that Penny was among them.

How could he speak with such conviction when they both knew it was an act, Tara wondered, laughing but saying nothing. She would have to tell him tonight, before the hoax continued any longer!

At dinnertime when the older set arrived, the party moved indoors, and after dinner there was dancing. For the occasion Mrs. Lownes had managed to engage a small classical revue as well as a rock-'n'-roll band from the university, so everyone's taste was satisfied. Again Tara thought somewhat guiltily of the expense and wished she could enjoy the party as her mother meant her to. In terms of society parties she knew it was a smashing success.

Dennis stayed by her side all afternoon and sat beside her during dinner. He was the most attentive of fiancés, charming everyone, especially her mother, who was so pleased she forgot to continue being so distant with Penny. But after one token dance Tara suddenly found Dennis gone. She danced with her father, then with a succession of friends, and still Dennis hadn't returned. She fervently hoped he hadn't disappeared for good. Perhaps he'd slipped out into the garden for a breath of fresh air. As she thought of it, Tara decided to do so herself. It would be nice to have a few minutes alone to prepare for the ordeal ahead.

She slipped away unnoticed. The garden was cool and sweet in the gentle spring night. No sign remained of the many tables and chairs; the caterers had vanished indoors along with their paraphernalia, including the trellised roses. Only a few couples wandered around beneath the shadowed trees and Chinese lanterns.

Tara headed for a secluded corner that had often served as her thinking spot. She was about to pass through the blooming forsythia shrubs that hid the entrance, when the sound of low voices stopped her. Disappointed, she hesitated for a second, wondering where to go. Then she recognized Dennis's voice.

Curiosity made her peep through the bushes, and there before her astonished eyes were Dennis and Penny, locked in a heated embrace. They were making full use of the corner's seclusion, and Tara deduced that he and Penny must be well acquainted. Suddenly it occurred to her how much time he'd recently spent in Edinburgh. In four weeks a lot could happen. It obviously had.

Tara left much more quickly than she'd arrived. Up in her bedroom she sank down onto her bed in confusion. Her first real thought after witnessing that passionate scene was one of blessed relief. It would be so much easier now to call the engagement off! Dennis would be as willing as she was, and now there would be no talk of last-minute jilting!

No sooner had she rejoined the party than Dennis was at her side again. Tara expected some change in his manner. Surely he wouldn't keep up the pretense after what had happened! But he did. If anything, he seemed more loving and more in love with her than ever before. He gazed at her fondly, insisted on keeping his arm around her waist, whispered sweet nothings in her ear like an infatuated schoolboy.

At first Tara was curious. How could he kiss Penny one minute and treat her this way the next? If she hadn't seen what had happened in the garden she would never have believed this was an act. But as Dennis grew more and more amorous she began to feel nothing but outraged disgust, and when he tried to kiss her ardently in front of everyone she just managed to brush him off. He had not changed his mind about their marriage. That was abundantly clear. But why? Why? He tried to kiss her a second time, and again Tara managed to evade him without seeming too obvious about it. Over his shoulder she caught Penny's eyes on them. Her cousin was smiling maliciously.

Finally the party was over. Mrs. Lownes was flushed and excited with the success of it all, and she and Janette Moreston were busily comparing notes. Penny was still saying goodbye to some young man when Tara decided it was now or never, do or die.

"Dennis, could we go into the garden for a moment?" she suggested in a low voice, smiling up at him. He looked at her in surprise, but when she tugged at his arm he came willingly enough.

She led the way to the same secluded corner before she said anything more. As they slipped through the forsythia shrubs she noticed that her fiancé looked slightly uncomfortable as he glanced at her. Then his manner changed completely.

"What is it, darling?" he asked smoothly, flashing the smile that made most women of his acquaintance weaken. "Want to get me alone? Is your frost melting already?" He flicked away his cigarette and reached for her.

Tara sidestepped him. "Not quite, Dennis." She went right to the point in a crisp, no-nonsense tone. "I'm not in love with you. You're not in love with me. It would be a mistake for us to get married, so I want to call the whole thing off!"

"What are you talking about?" he demanded, his voice suddenly three times as loud. "We're getting married, and that's that!"

"No! Our engagement is off. Finished! Why would you possibly want to marry me when it's so obvious you don't care for me? No, please don't answer. I don't think I want to know." She reached out to drop her engagement ring into his hand, but he pulled away. The large diamond fell into the grass, where it lay glinting like some evil eye. Tara left it there. "We're finished. I'm serious."

"Like hell you are! No...no bitch is going to jilt me!"

"This one is! There's nothing between us!" she cried. "Marriage takes a lot more than either of us is willing to give—my idea of marriage anyway. I wouldn't enjoy spending my life impressing your friends!"

"Don't you look down your nose at me! Don't wave your blue blood in my face! Isn't Brackenhill good enough for you?"

He was practically incoherent, beside himself with rage. Looking at his clenched fists, Tara felt a prickle of fear. She struggled to keep her voice calm as she answered, "Since I didn't have a hand in decorating Brackenhill, I'm sure any bride you pick wouldn't mind living there. In fact, I'm confident my replacement won't mind at all!" As those last words sprang out Tara felt immediate regret. She didn't want him to know she'd seen him with Penny; didn't want him to think that jealousy was the reason for her decision. But he pounced on her words.

"What do you mean by that?" His pale brown eyes narrowed as they glared at her. Tara didn't answer. In the dim light of the Chinese lanterns she saw him flush. "Who are you to talk?" he went on. "You.... You're as cold as a fish! So what *about* your replacement? And all the others, whom I'm sure somebody's told you about! Probably the oh so pious Yvonna! If you'd been as accommodating.... But no, not you! You're as old-fashioned as they come! Or maybe you don't have desires. Maybe you're frigid, Miss Lownes. How about that?"

"Oh, stop it!" Tara retorted. "I don't care about any others! I don't care, because I don't love you. You have affairs because you don't love me. So what more is there to say? Goodbye, Dennis."

"No!" he spat out, reaching for her.

Her eyes widening, Tara took a quick step backward. With a gasp she held out the chunky bracelet and her watch, dangling them in front of her. He snatched them away, throwing them down on the grass beside the winking diamond. As he determinedly reached for her again she was forced to take another step backward.

"I don't want to talk to you, I don't want to touch you and I *don't* want to marry you!" Tara enunciated, her voice charged with a crackling emotion. She stared at him for a distressed second, then turned on her heel and started running for all she was worth.

All the way across the wide lawn she never once bothered to turn around to see what Dennis was doing. She was through with him, and it was a sweet relief. A potent sense of peace welled up within her, pushing out her previous distress. Despite her panting breath, she wondered how she could feel so calm after breaking off an engagement. It was painfully obvious from her reaction that it had never been important to her.

She went directly to the library, where her parents were having their habitual nightcap. Just one more ordeal to go through and it would all be over!

"Mom, dad...." Her voice faltered as she saw the eager expression on her mother's face. Then, summoning strength, she plunged in. "The engagement is off. Dennis and I aren't going to get married."

To Tara's surprise her father looked intensely relieved. Her mother, however, seemed stunned beyond words, her hands trembling as her agitation increased. Tara ran to her and dropped down beside the chair. "Please, mom! Don't get all upset! It was never right. Really, I'm so happy...."

And she was. She felt as though the burdens of the world had just rolled off her shoulders. "I know you and Janette will be disappointed, but you'd have been more disappointed had we married and then... and then.... I can't marry him! I just can't!"

Mrs. Lownes looked taken aback by the desperation in Tara's voice. "Well, of course, dear!" she finally said, gathering her daughter close to offer unnecessary comfort. "My poor baby," she crooned, treating Tara like a six-year-old who had just scraped her knee. "I'm afraid I must have made things worse. What a busybody I am! But why...?" Meanwhile her husband shifted from one foot to the other, looking pleased, and for once as if he didn't know what to do.

Arthur came in with another round of nightcaps, for which Tara felt particularly grateful. Then she and her parents discussed canceling the arrangements and sending a discreet note to the newspapers to announce the end of the engagement. Arthur came in again to put another log on the fire—his way of listening in without appearing to—and it was all over. She'd been saved from a fate worse than death, Tara thought, and could even smile about it. She yawned and wriggled her toes as the heat from the fireplace toasted the soles of her feet. Then she smiled at her parents. For the first time in what seemed like years—two years, in fact—she felt completely happy and at peace with herself.

"Your inheritance does come to you today, my dear." Her father's words broke into Tara's reverie. "Have you decided what you want to do with it?"

A frown nicked her brow. "I haven't given it much thought. I, er, haven't been thinking at all in the past while. That is, not until about a week ago." She grinned widely, as she had often done in the past to get herself out of a scrape. "For the time being the money will stay where it is, in the bank. I don't know what I'm going to do now. I know I want more out of life than just serving martinis and—" She broke off, deciding to keep the part about warming the bed to herself. "And going to parties. But exactly what it is that I want. . . ." She shrugged her shoulders.

When Tara went to her bedroom a little later her cousin was there waiting for her.

"Oh, Penelope, I thought you'd gone to bed." Tara smiled at the voluptuous figure sitting cross-legged on her bed. At that point, she felt she could smile at anyone. The future spread before her, unknown and beset with question marks, but because of that it was exciting.

She went to her vanity and carefully removed the earrings her parents had given her for her birthday. They were small delicate studs, rubies embedded in gold flowerlike casings. Then she beamed at her reflection in the mirror, and wondered why Penny was so unusually quiet.

"So tell me," Penny said, as though on cue, "what happened out there in the garden. You look like a cat full of cream. Dennis must have said some awfully nice things!" Her voice was quieter than usual, and she didn't sound very cheerful.

"Well. . . ." Tara paused. "As a matter of fact, we decided to call our engagement off. You may be interested to know that neither of us cared enough for the other to go through with what would have been a dismal charade."

Penny's mouth dropped open. For a few seconds, she had the grace to look embarrassed, but that look was immediately replaced by something else. To Tara's surprise she looked vaguely disappointed.

"But why?" she finally spluttered. "Why?"

"I told you," Tara explained patiently. "I don't love him; he doesn't love me. It's as simple as that."

The disappointed expression hadn't left her cousin's face, and watching her Tara suddenly knew that Penny would have preferred stealing Dennis from her rather than having him free. The former represented a much bigger conquest. She hadn't thought Penny capable of such callousness, and for a moment she felt uncomfortably annoyed.

"Oh, really?" Penny was saying. "Aren't you even crushed?"

"No!" Tara exclaimed, recovering with a laugh. "There's nothing to be crushed about!"

"I would be," Penny affirmed. "I mean, having to give back that gorgeous diamond! Anyway, I suppose I'll have one of my own soon. There'll be plenty of men on the *Adventure Star*. And then, of course you never know, but I might get my diamond sooner." She sent Tara an arched look. "Mind you, I'd hate to miss out on the cruise—first the Mediterranean, then down to the Canaries.... Doesn't it sound like heaven?"

"What happens if you fall in love with the impoverished first mate and don't get a huge diamond? Then what are you going to do?" Tara asked, laughter evident in her voice.

"I certainly wouldn't marry him!" Penny sounded aghast. "I'd only marry a rich man!"

"But why is money so important? Doesn't love conquer all?" Tara asked. She herself wasn't sure that it did. She was having difficulty imagining how it would feel to be in love. Lately she'd been wondering whether the mad, passionate, starry-eyed version might not be a lot more fun than the companionship she'd considered marriage to be.

"Not in my books!" Penny replied vehemently. "Oh, I know mom and dad are well off, but *I* don't have a huge inheritance like you." She gazed moodily at Tara's back, a look the older girl caught in her mirror. "Of course, you can marry anyone," she went on. "The problem is you'll never know if they're marrying you or your money. By the way, do you know if Dennis is planning to play in the polo match on my birthday? I'd love to see him on a horse!"

"Why don't you ask him?" Tara smothered a smile; Penny was obviously smitten. She only hoped her cousin had the callousness to match Dennis's. Even if she didn't particularly like Penny she didn't want to see her hurt.

"Maybe I will...." Penny was staring dreamily out the window toward the shadowed shape of Brackenhill.

NEWS OF THE BROKEN ENGAGEMENT caused a veritable buzz of excitement. Tara knew everyone was itching to probe the whys and wherefores, but she didn't enlighten her friends. "We both decided it was best," she repeated over and over, "and no, we aren't dire enemies."

Dennis had given out a different version, she discovered, as her friends eyed her in disbelief. But they were careful not to let his version reach her ears through them.

No one seemed surprised when Tara couldn't be persuaded to go to even one party. A period of mourning was unanimously expected of her. Penny inevitably went everywhere in her place, under Mrs. Lownes's disapproving eye. Penny was also being very secretive about something, and Tara wondered if that meant she and Dennis were seeing a lot of each other. She didn't ask, however. When Tara did meet Dennis, he was civil, even friendly. But she was left with the distinct impression that underneath he was nursing a grudge.

Minutes and hours and days went drifting by. Tara felt suspended in a vacuum. One part of her life was finished, and now a new part must begin. But what shape would it take? What should she do? The only ⠶⠶⠶ she had decided was that she must leave Hampstᵉ⠶ d.

Shortly before the date set for Penny's birthday party, Yvonna asked Tara to go shopping with her in London. They'd just comfortably settled in Harrods for tea, when their conversation was interrupted by laughter from the next table. Even though neither of them could see their neighbors, they knew without question that it was Dennis sitting on the other side of the partition. Seconds later they recognized his companion. Penny's giggle, so much like Tara's, was unmistakable.

Yvonna colored with embarrassment and looked as though she would like to slide under the table. Tara just sat there, listening in astonishment.

"Darling Penelope, you're more lovely every day!" Dennis was saying.

Tara controlled the grin that threatened to spread over her face. Couldn't Dennis be more innovative, she wondered.

"Oh, Dennis—" Tara could vividly imagine Penny fluttering her eyelashes "—you're so wonderful! I only feel— Well, poor Tara!"

Yvonna choked on her tea.

"Umm. She was misguided, of course." Dennis sounded honestly aggrieved. "But what could I do? She literally threw herself at me, and because I've known her forever I thought we could make marriage work...."

"You must have gone through such torture!" Penny murmured sympathetically. "She's being very brave about the whole thing, you know. I mean, I couldn't possibly be if I lost you!"

Tara put her napkin over her mouth to stop the gurgle of laughter. Dennis has met his match, she thought ruefully. Penny can act as well as he can!

Yvonna was hastily gathering her purse, scarf and parcels, her gentle features as red as the Dutch tulips outside the window.

"Well, darling, Tara's not warmhearted, as you are. She's cold, even though she does look exotic with all that black hair. But there's no hot blood in her, I can assure you...." Dennis's next words were lost as they left their table.

"Oh, Tara!" Yvonna gulped when they were out of the tearoom. "I'm so sorry! None of us wanted to tell you that...that...."

Tara smiled wryly. Here she had so many friends, and not one of them believed her side of the story, not even Yvonna. What did they think—that she was lying to them? Restlessness spread through her like ripples on water. In the next second she had decided to leave Hampstead right after Penny's party, which left her only a few days in which to decide what she would do and where she would go.

On the Friday before the party, an answer to part

of her problem came in the shape of a letter from William Pillaring, her publisher. Would she be interested in writing a sequel to *Toodles, the Bear with a Bad Case of Big Nose*, he wondered. The market for such a book looked promising. Her response was anxiously awaited.

Tara couldn't imagine William Pillaring looking anxious at all, but at least someone other than her parents liked her books, and that was important. She read the letter several times, her brow puckering in concentration.

The more she considered the proposal the more sense it made. It was the obvious answer. And it fit right in with her decision to leave Hampstead. Books could be written anywhere. What was more, going off and writing a book would provide an opportunity to stand on her own two feet. She felt too mollycoddled at home, too protected. She would take the money she'd made from her books and travel somewhere. Start a new life.

Excitement overtook her like a tide, so powerful that even the arrival of her Uncle Albert and Aunt Dorothy made no difference to her mood. Usually when they came she felt a distinct decline in spirit.

Uncle Albert and her father immediately disappeared into the library for a quiet chat about their respective projects. Aunt Dorothy stayed in the parlor, talking in her rather high-pitched voice. Tara watched with amusement as her mother eyed the woman's freshly bleached hair, then marveled at the way she let Aunt Dorothy's pointed remarks pass over her head. After a while the conversation turned to the birthday party on the morrow. Penny herself was almost bouncing up and down with enthusiasm—more enthusiasm than even a polo party merited.

Tara floated euphorically through the next day, making plans, deciding on and then rejecting destinations, wondering what to take and what to leave behind. All around her the babble and gaiety of the polo game continued uninterrupted. She scarcely noticed when Dennis scored the last goal amid roars and cheering.

Tara chose to travel with her parents to the country club where they were to celebrate Penny's birthday, for she knew there would be an embarrassed silence if she went with her crowd. Even Yvonna was giving her a wide berth since that day in Harrods, and Yvonna had been her best friend.

The dinner was delicious, and the birthday cake drew numerous oohs and aahs. It was a huge affair with myriad pink-icing roses climbing over it. Twenty-one pink candles blazed from the top. There was an expectant silence as everyone waited for Penny to blow them out. She hovered dramatically over the cake, and Tara saw something glittering on her left hand.

When the cheering died down, Dennis stood up by her side and lifted his champagne glass. "Penny and I have an announcement to make." He paused theatrically, and the room was utterly quiet. "We have decided to announce our engagement tonight!" Supremely confident, he grinned unabashedly into the scandalized stillness. His glass and Penny's clinked together with a silvery tinkling sound.

Tara couldn't help but notice he avoided looking in her direction; for all his confidence, he didn't have the courage to look her in the eye.

Tara was one of the first to raise her champagne glass. Then came a babble of confused congratulations, and she felt herself being watched by scores of sympathetic eyes.

She knew she ought to be angry, but she wasn't. It no longer mattered what her friends thought. Yvonna wouldn't even look at her now! But Tara felt only a passing regret. In her mind she'd already said good-bye to the friends she'd known since childhood. Her intuition grasped the fact that their path and hers hadn't been the same since she'd gone to Europe with her father, and the split had finally grown so great that there was no point in continuing or attempting to revive their camaraderie, not even for appearances' sake. Nevertheless it all served to make her feel a bit lonely and frightened.

The ride home was strained. The only people in the car still talking to each other were her father and her uncle. Their wives maintained a strained silence. Mrs. Lownes was certain Penny had interfered in Tara's engagement; Aunt Dorothy thought so, too, but obviously didn't feel in the least sorry. Their bone of contention, Tara, sat between them and did her best to ignore the unpleasant undercurrents. She couldn't think of any way to smooth matters over, and all the way home she had to patiently bear Aunt Dorothy's triumphant glances.

She was in bed penciling rough sketches for her next children's book when Penny came sauntering in nonchalantly. She glanced quickly at Tara before dropping her silver mesh bag on the bed and plopping down beside it.

"It was a wonderful party, wasn't it?" she asked in a voice that was overly friendly.

"Perfect," Tara nodded, realizing immediately how uncomfortable her cousin felt. "And wasn't the game exciting? That time when we all thought Dennis would miss the goal!"

"Uh-huh." Penny shifted uncomfortably. Once again she seemed lost for words.

"By the way, congratulations, Penelope. I do wish you all the best," Tara added.

"Oh, Tara!" Penny wailed, her face flushed with guilt. "I felt bad about springing our engagement on you like that, but Dennis thought it best. He couldn't wait to let everyone know." She looked away and squirmed. "And...and he decided to, um, get married on the same day. I mean the first of June, your original wedding day. I hope you don't mind, but the arrangements.... And, well, it's so hard to book that particular cathedral in June. Your day was still open; Dennis said you wouldn't mind...."

"Of course I don't mind!"

"Well, you see, we had to let everyone know, since the wedding's so soon! And oh! Look at my ring! It's just a little bit bigger than yours was, isn't it—but not much!" she hastened to add. "I can't believe I'm going to be Mrs. Penelope Moreston!"

Better you than me, Tara thought as she smiled politely at Penny's eagerness.

"And oh, listen, Tara, I had the most marvelous

idea! I won't be taking the cruise now, so why don't you go in my place?''

Tara shook her head vigorously at the suggestion, but Penny rushed on.

"Oh, you must! I'd feel so much better, and your parents can afford it! And if you don't go I'll have to pay a cancellation fee! Daddy warned me when he bought the ticket that if I changed my mind I'd have to pay the fee myself! Besides, the cruise will make up for losing Dennis. There'll be all kinds of nice men on board! And do you really want to be here for our wedding? Think of what people will say!

"It's the perfect solution!" she went on insistently. "The ship leaves the day after tomorrow, on Monday, so you only have one day to pack...."

It wasn't just her welfare Penny was concerned about, Tara realized. Her cousin's conscience was bothering her, but with the cruise as a payoff, Penny must figure Tara would be more than compensated. The rather large cancellation fee probably had something to do with it, too.

Tara fervently hoped the younger girl wouldn't get hurt by Dennis's desire to get back at his ex-fiancée. Springing the engagement as a surprise to everyone and getting married to another woman on their original wedding day was exactly in line with Dennis's character. She hoped he wasn't marrying Penny out of vindictiveness, but that he truly felt something for her. Suddenly Tara wished she could say something in warning. But Penny would accept no word of advice; she would only think Tara was trying to get Dennis back.

Tara sighed and turned the idea of the cruise over in her mind. Well, she did want to get away from Hampstead, and as yet she'd come up with no alternative plan. The ship stopped in several ports, if she remembered Penny's description correctly. She could explore each one for suitability. Several of the towns along the coast shouldn't be too expensive to live in. She was going to be on her own, after all, and had to watch her money. It would be better if she settled quite far from home, Tara decided. That way her mother wouldn't always be pressing her to come back, to go out with bachelors whom she considered eligible.

"Okay, I'll go," Tara stated finally, and then had to laugh at Penny's obvious relief. "Monday, is it?"

"Oh, Tara, think of all the men! I almost envy you!" Penny cried.

"The last thing I'm going for is the men!" she answered dryly.

MRS. LOWNES WASN'T AT ALL PLEASED with Tara's decision when Penny broke the news at breakfast the next morning. Her hands went straight to her hair. Her husband merely smiled and said it wasn't such a bad idea, at which his wife gave him an annoyed glance. But Tara, once decided, was immovable, and her mother reluctantly helped with the hasty preparations for the cruise. Dresses, gowns, slacks and suits were pulled out of the closet, only to be put back in and then packed, after all. In the end Tara used the same battered pieces of luggage that had carried her throughout Europe, although her mother fussed and fumed over them.

"And I'm sure you'll be lonely!" she went on. "Oh, dear, we haven't time to buy new clothes.... And that nice-looking brother of Yvonna's is coming home next week! You won't know anyone on the boat! A whole month!" she protested. "There'll be no one to look after you...."

"Mother! I don't need looking after! I'll have a good time, really I will!" Tara said soothingly.

She was still reassuring her the following day on the deck of the small but exclusive three-hundred-and-fifty-foot *Adventure Star*.

"Bye, sweetheart!" her father said, enveloping her in his customary bone-crunching hug.

Her mother was pulling at a lace handkerchief, for her hairdo was safely tucked out of reach under a powder-blue hat.

"Bye, mom." Tara bent to kiss her cheek. "Will you please stop worrying? What on earth could possibly happen to me?"

"Yes, dear, of course...." But Mrs. Lownes was not convinced. Her eyes caught the white-uniformed figure of the captain, and she hurried toward him before Tara could stop her.

"Oh, captain?" Mrs. Lownes tapped his arm.

"Ma'am?" His beetling gray brows rose as he took in her anxious face.

"I don't like to impose, but—" she led him over "—this is our daughter, Miss Tara Lownes. Could you see that she enjoys herself? And doesn't get too lonely? So far away from home, you know...." Her blue eyes looked beseechingly up into the man's piercing gray ones. He glanced from her to her daughter, keeping his face remarkably straight as he saw the red flush that stained the girl's cheeks.

"Of course, Mrs. Lownes. We shall do everything within our power to ensure that your daughter enjoys her trip and doesn't get lonely. Mr. Lownes?" The two men shook hands.

"Thank you, captain."

"Captain Warren Baker, Mrs. Lownes." He smiled reassuringly and led the couple over to the gangway. The brass band on the pier had struck up a rousing and boisterous verson of "Bon Voyage." Streamers hung from ship to shore, with people hanging eagerly on to both ends. Reporters and cameramen swarmed over the Southampton pier, taking inventory of the VIP's and their assembled entourages.

Tara hung over the highly polished rail and waved to her parents, while the captain stood politely by her side. Moments later the horn blasted twice, and the strip of brownish water between ship and pier grew wider and wider until the streamers broke, to flutter off into the windy, gray spring day. When Tara's arm grew tired, and when she'd seen enough of the big tankers and freighters that lined other piers, she turned to face the tall man at her side.

"Er, Captain Baker, there's no need for you to watch over me! My mother is. . .overly anxious—"

"I understand." The man's lined weatherbeaten face creased in a smile, and the gray eyes now seemed a little less stern. "But if you do find yourself in need of anything, Miss Lownes, don't hesitate to call on me."

When Tara continued to look at him anxiously, he gave her a wink. "I know all about parents, Miss Lownes, and I can see you don't need a mother hen." This time his smile reached his eyes, and the whole aspect of his face warmed.

"Oh, good! That's a relief!" Tara laughed.

"Would you consider joining me at the captain's table for dinner?" he went on in his dignified tones.

"Oh! Y-yes, thank you," she stuttered in surprise. Surely there were more noteworthy guests on this cruise than herself. But he gave her no chance to say more and abruptly excused himself, walking toward the bridge with the sturdy relaxed gait of a man well acquainted with the sea. Tara, watching him with a half smile on her face, decided she would try to imitate that walk.

Then she turned back to the rail and watched the coast of Hampshire slip by with increasing speed. A vibrant thrill swept through her now that they were actually moving. Hampstead, Dennis, Penny—all those endless parties and gossip sessions were over! Finished!

She made a mental note of the countries the *Adventure Star* would stop in. She had visited most of the European ports before; between those and the countries farther south she would surely find a suitable place to settle down in for a while. But she would think of that later, she decided. Right now she wanted to see her cabin and change her clothes. Maybe she would wander about to get her bearings, practice that peculiar sailor's walk—and then it would be dinnertime. She knew she wouldn't have to change

again, because the first night on board was always in-
formal.

Her cabin, she found, was decorated in luxurious
shades of oyster white and pearl gray. The decor in
her suite, as elsewhere on the ship, was modern, with
chrome-and-glass side tables and swirling chrome
chairs designed in the shape of scallop shells. These
were offset by a plush sofa with overstuffed cushions. Subdued lighting came from tall rectangular
lamps. A weeping fig tree in a glazed pot offered
relief from the color scheme, as did the cunningly arranged abstract paintings. She had expected a berth
and a small shower; instead there was a wide double
bed draped in oyster-toned velvet with throw cushions in gray and blue. And the bathroom was full-
size, including a tiled bathtub as well as a shower.

Because her cabin was on the main deck facing
outward, she had three large portholes generously
swathed in tasseled velvet draperies. All the guest
cabins were above the waterline, but A-and-B-deck
suites below had only tiny round portholes. Tara
switched on the closed-circuit radio and turned the
dial to "Rock." Instantly the quick beat of a Rod
Stewart song filled her cabin.

A spurt of excitement overcame her, and she
couldn't resist dancing a few steps around her suite.
And she thought, *adventure, here I come!*

CHAPTER THREE

THE DAYS SLIPPED BY, and Tara, free-spirited, enjoyed every minute. One incident early in the voyage, however, caused her some distress, and later, when she overcame her initial embarrassment, provoked some in-depth self-examination.

She shared a table in the dining room with Dr. Hans Albert, a leading nuclear physicist in his eighties, who was on a holiday enforced by his doctor. The other celebrity was Fionna Genelli, an Italian movie star on honeymoon with her sixth husband. The latter fitted perfectly the description of a strong silent type. Although Tara was delighted to share a table with them, their conversation sometimes left her agog and at other times blushing furiously. But it was always interesting.

One day she was circling the greenery that partially obscured their table, about to join her companions for lunch, when she overheard them discussing her.

"I do believe she's still a virgin!" Fionna was saying not unkindly.

"And what's the matter with that?" asked her husband.

"Oh, darling, there's nothing the matter with it.

It's just so unusual in this day and age. She told me the other day that she was twenty-two!''

"I find her naiveté charming," Dr. Albert interposed. "Refreshing, actually. Something tells me, though, that she'll always have that air of innocence about her. Some people never lose it, whether they're six years old or sixty-five. It's in their character, their state of mind. She couldn't have chosen a better profession for herself than writing children's stories!''

They went on for a bit longer while Tara stood rooted to the spot in hot, all-enveloping mortification. She simply couldn't join them after that. Blindly she turned and found her way back to her cabin. By the time dinner was served that evening she'd regained her composure, but her self-examination went on for a great deal longer.

Okay, she was still a virgin. She hadn't until that moment even thought about just how unusual that was among her present companions. Yvonna was, too, she knew. But Yvonna was a minister's daughter, and perhaps that had something to do with it. Tara had no such excuse, and suddenly felt like a social misfit.

Was there something wrong with her, she wondered. Was she frigid, as Dennis had accused? Like Yvonna she had been strictly raised, although she'd probably been spoiled terribly at the same time. Then traveling with her father had closed the door on many opportunities for dalliance with the opposite sex, as had the fact of her becoming engaged. And with Dennis she had never wanted to go further than petting and kissing.... Tara was amazed at her stupidity in remaining engaged to him for so long.

Away from her home and parents she was finding out just how protective her parents had been; how they had sheltered her from hard knocks and reality. Out here in the world she felt out of her depth. Education she had aplenty. She'd studied everything from political science to philosophy, from the economics of a small business to the economics of a whole nation. Under her father's tutorship, on rainy afternoons in their library, she had been guided in her reading while he worked on his history novels. Of course she had picked up a good deal of history, as well.

All that erudition was fine, but Tara now realized that her practical knowledge of life was slight. She had some quick learning to do if she was going to cope on her own....

One of her challenges, she decided, was to get involved with a man. She would simply have to find herself a mate—temporarily, of course. There were certain specifications, naturally; her whole reason for the exercise was to gain experience, not to get herself into trouble.

Somewhat perplexed by her mission, Tara looked over the unentangled males on the voyage. Penny had been right in her prediction: there were many gorgeous men. After some diligent and determined pruning she had narrowed them down to ten possibles.

But when it came to following up their bold inviting glances with a smile of her own, she just couldn't do it. Every time initial contact seemed imminent she chickened out. The trouble was, she realized, she felt uncertain about each one of them. And she didn't want to start a flirtation with someone only to find he wasn't right, after all. It wouldn't really be fair to go around sampling kisses.

One day slipped into the next, and Tara's ambivalence continued.

As the *Adventure Star* stopped at Monte Carlo, Crete, Athens and Cairo, she studied each as a possible home base. The cost of living in some was prohibitive, she knew. The cruise was her last fling at her parents' expense, and once it was over she would have to watch every penny.

She was no nearer a decision on either home or mate when the liner set off down the coast of Africa from Tangiers. Hampstead had never seemed farther away.

The first of June dawned as they steamed away from Casablanca; it was as clear and beautiful a day as any they had enjoyed over the past week. Feeling luxurious and decadently lazy, Tara selected a chair in her favorite spot on the veranda deck beside the swimming pool, and prepared to sunbathe before the day became too uncomfortably hot. As she lathered on sun cream her thoughts flew to the church where she would have been married today. Thank goodness the lovely, centuries-old cathedral was now being filled with Penny's guests and not hers! She could imagine her mother sitting somewhat tight-lipped in the second pew, and at the thought a smile hovered around the corners of her mouth. Had Dennis got his rezoning law passed, she wondered. Had his little bribe done the trick?

Tara sank back with a sigh into the soft padded depths of the chaise longue. Perhaps she shouldn't return home with the cruise at all, not even to pack her things. It might be better to find a place directly and telephone home about her decision. That way she would avoid the inevitable lengthy argument with her mother.... She would have to contact her publishing house and ask them to readdress her royalty checks. That was all the money she would have to live on until her next book sold. Tara frowned. It was going to be difficult....

They had last docked at Casablanca. Next came Las Palmas on Gran Canaria, then on the return trip to England, a stop at Funchal on Madeira.

Las Palmas.... Tara turned it over in her mind. She'd been there with her father—only for two days, but she'd come away impressed. The spot was beautiful, and away from the city center, very inexpensive. The more she thought about it, the more it seemed a perfect place to dream up stories. Her passport was completely in order, so she should have no problems. She would do it, she decided. She would get off at Las Palmas and find a room for herself. Probably in a *pension*.

Tara was suddenly too excited to lie still and sunbathe. Instead she paced up and alongside the shiny brass rail, oblivious to the intrigued glances of fellow sun worshippers. The sea was unusually choppy but she scarcely noticed, for her practicing had paid off and she could walk the decks almost as well as the captain.

"Why is it that writers are always pacing?" Dr. Albert asked, falling into step beside her. "It must be a tremendous idea that's making you wear a rut into the deck!" His eyes were smiling from beneath shaggy white brows, and Tara thought irrelevantly that he would make a perfect Santa Claus. Whenever he chuckled his ample middle bobbed up and down in the most remarkable way. There was no question that the scientist had remained one of her favorite people on board.

"Well, yes it is," she admitted, laughing. Her thick hair shone in the sunlight and her eyes sparkled with suppressed excitement. A flush tinted her high cheekbones, making the delicate hollows below seem more prominent. As Tara gathered her hair up to let the breeze cool her nape, she was unaware that several of the male passengers were gazing enviously at Dr. Albert's stooped back, or that the doctor himself was wishing he were thirty years younger.

They turned together and walked back along the rail. "It is a tremendous idea," Tara repeated. "I've decided to set up shop in Las Palmas! Now that I've finally made up my mind my head's full of new plots for stories, and I can't wait to get started!"

Dr. Albert nodded his head a little wistfully as he listened to his companion's glowing commentary.

They had just turned to walk aft again when the steward came by to announce in his well-modulated voice that lunch was being served. When Tara and the doctor came back on deck an hour later, they immediately noticed that the weather had changed. Leaning against the brass rail together, they looked out over the endless choppy waves, crested now with foaming whitecaps. The sky had turned a yellowy gray, and the sun burned through the mottled haze as though determined to turn everything in its path to ashes.

"If my eighty-one years mean anything at all," the doctor rumbled, "I would say we're in for a spot of weather. *Meine Güte!* It is so very hot and sticky!" He loosened his colorful silk cravat and scanned the sky. "I'm glad Captain Baker is at the helm!"

Tara hadn't sailed enough to know the dangers of a storm at sea, and she smiled confidently. It would be fascinating, she thought, to have a real storm. Good material for a book, perhaps. . . .

A few hours later Tara was regretting her hasty assumption. She wasn't seasick, as most of the other passengers were, because for some reason her stomach withstood the jouncing. But one look at Miss Tillesby, an extremely wealthy and eccentric spinster who had befriended her, made it clear she was suffering some of the worst effects. The poor lady was green and white at intervals, and was repeatedly sick between moans. Tara stopped in at Miss Tillesby's deluxe cabin on the veranda deck to see if there was anything she could do to help. Most of the crew members were hopelessly busy, even though there were so many of them.

The first mate eventually requested that everyone stay in their cabins while the storm raged, and reluctantly Tara obeyed his orders. But she left her door open so that she could watch all the comings and goings. Restless, she went to a porthole and gazed out over the green water, which was tumbling and rushing past. She wished she could go up on deck to see everything better.

"Dinner will be served in your cabin tonight, ma'am." The chief steward appeared at her door for only a second, and then was gone, repeating his message down the hall. From the next cabin Tara heard an answering groan. If the situation weren't so horrible it would be funny, she thought, peering out at the sky. She was itching to go up on deck, unafraid yet in awe of the tempestuous wind that licked the white-caps into a boiling froth.

The next moment a towering wave hit the *Adventure Star* broadside. Tara skidded off her sofa and went sprawling across the oyster-white carpet. She got up shakily, deciding she was better off indoors, after all. Even the ship's stabilizers couldn't seem to prevent the side-to-side rolling motion.

When her dinner arrived Tara ate a few mouthfuls of lobster Newburg, but she found it tasted like saw-dust and impatiently pushed the tray away. How could anyone be expected to eat? The infernal tossing and pitching was getting steadily worse as the min-utes crawled by.

A few hours later everything that wasn't nailed down had been scattered across the cabin floor. One of Tara's perfume bottles had broken, the pungent essence making the whole suite reek. That was only a small nuisance, a mere pinprick of irritation in the ruling chaos.

Battering-ram waves punished the three-hundred-and-fifty-foot ship as though it were nothing more than a leaf atop the turmoil of raging water. Every now and then it felt as if the whole ship hung suspended in midair. Tara, wedged between the couch and the wall, waited in agony for each following downward crash and the fearful shuddering that would convulse the *Star*, as once more the water clutched it, shaking it from stem to stern with the ease of a mighty lion seizing a mouse between its fangs.

Over the tumult of the storm Miss Tillesby's piercing screams could be heard. Once she escaped from her cabin and stumbled up and down the gangways, eluding the frantic crew members who were trying to put her to bed again. Fionna Genelli and her husband had solved the instability problem by strapping themselves into their bed with sheets. They lay with their arms locked around each other as if prepared to die. Tara couldn't bear the thought of strapping herself to anything, but fortunately the little space between the couch and the wall held her securely. The larger space on the other side of her couch accommodated Dr. Albert. She would have gone mad, too, she thought, but for his calm philosophic acceptance of the storm. When their voices could be heard above the uproar they talked to each other across the intervening couch back.

Great sheets of water gushed sporadically down over the portholes, the boiling froth clearly illuminated by the rectangular lamps in Tara's cabin. Other than that there was little to be seen outside except an everlasting blackness stabbed occasionally by forks of greenish white lightning.

"The tropical storm season is months away!" Tara

shouted to the doctor in a three-second lull. "What in the world is going on?"

"Just another of nature's freaks!" Dr. Albert shouted back when the next opportunity came.

Grimacing, Tara braced her feet more firmly against the wall. The stomach-lurching sensation of free-fall was upon them. She tensed for the coming crunch. "Oh, *God*!" she muttered, as, this time, the terrible aftermath of shuddering was accompanied by a long inhuman groan that seemed to come from the very bowels of the ship.

"What was that?" Her white face rose above the arm of the couch.

"I'd guess it was metal straining against metal," the doctor replied thoughtfully. "These days they make hulls out of steel sheets of various diameter, riveted together. Steel has no give, or not as much—"

Tara missed the last of his scientific hairsplitting as the din abruptly mushroomed in volume. More time passed, and a flash of lightning, striking too close, filled the room with intense white brilliance.

"If that chief steward says everything's fine just *once* more...!" Tara began, her jaw set against the terror building within.

"The poor fellow's only carrying out the captain's orders. He looks as frightened as I feel," Dr. Albert answered.

"That's it! I'm going to talk to Captain Baker. He'll know what's going on!" Tara crawled out of her cubbyhole on her hands and knees.

"Broken glass—right in front of you!" the doctor

bellowed above the tumult. "It's safest where you are! Stay here!"

Undaunted, she picked her way gingerly through the scattered glass shards. "I'm going! But I'll be back! Wait here!" Tugging the seat cushions off the couch, she pushed them over to the doctor for extra padding. With a quick, rather shaky grin for him she started off, half crouching, half walking. Her nightgown and robe hardly helped matters, and when she was reduced to a crawl they became a downright nuisance. Along the gangways she crept stealthily, for every precaution was necessary if she were to evade the eagle eyes of the chief steward.

Down the long hall, up the stairs, through the dining room and the lounge she hurried, at times hiding behind the exclusive chrome furniture to avoid the crew. She had to make it past the staff quarters, then up more steps that led into the wheelhouse, so she sped past the smaller and much less luxurious bedrooms. They were deserted, thankfully, except for four at the end, but their inhabitants were dead to the world and didn't even see her as she tiptoed past. Any sound she might have made was lost in the clamor of the storm anyway. She reached the narrow stairwell undetected and clambered up to the landing. Her hand was on the knob, when the urgent voice of the first mate stopped her short.

"Capt'n! Water's coming into the engine room!"

"The bilge pumps?" Captain Baker's cold calm tones cut through the first mate's rising agitation. Several explicit curses escaped his lips. "They can send men to the moon, and yet they can't design a decent bilge pump! Water in the engine room.... That probably means some casing has sprung loose in the ship's housing. How serious is it?"

"Both pumps are down," Smith said in a subdued voice.

"Right. Johnston! Take three men with you and man the bilge pumps!" The captain was addressing the second mate, and Tara scrunched herself against the wall as the door opened and Johnston charged past her.

"Smith, get on that radio and broadcast Mayday! If the bilges can't handle the water it could mean we've got big problems. There's a good chance of these waves getting worse, and I've seen steel casings torn right apart.... Damn! If that engine room floods we're minus our engines and our emergency power system. So get on that Mayday! What are you waiting for?"

"But...but is it that serious?" Smith protested incredulously. "I mean, it's a last resort—"

"Serious?" The captain rumbled. "What did they teach you in that damn school? Of course it's serious!" he roared. "If that engine room floods we won't be able to send out *any* messages, let alone a Mayday, and meanwhile this ship will be sinking. Sinking, you understand? We're in a tanker route. We have to warn other ships of our location, and the very real possibility of our becoming dead weight. If the worst does happen we may sink so far down that radar won't be able to pick us up on the screen. And I don't have to tell you what that means. On the other hand, being in a tanker route may have its benefits," he went on. "If we do need rescuing there might be a freighter close by. Hop to it!"

Tara, clinging to the rails as the ship bucked and rolled, slowly absorbed what she'd just heard. Seconds stretched into long minutes. She had more bruises than she could count from bumping against the walls and rails, but her discomfort was forgotten as Josh Smith's next words rapped out.

"Capt'n? Johnston reports no progress."

There was silence; the first mate didn't have to say anything more.

Tara's skin crawled. The engine room really was flooding. What would a ship do without engines in a storm like this one? Continuing silence from the wheelhouse chilled her to the bone.

"Damn!" The single loud exclamation after the eerie quiet made her jump, and she wondered what else could have happened.

"Damnation!" the captain repeated. "The port engine's down already!" Such a stream of cursing poured from the captain's lips that, absurdly, Tara found herself wishing for a pen to write it all down.

"Wind up to seventy-two knots, capt'n, and Johnston reports more water in the engine room." Smith's voice was plainly grim this time. "We're in the middle of it now. These giant waves are canceling our radar visibility."

"We won't have any radar soon anyway," Captain Baker commented wryly.

With one engine failing the *Adventure Star* was heaving drunkenly between the gale-force winds and the mammoth waves. In the darkened stairwell Tara started shivering uncontrollably, and wished for the warm sweater tucked in her bureau drawer.

"Hang on!" Baker roared. "There's one coming!"

Tara looped her arms around the rails and planted her feet well apart. Scarcely were the words out of the captain's mouth when she felt the liner lifting. . . and lifting. Then the stern dipped sharply, almost standing the ship on its end. Tara's feet swung out from under her with the violent force of the motion, and for one startled second her body was parallel to the floor. Her stomach filled her throat as the ship's bow swung level again in a dizzying arch, thrusting the stern back up and causing her knees to smash against the floor. The sound of breaking glass added to the universal din.

Her arms felt wrenched from their sockets, but still she hung on. A soft moan escaped her clenched teeth as she watched the lights in the wheelhouse dim, blink and go out. Beneath her in the crew's quarters all was plunged into darkness.

The starboard engine had died, Tara knew without being told. Josh Smith hadn't sent the Mayday a moment too soon.

"Light the auxiliary lamps! Hand them out to the crew!" the captain was calling.

How he could sound so collected Tara didn't understand. She was still clutching the rail as though her life depended on it—and she believed it did—when a match flared in the wheelhouse and the glow increased. The light was tiny enough coming through the small window of the wheelhouse door, but it seemed a balm, and she released her hold a little. From down below she could hear shouting and screaming from the passengers. The sick crew members were totally quiet, however, and Tara wondered if they thought their prayers had been answered and they were dead at last.

Josh Smith thundered past with hurricane lamps swinging from his arms. He handed the lights out to the babbling stewards, who had come charging up the stairwell from the crew's quarters. Then he went back for more, which he also handed out. In all the hubbub no one had seen Tara, still sandwiched behind the door.

"The passengers are panicking, capt'n!" another voice reported. "They've left their cabins and are gathering in the Polaris Lounge. Chief steward says Tillesby's flipped her bloomin' lid! She's been trying to get out and throw herself overboard, and it's taking two stewards to hold her down. Too bad she never got married!"

How can he joke at a time like this, Tara wondered bitterly. Her grip had loosened considerably, and when the next wave hit she fell against the rail and struck her chin. When she drew back she tasted blood on her tongue. Oh, Penny, she thought, if you only knew about your fabulous cruise!

"Thank God we set that course change when we did!" Josh said, sounding surprisingly levelheaded. "How far do you estimate we are from Madeira, capt'n?"

"About fifteen, sixteen knots," Captain Baker replied. "Look on the bright side, Smith. Barring a tanker collision, we should make it. If we can just hang on like this we'll last out the storm, which, at the rate it's going, is in an awful hurry to get somewhere! The worst of it is moving off, I'd say. There's just one more thing: let's hope we don't shift any farther southwest. Those Deserta Islands off Madeira have some wicked reefs.''

Tara swallowed a few times. Was it Friday the thirteenth? No, she answered herself, it was still June the first, her supposed wedding day. She could have been married by now, safe and sound in Hampstead. But, she realized in amazement, she'd rather be here than there! The realization gave her some measure of calm. The *Adventure Star* was powerless—without radio, without radar. They were sinking in the middle of a main tanker route as well as drifting toward dangerous reefs. And yet the realization that she'd escaped from Dennis made her happy. *I'm going daft!* she assured herself.

Ludicrously, she giggled as she wrapped herself around the rail, ready for another monstrous wave. The upheaval this time was a little less chaotic. Then, unsteadily, she let go and grabbed at the wheelhouse door. At least she wasn't sick. Maybe there was something she could do. At a time like this surely all help would be accepted!

''Er, hello!''

Captain Baker and Josh Smith both swung around to face her.

''Before you start yelling at me for coming up here,'' she added defensively, ''I've come to see if there's anything I can do to help. I already know what's going on! And for goodness' sake, don't just send me back to my cabin or I *shall* go stark raving mad! I think I'm halfway there already. You see, I just discovered I'd rather be here than getting married, as I was supposed to be doing today. So if I can't do something I'll probably go right off the deep end! No pun intended.''

Captain Baker had frowned at the outset of her speech, but now his face broke into a lopsided grin. "That's about the craziest thing I've ever heard! You're the first woman I've come across who'd rather be on a sinking ship than getting married—'' He broke off as he realized what he had said.

"Oh, don't worry, captain, I heard everything. I was behind the door, you see," Tara finished.

"Well, I'll be damned! I guess there's no privacy anywhere. But I do have a job for you, if you think you can handle it." He looked a little doubtful. "It's Miss Tillesby... but I suppose you heard that, too?'' Tara nodded.

"Did you know you're one of the few people she trusts on this entire ship?'' he went on. "She told me that a couple of days ago, after that breakfast when she complained about her eggs. It's taking two of my crew to hold her down, and I could use those able-bodied men elsewhere. If you could try to calm her down...."

"Of course, but is that all?" Tara asked.

"All?'' Baker laughed for the first time in what seemed like days. Then he grabbed for support as the ship rolled to port. "It takes two men to hold the woman down, and she asks is that all! Yes, that's all,

Tara!'' He'd forgotten his usual polite title, Miss Lownes. ''And now, dear girl, see what you can do.''

''Yes, captain,'' Tara replied meekly. But she was smiling as she left the wheelhouse. Reaching with both hands in the darkness she eased her way down the stairwell where she'd spent so many terrifying minutes—or was it hours? Peeking into the staff bedrooms as she went, she noted with relief that everyone there was alive and back to their moaning. Then she made her way to her suite, anxious to tell Dr. Albert all the news.

The next three hours were hectic ones, but Miss Tillesby finally fell asleep on a couch in the Polaris Lounge. From time to time she half woke, and Tara would have to hurry over to the davenport to soothe her again. The other passengers were all in the lounge, too. None of them dared return to their cabins. Although the lightning had stopped some time ago and the force of the wind and waves had abated, the general morale was not good. The *Adventure Star* was slowly but surely settling down into the dark water.

Dressed in pajamas and dressing gowns, they made a funny-looking group, Tara thought humorlessly. Only, Miss Tillesby was sleeping. Everyone else couldn't have been more wide awake. One auxiliary lamp and a chain of red cigarette tips provided the only light. All the other lamps, Tara knew, were hanging outside on the ship's rigging, high above their heads. They were the only protection against a possible tanker collision, the only beacon to guide a rescue ship to them. Tara peeped out the window, but only her blurred reflection could be seen.

Another hour had passed, and the liner was an hour deeper into the inky tossing waves. There was no sign of rescue. Those of the crew who weren't suffering from mal de mer passed around coffee and hot chocolate. The passengers talked among themselves in low nervous voices. It became apparent that many of them were wondering whether they should gather together their valuables from the lower decks.

"Stay where you are!" the chief steward ordered, carrying a heap of life jackets into the lounge. "The staff has already made a search through your cabins and has put all jewelry and personal valuables into the purser's vault. B and C decks have been closed off...."

A few passengers objected, so he went on to explain in a tight tired voice, "The vault is waterproof, and the cruise attendants knew what to collect. In any case, your possessions are all insured, and if there is any damage or loss you will be fully reimbursed. The lower decks are succumbing to what is called, er, progressive flooding. All doors have been sealed shut to impede this process, but you must realize the danger. Unexpected things can always happen!"

He smiled ironically, placing the life jackets on a bar table and straightening his shoulders. "Now, I want your cooperation! After I leave you will put these jackets on. Remember to tie *all* the straps securely. You will assist each other as necessary." He stood aside as more of the orange jackets were brought in by lesser stewards. "I will return to check that my orders have been carried out. And I want none of you to leave this room!" He glared at the passengers to impress upon them the import of his words. "I have a checklist here. When I call your name please answer quickly and clearly!"

With an air of unreality the roll call commenced. The names read like a list from *Who's Who*, but the answers sounded hollow and oddly frightening in the dim room.

Tara shivered in sudden apprehension. When her turn came she said, "Here," but no sound came out. She said it again, and then spoke up for Miss Tillesby, who was at that moment sound asleep.

Everyone was present and accounted for. With a final nod the chief steward turned on his heel and left.

With her hand on Miss Tillesby's shoulder, Tara happened to glance out the window. Through the blackness of the night she could just see the crew undoing clamps that held the davits in place. Now at a moment's notice lifeboats would be swung out over the water. Did the captain think they would be needing them...?

She shook Miss Tillesby's shoulder and quickly slipped the orange jacket over the woman's touseled head before she knew what was happening to her. Tara was tying her straps securely before the spinster had an idea of what was being done. Myopically staring around her, the older woman sat quietly as the chief steward came back to check that all the jackets were on. He noticed Tara's straps weren't yet tied and told her to secure them at once. Then he suggested that everyone sit down and rest if they could, and with a smile that failed completely he left them again. It was at that point that Miss Tillesby began to shriek. In calming her Tara forgot all about her straps. . . .

She walked Miss Tillesby up and down one of the aisles, trying to quell her spiraling hysteria. Dr. Albert walked on the woman's other side, his hands shoved into his pockets and lines of fatigue marking deep grooves in his brow. Up and down, up and down they paced the length of the lounge, while all around them gold lighters flared and cigarette tips glowed in the eerie semidarkness. Many of the crew had now joined the passengers; there was nothing more they could do.

Another hour passed. Miss Tillesby had relaxed sufficiently to lie down again on the davenport, but she kept a tight hold on Tara's hand, and from time to time whimpered and shivered. Among the passengers the topics of conversation had gone around the world and back again. The New York Stock Exchange, dung beetles in the lower Sudan, union demonstrators in Italy, haute couture in Paris—all were thoroughly discussed in a tense hurried way that revealed growing fear and restlessness as minute after minute ticked by. Passengers and crew had no sign that the Mayday had been heard, let alone that a ship was coming to their rescue.

A deck was flooded. The whisper spread like wildfire through the shadowy Polaris Lounge. How long would it be before the main deck was beneath the waterline? Tara's skin crawled when she thought of sea water seeping into her oyster carpet, creeping up the slim trunk of her weeping fig. And after that... the veranda deck?

The deck's beautiful grand ballroom awash with black water.... She had danced there only last night. Before her eyes swam a vision: swirling skirts and sparkling diamonds under enormous chandeliers; chrome-and-brass tables with gleaming glass tops; floors, walls and heavy velvet draperies, all providing a perfect foil for gaily colored dresses and the vivid faces of glamorous women and handsome escorts in white ties and tails.

All around Tara the conversation continued, like the rush of water over a million pebbles. Faster and faster the words spilled out. Topics were picked up and dropped: chances of another coffee-crop failure in Brazil; Fionna Genelli's new motion picture; who was Prince so-and-so dating this week; the growing unrest in South Africa.

Some passengers sounded nostalgic as they reminisced. In some, fear turned into a brittle but brilliant wit; in others a biting sarcasm. Some were angry; some were close to tears; some actually laughed nervously. Tara watched silently from her spot on the davenport, her dark, smoky eyes quiet, somber and afraid. Time stretched with the tension of an elastic band. Seconds were minutes. Minutes were hours.

Some time later the hair on her nape started to prickle, and she knew uncannily that the main deck, and her suite with it, was under water. Of all things, the thought of her fig tree being submerged had the power to bring tears to her eyes. She blinked them back fiercely. It wouldn't be long now.

For what seemed like the hundredth time she wiped the sweaty palm of her free hand on her silk robe. She felt clammy and cold all over. Miss Tillesby was suffering another attack of the shivers, as well. Dr. Albert had just sighed deeply when the door opened and Captain Baker entered.

"Into the lifeboats!" His sonorous tones rolled through the lounge.

Instant pandemonium broke out, but the captain was ready for it. Cutting a swath through the frenetic crowd, he divided them into two groups. The first mate took charge of one group; the captain the other. Tara wrenched a wide-eyed Miss Tillesby from her stranglehold on the davenport and dragged her along with the captain's group.

Once outside, with the chill wind stinging their faces and the starless night black and thick around them, Miss Tillesby twisted away from Tara. With sudden vicious strength she tore herself loose and ran blindly down the deck away from the lifeboats. Tara, chasing the woman, just managed to yank her out of the way of an exploding shell that housed an inflatable life raft. The raft, once free of its restrictions, burst into its full proportions in a matter of seconds.

Afterward Tara could never remember how she got the older woman into the lifeboat. The only thing she did recall was that they were the last ones aboard. Seated on the wooden bench at the stern of the boat, her arms wrapped securely around her charge, Tara's head cleared somewhat. Her group, she saw, had filled two boats, the first of which was already bobbing in the waves ahead of them. Captain Baker stood alone on deck, a solitary figure.

Tara's eyes were irresistibly drawn into the murky depths of the water. Wavelets were just beginning to ripple over the veranda deck. At first they trickled into the swimming pool, but as she watched the trickle turned into a stream, then a rushing surge. From the other side of the ship two red flares arched and split the black night sky.

At a nod from Baker the davits were inched out and away from the ship. With a last cursory glance around him the captain swung himself into the boat. He shot up one red flare. The purser, in the boat behind them, added his to the night.

Tara caught her breath. The chill blackness that enveloped them was truly eerie. With sight restricted, sounds multiplied their impression. All around her people were sobbing and moaning. There was a sucking gurgling noise close by as water crept under the doors of the grand ballroom. She clung to Miss Tillesby, who was lost in a paroxysm of weeping, and Tara wished she could put her hands over her ears.

As the greedy waves swirled higher and higher around the ship her own eyes filled with tears. The chandeliers were visible one moment; the next they were gone. Rubber rafts and other pool toys were lifted off the sun deck by encroaching waves. It wasn't until she tasted the saltiness of her own tears that Tara realized she was crying.

Through a sort of fog she heard a chorus of hoarse

cries and shouts from the boat behind them. In the next moment the purser let off three red flares in rapid succession, and through the ensuing bedlam Tara dimly perceived that a rescue ship had been sighted.

The sudden tumult, however, jolted Miss Tillesby out of her weeping fit. She took one startled glance around her, then an ear-piercing scream tore from her throat. It was all but drowned out by the wildly excited cries of the other passengers, many of whom were jumping up and down in crazy glee despite the captain's efforts to make them sit down.

The lifeboat was rocking dangerously in the water. Miss Tillesby lunged away from Tara, then threw herself back in an attempt to free herself. Without the frantic woman to hold on to for support, Tara slipped on the wet planking of the boat and fell into the water.

Incredible darkness closed over her head. When she came back up the lifeboat was a few feet away. Tara screamed and screamed for help, but everyone else was yelling, as well, and no one heard her. A wave surged up under her, throwing her head over heels. Before she knew it her life jacket had slipped off her head. She grabbed at it desperately, but it bobbed away out of her reach.

For a few chilling moments the heaving water tossed her about like a cork, tangling the flowing sleeves and skirt of her silk robe around her arms and legs. Then Tara felt herself being pushed mercilessly under by a heavy wash of salt water. Panicking, she tore at her gown, but the ribbon sash was firmly knotted. At every attempt she made to swim the surging waves negated her strength. And each time she surfaced the lifeboats were farther away.

Then she went down without having caught a lungful of air. The bitter taste of salt water bubbled down her throat. *It's over,* she thought. *My life should be flashing in front of my eyes.*

There was something in the water above her, something big and soft holding her down. It was keeping her from the vital air above. She pushed at it with the remaining strength in her arms. Her hands felt the texture numbly. It was rubbery, and...and yes, it must be! It was one of the life rafts.

Tara's lungs were bursting. Feebly kicking her legs, she slipped to the surface beside the bobbing raft. With her last ounce of strength she grabbed at it, and once her lungs were full, pulled herself over the side. Too exhausted to feel any relief, she slumped backward onto the soft slippery floor of the raft, and then a darkness deeper than the night closed over her.

The raft turned and tossed on the waves, and now and then a spurt of foam sprayed over its unconscious passenger. In the aftermath of the storm the winds forced the raft ever farther west. The captain had been right in his estimation that the ship was within fifteen knots of Madeira and its rocky shoreline. After both engines had died, the *Adventure Star* had drifted even closer. Now the raft was closing in on the Desertas, a string of small uninhabited islands just southeast of the Madeiras. And an hour later, as the eastern sky was beginning to change from pearl to pink, the raft caught just inside one of the reefs and hung there.

The tide was moving in, and it threw the snagged raft onto its side. Tara, still unconscious, fell out. Jagged edges tore at her filmy nightgown and the soft whiteness of her skin. The storm-charged surf rolled her over on the sand, ever closer to the shore. . . . until at last it left her up on the beach, where she lay quiet and unmoving.

CHAPTER FOUR

LAYERS AND LAYERS OF DARKNESS, one on top of the other, suspended Tara in a twilight world. She drifted through the night seemingly disembodied, until the black ascended into gray, then a lighter gray. A floating euphoria. . . .

She blinked her eyes. Heavy incredible warmth weighed her down. She felt snug and comfortable, and totally numb. Drowsiness made keeping her eyes open difficult, and when she did manage, everything was blurred. Vaguely she discerned a face through the mist: lean, dark; a sudden glitter of midnight eyes intent upon her. She tried to focus on that face, to see it more clearly, but the image faded and became distorted as though she were looking through rain- lashed glass. Her eyes closed helplessly. On the brink of sleep, sure hands touched her; a hard sinewy arm went around her back to lift her off the pillows. Her head fell back and was then cradled against a shoulder. . .broad, warm, comforting. Instinctively Tara nestled closer, not knowing or caring who it was that held her.

If only she could go back to sleep! But the man was holding her bruised chin, forcing her mouth open. A thick wooden spoon went between her lips, and a hot sweet liquid burned down her throat. It felt oddly soothing until she tasted the milk. Then she tried to get away from the spoon, but it kept coming back. And too weak to resist that imperative hand, she swallowed everything that was given her. Finally the spoon went away and didn't come back. She was asleep before he laid her back onto the pillows.

When Tara wakened the second time it was morning. The early sun shone over her bed, making a pattern of shifting leaves on the thick sheep's-wool blankets. She blinked, narrowing her eyes against the brightness. The mist in front of her eyes was gone, but her head was a vacuum. It felt fuzzy and detached from the rest of her.

Listlessly she noticed that directly beside the bed was an old rocker, and that on it, upside down, lay a large book. At the foot of the bed more thick, studious-looking volumes filled a makeshift shelf. A coil of rope hung on a wooden peg on the rough plank wall.... She yawned widely, willing her sleep-filled eyes to stay open. Somewhere behind her she heard a movement: the floor creaked and a kettle made contact with a stove. She didn't have the strength to sit up and find out who it was, for she felt too tired even to be curious. The hot sunlight forced her eyelids to close, but they flew open immediately when a hand touched her shoulder.

The shock of midnight eyes again. The lean dark face, now sharp and clear in the brilliant light. A smile flashed, white and vital. Overwhelming. Tara pushed herself deeper into the pillows, confusion chasing over her. This man made a mess of her

senses. He towered over her bed like a giant...an
unknown force. Tara firmly shut her eyes. He would
go away if she couldn't see him.

But the mattress sagged and he sat down. She
opened her eyes halfway with unaccustomed timidi-
ty, to see a long brown arm set a bowl down on the
rocker. She was lifted, cuddled into a wide curve of
shoulder, and another sinewy brown arm held her
there securely. She dimly remembered going through
this procedure before. It hadn't been unpleasant, so
she relaxed against him. Then she remembered the
milk. She eyed the bowl suspiciously and recoiled
from the wooden spoon when it reached her lips.

"Open up or I'll make you do so!" he growled in a
deep voice.

Aghast, and fearing that he really would carry out
his threat, she opened her mouth immediately. A
look of distaste crossed her features as she tried to
swallow the mouthful without tasting it.

"Yech!" she cried as the spoon moved away.
"Please, please, I despise milk!" Her weak voice
trembled with impotent rage and protest.

He took no notice. The spoon came and went,
came and went. Tara conceived an intense dislike for
the man—her tormentor—as she swallowed the
whole sticky bowlful of hot milk and honey.

The man's hard, close, physical touch was making
it increasingly difficult for her to breathe regularly. It
was as though she had a sudden touch of claustrophobia. That, combined with the indignity of his first
words and with his complete disregard for her protest, left her seething within the circle of his arms.

The milk at last was exchanged for bite-size mounds of fluffy scrambled eggs, and she took a closer critical look at the hand that held the wooden spoon. Long lean fingers, strong-looking, well kept. They were hands with plenty of character, rather like the rest of him, and as sun darkened as his face. She trembled involuntarily, scorched by his irritatingly assured manner, and the arm around her tightened. It hardly helped matters. She would feel much better if he were across the room.

It was the aroma of coffee that woke her in the early afternoon. Tara lay contentedly with her eyes shut, sniffing appreciatively and expecting Arthur to call her to breakfast. Then she opened her eyes and gasped.

Shocked remembrance swept the last remnants of sleep from her. Hampstead...hundreds of miles away. Dennis. Penny. The *Adventure Star* sinking into inky waves. Miss Tillesby's crazy face inches from her own. The raft...the raft! Where on earth was she? Where was Captain Baker?

She propped herself up feebly, tentatively, on one elbow. Her wide eyes circled the tiny cabin.

The bed was wedged into an alcove. Around the corner, along the wall, was a cast-iron wood stove, the kettle sitting complacently upon it and emitting the exquisite coffee aroma. Beside the stove was a wide shelf holding a large, chipped porcelain bowl and a few spices in glass jars. An icebox, obviously an antique, but still in working order, stood nearby. There was an old oak table big enough for two, with drop leaves for extra company. On the wall opposite

Tara was a huge rough-stone fireplace, two worn easy chairs and a rocker. The door to an adjoining room was slightly ajar, and a couple of fishing poles stood in the corner. On the other wall were more shelves, more books; a battered hat with fish hooks hanging from the brim; a heap of rolled maps and charts, plus a few pens and pencils in a mug with a broken handle. Another door obviously led outside, for there was a crack of golden light between it and the door frame.

The rest of the wall space was almost entirely taken up with large paned windows. Tara could see magnolia trees and jacarandas crowding around the cottage. Between the branches gleamed a clear blue sky, and off in the distance a wonderful expanse of delphinium-blue water. Where on earth was she, she wondered. An island of sorts?

Frowning, Tara dropped back onto the pillows. The abrupt movement made her aware of a number of aches and pains. She groaned, reached up to scratch her shoulder, which was itching unbearably, and noticed she was wearing a man's shirt. She stared at the rolled-up sleeve, then pulled her other arm free from the covers. Yes, it was definitely a man's shirt.

Was it his? Startling questions arose in rapid succession. She huddled deeper under the blankets, then tried again to scratch her shoulder, but couldn't because of the bandages. Further investigation revealed two more bandages, one on her side and one on her right thigh.

Tara sighed deeply, vexed beyond memory. It was one thing to be rescued by a handsome, irritating, mysterious man; quite another to think of him undressing her and applying bandages. Why weren't there more people around? Where was she? And more importantly, who was he?

Perhaps—the thought pleased her—perhaps she had dreamed him. That might explain her claustrophobia and shortness of breath when he was near. For she'd never felt that way before when confronted by a man, and there had to be some reason for it. Yes, that was it. He was a figment of her dreamtime imagination, a product of muddled thinking. Any moment now a nice buxom old woman would come ambling in.... Tara settled down to sleep, feeling immensely relieved. When the crack of light beneath the door widened she looked up casually.

There he was, in flesh and blood. Tara felt unaccountably annoyed with him, against all reason. No man had the right to disturb her sense of balance as he did, to look so uncompromisingly masculine, to radiate that aura of control and authority as a matter of course. His very presence intimidated her. A man like this would take any girl's breath away, she thought grudgingly. He had already wreaked havoc with hers.

Her sense of humor suddenly took over, and she smiled wryly to herself. Most likely he had so many female admirers he wouldn't have time for another, especially one as bedraggled as she was.

Tara continued to study him with avid curiosity through lowered lashes, pretending to be asleep. He was an enigma, she decided at last; she couldn't explain him. A shabby denim shirt covered powerful shoulders; worn jeans fitted over lean hips and long straight legs. He was barefoot, too. His hair was as black as hers, but there the resemblance ended, for his was a heavy mass of jumbled waves and curls that reached the back of his collar. He had an unusual face, rather like a chiseled sculpture: a high smooth forehead; thick black brows; disturbing eyes with lashes too heavy for any man; an aquiline nose; and a firm mouth, the top lip almost straight, the bottom one sensuously full. Below, a hard square jawline was covered in about two days' growth of beard. He looked perfectly at home in this rude setting, yet he would probably look at home anywhere, she decided. Worn denims or a gray flannel suit would make no difference to him.

"You can wake up now!" There was an ironic gibing tone to his voice, a wry twist to his lips. He'd known all along she wasn't asleep, and wild-rose color stained her cheeks at having been caught. His tone was deep, resonant, filled with lazy offhand amusement. "Have you finished your inspection?" He almost laughed aloud. "If so, it's time to eat. I think you're well enough now to sit up by yourself!"

For some reason Tara felt that he was subtly taunting her. He probably thought her a prudish female; yet even he would have to admit her situation was highly irregular! She was wearing his shirt, after all! Was entirely at his mercy, without a clue as to where she might be. Defiantly she lifted her chin in what was an unknowingly vulnerable gesture.

"I would like some coffee, if I may," she said, her tone determinedly polite.

Then he did laugh. The carefree male sound sent a surge of blood through her veins and into her cheeks.

"Hmm, you really are awake! Last night you weren't nearly as reserved as you are now. I like you better half-asleep!" He tilted his head to one side, and a mocking smile played at the corners of his sensuous mouth. "But no, mermaid, that wide-eyed, black-magic stare isn't going to get you any coffee. No—" he had a faint trace of an accent, she noticed through her vexation "—milk and honey is what you get!"

Her temper flared at his cheerfully patronizing tone. Tara felt as though she'd been receiving a fierce electric shock ever since first setting eyes on him, and now seemed as good a time as any to let him know she was equal to it. She started off in her most dignified disdainful voice, "But I hate milk! I tried to tell you—"

"It didn't do you any good then and it's not going to now!" He had the effrontery to grin at her irritation. "You're at my mercy and you'll take what I give you." Then his tone changed, as if he were coaxing an overindulged child. "You were such a meek little thing only moments ago. Try to recapture that mood!"

A spitting cat, that was what she felt like, even though it was illogical. She owed him her life, that was clear. She should feel thankful, grateful, indebted even! Then why did she want to throw something at him? Everything he said made her hackles rise. He seemed to sense how she reacted to him and was intentionally poking fun at her. A clash of personalities, she decided; antagonism right from the start. They weren't destined to become friends.

There was a mutinous gleam in her liquid dark eyes when he put a large mug into her hands. It was brimful of milk, but she gulped it all down as quickly as she could. She even managed a dutiful "Thank you." The man's dry smile registered his disbelief in her sincerity and set her teeth on edge.

Her lunch of fresh rock cod was delicious, though, and Tara ate almost all of her enormous portion, trying not to show how much she enjoyed it. "Thank you," she said again, sincerely this time, as she pushed the rough pottery plate away.

"Finish it! Now!" he clipped.

"Or you'll make me do so?" Tara's eyes were as fiercely indignant as her tone, but he remained implacable, looking as though he fully intended to carry out his earlier threat. She quickly picked up her fork, and had an urge to throw it at him when he chuckled at her haste. Master of the moment, he sat there and watched the cod disappear off her plate with the intensity of a scientist watching an experiment.

Her distrust of him didn't lessen after the large meal, even though a feeling of sleepy contentment overcame her. She'd wanted adventure, and she'd got it! Now that she was through the worst she had to admit it was fun. Better than Hampstead by far—except, of course, for Him. He was something she hadn't bargained for when she'd set out in the world—but then, neither had she expected the *Adventure Star* to sink!

"What's your name?" she asked abruptly, trying

to smother a yawn. It seemed like a good time to get to the bottom of her mysterious rescue, to find out exactly what had happened and to decide what to do next. Something told her the sooner she got away from this enigmatic fellow the better off she'd be. If only her mind would work a little faster....

"Jorge."

"Oh. Jorge what?"

"Jorge Emmanuel Valente de Silves, my lady." His wry smile mocked her.

"Oh!" It was a soft cry of dismay. Valente de Silves...a Portuguese wine with a worldwide reputation. "Not the same...?" Her voice sank in disbelief.

"Just about everybody recognizes the name," he answered lazily.

Tara groaned weakly. The Valente de Silves family! The next time she asked the powers that be for adventure she would be more specific, she vowed. To land in the lap of one of the oldest, most aristocratic families in Europe was not something one did every day. And certainly *not* in a nightgown!

One member of the family or another was always being written up in the society pages, although Tara couldn't remember ever reading about Jorge. Perhaps he was the black sheep of the family, she decided, and didn't like that kind of publicity. She hoped so, for her advent on the scene was likely to produce some rather inglorious headlines. In her mind's eye she could see them now: SHIPWRECKED SURVIVOR LANDS ON VALENTE'S ISLAND IN NIGHTGOWN. And in smaller letters: Spent three days alone together.....

She sighed dismally, but midway the sigh turned into a wide yawn. In vain she tried to stay awake, for it was now of the utmost importance to get away from Jorge Emmanuel Valente de Silves. However, the folds of sleep weighed heavier and heavier.

"I don't want to stay here with you!" she mumbled. "I won't, you know. I'll get away. I'll leave in the...morning...."

IT WAS EVENING when Tara woke up again. The westering sun painted a thick golden sheen on the rough walls of the cabin, turning it into a sumptuous gilded parlor. From where she lay she could see Jorge's shadow, long and black, on the plank floor.

After struggling to sit up she peeked around the alcove's corner. He was peeling potatoes over the chipping porcelain bowl. That brought an instant smile to her lips, a sparkle to her eyes. She was feeling much better—more like herself—and was ready to tackle even this formidable Valente—man. Awesomely handsome though he might be, she thought grimly. Intimidating, too—but to lesser persons than her, now that she had her wits about her. Her earlier lack of capability could be excused; she'd still been recuperating. He hadn't got the better of her yet! And somehow she would get herself out of this mess without appearing in every newspaper across the country. It really shouldn't be too difficult.

"Hello!" she called cheerfully, ready to be friendly now that she felt equal to his profound attraction, equal to the challenge of his arrogant manner.

"Welcome back, mermaid," he answered, his

teeth flashing white against the burnished bronze of his face, and his eyes crinkling at the corners when he smiled. Tara felt unaccountably short of breath. "I can see you're wide awake now," he continued with lazy amusement, while his level assessing glance seemed to see right into her thoughts. "Has the meek, oh so polite child vanished for good?"

"You...you're supposed to be nice to invalids, didn't you know?" Tara snapped, hiding behind the only defense she could think of at a moment's notice. She didn't know why, but for some reason she felt inordinately sensitive. The least amount of teasing from him sent her usually mild temper flaring.

"For heaven's sake, why?" He was laughing at her. "Didn't anyone ever tell you not to bite the hand that feeds you? You know, you must have been an awful brat—thoroughly spoiled by mama and papa, I suppose?"

From the tone of his voice Tara knew he wasn't supposing at all; it was a bald statement. One that Tara had to admit was partially true, but it didn't give him the right to say so! Instantly her friendly feelings were gone. All the important questions she'd been going to ask faded into insignificance. He had such a dreadful knack of being able to put her down! And at the same time he was so extraordinarily, irritatingly attractive! Jorge Emmanuel Valente de Silves was definitely not from the same mold as most men, and she sensed that that in itself was dangerous to her equilibrium. She longed to ruffle him as he ruffled her.

"You are the most high-and-mighty man I've ever

had the dubious pleasure of meeting!" she retorted with nervous intensity, trying to appear icily condescending. "I suppose I should say 'thank you,' since you saved my life. Well, thank you very much! I want you to know I do appreciate that. But I simply can't be everlastingly grateful. I simply can't pay homage at your shrine!"

"I was wrong," he stated calmly with barely concealed humor, "when I said you must have been a brat. You still are one! Ill-mannered, too! Why in heaven's name your parents ever let you out of their sight is beyond me. Anyone with one eye shut could see you're not capable of taking care of yourself—"

"I can hardly be blamed for the storm, can I?" Tara interrupted sharply. "Or the lousy bilge pumps! Captain Baker didn't have your opinion of me. He— Miss Tillesby— I wouldn't have fallen overboard if she hadn't pushed me!"

"You fell off a ship?" His tone was incredulous and edged with unkind laughter.

"Off the lifeboat!" Tara's sense of humor had for once deserted her. "And I didn't fall; I was pushed!"

"What happened to—"

"The ship sank!" she said, cutting him off. "There was a terrible storm, and our ship sprang a leak," she explained patiently, as though to a child; she was going to give him some of his own medicine. "The bilge pumps failed. First the engine room flooded, and then the whole ship began to sink. When the main deck went under we all got into the lifeboats. Miss Tillesby shoved me overboard. With all the noise and confusion, no one noticed I was gone. I found a rubber raft and climbed aboard. That's all I remember. Now, if you think that shows carelessness on my part, so be it!'' She suspected there was a twinkle in his eye and disliked him all the more for it. "Don't you believe me?'' she demanded.

"Of course I do, mermaid! I caught the storm here, and it damn near blew my roof off. By the way, your raft snagged on the reefs just past the beach. I saw it there yesterday morning when I found you.''

"When you found me....'' Tara echoed. "By the way, what happened to my, uh, robe and night-gown?''

"There wasn't much left.''

He strode to the door, to return with a handful of filmy scraps, still wet and sandy. Tara swallowed at the sight and inwardly thanked him again for finding her. To die alone like that would have been horrible. Again the awesomeness of her adventure, or rather misadventure, struck her. And it wasn't over yet; it wouldn't be until she said a final thank you and goodbye to this man. She stared at him, vaguely distressed.

The only things she possessed now were her panties and her ruby earrings—not much to go on. But at least they'd escaped the fate of her gown, and that was something to be thankful for. The panties would probably be uncomfortable and stiff from the salt water, she surmised, just as her hair was. What a mess she was in! But more important, how was she to get out of it? The problem seemed terribly difficult all of a sudden—too big to deal with. And she was too tired to try.

"I have to change your bandages," Jorge said abruptly. He'd been standing there watching the fleeting changes of expression across her troubled face. "And it will be easier for both of us if you don't argue. Just think of me as your... family physician." His eyes flashed over her pale creamy face; her dusky eyes, too large and shadowed; her tangled hair spread like a dark cloud over the pillow. The dejected slump of her shoulders was almost lost in the folds of his shirt, and she seemed dwarfed in his large bed, her slender shape barely visible under the thick sheep's-wool blankets.

"Couldn't I do it?" Tara asked after a pregnant pause.

"No. You're hardly in any condition to. Besides, it's a grim sight, and you still have to eat your dinner. There shouldn't be any scars," he amended quickly when he saw alarm spread over her face. "I studied a bit of medicine once, and—"

"You're a doctor, too?" Her tone was sarcastic, the result of an engulfing wave of shyness. This stranger had seen her stark naked! "My goodness, but aren't we talented!"

The remark slipped out in one awful second before Tara could stop herself. Had she gone too far? One didn't insult a man like Jorge without just cause, especially not when he'd just saved one's life. She noticed a sudden hard glint in his eyes, a flicker of cold flame in the midnight black, and she felt panic rising within her. What did she know of this man? Would he retaliate?

"No, I'm no doctor," he drawled smoothly, glossing over her indiscretion like a steamroller over an ant. He sat down on the bed. "For such a pint-size thing you have an oversize temper! Now shut up and behave, or I'll throw you back into the sea!"

Tara, shamefaced and gritting her teeth, lay perfectly still as he drew down the blankets. Then he took fresh bandages, antiseptic and salve from a cupboard under the bed and put them beside her.

She stared agitatedly at him, watching each professional movement. She was fascinated and repelled at the same time—torn between the two. As the cotton on her thigh came off she bit sharply into her full bottom lip, willing herself not to look. The small cry of pain she choked back came out as a muffled whimper. His eyes flicked up and over her like the touch of a light hand, and she couldn't control the shiver that raced down the length of her body as his warm hand closed over her thigh.

"For heaven's sake, haven't you been touched by a man before?" He paused, studying her. "You really are an innocent, aren't you." His lips twisted.

She gazed at him mutely, hotly embarrassed and unable to explain her telltale reaction. How could she protest that it was involuntary, that his overwhelming masculinity wasn't comfortable to be close to?

He sighed impatiently, finishing the chore as quickly as possible. Tara's bottom lip felt lacerated by the time it was all over. But she hadn't succumbed to her embarrassment or pain; she had too much pride for that, and tears had never been her style. In relief she eased herself back against the pillows, aching in every cell.

Jorge didn't move but stared down at her, still frowning. His keen eyes searched her face and seemed to probe her innermost self with a dark forceful intentness. An indefinable tension bore down on her, eclipsing her rational mind, seeming to envelop them both in delicate mesh threads. Tara felt like a piece of brittle glass that might shatter into a million bits if he continued to stare at her in just that way.

"Better?" His voice, taut and clipped, broke the illusion. He rose from the bed.

"Yes, thank you." She cleared her throat, making an effort toward normality. "I don't feel so itchy."

"You're healing." His glance was swift and sardonic, penetrating in its clarity.

"Is there a bathroom?" She slowly recovered her composure. There was an audacious tilt to her chin as she returned his look. "I would like to brush my teeth."

"Through there," he said, waving a hand. "There's an extra toothbrush in the drawer. You'll find plenty of soap and towels, but no luxuries."

"I didn't expect any," Tara replied tartly, and before he could help her, swung her legs off the bed in a neat concise movement. She would have liked to walk proudly and disdainfully across the room to the bathroom door, but her very sore right thigh made that impossible. She had to content herself with a dignified limp. A faint malicious smile curled his lips as he watched her uneven progress, and Tara slammed the makeshift bathroom door to shut out the cool blackness of his gaze.

Having a sponge bath helped the way she felt, and

so did brushing her teeth. But Jorge's comb would not go through the tangled stiff mass of her long hair, and she finally gave up trying to force it. Nothing but a shampoo would help, and she felt too weak to attempt that.

During her ministrations she devised a new battle plan. Cold politeness was the answer. She must not let him affect her so strangely; throw her so completely off balance; give her such a case of jitters. His peculiar blend of charm and hard arrogance would get nowhere with her. She had to maintain an even keel, for this irrational seesaw of attraction and antagonism wasn't safe. A man as exciting, as intriguing as he was would never be *safe*. Vaguely she sensed that he could have a lingering effect on her life, and she felt frightened at such an implication. The sooner she saw the last of him the better. She needed a clear head to organize her new life. He was an unnecessary complication. . . .

Jorge was whistling when Tara opened the bathroom door. For a moment she remained where she was, leaning against the doorjamb looking young and almost unbearably slender. He was bent in front of the fireplace, adjusting a rack into grooves in the stone. He placed the peeled potatoes on it, then cranked the spit, on which a plump succulent duck was roasting. Drops of fat spit and crackled as they fell into the flames. Slowly turning his head he looked up at her, and the curve of his lips deepened.

"Very arresting," he commented dryly.

"Do you have a hairbrush?" she asked, ignoring his own touch of sarcasm. "Your comb didn't go very far."

"I can see that. Don't worry, mermaid. There's no one here but me to see you." Again that mocking, slightly insulting intonation.

"I'm not concerned with my lack of beauty!" Her temper blazed up, but in a second she had it under tight control. "It's mere cleanliness and comfort I'm after. And if these knots get much worse I shall have to cut it all off."

"Hmm, that would be a pity. But whoever said you weren't beautiful?" His voice was full of blank spurious innocence. "Surely not me! I couldn't tell such an outrageous lie!" He placed a chair in front of the fireplace and motioned her toward it. "Come here."

Warily she eyed him. "I promise not to pounce!" he said somberly, though his eyes danced like twin flames. "Just come over here like a good girl, and Uncle Jorge will take care of you." He laughed in his throat, and suddenly Tara hated him. "Spitting cats don't get any supper," he added warningly.

That did it. Tara's carefully controlled temper exploded like a rocket.

"It just isn't going to work!" she cried passionately. "I'm just not able to maintain any degree of civility with you!" She drew a shaky audible breath.

The last rays of sun caught her face and the slender column of her throat, highlighting the hollows under her cheekbones, the iridescent sheen of her satin-smooth skin. At the base of her throat a vein throbbed painfully. Jorge's eyes slid over her, keen and amused, noting how the shoulder seams of his shirt hung almost down to her elbows, how the shirt-tails reached well down over her thighs.

"It's difficult to believe you mean business in that outfit," he drawled with superb equanimity, "but you're giving it a pretty good try! You have—excuse the expression—guts to match your...volatile temper. I'm impressed! In fact, I'm admiring. I realize now why Captain Baker—was that his name—had such a high opinion of you!"

He held out a blanket to her. There was nowhere else to go, so feeling absurdly defeated, Tara went over to him. He wrapped the blanket around her shoulders, then pushed her into the chair. Inwardly unsettled, she watched him place the table behind her; then, upon it the chipped porcelain bowl, towels and shampoo.

She realized then what he meant to do, and that she would rather be thrown back in the sea than have Jorge Valente wash her hair. She reared up, but his hands clamped down on her shoulders, forcing her back into the chair.

"Bully!" she hissed at him.

"I've been called a few names before, but never that!" She could hear his smile, even though she couldn't see it. "Relax, *querida*, and pretend you're at the hairdresser's."

"Did you study hairdressing, as well?" she asked, her voice scathing.

"And do you bite the head off every man you meet?" His long fingers settled around her throat and rested there for a few tantalizing seconds before he pulled her head firmly back.

Despite herself Tara enjoyed the sensation his hard fingertips, moving rhythmically over her scalp, aroused. It was oddly soothing, strangely intimate. An ordinary occurrence such as washing hair was suddenly charged with magic, just because he was performing the task.

"Speaking of children, how were you christened?"

"Tara Cybelle Lownes."

"Hmm.... It's suitable. And our Captain Baker thought so, too?"

"Captain Baker is a wonderful man! He practically saved all our lives!" she answered warmly, overlooking the probing sarcasm of his last question. She was carried away on the discovery of something new in the world of washing hair.

"And how do you know the others are all alive?"

It was a ghastly question, for Tara had never considered that possibility. Of course everyone else was fine! Hadn't they spotted a rescue ship just before Miss Tillesby pushed her out of the boat? She related the story of those last dramatic moments.

"What was the name of your ship?" he asked.

Tara told him, somewhat bitterly.

"The *Adventure Star*!" he exclaimed. She knew what he was thinking: that she'd traveled on the most expensive elite cruise ship she could find for Penny's reason—to find a rich husband! If the implication hadn't made her so angry, she would have laughed at the irony of it.

"I see!" There was a wealth of meaning in those two short syllables.

"You don't see at all!" she snapped, flinching as the cool rinse water tingled over her scalp. "My cousin was going on the cruise, and at the last minute she decided not to go. I know what you're thinking, but a rich husband is the last thing I'm after!''

"A poor one, then?"

She gritted her teeth. "Why do members of the male sex consider that females are always dying to get married? I, for one, am not, and I doubt that I'm an exception. I have too many other things to do."

"Like playing games with your undoubtedly large circle of admirers?"

"I was on my way to Las Palmas!" she snapped. He was infuriating, shampoo or no shampoo.

"'Curiouser and curiouser!'" he quoted. "And just exactly what were you going to do there?"

"*Toodles, the Bear with a Bad Case of Big Nose*, book two."

There was silence from behind her. He thought her slightly concussed, perhaps? Tara started laughing.

"Would you have the grace to explain?" he asked in his deep voice.

"I write children's stories, you see—so I'm not entirely useless, as you seem to think. Book one received 'favorable response,' and my publisher asked me to write a sequel." Satisfaction was evident in her voice.

"How very interesting!"

To her consternation, and then awakening delight, Jorge started combing out the tangles in her waist-length ebony hair. Tara suddenly felt as she imagined Cleopatra would have felt had Mark Anthony done the same for her: exquisitely regal, and at the very least, lovely enough to win a beauty competition against the legendary Helen of Troy. It was a new feeling for her, amazingly heady, spreading pleasurable effervescent warmth right to the tips of her fingers and toes.

"I should like to read a copy."

That stopped her short. "You can't be serious!"

"Perfectly serious, Tara! But what do your parents think of Las Palmas?" That horrible mocking laughter was there in his voice again, relegating her to the level of a twelve-year-old who had just run away from home with a few possessions tied in a red kerchief.

Her vision of Anthony and Cleopatra shimmered like a dream, then faded into the rough board walls. Tara felt bereft, as though a limb had just been torn from her. In consequence, she overreacted to his question.

"For heaven's sake, I'm not a child! I'm twenty-two, and contrary to your low opinion of me, perfectly capable of taking care of myself! It's only freak storms and bilge pumps and Miss Tillesbys I have trouble with!" *And stupid romantic visions of Anthony and Cleopatra,* she reprimanded herself.

"What was the matter with Miss Tillesby?"

"She's neurotic to begin with, and when the storm hit she just flipped right out." Tara's tone was completely opposite to what she was feeling. "She told Captain Baker she didn't trust anyone but me, so I took care of her. Or rather, she took care of me."

"Ah! The mighty Captain Baker again."

"You're determined to annoy me, aren't you? You're implying—"

"Sit still, can't you?" he cut in. His lean, very

capable fingers tugged against the knots in her hair.

Tara subsided into a brooding silence. She determinedly put Anthony and Cleopatra behind her and forced herself to think happy thoughts. The rescue of the passengers and crew by that other ship, for example....

"Oh, my God!" she exclaimed.

"What is it now?" Jorge asked impatiently. "Surely I'm not that rough?"

"My parents! How long have I been here? They'll think I'm dead!"

"Most likely they do!" His tone was dispassionate.

"How can you be so...so.... You may not like me very much, but I assure you, they do! Let go of my hair! I've got to telephone or wire—or something!"

"You can't. I have no telephone and no telegram service here. I'm sorry, Tara."

"But where on earth are we? There must be something! A car...a horse?"

"This is an island called Chão. It's one of the Desertas, off Madeira. We are the only two living things here except for the birds, the seals and a wild goat or two. The Desertas are...deserted. I bought this island ten years ago and purposely left out telephones and radios."

"But how do you get here? By boat?"

"Emilio flies me in. Once I'm here I stay until he comes back."

"You must really trust him, this Emilio. By the way, who is he?"

"My butler. This time I arranged to stay for only four days, so you're in luck."

"Four days!" Tara cried in dismay. She was so upset she forgot to even smile at the incongruity of a flying butler.

"You've already been here for three, so Emilio comes tomorrow. As soon as he lands I'll radio in. That's the best I can do."

Tara twisted around to look at him, but his glittering black eyes met hers directly. So she really had been here for three days. Her sense of time was completely distorted, as was everything else. It was curious, the effect he had on her, almost making her believe in magic. She'd even forgotten about her parents until this moment. How did he do it?

"Don't look so panic-stricken, mermaid. So far you're only missing—not dead. They won't believe you're really dead until they find your body, and they're not likely to, are they? Don't think about what they're going through now. There's nothing you can do about it! And stop looking at me like that or I might do something we'll both regret!"

Tension crackled between them. A hot quick tingle swept down Tara's spine; the magic returned with a rush. She could not pull her eyes away from his. She was mesmerized, hypnotized. Fear sent her heart racing. He must be a sorcerer, for what else could explain the wild passions conflicting within her?

Jorge expelled his breath in one short burst of impatience. Then his mouth covered hers—hard, knowing, forcing her lips apart with sure deliberation; forcing her head back until it felt like her neck would snap. Raw sensuality.... Never had any man dared kiss her in this fashion! Tara wrested herself away from him, breathing heavily, and put the length of the room between them. The blanket slipped off onto the floor.

"Is that what you wanted?" Jorge asked. His eyes glowed darkly, a tinge of savageness evident. But his voice was cool, detached, sardonic. As usual, he was in control, whereas she felt stricken. His keen gaze raked her from head to foot, and she started shaking in a high pitch of agitation.

"What do you mean, what I wanted!" she gasped.

"If the look in your black-velvet eyes meant anything, just what I said. Play with fire and you'll get burned." His voice was dangerously soft. "I'm not one of your grammar-school boyfriends, *querida*, so don't tempt me."

As he advanced, Tara backed away. But he merely picked up the blanket, settled it around her shoulders and held it together in the front.

At the same time he drew her toward him. "Don't look so frightened. I haven't yet stooped to seducing babes in arms. Neither am I likely to."

Then he shoved her gently toward the chair. "Now sit down and let your hair dry. Don't say anything—just behave!"

CHAPTER FIVE

TARA DID AS SHE WAS TOLD, looking everywhere except at Jorge. Her anger was cooling, but oh, how she despised him! Hated him for kissing her the way he had. Hated him because he knew she wanted to be kissed. Hated him for the strange illusive happiness he had given her and then snatched away. But most of all she loathed herself for responding to his kiss. She'd been like a quivering lump of jelly, she thought disgustedly. Her bones had dissolved under his blue black spell. Midnight magic; it was deadly.

She pulled the blanket tighter, shaking her head to make her hair dry faster. What had happened to her willpower during those few seconds when his mouth had covered hers? Never before had it vanished so completely, like morning mist before a blazing sun. And right now she needed it more than anything; needed it to get her through until Emilio came. She wasn't going to get very far if she melted into a pool of water, or started fantasizing about Anthony and Cleopatra every time Jorge looked at her! She darted a swift venomous glance in his direction. If only tomorrow would come quickly. If only Emilio, the rather bizarre flying butler, would rescue her from this island and from Jorge Emmanuel Valente de

Silves! She didn't spare a thought for what she would do once Emilio rescued her, or where she would go without clothes or money.

Then an awful thought struck her. "Are you married?" she asked before she could stop herself.

His eyebrows shot up. "No, I'm not. Nor am I affianced. Why? Are you going to try for the position?" The familiar glimmer of amusement entered his eyes as he watched her, waiting for her answer.

"I only wanted to know if I could dislike you a little more," Tara retorted with spirit. "If you were married...."

"My kissing you would amount to a double crime?" He laughed with genuine amusement, then sobered slightly. His eyes came to rest on the full curve of her mutinously set lips, and his voice became mockingly serious. "If ever I did take that formidable step and got married, there would be no need for...philandering—no matter how many fragile mermaids crossed my path."

"Oh, heavens, I do pity your choice, though! I wonder if the poor thing has an inkling of just what's in store for her!"

"I don't think she does...." He was staring at her in a most unsettling way, his eyes tracing the line of her brow, the smooth curve of her determined chin. Tara bit her lip in vexation.

"How could she?" he continued lightly. "And who knows, but the 'poor thing' just might like it. Fire burns, but it also keeps one warm!"

"I don't think I'd chance it."

"Since I'm not exactly eager to marry, and you, by

your own admission, aren't either, there's not much chance of your having to chance it, is there?''

Tara didn't say anything, mainly because she couldn't think of anything scathing enough to say. She didn't have much practice at male/female verbal battles and she was sure she would lose this one, just as she'd lost all the others to date. It was demoralizing to lose every time. Always she'd been the one in cool calm control. But that was before she'd had the mischance to bump into this character. She slanted a glowering look in his direction and got a chuckle in return.

"Can't think of anything to say?" he asked. "Are you finally learning that it doesn't do any good to fight?''

At that Tara found her tongue. "Are you implying I should just take everything you dish out?"

His voice was a slow even drawl as he answered, "You asked for what I gave you!''

TARA REMAINED STUDIOUSLY POLITE throughout the roast-duck supper. She couldn't even bring herself to praise Jorge's cooking, although the meal was superb. If she hadn't been so hungry she wouldn't have eaten at all, she thought childishly, a heartfelt sigh escaping her.

Jorge's eyebrows lifted at the mournful sound. He noticed the dark smudges beneath Tara's large eyes, the slight trembling of her hands that she couldn't hide. "Finish your milk," he prompted.

Tara did so without a murmur. She was too tired, too dispirited to argue. She needed time to draw upon reinforcements. After a good night's sleep she would be able to stand up to him, she assured herself optimistically. He wouldn't affect her at all then....

She blinked with amazement as he set a mug of steaming coffee in front of her. Looking up quickly into his copper-dark face, she murmured, "Thank you." She had to struggle to maintain her even polite tone. The effort almost choked her, but she had enough savoir faire to carry it off. There wasn't a person on earth who could reduce her to complete defeat, and her deceptively calm conversational tone restored some of her usual self-confidence. "Tell me, do you come here often?" she added.

"When the mood takes me. It's a good place to think, you see. No interruptions."

"I certainly showed up without a welcome," she said ruefully. She wondered what she must have looked like when he found her, and the thought made her squirm inwardly.

"I thought I was going to be the first documented case of a man actually finding a flesh-and-blood mermaid." A smile flitted over his features.

"I'm sorry," Tara said irrelevantly.

"I'm not. It's been most entertaining!"

She flushed, the rosy color staining the pallor of her face, dusting her wide cheekbones and complementing the deeper rose of her lips. She quickly decided to change the topic, and carried on in her best art gallery-committee tones. "Do you live in Portugal?"

"Off and on." Jorge was looking at her through half-closed eyes, and it was impossible to read his expression. He seemed to be very close to her, yet he was actually sitting across the table. "That's where my family lives."

She knew that. Some members of the extensive de Silves family lived in Lisbon; others in Vila Nova de Gaia, a small town farther north in the heart of the wine district. The head of the family lived in Vila Nova de Gaia. "Your family?" she prompted.

"The usual. Father, mother, my younger brother, José, and a very much younger sister, Juana. Our mother continued the Valente tradition by starting all our names with *j*. And then there are reams of uncles and aunts and cousins in Lisbon."

Well, that answered that, Tara thought. His father was João Valente—Duque Valente de Silves! Who *hadn't* heard of him? Tara had never seen a picture of his mother in the society pages, but what she'd read of Nona Valente sounded formidable: soirées with Princess so-and-so, charity balls that Tara's own mother would give her eyeteeth to organize.

In her mind's eye she saw the *duquesa* as a tall spare woman—all patrician nose, cold gray eyes and heaps of heavy gold antique rings. The very image was daunting. If Tara could just slip quietly away from this dreadful contretemps she might escape the notice of this formidable family. Hopefully Emilio would prove helpful....

Clipped tones, accompanied by one black quirked eyebrow, broke into her reverie. "And what about your own family?" he asked.

She quickly filled in some sketchy details of her life. Besides her parents the only other relatives she had were her Uncle Albert and Aunt Dorothy, and of course, Penny. She mentioned her grandmother, but not the inheritance. Nothing about Dennis, either, and she made a rather obscure reference to Hampstead. But Jorge was insistent. He wanted to know what her father did and what her mother was like and where her relatives lived.

Tara found herself describing Uncle Albert warmly. Aunt Dorothy she treated as nicely as she could, although she hesitated a couple of times in midsentence. When she did she thought she caught an annoying twinkle in Jorge's eyes. "And Penny's very beautiful, with blond hair and blue eyes," she finished vaguely, still using her art gallery tone.

"You're leaving out a lot, aren't you?" he stated. "Penny's the one who was going on the cruise?"

"Yes."

"Why didn't she go?"

Tara sighed. "She decided to get married instead."

"Ah! So that meant she didn't need the cruise."

Tara sent him an exasperated glance, but her tone remained level. "There was only a reservation for one."

"But why did you go?" He was extremely persistent.

"I...I had to find a place to write my book, anyway, and since the *Adventure Star* stopped in a lot of ports...."

As his eyebrows rose she stopped speaking. Why did she have to explain everything to him, she wondered. She could see he didn't believe her.

"I wanted to be on my own," she continued impulsively. "Away from home. Away from my mother and her never ending string of eligible bachelors! I love my mother dearly, but she.... Well, she thinks I'll only be happy when I'm married. She doesn't understand that writing is important to me, nor that I want—" Tara broke off abruptly.

"What do you want?" he prodded.

She shook her head. She wasn't going to be cross-questioned by this man when he refused to divulge more about himself. "I'm tired," she stated. "All this talking I find quite exhausting all of a sudden."

There was a sardonic twist to his lips as he pulled the thick blankets firmly around her shoulders after she'd climbed into his big bed. He stood there looking down at her with narrowed eyes. In the shadows he seemed to be made of stone, impassive.... There was no soft spot, no chink in the impregnable armor. He was unknown, uncharted territory.

For a paralyzing moment Tara thought he was going to bend down to her, but instead he turned on his heel and walked across the room. Picking up the rocking chair, he brought it over to the bed. Tara watched him suspiciously as he sat down facing her.

"Now, tell me all about the storm and the subsequent events," he ordered in an unusually pleasant tone of voice. "If you're really so tired you can nod off right where you are. Start at the beginning."

"And finish at the end?" she quipped. "Oh, very well!" Sighing, she paused for a moment. Then she turned on her side and propped her head on one hand. "What day is it today?"

"June the fourth."

"Okay. The story begins the morning of June the first." Tara's talent as a raconteur was immediately in evidence. As she painted a vivid picture of the events of that fateful day, Jorge Valente sank into a comfortable slouch in his rocking chair. His gaze seldom left her expressive lively face.

"Then I must have fainted," she ended almost an hour later. "Because the next thing I remember is... is that huge bowl of hot milk! And milk is bad enough cold!"

"Maybe so," he replied, grinning. "But milk is good for growing bones and teeth. Didn't you know?"

He meant to get a rise out of her, she saw. Tara compressed her lips and said nothing.

She was again struggling inwardly against a distinct sense of claustrophobia. But how could she possibly feel closed in, she wondered. There were only the two of them on the whole island, which was far out in the sea, surrounded by space and more space.

That was just it; she couldn't get away whether she wanted to or not. A tenuous excitement was spreading through her despite her efforts to quell it. She and this stranger were completely, entirely alone, rather like Adam and Eve. Almost anything could happen....

"You're not going to snap my head off?" His easy drawl interrupted her line of thought. "Surely I've given you enough time to find a suitable retort?"

"Go pick on someone your own size."

"Touché!"

To her surprise they were suddenly laughing together. Easing his long length out of the rocking chair, Jorge bent over the bed, pulling the blankets back up around her shoulders and pushing her down to a lying position.

"It's time for all sweet young things to be fast asleep!" he murmured with a quizzical smile. In the gentle shadows shed by the kerosene lamp his teeth looked very white and his skin very dark in contrast.

"Where are you going to sleep?" A band of excitement tightened around Tara's chest. For a brief moment there was silence as his eyes caught and held hers. "It...it doesn't seem fair that I've annexed your bed," she explained, her tone light and nonchalant.

"Are you offering to share it with me?" His voice was like a brush of soft velvet against her skin.

She swallowed in panic. "Well, uh, not exactly...." Her confident tone trailed away into an uncertain whisper.

He paused before speaking, his black eyes minutely examining her face in the dim light. "You're younger than I thought." There was no censure; it was only a bare statement, softly spoken. "Don't worry about me, mermaid. I often sleep out under the stars."

He extinguished the kerosene lamp. In the doorway he turned back to her for a moment. Tara saw only his black silhouette against the star-studded sky before he shut the door and was gone.

The next morning Tara tried every ploy she could think of to get out of bed. But Jorge remained firm—unconcerned, even—and merely said she was the worst invalid he'd ever had to deal with. She had her breakfast in bed, swallowing large lumps of resentment with each mouthful of food. The sun felt hot through the blankets, hot on her skin, and the air was heavy with the tantalizing scent of flowers. Through her open window she heard bees droning by, saw the sea gulls and sandpipers far down by the water's edge, glimpsed the flicker of wet gleaming pelts in the everlasting blue. Seals! She heaved a sigh.

"Thank you for breakfast." She made her voice as bland as possible. "I'm so grateful!"

"Now that's highly unlikely. From the sparks in your eyes I'd say you're in the throes of another temper tantrum. You are an ungrateful brat, as I've mentioned before!"

"I try and try and try!"

"Perhaps what you should try is a change in tactics." He was smiling irresistibly.

"Nothing works with you," she retorted, but despite her sour mood she had to smile, too.

"And you are further ahead than you think, mermaid." He took the plate from her and exchanged it for a mug of coffee. His hand touched hers momentarily, and Tara drew quickly away.

She watched him as he walked away. Lithe, effortless movements, a tigerish grace.... He collected his rumpled fishing hat, a hand net and a small pail, then turned in the doorway. His eyes narrowed slightly as he glanced at her, and something indefinable glinted in their depths.

She couldn't resist the impulse to taunt him, and said childishly, "I hope a fish bites you, Mr. Valente

de Silves!'' Her crimson lips curved in an unconsciously provocative smile.

Jorge's mouth turned up wryly. ''If you so much
as dare get out of bed, mermaid, you'll find the day
of retribution is closer at hand than you expect!''

''It wouldn't surprise me!'' she answered. She
thrust her hands petulantly into her hair, pulling the
heavy strands up and off her nape. She let them fall
in one quick decisive gesture. ''The message is re-
corded if not understood, Mr. Valente de Silves.''

''Mr. Valente will do.''

His dark meaningful glance made her sink farther
down in the bed. With soft vehemence she swore at
the closed door. She felt so foolishly young and defenseless, so outmaneuvered! Damn the man! If only
she could once and for all make up her mind about
whether she liked or disliked him! It would make
dealing with him so much easier. But the conflicting
emotions that he aroused within her were equally intense. . . .

Her eyes turned longingly to the window. She was
aching with boredom; without him the cabin seemed
bare and dull. She shifted impatiently, yanking at the
folds in the blankets, then prepared grudgingly for a
long vigil.

The large showy blossoms of the magnolia trees
outside her window made splashes of delicate color,
and the periwinkle blue of the Brazilian jacarandas
appeared bright beside them. Tara could smell
honeysuckle but couldn't see the blooms. Bougainvillea rambled up the wall around her window, and
she stretched her arms to the utmost, wanting to

touch some of the brilliant red flower bracts. An exotic paradise, this Robinson Crusoe island she was on.

Butterflies floated past the window, dancing a complicated minuet in the balmy ocean breeze. Far below, two spindly-legged cranes had joined the sea gulls and sandpipers, their plumage glistening blue gray in the sunlight. And the sand looked positively delicious—a licorice ice-cream curve of beach licked by sapphire waves, which pounced upon each other in their hurry to get to shore. She breathed an enormous sigh of protest, closed her dark eyes only for a moment, and awakened to find lunch sizzling on the wood stove.

"What did you catch?" Tara asked eagerly. She twisted around in bed, pushing her fingers through her hair to tidy it. A delicious aroma was making her weak with hunger. It didn't seem possible that she'd lost any weight in so short a time, yet she had. And she was famished. Another storm would blow her away.

"We're having smelt for lunch, mermaid, and not one of them tried to bite!"

She looked at the back of his head, at his blue black, windblown curls. "They were too frightened, of course!" she retorted, grinning widely. She did feel better today.

"And you? Are you frightened?" he asked, eyeing her quizzically.

"That's an unfair question! Presumptuous, too."

"You can't have it both ways!"

His smile flashed white, compelling. His magnetism was strengthening its hold on her by the minute, she realized uneasily. How could she ignore it? Even talking with him was an excitement of sorts. But then, danger was always exciting. . . .

"But you can, seeing as how you're a man?" she taunted. "I've noticed that since I got here I've been following a lot of orders!"

"Your tongue certainly does run away with you—a most charming fault!" Jorge stated obliquely.

"Do you expect me to rise to that? I wouldn't touch it!" she replied scornfully. "Are you naturally bellicose, or do you turn it on and off as the moment suits you?"

"Where did you learn to talk like that? Don't you know honey draws more bees than vinegar? You should try it sometime."

"Now what would I want with a swarm of bees?" she asked innocently. "I prefer to go through life unencumbered by a following of. . .drones." She had to laugh. "Besides, I doubt that honey would sweeten you. You're much too. . .too domineering."

"Most women need a firm hand or they simply run amok."

"Oh! And what a charming way you have of expressing your opinions, Mr. Valente!" Tara refused to become ruffled by his teasing. Their verbal fencing, while fun, might end in unforeseen complications; she was going to take the safe route, she decided. Jorge had much more experience than she. She sensed that under his mocking, faintly derisive inflection he possessed a sure knowledge of women, rather like a maestro's knowledge of his orchestra. Her lips twitched at the simile; she could just picture the many women who would dance to his tune. A man like him always drew a crowd.

"You won't even nibble the bait? You disappoint me, Miss Lownes. I thought you were spoiling for a good fight."

"Don't judge others by your own feelings! And you have an unfair advantage. I can hardly look properly angry lying in bed. Besides, it's your bed, your shirt, your house, your food! I daren't incense you too much."

"I didn't think little details such as those would hinder you. You have a way of speaking your mind, and damn the consequences! Now wipe that holier-than-thou look off your face and put these pants on."

He threw a pair of his denims onto the bed. Then he uncoiled a loop of rope from the peg, judged a length and cut it off. He put that on top of the pants, then added a bulky fisherman's-knit sweater to the heap. With a cryptic smile he left the cabin.

Tara was out of bed before he'd properly closed the door. The rope, she found, held the denims up quite well, and it was exactly the right length for her to tie around her slender waist. Uneasily Tara wondered how he'd been able to judge so well. When she rolled the pant legs up halfway to her knees, she noticed that her toenails were still painted a bright cherry red—a provocative color, the manicurist on the ship had assured her. Then she pulled the sweater over her head. It was a ponderous affair, and the bottom almost met the rolled cuffs of Jorge's jeans.

Dressed at last, Tara opened the door and ventured outside, feeling as though she were part and parcel of a mysterious game in which there was no set of rules, no definite ending, no way of telling who won or lost. The Robinson Crusoe island heightened the effect, and the stillness of it made the feeling electric.

Chão, she noticed as she gazed around her, was a towering slab of black volcanic rock strewed with boulders. At the top it was ridged and seamed with granite, and with finer-grained basalt farther down by the water's edge. Pockets of vegetation thrived in small soil deposits, black and enriched. The terrain seemed to produce greenery wherever there was enough earth to bury a seed. Magnolias and jacarandas, bougainvillea and honeysuckle, oleander, hibiscus and hydrangeas grew in explosions of color against the austere background of ever present rock. Salt-brittle grasses sprang up in spiny patches closer to the water's edge, and giant heather grew where nothing else would, with great twisted stems as tall as trees bent over like hunched old men. In some places the rock plunged vertically into the sea; in other places small scalloped beaches ringed it in crystalline gray sand.

Tara circled the cabin. Straight below her, about a hundred yards away, was the licorice ice-cream beach she'd seen from her window. She saw now that the cabin was built on a high natural platform that sloped quickly up toward the north, providing an efficient buffer against the most violent sea storms. She walked farther around the cabin, and was suddenly overlooking the sea again. The island was extremely

narrow! To the south, barely visible over the rocks
and boulders of Chão, the string of Desertas continued like the humps of some prehistoric sea mon-
ster, poking up through the plate-glass sea.

Tara took a deep breath, relishing the salty tang on
the warm breeze. The sun poured down over her like
liquid gold. How glad she was just to be alive! She
expelled her breath slowly, easing the slight pain in
her chest. Jorge was probably right in insisting that
she wear his sweater, as pneumonia was unpleasant
at the best of times. But it was so unbearably hot!
She pushed her hair back behind her ears, looped it
into a knot and went looking for her rescuer.

Lunch was served on a large sun-baked slab of
rock. The meal consisted of the butter-fried smelt,
cucumbers, cherry tomatoes, raw fresh pieces of
cauliflower; a thick crusty loaf of French bread and
sweet butter. But best of all, Tara's milk was replaced by an elegant, tulip-shaped glass of pale sparkling wine.

"I take it you're pleased," Jorge said as, after
she'd done justice to the meal, she gave a long contented sigh.

Her eyes twinkled at him. "Heavens, yes! You're a
marvelous cook, even though you fall short in other
areas."

He threw back his head, laughing. "You do get the
odd hit home! All that salt water must have sharp-
ened your tongue, while it did nothing for your manners. Some day, *querida*, some man is going to take
you to task—and I don't envy him his lot. You're interesting, yes. Entertaining, yes. Beautiful, yes.

Quiet, no! And one can forget peaceful altogether! You'll keep the poor blighter hopping!''

"Perhaps your 'poor thing' and my 'poor blighter' should get hitched, since neither of us is likely to bring their romantic dreams to fruition. We're both dedicated bachelors, Mr. Valente, and I like it that way!''

"Did I say I was a dedicated bachelor?''

"No, but you hinted as much. Aren't you?''

"My, er, mother is a lot like yours, Tara, with her marriage-minded ideas. I daresay one of her protégées might stumble across me in a weak moment.''

"I find that hard to believe—the weak moment part, I mean. You are like this rock we're sitting on. Besides, why would you want to get married? You strike me as totally self-sufficient!'' Light sarcasm tinged her tone.

"Even I can't produce a son on my own,'' he drawled in wry humor, his black eyes shimmering over her. "And I want a son to carry on what I've built up.''

"What exactly have you built up?'' It was a leading question. Hoping he would answer, Tara made it sound coolly offhand. She was immensely curious and he was very reticent. She dropped her eyes, pretending to concentrate on a honeybee that was up to its back legs in a hibiscus blossom. Her lashes made thick and spiky curves on high slanting cheekbones.

"This and that,'' was the noncommittal reply. He grinned when her eyes flashed up at him. "It doesn't work; I'm impervious to velvet eyes and flower-petal lips. . . .''

"There you go again! You're trying to irritate me, it's obvious!"

"I was just being complimentary, and still you find fault!" he answered. "It's a pity you've taken such a strong dislike to me. I can't for a moment think why you have!"

"I could spell it out for you, but it would bore me to tears! Some other time, perhaps?"

"I'll hold you to that!"

"Fine!" she retorted rashly.

He replied to that with a slight smile, pinning her gaze. "And I get to choose when at my own discretion...right?"

Tara had the uneasy suspicion that a trap was being set. She stared back at him in deep contemplation.

"Right?" he prompted softly.

"Since I'm going to be pointing out your...foibles, I suppose that's only fair," she finally granted.

She tried to inject dislike into what was a certain unwanted admiration for the man. She wouldn't succumb to his considerable charms; she had too much common sense for that. It would be pure folly to fall for Jorge! Especially since she was so inexperienced. Pure idiocy to dream of Anthony and Cleopatra! And she'd already learned her lesson. She could still feel the burning quality of his lips....

Tara shook her head as though to shake him off, and her hair slipped out of its knot. The wind caught it, swirling it around her slender shoulders like shimmering black silk. The sun slanted obliquely across her face, highlighting the smoky depths of her eyes and turning the tips of her dark lashes to fine gold.

She stirred restlessly under Jorge's perceptive gaze. She didn't trust the deviousness of his smile; he had the look of a man who always got his way. For a moment she knew a devastating uncertainty.

Her eyes flew over the individual features of his face. How could she ever forget one of them? They were lodged in her mind as though carved in stone. What hell this man could play with a woman! Midnight magic in his eyes.... That smile, perpetually mocking, and yet with an elemental sensuousness that robbed her of her peace of mind. Her heartbeat quickened slightly. She put her hand to her throat in a defensive, purely feminine gesture. His eyes glittered suddenly, and Tara had the distinct vision of a tiger about to pounce on unsuspecting prey. She leaped to her feet.

"I'll never understand men!" she stated resolutely, avoiding his astute gaze. She gathered the plates together with nervous intensity, banging one down on top of the other. Action helped to release her mounting tension.

"Leave them!" he ordered.

Tara's eyes flickered over his lean hard body, his dark exciting face. Defiantly she reached for the wineglasses.

One of his hands snaked out and grasped her wrist in a steely grip. He pulled her quickly toward him, and the protest died on her parted lips. As he swung her down beside him, her ambivalent feelings for him mingled and merged until she could no longer tell one from the other. Then his head came down, blotting out the sun, and he was kissing her. . . kissing her until she felt nothing but the full weight of his hard male body and the searing exquisite heat of his mouth. Her body became fluid and yielding; her soft mouth clung to his. She was no thinking creature, but a woman obsessed by a man, drowning in midnight magic.

When his mouth left hers Tara felt shipwrecked once again. She was weak willed, she knew. She didn't even have the strength to resist the man when she wanted to!

His dark eyes held hers, daring her to look away, glinting with a peculiar blend of arrogance and tenderness. Her returning gaze was shadowed, the jeweled irises cloudy with new sensitivity. Deliberately he wound one hand through the abundance of her hair, forcing her to lie still beneath him. And with the same careful deliberation he began kissing her face and then her throat. . . never hastily or hesitantly, but with a languorous sensuality and a totally unexpected intimacy. Her hands clutched at his denim shirt and the muscles underneath. Her breathing became more and more shallow until she barely seemed to be breathing at all. Every cell in her body was caught up in the kisses. Slowly her tense grip softened as she sank into blissful acquiescence. Now she was holding him to her, her arms winding around his broad shoulders. . . .

Suddenly he raised his head, listening. "Emilio's coming," he breathed. His smile flashed down at her. "Just your luck!" He laughed deep in his throat, a disturbing sound to her senses, but one which nevertheless brought the world back into focus. He stood up, swinging her with him.

Now Tara, too, could hear a faint hum, barely louder than the droning of the honeybees. She scanned the sky, purposely turning away from him, for the change back to ordinary day was too abrupt for her. His arm tightened around her shoulders, however, as he pointed her toward the northeast. She followed the direction of his arm and saw a speck against the deep blue sky.

In a few minutes she would be leaving.... A tremor rushed through her. Unconsciously she leaned slightly against Jorge. She might never see him again! But she wanted to tell him so many things. Endless thoughts ran through her head...dreams, half-wished possibilities. Now that the time had come she didn't want to go anywhere!

She felt unbearably moved, and at the same time confused over what to do next. Her life would never be the same, she knew now, her intuition clearly grasping the fact. For the first time she realized just how precious life was. And for the first time, here with him, she realized a lot of other things, as well. How vastly different kissing could be by simply changing partners! It staggered her imagination. Dennis had never inspired her to such heights; he subsided into the shadows beside Jorge Valente's blazing passion.

Tara drew a long breath and let out a shuddering sigh. Yet *he* appeared unchanged. He looked as though their recent embrace had never happened, as though her unquestionable, almost wanton response was a figment of her imagination.

She obeyed an irresistible impulse. "I didn't ask for it *that* time!" Her lips pouted enticingly, and there was a faint malicious sparkle in her fine dark eyes.

"That's debatable," he drawled back lazily. His glance skimmed over her flushed cheeks, the deeper crimson of her mouth, soft and full and warm from his kisses.

"Then why did you do it?"

"Let's say I was just passing the time of day...." His voice trailed off tantalizingly.

Tara moistened her lips with the tip of her tongue. Really, he was infuriating! If she wasn't so afraid of his retaliation she would push him into the water.

"Don't do it, *minha querida*." He read the savage gleam in her eyes accurately, and his grip on her shoulders tightened. "You'll regret it." His voice was deep, gently baiting, almost caressing in its quality. She slanted a baleful glance at his hard chin, on exact eye level with her lips. It was almost hidden beneath the now curling growth of beard. She wanted to touch that crisp black hair....

Aggravated with herself most of all, she turned resolute eyes to the sky. "It's a helicopter! Your butler flies a helicopter?" she asked, incredulous.

"What did you expect? A giant eagle with Emilio perched on his back?"

"With you, nothing would surprise me! But your own personal helicopter.... The wine industry must be booming."

"Neither inflation nor overpopulation are detrimental to the industry. The more people there are, the more wine they drink. The more problems those people have—''

"The more wine they drink!" she repeated. "You're very cynical, and hard as nails, Mr. Valente.'' She shifted restlessly, for the claustrophobic effect was once more upon her. Her hair fell forward in a solid sweep of black.

He slid his hand under her chin and forced her head up, so that she had to look at him. "It's my family that's in the wine industry, Miss Lownes, not me. And every coin has two sides. . . .'' His thumb moved slowly, deliberately, along the bottom curve of her lip.

"I think you'd be the same—just plain hard—heads or tails. But I don't really feel compelled to find out,'' she finished swiftly, backing away.

His brilliant black eyes were twinkling as he released her. The fine line of his nostrils flared for an instant. "You'll have plenty of opportunity to find out, mermaid.''

"What do you mean?'' She swung to face him, surprised.

"I'll tell you later. But if you keep walking in that direction Emilio is bound to land on your head. Come here.''

For once she didn't argue, but followed him a short way from the plateau. Stones dislodged by their feet went bouncing down the incline, clattering musically against the rock to end their brief melody with a splash into the water.

They stood silently, close together since there was little room, to watch Emilio land the helicopter.

Tara's eyes widened as the gleaming silver beast settled into position, the blades flashing like knives in the sunlight. The vortex of wind whipped her hair away from her face, skeining it across Jorge Valente's chest. He caught a few black silk strands and absentmindedly twined them around his strong nimble fingers.

CHAPTER SIX

PREPARED AS TARA WAS for the unusual, Emilio was still a shock. He was a small wiry man with dour eyes and a long sepulchral face. He said no more than was absolutely necessary. His manner was stiffly correct, and Tara, studying him curiously, decided that he was starchier than an English butler in even the most rigid of households. He didn't smile at her, nor did he show any surprise at finding an unknown woman sharing his master's island and wearing his master's clothes. Whatever his thoughts, he kept them well hidden behind an impregnable mask.

Jorge climbed immediately into the cockpit of the helicopter and radioed word of Tara's safety to the air tower in Madeira. He gave instructions for messages to be sent both to Hampstead and to the *Adventure Star*'s headquarters in Southampton.

Meanwhile Emilio busied himself clearing away the luncheon dishes. Tara followed his progress with amazed eyes. Here she was, in the middle of the most remarkable adventure, and he didn't seem to notice! Arthur had a penchant for looking uninterested, but he wouldn't have been able to contain his curiosity.

A frown settled on her brow. Emilio didn't appear at all helpful.... She began to realize just what a fix

she was in. Certainly the butler would take her somewhere—but where? To Madeira, most likely, to drop
her off at the British embassy.

That would involve so many endless questions. Reporters would be swarming all over the place as soon
as they heard that the last passenger from the *Adventure Star* was miraculously alive and well. She'd
probably already been mentioned in the papers as
missing. Damn, what a picture she would make in
Jorge's trousers and shirt! People would draw
enough conclusions from that alone. Tara didn't
wonder why she was so concerned about what people
would think, when she never had been before. Just
now it seemed of the utmost importance that no one,
except maybe her parents, find out where she had
spent the past couple of days, and in whose company. The whole situation felt too private for public
eyes.

Perhaps she could bribe Emilio, she decided. Get
him to let her off at some out-of-the-way place. But
of course, she had nothing to bribe him with! She
needed money herself, and certainly didn't have any
to give away. She had set off from Hampstead prepared to count pennies, but not to this extent! She
took another long hard look at the butler and decided
that not even her ruby earrings would sway him. He
personified loyalty. Wherever Jorge told him to take
her, he would take her.

Why hadn't she thought of these complications before, she wondered. Then she realized why. She'd
been in such a hurry to get away from Valente she'd
forgotten the practicalities. She couldn't even think

properly when he was around. She had to get away, if only to preserve her sanity. And one of these days she would have to talk with her parents about the way they had raised her, for they seemed to have left out a lot of pertinent information. Her mother, for instance, had never told her about the Jorge Valentes of the world during her attempts at sex education. She must be behind in her emotional growth, too; how had they missed that?

Then another thought struck Tara. The Portuguese weren't as liberated as the English. Young women still went around chaperoned. They didn't go off by themselves, and certainly not in the company of a male. How would Jorge's family react to her present situation? At that moment Tara would have liked to crawl under a rock.

Emilio came out of the cabin and shut the door firmly behind him. The look on his face told her that everything inside—and that meant everything—was in exactly the right place. The wineglasses had been thoroughly checked for water spots, and not a speck of dust marred the now gleaming stove top. *I'm caught between the devil and the deep blue sea,* Tara groaned to herself with a kind of sour humor.

Jorge swung out of the cockpit and strode over to her. "Your parents should—whatever's the matter now?"

"Oh, uh, nothing," Tara muttered weakly. She felt utterly miserable. "Where. . .where's Emilio taking me? You won't make him take me to the British embassy, will you? I couldn't stand the reporters! And please, not to your family. Your mother. . . . I mean. . . if you could let me off somewhere. A pawn-shop. . . ."

"A pawnshop? What the devil would you want with a pawnshop?" He was regarding her with al-most comical amazement.

"Well," she said, fingering her earlobes, "I need some money. I mean, I need a hotel and clothes, and I don't want to go to the embassy! I know that's where one goes in such a situation but—"

"I'm not taking you to the embassy. The thought never entered my mind! And I'm certainly not taking you to any pawnshop! You are crazy!" Jorge uttered an exclamation of impatience and took her gently by the shoulders.

Tara didn't know how it happened but suddenly she was in his arms, with Emilio standing gravely in the background pretending not to notice. She hid her face in Jorge's shirt. She was feeling close to tears, and it would never do to cry. But neither should his arms be wrapped so tightly around her. Was this his way of saying goodbye? She pushed against his chest, but he didn't loosen his hold.

"I'm not crazy," she insisted staunchly, her voice muffled against his shirt. "And what's the matter with a pawnshop? I'm not going to offer myself, only my earrings!" Did he have to squeeze the last breath from her body? It was all his fault, she thought irra-tionally; he represented most of the problems she had. Her voice rose a note as righteous indignation threaded through it. "It's all very simple, really. Emilio can fly me to Funchal on Madeira. He can go and pawn my earrings; then he can buy me a dress

and some shoes. And that's that! I can take it from
there."

"Emilio's not taking you anywhere!"

"But—"

"Tara! I'm taking you with me to Minha Casa!"
He seemed angry. "You're my noblesse oblige, unfortunately! If I let you go to Funchal you'd be just
crazy enough to get yourself into some kind of trouble, and I'm not taking that risk. A pawnshop! I shall
see you safely back to your parents, and that's that!
You're the most featherbrained unpredictable—"

"I'll thank you to keep a civil tongue in your
head!" she retorted.

Jorge's anger turned to astonishment, then outright amusement. He started to laugh. His shoulders
shook, and his voice when he spoke was a laughing
drawl. "I'll say one thing for you: you do keep me
entertained! You're an amazing female! Absurd, but
amazing. All right," he continued with a sigh of protest, "what's on your mind now?"

"Rebellion. Or mutiny. I'm not sure which."

"Neither will get you very far! Just come along
like a good girl. You have no choice in the matter
anyway. Swallow your, er, aversion to me for a few
days and we'll get along fine. I'm your Uncle Jorge,
remember? Patron saint of fragile mermaids."

"A saint is the last thing I'd call you. And is it
customary for uncles to hold their nieces in just this
manner?"

"Would you rather sit on my knee?" His lips were
twitching wickedly at the corners, his eyes crinkling
as his smile widened. Emilio, Tara noted, looked as

though he were taking in a boring political speech. She sent him an exasperated glance, although she couldn't think of any way the butler could help matters.

"I suppose I should submit gracefully?" she asked. *For now,* she added to herself. *But wait till later....*

"You've got it."

"All right, then." She had to bend her head back to look up at him. "But I want to get a few things straight first. What's Minha Casa? If that's where your family lives you'll have to drag me there forcibly, because I won't go! What I would like to do is disappear quietly into the woodwork, never to be seen or heard from again. By you, that is." Her hands were still spread out on his broad chest. She resolutely denied herself the very real pleasure of relaxing against him, of feeling his brown chest under her cheek, of succumbing to the vibrant body heat that flowed into her at his closeness.

"Are nieces normally so nasty to their benevolent uncles?" He let her go, but her hair had become snagged on one of his buttons. He extricated the strands with deliberate slowness, keeping a sharp amused eye on her averted face. "Minha Casa is where I'm living at the moment. And if you want to disappear into the woodwork, it's the perfect place to do so. There are no reporters for miles around, if that's what you want to avoid. But you'll have to put up with me! I'm not so benevolent as to let you have the place to yourself. Besides, your parents have already been told that that's where you're going."

"Oh, I see." Tara's hair was finally restored to her. Her smoky eyes flashed over his burnished bronze features, his brilliant midnight eyes. So she wasn't to say goodbye to him yet.... Oh, but please, she prayed silently, it had better be soon. Now that she wasn't saying goodbye to him she wanted to!

She stared moodily at the helicopter, reading the stenciled words Lazelle Turbojet over and over again while the men prepared for takeoff. Then Jorge came up behind her and lifted her into the cockpit before she even knew he was there. He swung up beside her.

Just before Emilio climbed into the control seat she caught his surreptitious glance at her baggy clothing, and couldn't resist smiling to herself. The butler wasn't totally devoid of curiosity, and that was the first auspicious sign she'd had from him all day. It cheered her slightly. But what an odd person he was! A flying butler! She'd never heard of such a thing.

The engines caught with a deep-throated roar. Moments later they were airborne. Gulls veered away on either side of them, screeching raucously. Chão was looking smaller by the second; the ocean larger, a fantastic expanse of muted blue and green rippling away in every direction. The higher they went, the brighter the sunlight became, until the very air itself seemed full of gold dust.

Madeira was a patch of viridian and white; Funchal a scrap of creamy yellow and pink. They flew over the island of Porto Santo, and Tara had a closer look at the same colors, now broken up into recognizable stretches of forest, beach and city streets. She drew a breath of pure pleasure and realized she could think of no other place she would rather be at this moment, even with Jorge and Emilio. How could anyone stay depressed up here?

She twisted in her seat belt to face Jorge, and her soft lips parted in a happy, instinctively sensuous smile. Her fine dark eyes, large and liquid, shimmered as they touched on each feature of his face.

His voice was deep and quiet and lazy as he said, "Sometimes I get the distinct impression you don't dislike me as much as you would have me believe."

Instead of answering his indirect question, Tara laughed. Emilio, however, remained as somber as ever. Even when Jorge related to the butler Tara's highly unusual arrival on Chão, Emilio merely nodded. He hadn't said a word by the time the Moroccan coast came into sight an hour later, and he was still silent when the landmass of Portugal appeared as a sliver across the horizon. If Tara hadn't already heard him speak she would have thought him dumb.

She herself made up for Emilio's silence by pumping Jorge with innumerable questions. He, for once, was in a pleasant mood and indulged her. In due course she learned that Minha Casa was a house, or rather an old-fashioned villa, set in the rolling steppes of one of the old family estates. The estate itself, named Quinta das Valente de Silves, was situated at the southwestern tip of Portugal, in the Algarve district. It had been sold by Jorge's grandfather to the d'Cimbriannis when Jorge was born, and consequently, to be closer to their miles and miles of fertile vineyards, the Valente de Silves family had moved from there to Vila Nova de Gaia.

Tara sank into a reverie induced by Jorge's words as he unfolded the story. In her mind's eye she could see the events as they happened.

Conte d'Cimbrianni, then fifty years of age and last in the line of a wealthy Italian family, had fallen in love with an aristocratic Portuguese woman while on holiday. He married her, deciding to settle in her native country. Unfortunately he died a violent death shortly after purchasing the estate. He was gored by a bull, one of the animals specially bred for the bull-ring on the *quinta* property.

His wife, Ernesta, a frail woman even then, had immediately left the estate to take up residence in Albufeira, a small town down the coast toward Spain. Much younger than her husband, she had been expecting their first child, and five months later a girl, whom she named Angelica, was born. Contessa d'Cimbrianni visited the estate from time to time after her husband's fatal accident, but she never stayed for long. Nor did she know how to administer the thousands of acres the *quinta* represented. She had no head for business, she insisted, and further-more she refused to have anything to do with money matters—to the point of avoiding the handling of coins and bills! Her eccentricity she explained away by saying that she'd never had to touch money before and she wasn't going to start now. Besides, money was quite vulgar!

So Minha Casa was left deserted, and the immense gardens around it slowly turned into wilderness. The *contessa* hadn't bothered to hire an overseer to man-age the farms, orchards, vineyards and fisheries. The peasants, left on their own, struggled loyally through the next twenty years to keep the *quinta* prosperous, but slowly Ernesta's income from the estate dwindled. She took little notice of the fact, and even stopped her visits.

On her twentieth birthday, Angelica, the daughter, married a handsome but opportunistic fisherman. The wedding took place against her mother's wishes. However, shortly afterward Contessa d'Cimbrianni put her new son-in-law, Mario Resende, in charge of her numerous business interests, including the Quinta das Valente de Silves.

The first thing the young man did was sell almost all of the estate's famous line of purebred bulls, classic Arabian horses and prime dairy cattle for quick cash. Not a penny went back into the estate. Then he demanded from the peasants twice the harvest that they had previously produced. Not one inch of the *quinta* escaped his grasping hands. The orange, lemon and lime groves, the vast orchards of peach, tangerine and pomegranate trees were harvested year after year without necessary care, without being fertilized, without new trees to replace the effete. The almond groves were treated in similar fashion. The cork-oak plantation was overharvested. Not one fishing ketch was replaced, nor were boards provided to replace those that were rotting. The nets were repaired, then repaired again. The irrigation system grew out-of-date and fell into ruin. And still Mario Resende demanded an outrageous income from the estate without putting a penny of capital back in.

Under his authority the peasants received the bare minimum of schooling. More than half of them were illiterate. They were without medical attention and most of them had never seen a dentist. Too poor to leave home, they accepted their lot fatalistically. Indeed, most of them had nowhere else to go, nor did they want to leave. The *quinta* had been their home for generation after generation.... Today, thirty-four years later, the once beautiful bountiful *quinta* was in decay.

"Oh, my God," Tara breathed as Jorge finished his shocking tale. She was at a loss for something else to say. Poignantly she felt the fate of the peasants, the hard grasping cruelty of a man she'd never met. "But why are you living at Minha Casa now?" she finally asked.

Jorge Valente smiled, but there was a grim cynical twist to his lips that made Tara glad she wasn't this Mario Resende. Never, she vowed, would she do anything that would provoke Jorge into real anger! She shivered slightly, for the thought of him in a rage was unnerving. Those midnight eyes of his could burn holes right through one, could do untold damage.

When Jorge spoke, however, his voice was light and easy, dispelling her misgivings. "I own a hotel in Sagres. I stopped there for a meeting with my architect to go over the renovation plans, and I couldn't resist taking a look at the old *quinta*. I'd always been curious about it. To make a long story short, I found my way to the fishing village and talked to some of the older folks—men who still remember my grandfather selling the estate to Conte d'Cimbrianni. That's when I heard all the sordid details.''

His hand slowly clenched, and Tara almost felt pity for Resende. ''Unknown to me, the peasants held council. And the next day they requested that I make an offer for the estate to Contessa Ernesta Angelica d'Cimbrianni....''

"And you agreed?'' Tara would have jumped up with enthusiasm had the seat belt not held her firmly in place. ''That's what you were doing on Chão, isn't it? Thinking it over. You told me that's where you go to think when you don't want interruptions, remember?''

"I remember.'' The look he gave her brought a sudden flush to her cheeks, and she subsided back into her seat. She had the distinct feeling he was not thinking of her advent on the island, but of the kisses they'd shared earlier that day. Confusion washed over her. He had, most definitely, left his stamp on her skin, on her mouth. Her lips trembled slightly at the remembered ecstasy, and as they did his eyes fell from hers to linger on the full curves, noting how the tip of her tongue moistened them when she was agitated, as now. He smiled faintly, as though satisfied with some inner thought, and his smile sent a prickle of apprehension through her.

"What are you going to do? Are you going to buy the *quinta* or not?'' she asked hurriedly, hoping to divert his keen attention from her mouth.

"I've been to see Contessa d'Cimbrianni. She's agreed to sell—if I want the place.'' He paused for a moment. ''The poor woman lives only for the past.

And from the condition of her villa in Albufeira, I'd say Resende is squeezing *escudos* not only from the estate, but from her other interests as well. I'd be surprised if she sees more than ten percent of her actual income. The remainder must go straight into his pocket."

"Do Mario and Angelica live close to her?"

"No, they live in Lisbon. And if they visit her more than once a year, I'd be surprised about that, too. She's a very lonely woman and appears much older than her fifty-four years. She speaks of her Antonio as though he were still alive. She does it for company, I think."

"Oh...." Tara breathed. She'd always been susceptible to sad stories; had always wanted to rush in and help. "But what have you decided to do?"

"It isn't just a question of buying the estate, Tara. It could take years before the land is productive, and the place will take a tremendous amount of capital to rebuild. And then there are the peasants. I would have to take on all responsibility for them; they would expect it of me. Before I eat, they must eat. Before I sleep, they all have to have beds. I'd have to be their lawyer, judge, policeman, marriage counselor, father confessor, merchant—and a good example to top it off. My life won't be my own!"

That wasn't true, Tara thought. His life would always be his own; he was that kind of man. She sighed. "I think you've already decided to buy the *quinta*—" she said with a grin, "and what you're doing now is trying to convince yourself that you haven't gone completely mad."

Jorge gave her a long look that she found vaguely disturbing. There was an odd shift in his manner. Something indefinable had charged the air between them, but when Tara tried to put her finger on it the elusive feeling vanished.

"It's an enormous challenge!" she added on a teasing note, "but then you strike me as a man who loves a good challenge! Besides, it's obvious that those peasants still think they belong to you, in a way. Otherwise they wouldn't have approached you. You would have inherited them along with the land had the sale all those years ago not complicated matters. And now they want you to *un*complicate matters. How can you possibly resist? It sounds thrilling!"

He chuckled at her eagerness, then sobered slightly. A frown hovered between his straight black brows.

"And if you don't have the necessary capital—" Tara was carried away by her own excitement for the project "—you could always approach your father."

"I don't need subsidizing," he informed her.

"Oh. Your hotel business is lucrative?"

"When business is properly managed it always is," he answered dryly.

"Oh," she said again. "Does your father mind? I mean, your not taking an interest in his vineyards?" Perhaps she shouldn't be asking him such personal questions. After all, she hardly knew the man, and they couldn't exactly be called friends. But her curiosity, when it came to Jorge Valente, was insatiable.

"Let's just say he didn't approve!"

"Ahh! You are the black sheep, then! Just as I thought."

"Sometimes you think too much, mermaid! And sometimes not enough."

"I'll never be able to win your approval, will I?" she asked, more wistfully than she realized.

"It's hard to say. Why? Do you want to?" he finished softly.

She swung her head away from him, pretending sudden interest in the sun-struck sea far below. She could see the helicopter's shadow rippling over the waves.

"Heavens, why should I want your approval? We'll only be spending a few more days in each other's company, and I daresay I'll survive without it!" She made her voice deliberately noncommittal, injecting a tinge of boredom for good measure. Then she turned her head to catch his reaction, demurely lowering her thick lashes in a falsely innocent gesture. Even through the veil of lashes she could see the glitter in the depths of his eyes as he leaned quickly toward her. "The devil made me say it!" she added hastily, her nonchalant attitude vanishing in an instant.

He chuckled richly, enjoying her retreat. "We're going to get along like a house on fire, *minha cara*," he drawled in his deep voice. "Or maybe like a whole forest on fire."

"An apt description!" she returned crisply. "I can just see the sparks fly!"

"And you haven't even come close to the flames yet...."

She wished he wouldn't speak like that; it did disturbing things to her pulse. What a low voice he had, so deep throated. She could just imagine him growling like some king of the jungle. The picturesque simile brought a quick smile to her lips.

"Here we are, rational adults—" she pretended to look perplexed "—and yet it appears we enjoy provoking each other for no reason. Now what do you suppose is the cause?"

"Rational is not the first thing I would describe you as!" Jorge replied enigmatically.

"I'll have you know others have had much more complimentary opinions of me!" she parried.

"Here we go again with the mighty Captain Baker!" he sighed with exaggerated protest, his eyes laughing down at her. "You have a one-track mind, mermaid."

"Since I hold Captain Baker in high regard it's natural for me to value his opinion," she replied loftily. "And it gives me immense satisfaction to say that he thinks very well of me, indeed." She wasn't absolutely sure of this, but thought it was a safe bet. "Not to mention Dr. Albert. He rather likes me, too, I think."

"No doubt most members of the male sex would find you attractive. How about the females?"

"Miss Tillesby thought I was trustworthy," Tara answered, "as I've already told you. And Fionna Genelli seemed to like to talk to me. There was one woman—when I was growing up—who called me a demon more times than I care to remember, but that's neither here nor there. I didn't like her much, either."

It was with pleasure that Tara realized Penny now

had to deal with Janette Moreston as a mother-in-law. Envisioning Penny and Janette eye to eye at the breakfast table made her giggle out loud. Suddenly Tara wished she could share her secret amusement with Jorge. But that would mean talking about Dennis, and for some reason she didn't want this tall dark man with the midnight eyes to know she'd been engaged to a person as soulless as her ex-fiancé. Jorge himself definitely had plenty of soul, she thought, staring at him somewhat absentmindedly as she pondered the thought.

Soul, yes, and a whole lot of other attractions, if she was honest enough to admit it. She felt she'd only scratched the surface where he was concerned, and she wished a little wistfully that they had more than just another day or two to spend together. Another week on the island, for instance. . . .

Her lips parted at the thought, and her eyes clung to his rather splendid profile. Then an idea clicked on in her head like a two-hundred-watt light bulb: he was without a doubt the perfect mate. She couldn't have dreamed up a more wildly attractive, virile male. And there she'd had all that time on the island and she'd wasted it, arguing with him! But one couldn't rush something as delicate as love. She couldn't just offer herself on a plate. Tara's lips twitched into a smile. She was almost tempted to try it, purely to see his reaction.

Jorge's eyes swung away from the seascape to capture hers in the middle of their prolonged appraisal of him. As his gaze pinned hers, a faint tantalizing blush washed over her face, and her eyes, light with barely contained merriment, laughed back at him and hinted a challenge.

He said abruptly, caustically, "I'd just love to know what's going on behind that flower face, but I don't dare hazard a guess. Looking at you, I'd say that rampant imagination of yours has pulled out all the stops! I doubt even the sky's the limit where you're concerned!"

"How can one concoct children's stories when one is limited to the ground?" she replied airily. A last quick amused smile curved her lips before she turned from him. There was a well of silence as he contemplated her shrewdly.

"I suppose your manuscript for *Toodles*, book two went down with the ship?"

"That's right. I didn't take any luggage overboard with me, you see. Even my life jacket executed a swift departure once I was in the water. Now there I was careless, I must admit!"

"What? No excuse?" he taunted lazily.

"None. I simply forgot to tie the straps, what with the excitement Miss Tillesby was causing," she said with an ironic smile.

When they landed Jorge swung out of the cockpit and turned to help her down, his long fingers tightening around her narrow rib cage. Shortly before touchdown they'd flown over Sagres, and Tara was still preoccupied with what she thought of in her mind as a welcome from an old friend. The little town, cresting the cliffs of Ponta de Sagres, had winked on its lights just as they flew overhead. Dispelling the twilight that blue-shadowed its narrow streets, clusters of lights had sprung up in twos and threes: tourist hotels had suddenly blazed like mushrooming clouds; neon signs had blinked and then turned on their steady glow of red and yellow, orange and green. Off to their left the lighthouse at Cape San Vincente had beamed its powerful ray in a wide semicircle over the Atlantic waters a steep three hundred feet below.

And now they were at Minha Casa. Tara straightened her shoulders as her feet touched the ground. Valente's face was in shadow, his head and shoulders canceling out the moon rising behind him. Emilio slipped out of the helicopter, barely seen and barely heard, and melted into the darkness that gathered as night closed about them.

"Welcome home," Jorge murmured, releasing her, then stepping back a pace.

The full moon, round and rich, spread its light over her, and looking eagerly around she made out the dim lines of an overgrown garden, the crumbled stone of an old goldfish pond long since dry. A climbing rose, its colors indistinguishable in the moonlight, tumbled in waves of blossom over a high-backed marble bench. Immense evergreen oaks marched ahead of them in a stately avenue. Poplars and beeches and chestnuts, their leaves dappled with silver light, grew in less formal clusters and formed a solid screen at her back. The air pungent with the night-released perfume of roses, unseen bougainvillea and fuchsias, and the hardy earthy scent of geraniums. The intermingling salty tang of the ocean spiced the air and brought two-year-old memories crowding in on Tara. She shivered with delight.

Minha Casa, when her eyes first alighted on it, appeared to belong in a North African Casbah, a Moorish stronghold enclaved in Christian land. *Arabian Nights* immediately flashed into her mind as she stood gazing at the structure in stupefaction. Nothing Jorge had said had prepared her for it—a crenellated fortress with enchanting onion-shaped domes and narrow stairways climbing steeply to flat terraced roofs! Several of the grills hanging over the deeply inset windows were crooked, painting irregular black shadows on the once white walls. But what walls! Thick and massive, they were interspersed with slabs of steel-gray granite in an intricate design that blended architectural grace and strength.

What did one wear in such a place, Tara wondered, feminine in thinking she had nothing with which to grace the villa. It seemed only proper to have a samite shift, thin gold ankle bracelets, a heavy bejeweled collar extending to the shoulders and a great emerald teardrop glistening on her forehead. So involved was she in her imaginings that she could almost hear Eastern music weaving through the night.

"It's too early to fall asleep, mermaid." Jorge's voice, faintly indulgent, brought her straight back to earth.

Her lips formed a soundless "oh" as she swung to face him. "It's...it's...." She waved a hand helplessly.

"It's a nice old place," he agreed, then grinned

suddenly. "I'm so glad you approve, Miss Lownes. I thought you'd like it, for it suits you!"

"It's like stepping into a fairy tale!"

"Complete with a big bad wolf?" He laughed under his breath. "Come inside."

He drew her after him until they reached the outer wall. There he lifted a curtain of rioting bougain-villea that all but hid an inset doorway.

Tara found herself in a large forecourt, where the floor and walls were totally paved in *azulejos*, the Algarve's colorful ceramic tiles. The amassed flowers and shrubbery and the darkness hid some of the shabbiness. A dry fountain stood in the center. From niches in the walls graceful statues of Muslim origin smiled benevolently. Elegant torch fixtures hung like coat pegs all around, while carved white marble benches provided stately seating arrangements. The outer wall rose straight up from two stories, though the other three walls that surrounded the courtyard opened into galleries on the second floor. The filigree woodwork shielding the galleries must have original-ly protected household ladies from roving male eyes.

Jorge stood silently behind Tara's shoulder, and she could feel his eyes on her. She took a deep breath, and touched by a profound sense of imminent dan-ger, resolutely walked around the marble fountain to the immense double doors that led into the house proper.

Her hand was already outstretched, when the doors creaked open and the bent figure of a woman was silhouetted in a single shaft of light piercing through the darkness from within.

"This is Ashta," Jorge said by way of explanation as Tara stared in alarm at the old crone, who immediately started speaking Portuguese. "She's glad I'm home." A sardonic note crept into his voice as he added, "And she's quite pleased to see I've brought a woman back with me." He in turn spoke to the old servant, his Portuguese so quick and fluid that Tara didn't understand any of it.

Ashta cackled, exposing a toothless expanse of pink gums. Her hands, knotted with rheumatism, punctuated her laughter, and the mass of wrinkles in her face changed direction like a mobile relief map. Between the folds of brown weathered skin two eyes as bright and black as berries sized Tara up with keen precision. Tara felt a measure of relief when Ashta seemed to approve of her and stood aside to let her enter.

The aroma of hot and spicy food immediately assailed her nostrils as she walked into the massive entranceway, which soared straight up three floors, peaking in the largest of the onion domes. She realized then how hungry she was. If she had felt more at home she would have eagerly asked, "What's for dinner?" Instead she caught her hands behind her back and stood waiting with the polite and innocent patience of a schoolgirl.

Jorge gave her a quizzical look, smothered a grin with some difficulty, and then propelled her down the dark shadowy hall to one of the innumerable double doors that flanked either side. She caught a quick glimpse of the two of them in a huge gilt mirror.

Then, as if on cue, the doors were opened from the inside by Emilio. He inclined his head slightly as Tara stepped into a small *sala*. She was getting used to Emilio's perfectionism, but after she'd passed him she couldn't resist swinging around for another look.

He was now dressed in full butler regalia, his linen spotless and crisp, his superbly tailored suit pressed and without a mote of lint to mar the velvety black. How had he changed clothes so quickly? Not a hair on his head was out of place, and he was looking as bland and unruffled as always. He made her feel positively scruffy in her baggy jeans and sweater, with her bare feet and windswept hair. Her chin went up a few degrees, and she wished she had at least a tube of lipstick for moral support. With conscious effort she subsided gracefully into the chair that he held out for her, while her thoughts ticked over with the rapidity of typewriter keys.

Had she been wise to let Jorge bring her here? What was she letting herself in for? Where could she buy clothes? Exactly how far away was Sagres? What would it be like living in this...this seraglio with only Jorge Emmanuel Valente de Silves for company? Emilio couldn't be called company. Ashta was still a question mark, although Tara had passed the first test with the old woman. Just how close were the closest neighbors? Her misgivings swept down on her like an avalanche.

Mainly to avoid looking at Jorge, she glanced around the dusty *sala*. Absentmindedly she noted and appreciated the cabinets with their mozarabic inlay, the priceless Chinese porcelain behind leaded glass doors, the thick and wildly colorful Persian carpet, the filigree brass lamps and the ornate *azulejos* fireplace suggested part of a likely setting for a Hitchcock movie. Any moment now the villain would come stalking in. Or maybe he was already in the room. Was the place just as Jorge had said—a fairy tale complete with a big bad wolf? And then she did look at Jorge, her eyes wide and poignant, as though she expected him to turn into a werewolf before her very eyes.

He stared levelly back, making Tara feel slightly embarrassed. She chided herself for her vivid imagination. Was it the by-product of writing books, she wondered. Her head was so often in the clouds, so often in fantasy worlds of her own making that her fantasies sometimes ran away with her. She smiled tentatively at Valente, and got only the quirk of an eyebrow for answer.

He was a difficult man to get to know, she realized. Instead of lessening, her curiosity about him was growing, and she wondered uneasily if that was significant. Perhaps she should try to squelch her interest and treat him as though he were just any other person. But she'd already tried that, she reminded herself, and it hadn't worked. He just wasn't an ordinary person, not to her. He was larger than life somehow—a study in controlled vitality, sense of purpose, raw male power.

For the first time in her life she really was a little intimidated. It was an uncomfortable state of affairs, and she wished she could rise above it. He could be inordinately annoying. He could play on her emotions as though they were a keyboard, and she didn't approve of that at all. While he was perfect in one sense, something warned her that he was potentially dangerous in another. She had just better watch her step....

Emilio interrupted her cogitations when he began pouring wine into a crystal goblet—probably eighteenth century, she decided absently. She recognized the wine immediately by its sparkling fruity-green color. It was *vinho verde*, the Algarve staple, and an excellent wine. A few sips later, she slowly began to feel a bit more relaxed. But she still hadn't spoken a word to Jorge. Her tongue seemed to have gone on vacation, and for the life of her she couldn't think of anything to say. She, who'd been brought up on the social art of small talk. She remembered all the afternoon teas her mother had hostessed, and the way she'd always been able to hold her own at those gatherings.

The silence lengthened. Warmed by the fire crackling in the hearth and the heady wine, Tara made a movement to pull off Jorge's bulky fisherman's-knit sweater. Emilio was at her side in an instant assisting in its removal, acting for all the world as though it were an ermine stole and she a reigning queen. She was used to the rather paternal deference that Arthur bestowed on her, so Emilio's manner continued to take her by surprise. Hastily she stuffed her shirt into her rope-tied jeans, determined that Emilio would not help her with that also. Then she glanced suspiciously at Jorge to see if he was smiling. Ever since he had saved her life she felt he'd taken the control of it right out of her hands.

He wasn't smiling, but he was watching her, and the expression on his face was potently disturbing. Tara didn't know how to account for it, nor what it meant; she couldn't remember ever being looked at in just that way before.

Concentrating on the filigree pattern of soft light that the lamps sent shimmering around the *sala*, she sipped more wine, still feeling absurdly tongue-tied. Emilio refilled her goblet, and she noted with consternation that Jorge's was still over half-full.

Quietly and precisely Emilio put place settings before them: hand-painted paper-thin china and heavy silver flatware evenly spaced on either side of the plates. Her father would know the history of these place settings, she thought irrelevantly, and immediately after wondered what he would think of Jorge Valente.

Their first course arrived promptly; steaming bowls of spicy hot *caldo verde*, a long-simmered soup of vegetables and fragrant herbs, which Tara had tasted the first time she'd visited the Algarve. After that there were crisply grilled fresh sardines and deep-fried oysters, a large round of goat's-milk cheese and heavy slabs of coarse, whole-wheat bread with freshly churned butter. It was typical peasant cooking, and Tara loved it. The Portuguese meal tasted even more delicious than she remembered, and she silently congratulated Ashta. Emilio refilled her goblet several more times without Tara's noticing.

Her mood also mellowed without her noticing. Although she and Jorge didn't speak, the silence eased into a comfortable one that was far from dull. Dashes of inexplicable excitement occasionally tingled down to Tara's fingertips. Her bare, dusty pink toes curled around the rungs of her rococo chair. She felt very much alive and self-aware, not something she could explain as being caused by the wine alone. Slanting a look at Valente through thick curling lashes, she pursed her lips thoughtfully. He possessed a decidedly dominant personality, she concluded. His presence filled the room as it seemed to fill her. Her unease and gradually growing contentment were now a mingled force, and she couldn't quite decide which one had the upper hand.

"Had enough to eat?" At last he broke the prevailing silence.

"Yes, thank you." She half smiled and sipped more wine.

"We'll have dessert, Emilio," he said quietly. Then to Tara he murmured, "Am I right in thinking you have a sweet tooth?"

"Yes," she admitted.

Their dessert turned out to be a sugary sweetmeat of definite Moorish heritage, a combination of powdered almonds, eggs and figs that Ashta had shaped into delicate flowers and birds. Tara nibbled a rose and drank strong Turkish coffee from a tiny eggshell cup.

She would have loved to stretch and yawn, a long extended stretch like the ones cats took when they curled up before a hearth. Emilio's presence daunted her, however; he would think she lacked manners! By now slightly tipsy, she considered the situation. If Jorge's heavy old sweater merited ermine-stole treatment, perhaps a stretch of hers would be regarded as an elegant royal gesture.... She started by uncurling her toes, then her knees. Working upward, she felt immense satisfaction, mostly at the luxury of flouting de rigueur etiquette.

Emilio didn't bat an eyelash. As Tara finished her yawn a fit of giggles bubbled up in her throat. How the matrons of Hampstead would envy Jorge his butler! She began to like Emilio a little better.

Her eyes slid over to Jorge and intercepted a look on his lean dark face that made her catch her breath. Her low laughter stopped abruptly. Her recent actions had obviously affected Valente differently than they had his butler. A sudden glitter of desire betrayed his inner feelings and gave Tara an insight into his mood of the evening, as well as into the peculiar way he had looked at her earlier. At first she felt surprised, then intrigued. Never before had she been quite as aware of the power of her femininity. Nor had she known what a mere lazy stretch could do. So Dom Jorge Emmanuel Valente de Silves wasn't totally impenetrable after all! He was more attracted to her than he let on....

"Do you share your jokes or do you usually keep them all to yourself?" His cool tone belied the black fire in his eyes, and she decided it wasn't at all safe to be here with him. If anyone did any seducing it would be him! She threw her head back, sending the heavy silk mane of hair over her shoulders. Her dark eyes regarded him unselfconsciously.

"Oh, I'm not at all selfish," she assured him, her tone slightly husky with undercurrents of excitement. "I'm full of admiration for Emilio," she explained, "and I was just imagining to what lengths the women in Hampstead would go in secreting him away from you!'' Just as she'd made up her mind that Emilio never smiled, she noticed the corners of his mouth quiver just a very, very little.

Valente was frowning at Emilio, frowning but still half smiling in such a way that Tara stared at him in sudden fascination. Somewhere inside her head a little warning signal switched on, blinking like a red traffic light—but only faintly, as though halfhearted about doing its job.

Ashta came into the *sala* in a spotless white apron that almost swallowed up her small bony frame. As usual, she was smiling. Out of the ensuing rapid Portuguese, Tara understood one word—*cama*—and from that deduced that a bedroom had been prepared for her. A vague instinct of self-preservation caused her to smile and nod her head, intimating she was eager to get to bed. She felt she was being bewitched by Jorge Valente and that she needed to get away before the spell became complete. She was aware that it was a back-door escape, and that she had used this ruse before. But at the moment it seemed wise to get away from the lord of the manor, and she nodded her head once more. As if he understood exactly what was going on in her head, Valente's eyebrows went up a fraction of an inch, but she did not care. Sometimes it was wiser to retreat, and this was one of those times. She smiled amiably at him.

Ashta beamed toothlessly. She was pleased by Tara's eagerness to see her allotted bedroom, and with a meaningful look at Valente she patted Tara's shoulder, motioning for her to follow.

All the way down the dark hall Tara sensed Jorge's presence behind her, keenly felt his eyes on her back. She wished he had stayed behind in the *sala*. Then she tripped over a turned-up edge of carpet and stubbed her toe against the banister post. Swinging around, Ashta held her coal-oil lamp high. The feeble beams of light revealed Tara leaning weakly against the post in silent distress. When Jorge swung Tara up in his arms as though she were no more than an unresisting sack of potatoes, Ashta nodded her approval. Agilely the old woman began to ascend the cavernous stairwell ahead of them, the light from her oil lamp flickering her dried-apple face.

Tara looked into Valente's own shadowy features, so close now, and noted the deep cynical twist to his finely cut lips, the arrogant nose and the high cheekbones. She didn't look up as far as his eyes. Her breathing became shallow and quick, and she could feel the steady beat of his heart near her shoulder. The stairwell wound around and continued upward, and an irresistible impulse was triggered in Tara. Feeling safe with Ashta now a proven ally, she followed her instincts and wrapped her arms tightly around Jorge's neck. The fingers of one hand rested on his nape underneath his black curls, and her warm touch there was not altogether impersonal. A wide grin spread across her face.

Valente glanced down at her and shook his head. "I hope you know what you're doing." His voice was quiet and silky, yet with a rough undertone.

"I usually look before I leap."

"Usually?"

"We can't all be perfect!"

"You'd better learn not to rely on Ashta; she won't always be handy!"

"I promise to mind my p's and q's."

He laughed low in his throat. "That I'd like to see! I'd say you were totally out of control!"

"Out of your control? I should hope so! I wouldn't have it any other way."

He laughed again and his arms tightened around her.

"I'm not one of those women who appreciates a firm hand! You obviously get your own way much too often, so some humble pie might possibly have a salutary effect."

"Ahh! The kitten finds her claws!" he smirked.

Tara longed to wipe that expression off his face. "Put me down! I don't like being carried about like a...a recalcitrant brat."

"Not on your life! You're safest where you are right now." His arms fastened even more securely around her, holding her now as a woman and not as a sack of potatoes. "And don't jiggle!"

"You're taking some perverse pleasure out of this, aren't you? Just because you have all those marvelous muscles, you think you can subjugate me!"

"Exactly! When you want to you learn quickly, *minha querida*!"

Ashta suddenly turned and held her lamp up close to their faces, precluding the remark Tara was going to make. She was cackling quite merrily, and Tara wondered why. The old woman's free hand gestured widely as she talked. She had stopped at a bedroom door and was obviously explaining the propriety of Jorge's not taking one step farther. Tara's ears were becoming more attuned to the sound of Portuguese, but even so she missed a great deal of what Ashta was saying, and felt annoyed when Jorge laughed heartily before he set her on her feet. He kept his hands on her arms until she steadied herself, but he still seemed quite amused, clearly at her expense. She looked up at him with reproach in her wide eyes when he didn't explain the joke, but it only made him laugh more. A stab of aggravated fury took hold of her. He missed nothing, of course—not the vivid flush on her cheeks, nor her shimmering smoky eyes suspiciously bright with angry tears.

"How very intriguing!" He bent closer, pinning her gaze.

"Oh, for heaven's sake, will you stop being so smug!" she retorted passionately. She shivered. Her voice sounded low and urgent and choked even to her own ears. She drew herself up to her full height; she would rather die than lose face entirely, especially in front of him, Jorge Emmanuel Valente de Silves! It just wasn't fair. But then, life could never be explained in terms of fairness.

She curbed her violent emotions and assumed a sweeter tone. "Your home is admirably suited to your temperament, Dom Valente. All the same, I expect I shall have a good night's sleep. Thank you so much for your gracious hospitality!"

He was leaning against the doorjamb, his amazing eyes staring into hers. "And what a temperamental spirit you have," he drawled succinctly, deprecatingly, his voice sending pinpricks down her spine. "It's a good thing you're so ravishingly pretty; it's your only saving grace." His teeth gleamed savagely white against the sun-dark bronze of his face. He was studying her with a cool sensuality that set her heart beating like an agonized trapped bird.

"Do you like your women tame and amenable?" she asked rashly, scornfully.

"At times." His eyes swept down her slender form, swathed from neck to knees in his shirt and trousers. A smile tugged at the corners of his mouth as he said good-night. Then he turned on his heel and vanished down the gloomy hall. He, of course, would not trip over the carpet, Tara thought as she closed the door with a petulant bang.

Safely inside she leaned against it, catching her breath. She felt physically and mentally exhausted. Her emotions had gone through so many ups and downs today. One minute she quite liked Valente, and the next she couldn't get far enough away from him! She would have to make up her mind one way or another, for she simply couldn't take this hectic confusing seesaw ride much longer....

It didn't take Tara long to prepare for bed, since she had none of her creams, lotions or scented bath powders with her. She shrugged into a nightgown of coarse woolen weave—probably one of Ashta's, she thought, for it was much too short for her. Once on it felt wonderfully warm and cozy. Ashta had already turned back the heavy rose counterpane and was plumping the pillows on the huge canopied four-poster bed. Tara's bare feet sank into the soft pile of the old Persian carpet as she crossed it, and then she gratefully lay down on the old-fashioned mattress.

"Not cold?" Ashta asked in her broken English as she pulled the blankets right up to Tara's chin.

"Oh, no! Thank you very much." Tara smiled warmly and was rewarded with an answering beam.

"Good. Much good. Nice you come. You laugh at dinner, no? I hear you laugh. Good. Not much laugh here. Now you come, much laugh, yes?"

Tara was certain she had indeed found an ally in the old woman. Eager friendship exuded from her, and the warmth of it took Tara by surprise. "Oh, I hope so!" she answered, not knowing what to say. "I laugh a lot anyway, and—" She stopped, then spoke more slowly. "I like." She pointed at the walls, gesturing to include the whole house and Ashta, as well. "I like much. Happy here."

Ashta nodded vigorously. "You stay, yes? Stay much...time?"

"For a while." Tara answered, and then realized the woman didn't understand her. So she repeated the word "time," and held out her hands to resemble a certain length, hoping that would do.

Ashta looked disappointed, but then brightened to say with evident satisfaction, "Yes. Much time. *Senhorinha* stay much, much time. Good. Dom Valente he good man; he happy now. Yes?"

"Uh...." Tara was stumped. "Dom Valente good man, yes," she finally said for want of something better. "You happy he come?"

"Yes!" Ashta said with unmistakable emphasis. "Much good!" And she waved her arms around to encompass what Tara took to mean everything and everyone for miles around. "Dom Valente come home. Much good."

Tara could agree with that. A few minutes later, when she was alone, she had just enough time to murmur "much good" again before she fell asleep.

CHAPTER SEVEN

IT WAS LATE the next morning when Tara woke to find Ashta beside her bed. A small silver tray was balanced in her gnarled hands, and her berry-black eyes looked even brighter and sharper in the light of day. Tara gladly accepted a steaming cup of aromatic coffee, and then looked askance at the stack of telegrams the servant woman handed her. After several attempts in broken English to explain that they had just arrived, Ashta managed to get her message across. Then she scurried away to run Tara's *banho*, her bath.

Tara flipped through the pale yellow envelopes, noting the names: Captain Warren Baker, Dr. Hans Albert, Fionna Genelli and a Mr. Oliver Breakwell, president of the *Adventure Star* shipping lines. Two or three of the letters were from leading newspapers, no doubt asking for exclusive interviews. There was one from William Pillaring, and even one from Miss Tillesby. Tara sighed happily and settled down to read the lot, starting at the top of the pile. Captain Baker was unusually verbose, especially since it was a telegram, and she realized happily that her statement of his opinion of her had been correct. He went on to say that they had all been rescued by the freighter they had sighted, and that a few sniffles and one case of nerves—who else but Miss Tillesby—were the only physical aftereffects of the disaster. Miss Tillesby's telegram was the shortest of the lot, and in it she apologized three times.

"Has Jorge had breakfast yet?" Tara asked finally, jumping up. She had no idea of the time.

"Dom Valente go. Help...cow?" At Tara's blank look Ashta struggled further. "Cow, er, baby trouble. Much bad. Dom Valente go help. Much... kilometers." She pointed vaguely. Then, as though she'd rehearsed the next lines, she said, "Home for tea. You are to rest. Telephone from parent soon. Doctor after...after lunch." And she beamed with the pride of accomplishment. Then she produced a skirt, a blouse and sandals of definite peasant origin. "Pants much bad. *Senhorinha* put...?" She held up the skirt.

"Skirt," Tara supplied the word, looking closely at the embroidery along its wide hem and waistband. It was beautifully worked, and the black homespun cloth set it off to perfection. The gathered blouse was of white cotton and delicately starched, but the sandals she knew at a glance were much too large.

After her bath Tara took a more detailed look at her bedroom. French doors along one whole wall led out into the loggia, or gallery, that overlooked the courtyard below. This screened loggia opened onto the hallway outside her bedroom and then fronted another bedroom opposite Tara's. On the other side of her room a door, when opened, revealed a narrow stone staircase that led down to the main-floor terrace. It also continued up to a small walled-in garden on the flat roof above, but that garden was in complete ruin.

Tara's room, however, was still majestic, with elaborate rococo furniture and delicately tinted plaster walls, only a little faded. The beams in the ceiling, as well as the doors and window frames, were carved in the intricate baroque fashion that she'd often seen in the Algarve before. Rose damask draperies were swept in billowing curves from the windows and attached at the sides with long gray blue tasseled cords. Sybaritic splendor—that was the best way she could describe it.

She went downstairs barefoot, much to Ashta's dismay. It took a long time before the woman understood that Tara was really quite pleased to walk around without shoes. Even so, Ashta shook her head every time she caught sight of Tara's bare feet. And then, to perturb the old woman still further, Tara insisted on eating breakfast in the kitchen. She translated Ashta's protests to mean that no guest of the manor had ever at any time eaten in the kitchen, and what would Dom Valente say if he found out. It just wasn't done; nobody but servants ate in the kitchen. There was more, but Tara couldn't unravel it all.

"Dom Valente doesn't have to find out, does he? Besides, why should he mind?" Tara smiled placatingly and settled comfortably at the big kitchen table, then went over what she had just said in her own stumbling Portuguese. After that, with much gesturing, she learned that Emilio had gone with Jorge to solve the "cow trouble," and that her parents would call her at twelve o'clock.

Meditatively sipping her third cup of Ashta's delicious coffee, Tara gazed out the wide, open window at the briers and flourishing weeds that had once been a vegetable garden. She felt beautifully rested and refreshed. In the calm, glorious morning sunshine she found herself wondering why she let Jorge upset her so much. Her violent moods seemed quite irrational and silly now. In fact, she had let the man upset her ever since they'd first met, and there really wasn't a logical explanation for it. She must have been very tired. . . .

She blushed when she remembered the way she'd put her arms around his neck the night before, deliberately and inexcusably teasing him. Why did she want to provoke the beast in him all the time? Well, she rationalized quickly, he was the one who started it, in most cases anyway. He had deliberately irritated her right from the beginning, when she'd been perfectly willing to be friendly. But now that she was feeling better and was in full control of all her faculties, their heretofore turbulent relationship would settle down; she was sure of it. At the very least, since she couldn't speak for him, she would do her part.

In this mood Tara felt almost like a missionary sent to soothe the heathens. And who knows, she asked herself. Anything could happen in a place like this, and by the time she left, it might have. . . . It was a pleasantly captivating thought.

All the unexplainable feelings she had when

around Jorge Valente she dismissed as merely the workings of an overwrought mind. One could imagine anything when one wasn't feeling well. Traitorously, his dark face swam before her eyes, and she hastily blinked it away. Her faith in calm waters wavered and then reasserted itself. She would surprise him. She would not become angry when he poked fun at her. Instead she would be the very model of a pleasant guest. And she would see what happened. It didn't really matter what he thought of her. He treated her like a child, but the desire in his eyes showed his inner feelings to be rather different. If she was wrong, in a few days she would walk out of his life. And then... then she would find the place to rewrite her submerged *Toodles*, book two, and Jorge Emmanuel Valente de Silves would become just another one of the figures connected with this adventure.

Certain that there were no loopholes in her reasoning, Tara happily accepted another cup of coffee and sank back in her chair. She put her feet up on another chair as she watched Ashta's preparations for their evening meal, sniffing contentedly at the faint salty tang in the air. She couldn't be more satisfied with life in general, she concluded.

Then the telephone rang. Tara shot out of her chair and ran down the hall to the *sala*. There she looked around, trying to locate the telephone, which rang insistently. Finally she spied it wedged between a stack of ledgers and some official documents that cluttered a huge ornate desk.

The first few minutes of conversation were totally

incoherent. Mrs. Lownes couldn't decide whether to laugh or cry, and Mr. Lownes tried vainly to soothe his wife and talk to Tara at the same time. They both became quite silent, though, when she related what had happened to her and the subsequent events that had brought her to Minha Casa. Even to her own ears the story sounded strange and unbelievable.

"Are you quite all right now, my dear?" Mrs. Lownes sounded weak and rather faint. "Are you comfortable there? Do you have everything you need? I mean, a man doesn't know—I mean, Jorge Valente sounds very nice but...your bedroom may be drafty! You know how old houses are! Are you eating the right food? Have you been drinking the water without boiling it? Ashta sounds charming but...but does she know how to take care of invalids? And what do you have to wear, Tara, darling? Oh, dear! This Jorge Valente.... No one knows very much about him. I mean, his family is certainly respectable, but he's something of a recluse, isn't he? Is it quite safe—"

"Oh, mother!" Tara cut in, laughing. "I'm not an invalid, even though a doctor's coming to see me after lunch. I have nothing more than bruises and a few scrapes, and I'm eating well. My bedroom is not drafty, I've been drinking wine mostly and Ashta takes very good care of me. In fact, she won't let me do anything for myself. I'm being pampered to death."

"Wine? Nothing but wine? Is he plying you with *wine*?"

"Mom!" Tara chuckled. Her mother was acting

true to form. "He's not plying me with anything! And he's very respectable; I'm sure you'd like him. He's been the very soul of consideration. Why, he even washed my hair!"

"He what?" Tara held the receiver from her ear as her mother's voice rose.

"Yes," she interrupted again calmly, "a truly charitable gesture. He's...he's...." She struggled to find the right word that would explain Jorge and yet put her mother's fears to rest. If she confessed what he was really like her mother wouldn't sleep a wink! "He's kind!"

"Yes, indeed! Struck me that way when he called us this morning." Tara took the receiver from her ear again to look at it in surprise. "You couldn't have chosen a better person to come to your aid."

Was that really her father's voice coming steadily over the wire? Well, Tara thought peevishly, Jorge had certainly won her father over in an admirable hurry! If she had her choice of rescuers it would not have been Jorge. Here she was, living in a strange man's house, and her father wasn't even concerned! She herself was plenty concerned about it.

"You'll be wanting clothes and money and whatever else it is women need." Professor Lownes was, as usual, his practical self. "Give a list to your mother and we'll send everything directly. Er, how long are you staying?"

"Just until I get the clothes and things. If you could send them right away I won't be staying here more than a few days."

When Tara finally hung up she bumped into Ashta,

who had been waiting, worriedly, right behind her.

"No, I'm not going home today," she reassured the old woman. "Me stay." Then she held out her hands and hugged Ashta impulsively, wishing she could take her along when she left.

It was a full minute later before Tara realized she'd forgotten to ask her mother about Dennis and Penny. She shrugged her shoulders, dismissing them. Their path was certain to go smoothly. Penny would love making martinis, and Dennis was sure to get his way. Thank God the picture didn't include her!

She had one foot out the door when the telephone rang again. "Oh, Tara, in all the excitement I forgot to tell you the most incredible news!" She could just see her mother on the other end, pulling and tweaking at her coiffure, which, curiously, didn't become disarranged in the slightest. "It's the biggest scandal in Hampstead since Lady Pritchard ran off with that American drummer! Dennis and Penny didn't get married! He disappeared the day of the wedding! Everyone was waiting at the church, but evidently his business in Edinburgh fell through and now he's penniless! It appears the company's been going downhill since Mr. Moreston died. Dennis laid more eggs than just this last one, and all the while he spent money as though it grew on trees. You can imagine what a shock this has been for Janette. There's a crowd of creditors after him, and no one knows where he's gone. He's left her to cope with everything! To think you almost married him! I shudder to think of it! Thank goodness you inherited so much foresight from Grandmother Lownes! And Penny, well, she's in tears now. At first she was furious that she'd given you her reservation on the *Adventure Star*. But after it sank she brightened right up! Which I thought rather indecent of her. What a strange girl she is.... Just like her mother!''

Tara grinned at that, then listened rather absent-mindedly to the rest of her mother's chatter. So the government hadn't changed the rezoning law, after all. How stupid of Dennis to sink all his remaining capital into acreage zoned for farmland on the strength of a bribe! But then, that was like him, she mused. He was often too sure of himself. Old Mr. Moreston would never have taken such unnecessary risks. And if Dennis's finances had been in bad shape, that explained his reason for wanting to marry her. Love obviously hadn't been his motive. Two hundred and fifty thousand pounds would go a long way toward paying off creditors. It might even get some new business venture off the ground. All the evidence clearly pointed to Dennis's avarice. She sighed deeply. The whole thing was distasteful. Her grandmother's inheritance proved at times to be an albatross around her neck.

How long would it take for her clothes to arrive, she wondered, her eyes roving over the lush tropical vegetation of the garden. She made her way to where the helicopter had landed last night, recognizing the spot by the marble bench smothered in a tide of full-blown roses. Close by stood a vine-covered statuette. Her fingers started to pull at the bougainvillea hiding it, first releasing the face and head, then working the clinging stems down over the shoulders.

One, two days for her clothes? Maybe more? It was too bad, seeing as she was here, that she couldn't start looking around for accommodation of her own. Las Palmas was out now, but that didn't matter. Somewhere in Portugal would do equally as well. In fact, she'd always had a hankering to come back here. But she couldn't start looking for a place to live without money or a decent set of clothes. Landlords would look askance at a would-be tenant who didn't even own a pair of shoes.

She pulled the sturdy vines down over the marble statuette's torso and yanked them away from its legs. Satisfied with her efforts, she straightened up.

Her eyes skimmed over the poplars, the seemingly endless avenue of evergreen oaks, the beeches and chestnuts, the exuberant growth of rioting roses and wild flowers. What rich vibrant color! At its finest the garden would be a paradise, and in the spring when the orchard along the garden edge bloomed it would take one's breath away! High above the orchards she could see mile upon mile of *charnecas*, Moorish heaths. Unirrigated and sun dried, the land varied between brown and ocher and the lemon yellow of thirsty scrub grass. Here and there a clump of sagebrush or a squat olive tree showed dusty green on the landscape. Past the *charnecas* the *serras* rose in desert-hued foothills. And all of it would soon belong to Jorge!

The vastness of the estate awed her. Used to living in the city, she couldn't quite imagine what it would be like to have all this space to roam around in. But after careful thought she decided that it could be very pleasant, providing one had someone to share it with. . . .

Frowning slightly, her eyes rose to the hazy outline of blue mountains just visible beyond the *serras*. The mountains were the barrier around the town of Monchique. Barely three thousand feet high, they sealed off the Algarve from the north. She'd traveled through them with her father two years earlier, but it seemed a century ago.

Just to her left was an oddly shaped, leaf-smothered lump. Hoping it was another statue, she went over to it. Sure enough, her fingers pulled and twisted at thorny brier stems to uncover yet another marble head!

Absorbed in her tasks, Tara didn't notice a lithe young man coming through the shrubbery toward her. Nor did she see him right away when he came to a stop directly in front of her.

"Oh!" she gasped when she looked up. "Who are you?"

"You are truly real!" he breathed, his beautiful dark Portuguese eyes melting all over her.

"I believe so," she replied, smiling a little.

"*Avó* told me of a young girl graciously snatched back from death by Dom Valente, but I scarcely believed her words! And here you are!"

"I wouldn't go so far as to say graciously!" she said wryly.

"What? I'm sorry, I do not—"

"Oh, never mind. But who are you?"

"I'm Ricco. Ashta is my grandmother. And you are Tara!"

"Er, yes."

"*Avó* said how delicate, how lovely you are, but I stand silent at your beauty! Yes...yes.... I can see how Dom Valente would mistake you for a mermaid. Your long hair, floating behind you in the water, the—"

"I don't think the actual situation was as romantic as you seem to think," Tara interrupted a shade repressively.

"Any situation would be romantic with you in it!" he replied robustly, not to be denied his fantasies. "I should feel like the luckiest man on the earth to be able to save you from certain death!" He approached the opposite side of the statuette, his hands resting beside hers on the bare marble head, his eyes staring down at her with warm enthusiasm.

"No doubt anyone would feel good to save someone's life." Tara removed her hands but smiled at him. He really was almost alarmingly good-looking, and rather aware of it. To change the subject she asked, "Do you work on the *quinta*?"

"Me? Oh, no, no, *senhorinha*! I am a cicerone!" He puffed out his chest.

"A what?"

"A tourist guide. In Sagres! *Avó* told me you are a writer. How is it that you are English, a writer, and don't know that word?"

"Uh...well, I expect there are a great many words I don't know," Tara answered, a little amazed by this young man. "You speak English very well."

He grinned widely at her; she had obviously said the right thing. "Yes, I do. I speak Spanish, French and Italian, as well. My German is...rough, I would say, but I practice every day with a German woman who I am escorting. She is greatly interested in Portuguese customs."

Tara wondered for a moment whether the woman might not be more interested in Ricco himself. But she said, "You know five languages? However did you learn?"

"I have what the English call 'the knack.' I'm good at it." He shrugged his well-built shoulders eloquently. "*Avó* has been the...the caretaker at the *casa* for as long as I remember. When I was little I used to spend most of my time in the library. There's every book in there one could want, including a vast number of books in different languages. Grammar books made it easy to learn. My accent improved once I became a cicerone and could speak to the people of the various nationalities."

"Ricco! You taught yourself! That's wonderful! But what happened to your parents?"

He shrugged his shoulders again. "They both died of the fever before I could walk, so *avó* tells me. I don't remember them."

"Oh, Ashta must be so proud of you! Five languages, and you're working on the sixth. Ricco, you must be very intelligent."

"I believe so," he replied, so unselfconsciously that Tara laughed. His brows beetled into a quick frown. "You find me amusing, *senhorinha*?"

"Oh, no, Ricco!" she assured him hastily, not wanting to hurt his feelings. "And why don't you call me Tara? That would be a lot nicer."

"I shall." He beamed at her, his good humor restored.

With a touch of old-world charm he held out his hand. A trifle uncertain, Tara carefully placed her fingers in his palm, wondering what he meant to do. Bending, he brushed his lips lightly over her hand before restoring it to her. Tara, taken aback, could only stand there looking at him.

"I would have preferred to kiss your lips," he pointed out, his eyes sparkling mischievously. "But not only would that have been too forward, it would also have been...crude."

Tara was glad he hadn't tried to kiss her mouth, but she had to ask, "Crude?"

"You belong to another man. I consider it crude to poach," he declared loftily.

"I see! Exactly whom do I belong to?"

"Dom Valente, of course!" He spread his hands.

"Oh, just wait a minute! I don't belong to anyone! He may have saved my life but that doesn't mean—"

"He has no designs on you?"

Tara stared at Ricco with her mouth open. "No, er, not that I know of. But that doesn't mean you can kiss me!" she protested as he took a quick step around the statuette.

"No harm in trying!" he smiled at her, his eyes sparkling.

"Yes, well. Perhaps we can just be friends?" Tara eyed him doubtfully.

He appeared disappointed by her suggestion. "For the present I shall be satisfied with only the crumbs of your affection," he began mournfully.

"Really, Ricco! You've been reading too many novels! Why don't you show me how to get to the beach from here?" she coaxed, since he seemed to be sulking.

He brightened immediately. "I have a free half hour before I must return to Sagres! Come, I will show you the path!"

Seemingly directed only by the faint swish of breakers against the shore, he plunged into the underbrush, chivalrously clearing the way for her to follow.

"This is a path?" she asked dubiously, winding her way around great bushes of cyclamen and hibiscus.

"Of course! See? Here's the bridge!"

It was a half-rotted affair, collapsed into a small rushing stream. He leaped over it easily, then turned to help her across. They passed a derelict gazebo with a crumbled roof, scrambled over a jumble of rocks, and then there was the sea, spread before her.

Exulting, Tara faced into the warm ocean wind. It lifted the hair off her shoulders and fanned it through the air. A sudden gust whipped the calf-length skirt up to her knees, and she laughed with pleasure. Her eyes eagerly followed the rough tumbling coastline of polychrome rock: now straight and high, forming cliffs with great boulders at the foot; now low and jagged and whipped by creaming waves; now vanishing altogether under white gold sand.

It was a place of harsh lonely beauty. Softened by the intense gold-hued sunlight, it took on a dreamlike unreality. Far places looked close, close enough for

Tara to reach out and touch. Rocks near at hand seemed far away, seen as though through glass. A kind of shimmering moodiness hung over the landscape, penetrating the very rocks themselves, so that they, the sand and the water seemed to be alive, to have a singular power to bewitch and delight the mind.

Tara had no idea how long she had stood on her rocky promontory when Ricco lightly touched her arm. Faintly, she heard Ashta calling her name. She abruptly left her reverie, realizing the doctor must have arrived. Ricco had to be off, too; he turned and waved strenuously before disappearing around the first bend in the beach. She waved back. Then, flying, she made her way through the garden maze and reached the *sala* out of breath.

"Hello, Doutor Couto!" She turned the full force of her smile on him.

A gray-templed, stoop-shouldered elderly gentleman, he gazed back, momentarily lost for words. "*Senhorinha! De Deus!* I expected to find you in bed!" He stopped to laugh, finding her smile infectious. "Jorge must be a better doctor than he supposes. He should have stayed in the profession but, ahh, he was so very headstrong then!"

"I don't think he's changed any," Tara said dryly.

"Perhaps not." The staid doctor was surprised to find himself beaming back at his patient. "Ah, well. Shall we get to the business at hand?"

He gave her a meticulously thorough examination. Finally, replacing his stethoscope and assorted paraphernalia in his black bag, he affirmed, "You've made an excellent recovery. Jorge knew exactly what to do. Bah! And now he is a hotelier!''

"You know him well, don't you?"

"Yes, indeed. I've been his *doutor* since the day he was born.''

"Oh. I . . . I thought you were from Sagres."

"No, no, *senhorinha*. Jorge sent for me. My practice is in Lisbon, but most of my clients are scattered far and wide. I enjoy the travel much more than being bound to my office. Now, *senhorinha*, although you feel well and look the very picture of health, there is the matter of your lungs. Not all is as it should be. A slight congestion, you understand— nothing serious if you treat it properly. A relapse could be very serious, though, and so I warn you. You are to have complete rest; no exertion for at least two weeks!" He paused to let that sink in. "I hope you are not planning on returning to England immediately. Our dry climate is much more suited to a rapid recovery. One must not trifle with the lungs!" He bent stern eyes upon her.

"No, indeed, Doutor Couto," Tara replied meekly. "I . . . I plan on staying . . . indefinitely."

"Yes?" the doctor looked more than interested.

"Not here! I mean, I plan on staying in Portugal, b-but not exactly right here." She blushed furiously, reading in the man's face an embarrassing assumption. How could she explain that she and Jorge didn't really mean anything to each other, as he obviously thought, without coming right out and saying so?

"Of course not, *senhorinha*," he said soothingly, but not at all convincingly. "And now I must go.

Give this to Jorge—'' he handed her a bulky envelope ''—and thank him for his kind dinner invitation. Alas, I cannot stay, for I have another appointment.'' He looked at her curiously for a moment, then smiled and was gone.

Tara let out a short vexed sigh. On the surface her situation could be misconstrued to mean almost anything. Ricco, too, had made assumptions. The reality was not at all what people thought, but would she have to explain that to everyone she met?

The grandfather clock chimed, and Tara gave a start. It was almost teatime, and that meant Jorge would soon be home. A thread of excitement spiraled up inside her, and without really realizing what she was doing she jumped out of her chair and hurried off down the hall. The doctor's words echoing in her mind forced her to slow her pace a little.

The huge double doors creaked as she slipped through them. Her bare feet made no sound on the courtyard floor but left smudged imprints in the dust. Tara looked down at her toes with childish pleasure. It had been years since her feet were this dirty.

The main road leading from the villa wound away between the tall avenues of evergreen oaks, and she set off down it. The air was dry, glimmering with heat. Tara drew deep breaths, trying to cure her ailment in record time. The powerful sun pressed down, making her back feel hot and sticky beneath the heavy fall of her hair. A ground squirrel scuttled over the road in front of her, then turned on its hind legs to stare at her curiously before diving into the underbrush. Other than that, there wasn't a sound or a movement. The countryside slept in the midday heat.

She walked on and on until beads of perspiration broke out on her forehead and her feet lagged. The avenue of oaks was a lot longer than it had seemed at first glance, and finally Tara stopped. Panting, she drew her hand across her forehead. A rest seemed necessary, so she dropped down against the trunk of an oak, whose comfortable curve accommodated her back. She closed her eyes—only for a moment to shut out the sunlight. Peace and contentment filtered through her senses, and a soft smile curved her lips. Her body went limp as she fell asleep. . . .

A rough hand on her shoulder woke her abruptly. Jorge was leaning over her, his face very near her own. Only it was black and angry and impatient. Tara felt the smile slip off her lips as this registered on her benumbed brain.

"What the hell are you doing out here!"

"Oh, hello. . . Jorge."

"Is that all you have to say? Hello?" He shook her again. "You don't even have a hat!" he accused.

"Oh. No. But I'm in the shade. Is it teatime? I came to meet you." Her smile returned of its own accord.

He gazed at her darkly, obviously not quite believing what he saw.

"You've shaved your beard off!" Tara exclaimed suddenly.

"You've shaved your beard!" he mimicked her words. "You haven't even the slightest bit of sense behind that flower face, have you?" His hands clamped fiercely around her wrists as he pulled her to her feet. "Get in the jeep!"

She watched him out of the corner of her eye as she went with him to the vehicle. He was quite out of temper. Had the cow lost her calf? Why else would he be so angry? She noticed that his denims were dusty and stained, that his work boots had known better days. Then Tara stared curiously at his chin, seeing it clearly for the first time. She liked what she saw... a lot.

She felt not the least put out by Jorge's foul temper, nor by Emilio's long dour face. "I've had a lovely day," she said conversationally, ignoring Jorge's black look as he started the jeep with a squeal of tires. Cheerfully she recounted her breakfast in the kitchen, her parents' telephone call, the meeting with Ashta's grandson and Doutor Couto's message. "How's the... the cow?" she asked at last.

"Well enough" was the grudging reply.

"And the calf?"

"Alive and kicking."

"That's wonderful! I thought perhaps it— Well, you do seem out of sorts and—"

"I seem out of sorts!" Exasperation showed clearly in Jorge's voice. "I find you lying under a tree, looking as though you're dead when you're supposed to be inside resting, and you wonder that I'm out of sorts!"

"But I *was* resting!"

He uttered a sound in his throat that was very much like a growl.

Tara's hand moved toward him, then stopped in

the air midway. "I didn't mean to worry you," she said, an impulsive smile curving her red lips. She was, she felt, the personification of a pleasant guest. Surely her good intentions would allow them to live in relative harmony, if nothing else.

Midnight eyes glowered at her from under frowning black brows. The flaring anger directed toward her was puzzling. She pondered it as they drove up the avenue.

Jorge stopped the jeep as abruptly as he had started it, then leaped out and strode around to her side. Tara swung her legs out, then just sat for a moment, staring at his furious face. She still was determined to be a pleasant guest, but a touch of defiance now mingled with her feelings. The air between them gradually became charged with a fine tension.

Coldly Jorge eyed her vulnerable slenderness, the soft rise and fall of her breasts beneath the thin cotton blouse. The velvety dark eyes staring back into his were guileless, hopeful, questioning. The full mouth seemed to be on the very edge of a smile, and the small feet were so dusty!

"Oh, God!" He threw up his hands and turned his back on her. With a muttered "why me?" that Tara only barely heard, he strode away from her into the courtyard.

Tara's smile broke out and spread into a wide grin. She jumped out of the jeep, then had to force herself to walk slowly after him.

When she entered the *sala* he was relaxing in a chair, and the look on his face told her nothing at all. She sat down opposite him but didn't say a word until Emilio wheeled in the trolley. She served coffee for them both with a steady hand, and only then asked, "Did you spend your whole day with the cow?"

His lips twitched with grim amusement at her polite tone. Sardonically he replied, "No, but she needed a cesarean. She'd never have made it on her own. First birth, you see, and she's smaller than most."

When Tara nodded, as though she knew all about farm life, he chuckled aloud. "It's too bad you couldn't have been there."

"Yes, isn't it," Tara gulped, trying to sound enthusiastic.

"I checked the cork oaks on the way back," he informed her, vestiges of amusement still glimmering in his midnight eyes.

"How were they?" She was trying to hold up her end of the conversation, but was finding it rather difficult to sound intelligent. She had no practical knowledge of agriculture, and yet she wanted very much for the conversation to stay on this impersonal level. She also wanted to hear as much as she could about the *quinta* and its related goings-on.

"Terrible. The bark's been stripped off twice in the past seven years, I was told. So it's no wonder."

"Ah!" she replied blankly.

He watched her discomfiture for a moment, then relented. "Cork, as you know it, grows on cork oaks as bark. This bark can be harvested approximately every nine years. If it's done too often the tree dies."

"Oh! Are they. . .?"

"No, not dead yet, but powerfully close to it." He smiled grimly as she digested the information.

"And the cow...? Was she one of your herd?"

"No, not one of the main herd. Not that there's much of a real herd left. Just a handful of mangy cattle, and those all steers. Quite useless for breeding, you understand. No, the cow in question belongs to Maria Duarte." At Tara's questioning glance he added, "She's one of the peasants."

"Ah." Again Tara racked her brains for something to say. Earlier in the day she'd had hundreds of questions about the *quinta*; now she couldn't remember any of them. With relief she sensed that Jorge was going to change the topic even before he spoke.

"You need clothes, shoes—surely a great many other things. Give your measurements to Emilio and he will run into Sagres to get what you need."

"No! I...I mean, I haven't any money. And although I appreciate your offer, I would prefer not to become more indebted to you."

"Don't be ridiculous! You—"

"I'm perfectly fine just the way I am!" Tara interrupted, struggling to maintain her earlier equilibrium. "I don't have to go anywhere, so these clothes will do for a day or so. My parents are sending my things."

He looked pointedly at her feet, so Tara tucked them quickly under her chair. As though he were dealing with a dense child, he sighed, evidently prepared to argue the point. Then he shrugged his shoulders.

"Have it your way! But don't come crying to me when you step in a patch of thistles!"

"You're the last person I'd come crying to!" she

retorted spiritedly, her eyes blazing, her manners giving way before her wrath.

Jorge returned her gaze, and for a moment she glimpsed a hard recklessness in him. It was as if he meant her to pay for something she'd done.... She took a deep breath and held it, wondering what would come next. He was so unpredictable. His attitude was so far removed from "calm waters" that she could only be rueful about her earlier plans. Now she saw plenty of loopholes in her reasoning.

"Stop holding your breath before you turn blue!" he said, his tone painfully scathing. "At times you're such a child—almost beyond hope!" His black gaze whipped over her, blazing down her body.

"Oh, don't be like that, Jorge!" she exclaimed.

"Like what?" There was a razor edge to his voice.

"So...uncharitable. We all have our faults, and although I try not to, I can't help it if I antagonize you! It seems there's nothing I can do to please you. There's nothing about me that you like!"

"There, at least, you're right! But not for the reasons you suppose!" he said enigmatically.

She gazed at him reproachfully, her eyes enormous with hurt. *"Bêsta!"*

"So now you've stooped to flinging insults...." His cool drawl infuriated her, choked her. She all but ground her teeth in helpless rage.

"Just to show you how very charitable I *can* be, get a hat from Ashta and be in the courtyard in ten minutes!"

He moved purposefully toward the door, his steps effortlessly graceful. At the door he turned suddenly to look at her, and the sunlight, slanting through the leaded windows, split into prism-bright colors and played over his face. It emphasized the glittering mockery in his eyes and the coppery darkness of his self-contained features. With a small grim smile he turned on his heel and left.

As soon as he was gone Tara's anger vanished, and she was left feeling like a deflated balloon. What was she getting so upset about, she wondered in confusion. She always seemed to be making adjustments, trying to make allowances for his moods. But he simply would not be accommodated, and now she didn't know what to think of Jorge. Nor did she know how to deal with him, and with his perturbing effect on her spirits. She could no longer deny that effect.

She had better put all thought of him as a potential mate right out of her mind, she decided. How silly to even consider him in the first place! That her body chemistry reacted to his was no reason to take the plunge—in fact, all the more reason to avoid it. Her mild infatuation with him would soon wither away if it was given no encouragement. . . .

"ON YOUR LEFT are almond trees; on your right, orange trees. Past the oranges are the lemons and limes, and finally, the pomegranates. On the other side, past the almonds, are the tangerines and peaches." Jorge spoke above the grinding gears of the jeep. His voice, devoid of emotion, was perfunctorily pleasant.

She had pleasantry to match his, Tara thought pee-

vishly, still smarting inside. She clung to her seat as
the jeep swung into a sharp ascent. The dirt road was
full of potholes, and the last rain had left it deeply
rutted. Cane grass, bluegrass and weeds grew on the
hump down the middle.

The evergreen oaks continued in a line up the road,
hiding the villa and its grounds as Jorge and Tara
drove farther away. Tara looked back and could see
nothing but shiny blue green foliage. The front view
was the same: acres upon acres of orchards spreading
out on either side with the oaks towering overhead,
their tops meeting across the road. It was so peaceful.
A softly flowing green tunnel dappled with golden
light.

Little green globes of unripe oranges dotted the
ground beside the road on her side. A great butterfly
of brown and dark orange velvet fluttered lazily by.
The tranquillity surrounding them grew and deepened until Tara felt lost in it. Jorge had sunk into a
reverie of his own; she doubted that he was aware of
her existence.

What a spell the Algarve cast! She'd felt it earlier
that afternoon, but it was eternally the same, she
supposed. Each part of the district had its own
peculiar charms, but all of it held a mystery, a sense
of timelessness, of history going on and on forever,
of old mixing with new in total harmony. Tourism
had spoiled some of that, Tara considered, but only
a little. Native Algarvians held to their ways, enjoying them and revering their time-honored customs.
In her heart she thanked Valente for wanting to preserve this part of the Algarve, without concrete and

neon lights and continual hurry. It would be a shame
to—

"We'll have to get a chaperon," he interrupted her
thoughts.

"Wh-what?" Tara didn't think she'd heard correctly. She swung to face Jorge, her dark eyes incredulous, her skin sheening in the amber light.

"A chaperon," he repeated. Mocking lights
danced in the depths of his eyes, which dropped
meaningfully for a moment to the youthful curve of
her lips.

Tara felt herself blush, and hated her lack of self-
control. She twisted away from him, but knew by his
soft chuckle that he had seen her heightened color.

"You get my point," he stated. "We must keep up
appearances. What would the neighbors think?"

"But there's Emilio and Ashta!" she protested,
carefully examining the trunk of a passing oak.

"But they're servants. They don't count as chaper-
ons. They work for me...."

"Now you're being ridiculous!" she said crossly.
"A chaperon! There's no way I would let you.... I
would never want to.... I mean, it's not as if...."
Her voice trailed away, and she blushed more furiously than ever.

"But *querida*," he drawled suggestively, "it has already happened! They say a kiss is just the beginning;
the thin edge of the wedge, so to speak. Hasn't your
mother told you?"

"Heavens, I have no desire to go into all that! You
wouldn't dare!"

"I might, if I'm sufficiently tempted."

Tara caught the meaningful nuance in his tone. "You're baiting me again," she declared sweetly, abruptly switching her mood. The silvery sound of her laughter fell around them. "I think I'm finally getting to know you, Valente, even just a little bit. But why can't you be nice? Oh, I know—don't say it! You have something against me, as you mentioned earlier! There's a fatal flaw in my character. You should tell me what it is; perhaps I can change."

He in turn threw his head back and laughed in rich enjoyment. "It would be as impossible for you to change as it would be for that almond tree to bear oranges!" His eyes sparkled with devilry. Suddenly he grasped her hand and kissed it warmly, right in the center of her palm.

Tara pulled away as though burned. She didn't dare meet the challenge in his dark taunting eyes. Some heaviness seemed to weigh her down. She struggled to rise above it.

"On second thought, I think a chaperon is just what we need to keep the peace between us. That way you'd have to be nice to me!" Laughter gurgled up in her throat. "I'd love to see that!"

"Hmm. I wonder." Incredibly, he smiled back at her. "I've decided upon Contessa Ernesta Angelica d'Cimbrianni. She's extremely respectable, she's lonely, she has a good grasp of what young ladies should and shouldn't do. And with her here, perhaps I can get the sale of the *quinta* finalized more quickly."

"Anything you say," she replied.

Jorge flashed her a sharp look. "Indeed! You have

had a change of heart! I wonder what brought that on?"

"I merely thought that, at this point in time, agreement was the wisest course to take."

"And what would you know of wisdom? Why, you're barely out of the schoolroom!"

"You're on *that* old treadmill, are you?" Again her infectious laughter broke out. "And you, with your advanced years, know it all, I suppose?"

"I've covered a great deal more ground than you have, mermaid." His teeth gleamed savagely white in the saturnine darkness of his face. With her eyes she traced the strong virile line of his brown throat, the clean broad width of his shoulders, the powerful controlled muscles. A soft sigh escaped her throat, a totally sensuous sound that she was unaware of. She felt him tense and turned to look questioningly at him, her eyes wide, her lips slightly parted—the picture of innocence. When he groaned her eyes widened still further.

"Now what have I done?"

"You wouldn't know; you're too young!" he returned bitingly. His lips twisted wryly and his eyes narrowed on her face.

In mystified frustration she shook her head, and her hair gleamed a dancing blue and black in the pattern of sun and shade.

Jorge swung his eyes back to the road, now dipping sharply downhill. The end of the orchard was in sight. Tara breathed a sigh of relief. Somehow she associated the end of the orchards with the end of the heaviness around her heart. She slanted a look at him, taking in the compressed lips, the jutting, iron-hard chin, and sighed again. The sound seemed to irritate him.

"Contessa d'Cimbrianni arrives tomorrow," he stated shortly.

"Have you asked her already?" she asked, trying to shift the conversation back to normal. The sound of her voice, calm and noncommittal, made her feel better.

"No! I'm just going to get her!" he snapped emphatically.

Tara eyed him warily. Once again he was like an angry bear. She tried to keep her face straight as she asked, "You're just going to bring her here whether she wants to come or not?" She couldn't keep the laughter out of her voice. "How tyrannical you are! Your ancestors weren't by any chance pirates, were they?"

She studied his profile with mock seriousness. "You know, of course, that these waters were once infested with pirates? With barbarian galleys? As far back in time as the Phoenicians and for centuries later—why, when the Christian cross replaced the Muslim crescent in Tavira and in Silves—the barbarians plied these waters, trading with the fishermen from Olhão and Albufeira for food and occasionally shelter! It was the Phoenicians who started it, setting up ivory and amber trading posts at Lagos and at the Faro marshes."

"What's this? Where did you learn so much about my country?"

Tara laughed aloud. "I know a great deal more

than you give me credit for, Mr. Valente de Silves! By the way, do you have a title? Conde de Silves sounds so lovely!'' She was teasing him gleefully. ''I shall have to address you as 'my lord' or— Say, you're not a duke, are you? No, you can't be, since your father bears that title. Thank goodness! Otherwise I'd have to say 'Your Grace'!''

''I don't have a title, not until I inherit my father's. And then it will be no more 'Jorge' this and 'Jorge' that! You most definitely will have to say 'Your Grace'! And while you're practicing it, you might as well learn some respect for your elders!''

He was assuming rather a lot, Tara thought—assuming that she would still be around at that distant point in time.

''Aren't we getting stuffy!'' she teased. ''You're not Your Grace yet, so don't put on airs!''

''Two hundred years ago, mermaid, I could have had you beheaded and quartered for that.''

''Aha! You *do* have a barbarian heart beneath that civilized veneer. I know your true colors now, Valente, and my mother told me never to trust a pirate!''

Jorge's laughter rang out clear and full. ''This is getting us nowhere!'' he finally stated, shooting her one of his dark-eyed glances.

''If we talk about it, perhaps we can sort it out,'' she suggested. ''Do you see what I mean?''

''Not very clearly! Anything to do with you, Tara, strikes me as highly chaotic! Now be a good girl and don't say anything more.'' His laughing eyes taunted her, while his voice became extremely impersonal, affecting the singsong rhythm of a tour guide.

"We are now entering the vineyards. You'll notice the absence of trunk supports. These vines were cultivated so as not to need them. Are you listening, Tara? As I was saying, if you'll look at the main stems of the vines, you'll see how strong they are—like small tree trunks. It took years of diligent pruning to produce that thickness, and during that time the plants were not allowed to bear fruit. Early this spring they were pruned again to reduce the number of buds. The shoots that develop from the remaining buds will be more prolific and will bear grapes of better quality than if all the buds had been allowed to remain. Pretty, aren't they?" He cleared his throat and continued in the studied voice. "Grapes are attacked by many insect pests, as well as by plant diseases, the most common of which are black rot and downy mildew. Unfortunately, these grapes have both. The ounce of prevention wasn't provided by Resende, so grape production will be down this year—"

"Jorge, stop it!" Tara protested weakly. "You sound like a grape-grower's almanac."

He grinned from ear to ear, looking for a moment like a carefree young boy. "Just giving you a taste of your own medicine, mermaid."

The vineyards were miles in width, Tara guessed, clutching her hat with one hand and steadying herself with the other as the jeep bumped and jolted over the ruts. They ran in a wide belt all around the orchards, Jorge had told her.

When they jounced over a particularly large rock,

she was thrown against his shoulder. Unseated, she clutched at him instead of her hat.

"My God, Tara, you choose the most unlikely times!" he yelped.

But she could only tighten her hold or catapult into the rear seat. She chose the former.

Jorge swore under his breath as the jeep veered toward the right ditch, then the left. Another rock caught on the undercarriage, and the vehicle came to a precipitate halt half in and half out of the right ditch.

"You see?" he asked grimly. "Chaos! You firmly believe in never a dull moment, don't you?" His arms swung her roughly onto his lap.

Her weight crushed her hat, for somehow it had got caught between them. The black peasant skirt had worked its way well up over her thighs and was wound in a most undignified manner almost up to her waist, leaving her long shapely legs in clear view.

"But Jorge—"

"But Jorge nothing!" His breath came out in a short explosion. "I have this uncanny feeling you've been wanting this all afternoon! You just don't know when to quit!" His voice held a deep rough vitality, an edge of ruthlessness.

"Jorge, you're being unfair!"

"Unfair, she says!" He groaned, striking his forehead with the palm of his hand. "So now that you're here, what are you going to do about it?" His black eyes glittered brilliantly into her own.

Tara moistened her lips, feeling suddenly and incredibly nervous. She expected to hear her teeth rattling in her head. "D-do?"

"If you don't have an answer, I have!"

"No. No, no, you mustn't, Jorge. No, really. It would be fatal!"

Inexorably his arms tightened. One hand wound through her hair to shape itself to her head; the other, curved around her hip, pressed her against him. Every nerve in her body pulsed with warm desire for him. "No." It was barely a whisper.

"You have the most inviting way of saying no." His voice softened to his own blend of mockery and tenderness. His lips brushed her own, so lightly that Tara wasn't sure they'd touched at all. "Either your tongue is lying or your eyes are, *querida*."

She shut her eyes immediately, pressing her lids down as though that would save her. But even halfway around the world she would not be able to escape his hold over her! She moaned softly just before his lips touched hers again. This time they lingered, and Tara had not an ounce of willpower left to push him away. It would always be the same. Her head said one thing; she did another.

He traced the full curve of her lips with his, and the resulting sensations made her forfeit her pride, her armor...everything. Her arms went up around his neck. For once her mind and body attained a shattering unity in wanting him, in unconsciously loving him.

When his mouth drew slowly away from hers she murmured a sigh of protest. His lips trailed across her face, over her slanting cheekbones, down her throat to nibble at a point just below her ear. She turned her head, her lips brushing across his tanned cheek in drowsy hunger as his hands molded her intimately closer to him.

Aching with need she sought his mouth, found it, and her lips parted unresistingly at the increased pressure. The world dropped away and fell out of sight. White-hot passion smoldered and swamped mundane reality. With her slender body arched against his, with her lips fused to his in warm pulsing sweetness, the thought of tomorrow, of the outcome of this moment of madness, never crossed her mind. In a vortex of emotion and sensation Tara caught one of his softly caressing hands. Guiding it over her body, she moved it to her breast, never once breaking contact with his ravishing mouth.

Immediately his long hand closed around the swell of flesh, burning an urgent heat through the thin cotton of her blouse, igniting a wild fire between them that raged through her blood. Within the suddenly iron-hard, demanding circle of his arms she trembled with delicious satisfaction from his lovemaking. Under his searching gentle fingers the tip of her breast hardened, and a deep-throated groan seemed forced from him. "I'm losing my mind...." His voice was thick, as though he was having trouble getting the words out.

She felt his withdrawal like an acute physical pain. "Open your eyes, Tara," he said a shade repressively, obviously unaffected by the emotions she was experiencing.

She shivered in reaction, leaning away from him, trying to fathom what had just happened. "Why? Why, Jorge?" she asked breathlessly, her voice husky and strange sounding, even to her own ears.

"Maldicao!" he uttered with sharp self-mockery. "I gave your father my word that I'd take care of you—and that's what I'll do!"

"Not every man would do the same." It was a stupid taunt. She hadn't meant to say it but his rejection of her was an open wound.

"I'm not every man," he retorted curtly. "I keep my word!" He fitted his hands around her waist and shifted her to the other seat, dropping her there unceremoniously.

"Why are you so angry?" she asked, pulling the peasant skirt well down over her legs until it hid all but her dusty feet.

"I have good reason to be," he stated cryptically. "Besides, as I've already pointed out to you, you're a little young for my taste! I think we've seen enough of orchards and vineyards for one day." He shot a black glittering look her way.

Tara's hair was tousled and her eyes a shadowed purplish gray. Her lips were set in a melancholy pout. She looked straight ahead, her eyes wide but unseeing, as though she were in a trance. He looked at her again, taking in every fragile detail. Without meaning to he drove perilously close to the edge of the road.

What was a little petting anyway, Tara wondered. Completely unnerved, she argued with herself all the way back to the villa. Obviously her infatuation for Jorge was stronger than ever. But that was no excuse for encouraging him! She writhed in her seat. If only he didn't know she wanted him to make love to her!

She'd made a complete fool of herself. Recently she seemed to have lost all sense of proportion. How, when, where had that happened? There was nothing the matter with her; the doctor had reassured her of that. So why did she feel as though something was wrong? Tears threatened, and she despised herself all the more. Terribly agitated, she blinked her eyes. Her stomach seemed tied in knots.

She flashed a baleful look toward Jorge. He seemed so cool, so uncaring. Her first impression of him came back: a granite wall with no chinks. He was a sorcerer towering over her, able to send her to heaven or to hell; and she a mere babe in the woods, trying to protect herself against his power.

With a massive effort she pulled herself together. She couldn't remain a child forever, but she was damned if she'd take the plunge into womanhood with him!

Barely composed, she preceded him into the villa. Looking neither right nor left, she headed straight for the kitchen. How she needed Ashta's gentle soul, her toothless but oh so sweet smile. For the moment Tara gave up being pleasant with her host, and totally vanquished the idea of being an ideal guest. She would damn Jorge Valente to hell first!

Jorge's eyes followed her, taking in the squared shoulders, the trim line of her back, the graceful step that swung her skirt softly, seductively around her legs. He took a deep breath, and expelling it very slowly, stepped into the *sala*. As he saw Emilio's long sour face bent over a stack of documents, his own expression was one of relief.

CHAPTER EIGHT

JORGE'S COOL BLACK EYES surveyed Tara from across the breakfast table, minutely, feature by feature. She fidgeted with her coffee cup, but managed to gaze archly back. The whole thing was that they were just not meant to get along, she reminded herself. It was in their stars; she'd felt that right from the beginning. They were poles apart and exploded whenever they got close to each other. Spontaneous combustion. So she would stay out of his way; it was that simple.

"You'll be leaving immediately to collect the Contessa d'Cimbrianni?" Her voice was an exquisite blend of natural charm and forced reserve.

"Yes, immediately," he murmured. "And while she's here dinner will be served around six. The *contessa* likes to go to bed early and to get up late. By the way, the cleaning women should arrive soon. Will you choose a bedroom for the *contessa* and have it prepared, Tara?"

"Of course." She smiled insincerely and was well pleased with her performance.

Jorge looked outrageously attractive today in his gray linen suit. Quickly she lowered her eyes. Had they been melting all over him as Ricco's had melted all over her? She was rather afraid they had. All she really wanted to do was lie back in her chair and stare at him until he came around the table to kiss her. Could she will him to do so?

"So...did you enjoy your walk with Ricco last night? You two seem to have hit it off rather well together," he said nonchalantly.

"Yes, I did, and yes, we have. He knows this property like the back of his hand. And I can see why he's making a success out of being a tour guide. There's a way he has of describing the simplest things. In English, even, and it's not his mother tongue. He's absolutely wonderful with words!"

"Indeed!"

"Did you know he speaks five languages and is learning another? And he taught himself!"

"No, I didn't know. You...find him charming, do you?"

"Who wouldn't? Don't you?"

"I wouldn't describe him in those terms exactly. He's a very personable young man, and I would say, from the little I've talked with him, that I find him to be intelligent and eager for life. He tends to be a little...a little...."

"Romantically theatrical, perhaps?"

"That's about it. Actually, you two are quite similar—And no, psychology is not one of my hobbies!"

Tara gritted her teeth and carried on as though he hadn't spoken. "I've met other people with the same trait, but with him it comes so naturally that I think it's part of his charm. He doesn't feel ridiculous saying things that would make most men blush. And I imagine most women would find that...."

"Appealing? Intriguing? Exhilarating? Embarrassing?" Jorge shot suggestions at her.

"Oh, no. His eloquence is always in the best of taste."

"I'm glad to hear that." Sarcasm tinged his drawling voice.

Tara's eyes flickered from the garden back to the terrace where they were dining.

"Exactly what is your point?" he asked when she met his gaze. "You are leading up to something, aren't you?"

"Well...."

"Yes, I thought so!"

"It merely crossed my mind that some formal education would not be wasted on him! And as he's sort of under your wing...."

"You think he should be sent to university?"

"Think of all that talent and...and eagerness. If it were channeled...."

"Er, yes. I am thinking of it! Ricco left school when he was ten. He would need tutoring before he'd be ready for any university. So, I will add finding a suitable tutor for Ricco to my list of things to do! No doubt there are a few others who need the same."

Intercepting Tara's astonished glance, he observed dryly, " 'The wealth of a nation is in its youth.' Haven't you heard that quote before in your discussions with your father? The *quinta* is a small-scale version of a nation, but I still intend not to ignore the kernel of truth."

"I do like the way you get things done!" she conceded, in as impersonal a tone as she could manage.

"Tell me something," he asked thoughtfully.

"If I can," she carefully agreed.

"You said Ricco knew this property like the back of his hand. How well does he know you?"

Tara's coffee cup stopped halfway to her mouth. Her eyes widened in shock as she stared across the breakfast table at him.

"You can't be serious!" she cried. With a bang she put down her cup and rose from the table, taking a few steps away. When she swung around she found him smiling widely, as if he couldn't help it. "You...you..." she sputtered. "How dare you insinuate anything? Just who do you think you are? I may be your noblesse oblige, as you once pointed out so ungraciously, but that hardly gives you any right to poke and pry into my private affairs!"

"Oh, it's an affair now, is it? You *have* got along well with him!" The brimming smile remained, setting her blood to a low seething boil.

"You're being deliberately obtuse!" she snapped back. "You know very well what I meant! And what possible concern can it be of yours whether I'm romantically interested in him?"

"I told your father I'd take care of you while you're here. I was merely carrying out my, er, duty," he finished mildly. "Steering you clear of harm's way."

"Duty be damned! Taking care of me! Why does everyone suddenly seem to think I need taking care of? I'm sick to death of being taken care of! I'm not a parcel to be kept in safekeeping!"

His laugh broke her train of thought.

"That's better," he said. "I hate it when you're being polite! I'd rather argue with you any day. Care for another cup of coffee? Yours must be cold by now." Around the edges of his mouth a smile lurked.

Tara stared at him in a sort of stunned helplessness. Mixed in with it was a good measure of her earlier wrath. Everytime he laid a trap for her she fell right into it. She could have kicked herself.

"Come on, Tara, sit down," he soothed. "You can't blame me for wanting to have one last spat before the *contessa* comes. After she's here we'll have to behave. No more tours of the vineyard without her glued to your side...."

How could she have imagined him for a mate, she wondered. Sheer and utter lunacy! One did not experiment with the likes of him; that would be like dabbling with the neutron bomb! Ricco was more in her line. But the problem was, she didn't want to make love with Ricco at all. Not the least little bit, although he was charming and sweet and entirely attractive. At long last she'd found one man she wanted, and he was.... She searched her mind for an adjective caustic enough to suit her mood.

"Don't look so heartbroken, Tara. It's only a little spat. Surely you're up to it? I thought you liked to fight. And one can enjoy an argument just as well sitting down!"

She sat down, picked up her freshly filled coffee cup and asked, "What shall we argue about next?"

"Well put. I stand reproved." He smiled tantalizingly across the table at her. "Shall we make up now? I understand that's supposed to be the best part."

After a startled pause Tara exclaimed crossly, "Oh, you're impossible!"

"Now I think I've heard that somewhere before." Then, at Tara's inquiring look he added blandly, "I believe my mother said it on the odd occasion."

Her disappointed grimace made him laugh. "The women of my acquaintance have found me irresistible on the whole, I assure you."

"If I were staying here long enough no doubt I'd learn to decipher when you're serious and when you're only trying to irritate me," Tara retorted. "That fine line escapes me at the moment, though."

"Now we are getting somewhere! Which would you rather it be?"

"I can't imagine why the subject gives you such fun!"

"Can't you?" His eyes shimmered brilliantly into her own. Then he pushed aside his cup, saying, "Well, I should be on my way. Mustn't be late for a *contessa*." A quick smile flitted over his face as he stood up. For a bare two seconds he was immobile. "I know I shouldn't," he said, "but to hell with it!"

Circling the table he grasped her chin, and bending, planted a very firm kiss on her mouth. His next kiss was as short as the first, but in that time erotically thorough. Tara was tingling inside as he walked away.

"Are you taking the Lazelle?" she called after him. "It's a perfect day for flying. There's not a breath of wind and not a cloud in the sky.... I hope you have a good trip!"

"I'll bet you do!" The irony in his voice seared

through her. Tara had a retort ready, but Jorge had already gone. She felt in a vicious temper and could have cried with frustration. And it was not even eight o'clock in the morning!

She thought she saw a whisper of a smile on Emilio's face when he came out, but it vanished so quickly she couldn't be sure. "I believe the women have arrived, *senhorinha*," he announced quietly. "Shall I introduce them?" The butler was his usual phlegmatic self.

BY ELEVEN O'CLOCK the *contessa*'s bedroom was finished, all except the bed itself. Freshly washed sheets were hanging outside on a prickly-pear tree, drying in the sun. When Tara had opened the linen closet with one of the keys on the huge brass ring that Emilio had given her, the smell of moth balls had been so overpowering that the sheets and pillow cases had required more than one laundering.

Santa, Rosa and Lianna, the three women hired for the day, had worked like troopers to get the room finished, Tara reflected, opening the last window to relieve the mustiness of the long-closed bedroom. Ashta had too. The parquet floor had been scrubbed, waxed and polished. The walls had been dusted. The ornate furniture had been rubbed down with lemon oil. The luxurious Persian carpets and the voluminous velvet draperies had been beaten to within an inch of their lives with a broom handle until not a speck of dust remained. The loggia itself had been scrubbed down, and more lemon oil had been lavished on the filigree woodwork that screened it from the courtyard below.

Tara had not been allowed to participate in the actual work. Not once had she come within two feet of a broom or a dustpan. Ashta and Emilio had both watched her like hawks, but she had managed to add in a few finishing touches: quick handmade pomanders of lavender to freshen the drawers and the wardrobe; and bowls of golden roses and wild geraniums for the night table and the vanity. She took a last appreciative look around the room. It had been satisfying to bring it to life again.

Her fingers itched to make further use of the brass key ring. If only she could open all the doors, return all the rooms to their original beauty. With Santa and Rosa and Lianna—heavens, wonders could be worked! They went about their given tasks with so much vigor, so much goodwill, that Tara could only feel amazed. And with what respect they treated her! It made her feel quite out of place, as if she were the lady of the manor. And twice she'd caught them looking at her and giggling behind raised hands when they thought she wasn't watching.

They were now in the kitchen taking a break. She could hear their vivacious chatter all the way down the hall, but it ceased abruptly as she entered. Talk about feeling centered out, Tara thought—not that she looked much different from them in her white blouse and black skirt.

Lianna immediately asked what they could do next; she had a good grasp of English and practiced it laboriously whenever a chance presented itself. She was also the most talkative of the three. When Tara explained that they'd already finished what they'd been hired to do, the woman looked pointedly around the kitchen. The brass mantelpiece was green, she noted, shrugging her shoulders and gesturing with her hands. And the floor.... It had been washed, but where was the polish? Where was the shine? Should rust be allowed to remain on the old wood stove? Ashta had done all that one old woman could do, but now they were here....

Tara alternately nodded her head and shook it, but Lianna kept right on with detail after detail that needed taking care of. In the end Tara gave in. And why not? As Ricco pointed out when he stopped in for lunch, the work had to be done anyway at some time or another. Whether she directed it or someone else did made no difference. And it would be something to keep her pleasantly occupied until her clothes arrived.

As a result, their work started again directly after the midday meal. Even Emilio seemed to approve, although he mainly kept to the *sala*, where he was typing page after page of intricate lists and figures. He came into the kitchen only to check on Tara. Jorge had obviously given the most explicit instructions concerning what she was and was not supposed to do.

At one point Tara poked her head into a deep cupboard, to discover several beautiful copper-bottomed pots and pans. She was just wondering to herself why Ashta didn't use them when Emilio informed her in precise terms that she must not strain herself, that it would be much better if she just sat at the table and didn't get her hands dirty.

Tara smiled and nodded, but as soon as she heard

his typewriter keys clicking again she was back in the cupboard. When he returned the next time she had all the copperware spread out on the kitchen table and was scrubbing industriously at the mottled green patina on a casserole dish. Tara gave him a bright, ear-to-ear smile, but his long face grew even longer.

And although the butler pursed his thin lips, registering extreme disapproval, there was nothing he could do. Tara was, after all, the reigning monarch, even though she was only a guest. And they both knew it. With a tight frown he disappeared back through the swinging doors into the *sala*.

As soon as the typewriter was heard, fiercely clicking with even greater speed, the Portuguese women all burst into giggles. Tara sent them a warning glance, and they subsided at once. She didn't want Emilio to dislike her more than he already did, and to encourage four women to giggle behind his back was no way to gain favor. Lianna and Rosa went back to scrubbing the stone floor with bristle brushes, while Santa renewed her attack on the stove. The latter was using her own special mixture of oil and fine sand; it worked wonders on rust, she had assured Tara earlier.

Suddenly a terrible commotion was heard from the pantry. What Ashta was doing to produce all that noise Tara couldn't imagine. Half curious and half afraid, she flung open the door, then stepped quickly back. The housekeeper, flailing a rolling pin in one hand and hopping from one foot to the other, was muttering viciously all the while. A mouse! Tara saw it scuttle between Ashta's feet. The rolling pin came down close behind it.

This time Tara didn't stop the shouts of laughter. She was giggling herself as she grasped the rolling pin from Ashta and pulled her out, firmly shutting the pantry door. Lianna volunteered the services of a cat, and Tara accepted before she even wondered whether Jorge would want one or not. When she opened the pantry door again the mouse was gone.

Despite Emilio's dutiful vigil over her the work progressed steadily all afternoon. When Tara remembered that the women hadn't taken a siesta, they just laughed and continued with what they were doing. She could not understand it, for siestas were religiously taken among the Portuguese. Yet her women wouldn't even slow down.

By the time the grandfather clock in the *sala* chimed four, the smooth stone floor of the kitchen had been polished to a high shine. The wood stove was a gleaming gunmetal gray, its brass handles and trim sparkling like gold in the afternoon sun. The ugly green mantelpiece was now transformed, to become the kitchen's focal point. The plaster walls had been carefully brushed down, but they still needed a coat of whitewash, while the crossbeams in the walls and along the ceiling had been lathered with lemon oil to bring out the dark richness of natural wood. Gleaming, the copper pots and pans now hung on pegs beside the stove. Each cupboard had been washed thoroughly inside and out. Every nook and cranny, every counter had been painstakingly cleaned.

One could actually eat off the floor, Tara thought with pleasure. The kitchen merited a full-page spread in a housekeeping magazine. It was an old-fashioned dream, complete with a separate vegetable sink and a huge worn butcher's block. She hoped that when Jorge modernized he wouldn't spoil its charm.

While Santa and Rosa washed and dried stacks of dishes, Lianna cleaned the *sala*'s china closet and drawers. Ashta and Tara settled down together at the kitchen table to begin the enormous task of polishing the silverware. During all the work, their chatter never stopped for a moment. Time flew by, and as the sun dropped slowly toward the horizon the stacks of clean shiny dishes and silverware grew. Emilio had by this time given up his constant watch over Tara and had retired in a huff to the *sala*.

It was six-thirty before Tara realized the time, and with an exclamation proclaimed work done for the day. She waved the women into the *sala*, where Emilio would sort out their wages, and then decided to help Ashta prepare dinner. With a *contessa* coming something special had to be whipped up, and it was already very late. She had begun to look through the available foodstuffs when she encountered Ashta, who was looking unusually adamant. The old housekeeper pleaded with her to do nothing but relax in the *sala* and drink sherry until Jorge and the *contessa* arrived.

Amused, Tara yielded. Despite what Jorge thought, she knew when to quit. She was on her way upstairs to change into a fresh blouse when Emilio returned from driving the women home. To hide the dirty marks on her blouse she crossed her arms in front of her as she called, "Oh, Emilio? Lianna is bringing me a cat. We have mice in the kitchen, you see, and I'm sure there are more in the cellar. She assured me the cat was a good mouser, and traps are so cruel. This way the mice have a chance to run outside, you know...."

"Yes, *senhorinha*," the butler replied in his dignified tones. "I understand perfectly. You want the cat to frighten the mice away, not to catch them."

"That's it." Tara beamed at him.

"Very good, *senhorinha*. I shall instruct Ashta to feed the cat well. That way we'll have no mice underfoot, dead or alive."

"Exactly. And Emilio...."

He'd turned to enter the *sala*, to go back to his typing, Tara presumed. The man was indefatigable, and she was beginning to understand his true worth. He was much more than a butler! "I...I wonder, uh, the women.... Are they coming back tomorrow?"

"Indeed they are, *senhorinha*. I took it upon myself to hire them for as long as you are here. I perceived that there was no other way to, er, keep you from the more arduous tasks." His critical eyes slid to the dirty streaks her arms couldn't cover. "And the work has to be done," he amended quickly, as if not wanting to appear entirely ungracious.

"Wonderful! Oh, you're a darling, Emilio!" Tara flashed him another wide appreciative smile and was off up the stairs with a colorful swirl of her embroidered hem. She didn't know that he looked after her and gave a long resigned sigh.

Fifteen minutes later Tara was sipping sherry, but not in the *sala* as Ashta had suggested. Instead she took a fine crystal goblet with her as she decided which rooms to tackle on the morrow. Naturally, it made sense to start on the areas they used the most. That narrowed the choice down to the *sala*, the downstairs and upstairs hallways, the stairwells and the bedrooms. Jorge had obviously moved in shortly before she herself arrived. The areas were basically clean; however, the vast stretches of paneling had only been dusted, not waxed, and the brass lamps all along the halls and stairs, although free of cobwebs, were badly tarnished. And the crystal that hung from each of the lamps, tinkling softly as one passed, would look so much nicer with a really bright shine. Although the electric power wasn't yet working, the villa had been wired for electricity, and each of the old lamps had bulb sockets neatly hidden inside. Tara had to climb up on a chair and hold up a candle to discover this, and that's how Emilio found her. He started to say something, but obviously thought better of it. With a blend of exasperation and amazement on his usually immobile face, he disappeared quickly the way he had come.

"Tara! I might have known I wouldn't find you doing something ordinary!" Jorge's deep tones stopped her short.

Feeling guilty, Tara clambered down off the chair. At the same time Emilio hurried out of his hiding place to meet Jorge and the *contessa*, looking woefully embarrassed at not being there to open the door in the first place.

"Hello." Tara said tentatively, giving a small welcoming smile. She noticed the spare, white-haired woman at Jorge's side, but had eyes only for him. "Oh!" she exclaimed then, realizing she still held the burning candle. In her surprise she dropped it and it went out, plunging the hall into darkness. "Oh, no...." Could she do nothing right?

"Come, Tara, it's quite all right," Jorge said soothingly. "Shall we go into the *sala* and finish our sherry there?" He pulled her up beside him, obviously stopping just short of laughing outright.

Tara followed him docilely, chewing on her lower lip. She felt quite the fool, and his patronizing tone didn't help.

In the *sala* introductions were made without further mishap.

"My dear, how pretty you are." Contessa d'Cimbrianni patted Tara's hand absentmindedly. Her blue eyes, the color of rain-drenched cornflowers, gazed at her kindly, if a little vaguely. "You're not at all like my daughter Angelica. You are as dark as she is fair. But what lovely hair—like a raven's wing, and so thick."

Tara murmured her appreciation of the compliment, feeling at a loss. The *contessa* didn't seem to be completely present. She carried with her a nebulous aura of past times and past people. Hardly chaperon material, Tara realized. There was nothing eagle-eyed about her. But, she reminded herself, the chaperon was for appearances only and not a necessity.

Smiling her warmest smile she settled the older woman in a chair. It was quite obvious who would be taking care of whom. Curiosity and pity touched her heart, striking more black marks against Mario

Resende, and now the *contessa*'s daughter, Angelica, as well. Tara sent Jorge a wide-eyed look, and his answering nod was barely perceptible. Noticing how the woman's hand shook as she lifted her sherry, Tara told Emilio that dinner could be served the minute it was ready. He nodded understandingly and disappeared into the kitchen.

Tara did her best to make the *contessa* feel comfortable. She started a light easy conversation, pulling out of her hat subjects that she didn't even realize she knew anything about. Injecting as many amusing anecdotes as she thought advisable, she was finally rewarded with an intelligent smile and a response that indicated the woman was at last completely aware.

Jorge could have helped some, Tara thought indignantly, flashing him a supercilious look. He merely lifted an eyebrow and smiled slightly in answer, whereupon she all but turned her back on him.

Ernesta was extremely fine boned, her paper-white skin so transparent that it seemed each vein showed through. Her very long hair was waved and braided into a most elaborate confection piled high upon her head. A mass of frills, her lavender lace dress was at least thirty years out-of-date, and her hands were heavy with rings. Indeed, jewelry seemed her passion, for she wore bracelets, necklaces and brooches, too.

At dinner Jorge resumed his role of host. He was so charming and attentive that the *contessa* blossomed like a rose before Tara's eyes. He'd never taken the same trouble with her, she thought resentfully and a shade uncharitably. But all in all, after it was over she decided dinner had been fun. And to her surprise the *contessa* did keep them from arguing, from striking sparks off each other. In that way she did her job remarkably well. What was even nicer, she did it unwittingly.

Presently Tara showed Ernesta to her bedroom, and then set about taking out the one million and one hairpins that the woman's coiffure required. Ashta offered to help, but Tara sent her away to relax for the first time that day. Emilio brought up case after case of the *contessa*'s luggage—hatboxes, suitcases, a jewelry chest. At last, after a great deal of fuss, she was settled for the night.

Tara went downstairs feeling excessively weary. She tiptoed past the *sala*, intending to share Ashta's leisure in the spotless kitchen. But it was not to be.

"There you are!" Jorge must have been waiting for her, she thought glumly as he firmly grasped her arm and pulled her into the room. "A nightcap? Ashta kindly brought me some coffee."

"Ashta's very kind," she agreed, saying the first thing that came into her head.

"And I'm not?" The amusement was ever present. She racked her brains to discover what he found so diverting about teasing her.

"No, I'd say you're very kind...among other things."

He placed a snifter of brandy before her and poured a cup of coffee to accompany it. "Cigarette?"

She accepted one, allowing him to light it. The match flame reflected in his eyes, glimmering in the black depths, etching the thickness of his dark lashes.

Settling back into her armchair, Tara sipped her coffee and tried to look relaxed and nonchalant. Instead, she appeared young and defenseless, as exotic as an orchid and just as vulnerable. Her great smoky eyes were innocently alluring, full of feminine secrets. Her skin sheened in the dim light of the Moresque lamps. Her soft ruby red lips were curved in a slightly melancholic pout.

The slow relentless rise of tension in the silky-smooth night air was familiar. Tara sensed the imminent danger. They were alone again, and that meant they were heading for another flare-up.

A moth drifted in through the window and was caught in the golden glow of a lamp. The sound of pounding breakers on the shore, on the rusty red rocks and sculptured cliffs, permeated the room. She was hypnotized by the steady beat of them, coming faster and faster. But it wasn't the sound of the waves, she suddenly realized; it was her heart. Reaction was setting in. Too much sherry, too much emotion, too much of Jorge altogether. He'd found some self-destruct button within her and was pushing it with all his elemental male power. Something was going to explode....

"Emilio tells me I am to be the proud owner of a cat," Jorge announced, his wry tone cutting through her thoughts.

She pushed down her inclination to run. Small wonder he thought her childish! Whenever he was close by she acted irrationally. "You don't mind?"

"Mind? No. A cat is the logical answer. And thank

you for directing the women today. Emilio tells me you get along well with them. It's obvious, considering the amount you accomplished.''

Tara flushed slightly at his compliment.

"He also tells me you insist on involving yourself in the work, contrary to doctor's orders,'' he went on.

"Does Emilio tell you everything?'' There was controlled antagonism in her voice.

"He keeps me well informed.'' To her surprise he smiled. The effect was of sunshine across a bleak landscape. Tara caught her breath and smiled back.

"He's a most efficient butler, among other things,'' she answered lightly.

"What is it, Tara? You seem troubled.'' The bluntness of his question caught her off guard.

"Troubled?'' she echoed, tricked into looking straight into his steady, all-seeing eyes. "Not—not really.''

"Then why do you seem on the very verge of flight? I'm afraid to blink my eyes in case you vanish!''

She could feel herself weakening at the sudden gentleness in his deep throaty drawl. One way or another she had to stop this eternal seesaw, this crazy up and down whirl. Somewhat desperately she searched about in her mind for a neutral topic of conversation.

"By the way, did Emilio also tell you that Ricco stopped by for lunch?''

"As a matter of fact, he did.''

"Yes, of course.'' She blinked and looked away

from him, fiddling with her brandy snifter, warming it between her hands. "I...I had a little talk with Ashta about Ricco when we were cleaning the silverware. I said she must be so proud of his accomplishments, but she just about jumped down my throat."

"Oh?"

"She's quite upset with him, actually. She says this guide job is having an evil influence on him. He won't listen to a word she says anymore."

"That's a normal part of growing up. Deaf ears turned to parental advice, whether the advice is worthwhile or not."

"Yes, but it's worse than that. She says being around people that have so much cash to spend—to splurge—has corrupted his mind. That he's getting greedy for quick easy money, for the high life he sees all around him. He's vowed to her that he'll get it any way he can. And that's what she's so upset about."

Jorge's eyes held hers for a long serious moment, then he said, "Go on."

"Well, she said she checked his wallet the last time she washed his clothes, and there was more money in it than there should have been. She also said the people he's guiding these days all seem to be women—no more families, no men. And these women all happen to be...older. And wealthy. Very wealthy. He was wearing a gold chain, of high quality, I can tell you, when he came to lunch today. Ashta told me later that they quarreled about it, and she made him take it off. She is afraid he's going to turn into...into a...."

"Gigolo?"

"Yes. Exactly."

"He didn't tell her where the gold chain came from? Perhaps he found it?"

"I think not, because he refused to tell her where or how or from whom."

"And she's tried to talk to him and it's had no effect."

"Right. In fact, she's afraid if she pushes too hard...."

"She'll push him right into it. Yes, I can see her predicament. And if I know you, you have a suggestion on the tip of your tongue, right?"

"Well, he may not listen to her but he might listen to you. He has a healthy respect for you, you know. He looks up to you, and while you are older you're still not ancient."

"Thank you, I'm sure!"

Quickly she glanced away from him, the color in her cheeks heightened. "What I meant was—"

"I think I know exactly what you meant, Tara!" Jorge didn't sound overly pleased. "But back to Ricco. I think the time has come to discuss plans for his education. If he were to realize a better life is in store for him he might be more...circumspect in his actions. And yes, Tara, I shall have a man-to-man chat with him while I'm at it. Are you satisfied now?"

"Oh, yes! Oh, thank you, Jorge. You really are kind!"

"I believe I'm beginning to hear that a little too often!" he replied dryly. "You have a rather strong affection for Ricco, don't you—seeing as you've only known him a couple of days? You take his concerns much to heart."

"Uh. . .well, he's such a sweetheart that I'd hate to see him ruined!"

He affirmed, unamused, "It hardly bears thinking about, I agree!"

"Now you're angry with me."

"Angry? Why on earth should I be angry? I'm only a little surprised that you show such concern for your fellow human beings." His shapely bottom lip had a definite cynical twist to it. Tara didn't like the look of it.

She swallowed the last of her brandy in a long gulp that burned all the way down her throat. Gasping a little over her good-night to Jorge, she slowly circled the couch in front of the fire, where he was half reclining.

"Tara?" It was a soft caress.

She stopped dead in her tracks. The skin on her back prickled, and when she half turned he was right behind her. Her shoulder brushed against his denim-clad chest—a chest with a deep V of tightly curling black hair and smooth, copper-dark skin. She stopped breathing, or felt she had. There simply wasn't enough air left in the room.

"Minha querida," he said to her, just above a whisper. One hand slid around her waist and the other around her throat. She stared up at his face in confusion. A deep-rooted instinct for survival flared into life, and she forced herself to think, to look before she leaped. And what she saw was all wrong. She closed her eyes fiercely. It was all wrong, and it hurt like hell. He had shown her clearly enough that while he might be physically attracted to her at odd moments, his prevailing opinion of her left something to be desired. And that wasn't enough. The realization that she wanted a whole lot more from him than just a one-night stand was abrupt and shattering.

"Oh, no, Jorge, don't do this," she whispered, breathless.

The touch of his hands instantly changed but they didn't leave her. "Why, Tara? I know you're a sensuous woman. And don't ask me how I know. I've had you in my arms before, if you'll remember."

"But that's no reason—"

"It seems a damn good reason to me. Surely someone in this world must be allowed to kiss you. If it isn't me who is it? There's no one here I think you'd care to kiss except for Ricco. Is it Ricco? He can and I can't? Just exactly how far has your relationship with him gone?" His hands tightened around her when she made a move to put greater space between them.

"I have no intention of telling you!" she gasped. "How would you like it if I began asking you private questions about your women friends—most of whom find you irresistible!" She flashed a quick look into his eyes. "I find Ricco fun to be with. I enjoy his company. There, is that enough for you?"

"And you don't enjoy mine?" he asked, his hands falling away.

"Let's just say that Ricco knows when not to push. And he knows how to make a woman feel good—whether or not—"

"I think that's enough!" Jorge interrupted. "You've explained yourself very clearly, Tara, so there's no need to repeat it!"

Her eyes flew back to his face.

"I won't push in the future," he observed quietly, one corner of his mouth lifted in a faint smile. "It was my intention to see whether we could make better sense if we tried talking in closer proximity, rather than across the room or across a table. I guess we just don't have much to talk about, either way."

She shivered at the hard cynicism in his voice, feeling as though he had physically repulsed her. She wished she could answer him, but the right words evaded her. And now, perversely, she ached for his arms around her, for the rough silk of his jaw against her skin. She shook her head a little wildly, spilling the ebony richness of her hair over her shoulders.

And it was too late now to make amends, to explain. . . to explain what? He looked as distant and as frosty as the glaciers to the far north. Her sixth sense told her he would not even try to touch her in the little time left to them. Something tenuous between them had been broken, and she could only hope that she'd be able to patch things up. . . somehow. But now was not the time to try; she could see that. Later, when he wasn't looking quite so grim, perhaps he would listen.

But if her clothes came tomorrow she would be leaving. She might not even get a chance to talk to him. But perhaps that was best, after all. She didn't really think he wanted to further their acquaintance, so what was the point?

"Good night, Tara!" It sounded pointedly like a dismissal.

"Good night, Jorge." Her voice was husky and

choked. She didn't trust herself to say anything more, and brushed past him. As soon as she was out of the *sala* she broke into a run and sped up the stairs as if the very devil were after her.

The stairwell curved in a complete circle before it opened out onto the upstairs hall, and with her head down to watch her step, Tara didn't see Emilio just beginning the descent, his arms loaded high with old ledgers. They ran into each other full tilt. The ledgers erupted out of Emilio's arms like lava from the mouth of Vesuvius. Unbalanced, Emilio teetered on the top stair, while Tara clutched for the banister, missed and slid bumpily down amid a snowstorm of loose papers and hardback covers. She stopped abruptly on the sixth stair by catching one of the balusters, then twisted around just in time to see Emilio lose his fight with gravity and plummet down to meet her.

The outraged look on his face was so hilarious, his sudden activity so uncharacteristic that Tara convulsed with helpless laughter as she hastily reached out to grab him. She caught his vest, heard the ominous rip of material, but managed to stop him all the same. Another look at him spread-eagled on the stairs amid all the papers sent her into further peals of laughter. Miraculously her tension vanished, leaving her feeling surprisingly good considering how terrible she'd felt only moments earlier. She rocked back and forth on the stairs, holding her sides. One last paper wafted gently down to settle on Emilio's stomach.

From below she could hear excited comments from

Ashta and lower terse exclamations from Jorge. They only made the situation funnier, and so did another look at Emilio's disgruntled face. He stared back at her incredulously and slowly shook his head in helpless amazement. At that moment their situation seemed to strike some soft spot within him, for he, too, started to chuckle, a rasp of dry sticks rubbing together. The very sound of his own laughter seemed to delight him, for he laughed all the more then.

All the merriment, however, seemed to widen the gulf between Tara and the master of the house. His final good-night to her was so remotely polite and so thoroughly chilly that she went to bed sick at heart.

It was almost noon on the following day before the *contessa* made an appearance downstairs. When she did she was wearing a floor-length, fluffy, ice-pink creation. Tara and her army of women had already launched an all-out attack on the downstairs hall, with its acres of carved paneling and its white-and-black marble floor. Tara herself was outdoors on the terrace that surrounded the villa on every side except the back, where the courtyard led into the house proper. Emilio had strategically placed her chair close to the kitchen door and yet in full sunlight. On the little round table before her and on the smooth stone floor of the terrace lay heaps of the brass lamp fixtures; a separate heap of crystals on the table sparkled like diamonds in the sun.

Tara blew some stray tendrils of hair off her forehead, and with a large square of flannel applied a few last whisks to a lamp. The day had started reasonably well, for Jorge was already gone when she came down to breakfast. Emilio had told her earlier that today Jorge was checking the remaining cattle, horses and bulls, and would be taking inventory.

Emilio seemed more disposed to be friendly after last night, while Jorge.... Tara shrugged her shoulders. What was the use of thinking about him? She couldn't banish his dark saturnine face from her mind, however, so the *contessa*'s arrival came as a more than welcome diversion.

Emilio placed the *contessa*'s breakfast on the table across from Tara, bowed slightly to the two women and then vanished back into the kitchen. Ernesta Angelica adjusted her pink mohair shawl more securely around her shoulders, then began, "Good morning, my dear. What a lovely day it is! It reminds me of when...." Her croissants and tea were long finished, her chair moved into the shade and the stack of cleaned lamps growing into a mountain— and still the *contessa* was enmeshed in memories. One story after another spilled from her lips once she realized she had an attentive audience. Tara heard of her childhood and of her courtship. She listened to all the little foibles of the *contessa*'s maid, who was on a well-deserved vacation, and the exact details of her hire years before.

Then the subject turned to the *contessa*'s beautiful daughter, Angelica, her dashing and oh so charming son-in-law, Mario Resende, and the lavish exciting life they led in faraway Lisbon. Tara heard about Angelica's wardrobe, which, she thought, seemed vast and extravagant and entirely out of line considering the poverty of the peasants here on the Quinta das Valente de Silves. A floor-length white mink cape stood out among a host of Angelica's other furs. There were endless pairs of shoes and matching bags, as well as evening gowns too numerous to count. Angelica seemed to share her mother's predilection for jewelry, since her wardrobe was embellished with a collection of gems that sounded like an absurd display of wealth. Indignation stirred inside Tara, who suggested that the money could have been put to better use.

But the *contessa* would hear none of it. She didn't seem able to grasp the reality that some people didn't have enough food to eat, and clearly disliked discussing such topics.

What with the *contessa*'s chatter, a brief afternoon visit from Ricco and the challenge of keeping her three women occupied, the day vanished for Tara. Before Santa, Lianna and Rosa left, the downstairs hall glowed from lemon oil and elbow grease. The carved panels in the *sala* were restored, in all their minute detail, to a honeycombed richness. The small but ornate table where they dined had been polished to a mirrorlike finish, and the high-backed matching chairs were a gleaming complement.

"Not bad!" Tara murmured out loud. The *azulejos* fireplace, which graced one entire wall, was an intricate panorama of deep and fresh vivid colors, and the aired Persian carpet, which seemed to reflect the tiles like a mirror, breathed life into the gold brocade curtains, old as they were. Tara herself had reverently dusted the heavy oil paintings, appreciating their antiquity and the passion of their religious scenes. As a finishing touch she had filled terra-cotta bowls with an assortment of flowers from the garden and had placed some of the Oriental porcelain pieces to better advantage on top of a cabinet. Not wanting to overstep herself, she had left Emilio's desk entirely alone.

Now the work was done for the day, and still her clothes hadn't arrived. There wasn't even a sign of the trunk her parents were shipping to her. With no means of dressing up for dinner, she spent the last part of the afternoon socializing with Lianna's cat and three nursing kittens. No one had had the heart to separate the kittens from their mother, and now Tara wondered uneasily how Jorge was going to like being the proud owner of four cats instead of one. As it turned out, they had one more day of grace before he found out, for just before dinner Emilio informed her that Jorge was staying overnight with one of the farmers to discuss further business matters.

When Valente took it upon himself to do something, he didn't waste any time, Tara reflected, feeling curiously let down because she wouldn't see him until the next day. But by that time surely her trunk would have arrived! At the same time Tara felt glad that the peasants would soon be rewarded for their years of labor. Jorge would see to it, she was sure. With a flare of revenge, unusual for her, she hoped that Angelica and Mario would be rewarded, too, but in an entirely different fashion!

After dinner Tara polished lamps until bedtime. Ricco and Ashta worked with her, and even Ernesta, wanting to be helpful, made a small contribution.

Meanwhile Emilio replaced all the delicate Moresque lamps in the *sala* and hallway.

For the most part Ashta didn't involve herself in the conversation. Ricco did the most talking. Tara came second, with the *contessa* a close third. Emilio said even less than Ashta did, restricting himself to monosyllables when asked a question. He came and went, carrying the lamps, and Tara had the impression he regarded the merriment that went with the work in lofty disapproval behind his impassive face.

Every time Ricco had had enough of the topic under discussion he would prod Tara for "good long words." When she couldn't come up with one in a split second he would shoot one at her, parading his learning. Sometimes he would tease her with suggestive words, his eyes bright with the fun he was having.

"And what does that one mean?" cut in the *contessa* at one point. "It sounds rather doubtful to me!"

"Tara will tell you. She's better at English than I," Ricco said seriously.

"Well...it means.... Ricco!" Tara finally protested.

His great peal of laughter started them all giggling, Ernesta and Ashta without knowing exactly why.

The following day, without Jorge around, Tara found she could concentrate much better on the work to be done. As before, the women arrived very early, and she set Santa to work on the staircase, while Rosa and Lianna started on the bedrooms. There were seven goodsized chambers on the second floor, not counting the master bedroom, the nursery with an adjoining room for the nanny and the schoolroom. By the time she'd opened all the doors with keys from the big brass ring Tara had stopped counting fireplaces. Each and every room seemed to possess one.

At the end of her intensely interesting survey she found one door still locked. From her calculations she figured it must lead into the turret, for the door was between that of the master bedroom, which was situated above the Grand Salon, and the *contessa*'s bedroom, which was above the *sala*.

Finding no key to open this door, she went down to ask Emilio about it. But Ashta informed her that he had gone to Sagres on business for Dom Valente, and to make inquiries about her trunk. Somewhat reluctantly Tara resumed her seat on the terrace amid the brass fixtures, and settled down for another day of Ernesta's stories. She worked briskly, however, intent on finishing the lamps. She'd been at Minha Casa for five days already, and by tomorrow at the latest her clothes would certainly have come. In the meantime she wanted to get as much work done as possible. Instead of an interesting pastime the project had become a personal endeavor to repay Jorge in a small way, and although Tara didn't want to admit it, she wanted to prove she wasn't as useless and spoiled as he seemed to think.

At one point her mind wandered from the *contessa*'s words, and she gazed meditatively over the wild jumble of garden. Her eyes were drawn to the ancient craggy oaks that towered over the supple poplars

with their slender white trunks. Her gaze went past
them to the edge of red rock that marked the beach.
The Atlantic shimmered beneath the sun. Far out she
could see fishing ketches—bright flecks of yellow and
red skimming over the blue green sea, their triangular
sails billowing out, rounded and full. She feasted her
eyes on the scene, thinking of how very recently
Jorge had decided to make this his home. Who would
he bring here to live with him? A strange kind of pain
stabbed through her and she began to wish for him to
return—if only to needle her!

Late in the afternoon when Emilio returned—with
no word of her trunk's whereabouts—the staircase
was all but finished and the master bedroom, which
Jorge used, was completely done. Tara had taken
only a quick glance into that room, for his presence
seemed inordinately strong there. Its dimensions
were awesome, and the little she did see was beautiful: the white ceiling rising into a peaked dome; the
wide symmetrical windows looking out to sea; the
huge brass bed intricately carved in an old-fashioned
design; and its lofty canopy. In the bathroom a
sunken tub was paved in blue, rose and gold *azulejos*,
with a hand-painted Oriental screen to pull around it.
Tara hurried out as though she'd intruded on Jorge
himself.

After a thorough search through the desk in the
sala Emilio came up with a handful of loose keys.
These he deposited in Tara's hand, his face as bland
and expressionless as usual over her latest interest.
To Tara's delight one of them fitted in the mystery
door, and with a creak that sent a shiver down her

spine it opened. The light that filtered in through the narrow stained-glass windows was dim; it turned the specks of dust in the air to gold. As she'd suspected a curving staircase wound upward, and without a second thought Tara took the stairs two at a time. She held her breath, not knowing what to expect. But when she reached the top she almost cried out with delight.

It was a small round room, but so pretty that it could have come straight out of a fairy tale, despite the accumulated dust. Even the windows were shaped to curve with the room, and each one was bordered in colorful stained glass. The view was an unobstructed expanse of garden edged by orchards, and on the other side, garden edged by the sea. It had obviously been a woman's room, because the furniture was dainty and feminine. On the seaward side there was a writing desk and a scroll-backed chair, accompanied by a delicate settee with harem cushions. Two tall narrow bookcases stood between the windows. Everything was in its place, as though the owner had stepped out for just a moment with every intention of returning. It must have belonged to Jorge's mother, Tara surmised, while blowing the dust off a gilt-framed picture.

Emilio had gone to drive the women home, and with Ashta busy in the kitchen preparing dinner it was no trouble for her to sneak up brooms, some rags and furniture polish. Ricco followed her up the stairs, protesting all the way. To him it seemed a crime to spend the evening cleaning the turret room. To her it seemed a crime to leave it neglected for even a day.

"Come, Tara, leave it!" he begged her.

"No, no. It'll only take me a few minutes. . . ."

"But I can't talk to you like this!" She was on all fours sweeping dust out from under the settee. "I like to be able to look into your eyes when we talk!"

She lifted her head to look at him. "Well, grab that other broom then and join me!" Flashing him a quick grin she was back at it.

Ricco slipped off the corner of the desk with an exasperated sigh and reached for the broom.

"You know, Tara," he said, meeting her eyes under the settee, "I may have been raised *pobre*, but it's been a while since I have had to sweep a floor!"

Absorbed as they were in rubbing the shine back into the rosewood furniture and in conducting Tara's first lesson in the finer points of Portuguese grammar, they didn't notice Emilio's return. Nor did they notice how late it was getting until the light began to fail.

"I'll bet you everyone's looking for us by now," Tara exclaimed at last, breaking into a rueful grin.

"And I would like to be able to tell them we were doing something other than cleaning house!" Ricco retorted. "*De Deus!* I shall have to run all the way to Sagres if I'm to make my dinner appointment! *Adeus!*" He gave her a hasty peck on the cheek and bounded off down the circling stairs.

Tara followed at a slightly slower pace. There was no one in sight. Slowing her walk further, she nonchalantly entered the *sala* just in time to hear Jorge mutter, "Where the devil has Tara got to now?" Catching sight of her, he snapped accusingly, "Where have you been?"

"I've been with Ricco, and we lost track of the time," she said, taking a deep breath.

His eyes were smoldering under half-closed lids. "You should have invited him to stay for supper."

"He had to run off to work."

"How inconvenient for you. Er, may I ask what you two were doing?"

"Doing? Nothing much...." She shrugged her shoulders.

"Nothing?" he snorted, eyeing her blouse. The *contessa* looked at him in shocked surprise.

Tara followed his eyes down to her white blouse. It was quite dirty, and in her hurry she had forgotten to change into a fresh one. She stared at Jorge in dismay, for the moment unable to defend herself.

"Well?" Jorge asked.

"Now be quiet, young man!" Ernesta said firmly. "Tara has done a lot of work today and she doesn't need to put up with you at the dinner table! What she has been doing is her own affair!" The *contessa* added in an aside to Tara, "In my day we did not get quite so dirty whilst courting...."

Tara closed her mouth in surprise. Had that really been the *contessa* talking—telling Jorge to be quiet? What had come over her? She beamed at the dainty, white-haired woman, then said to Jorge, "You know you are being very tiresome!" She looked at him just in time to see the smoldering in his eyes grow into a dancing fire.

"Aha! So today I am being tiresome? I seem to be taking a lot of abuse in my own household!"

"Correction! It is my house!" the *contessa* affirmed airily. "And don't look at me like that, young man. It will be yours soon enough. I know you want to sort out the final details, but I have no head for business; Mario kindly handles it all for me. I will not sign anything until he has agreed to the terms of the sale. Of course, the provision your grandfather made assures you that Mario will not sell to anyone but you.

"And now you can thank Tara for all her effort. I cannot think why you shout at her when she has worked so hard. There is really no need for her to lift a finger while she is here, and yet look at all she has accomplished!"

Tara smothered a grin by spooning onion soup into her mouth. This was a new side to the *contessa*, one she hoped would be more in evidence from here on in. She liked the old woman much more this way, and realized that Ernesta probably liked herself better, too. She looked positively refreshed by her outburst and attacked her soup with a great deal more appetite than she'd ever shown before.

"But all that aside, Jorge—" Ernesta stopped to pat her napkin elegantly against her mouth "—I am glad you want to keep the *quinta* the way it is. It would be a shame if what happened to Sagres happened here. Row upon row of hotels with those gaudy neon signs! It is just like any other tourist resort now. When I was your age, Tara, Sagres was one of the most delightful towns! And the *quinta* is a tourist attraction in its own right. Foreigners love to see a genuine Portuguese estate. The quaintness of the peasants...."

Jorge ate his dinner in glowering silence. From time to time Tara slanted a look at him through her lashes. Obviously their friendship was at a stalemate.

THE NEXT MORNING was a repeat of the two that had gone before. The women worked on Tara's bedroom, after which she had them scheduled to finish cleaning the upstairs hall. And if there was any time left they were to return downstairs to begin work on the library, which was situated on the same side of the hall as the *sala*. Tara had decided on the library next because the *sala* wasn't the ideal spot for Emilio and Jorge to work on the accounts. It was crowded there in the corner, and she was sure they would appreciate more space and greater privacy.

As she let herself into the library her eyes strayed longingly to the floor-to-ceiling books behind many leaded-glass doors. There were *azulejos*, fireplaces, at both ends of the room with easy chairs, swathed in dust covers, grouped around them. In the middle stood a long refectory table. Footstools were piled on top of each other in one corner. At the far side of the room was another door, and on her right French-style doors led out into the courtyard.

The far door, she found, led into a masculine-looking den. The dusty oil paintings there depicted hunting scenes, and the fireplace had an impressive marble mantel. The cool tiled walls lent muted shades of rust, gold and blue to the room. Tapestries rolled in moth balls formed a bulky heap on the desk, and the rest of the furniture was hidden beneath dust covers.

Tara wandered slowly back the way she had come. She had the urge to go for a walk on the beach, to go anywhere, but she sternly reminded herself that there were more brass lamps to polish. And so, reluctantly, she settled on the terrace for another day's vigil with the flannel rags. Although Emilio had gone with Jorge to examine the maize, barley and wheat crops, she knew she wouldn't have a chance to sneak upstairs to the turret to finish the cleaning there. That would have to wait until later when the women were back on the main floor.

She felt too restless to sit still, and entirely miserable with life in general, rubbed the harder on a lamp. She'd only seen Jorge once in the past two days, and then only at dinner with the *contessa* acting as a buffer. Contrary to making life simpler, his avoidance of her had backfired and made it more complicated. For he was avoiding her. Even though she knew how busy he was there was no mistaking it. She longed to kiss him, to fight with him, to do anything with him! This being left out in the cold was worse than any of their arguments by far. It was desolation.

With the least provocation she could have dissolved into tears right then and there. If only she could reword what she'd said in the *sala* a few days earlier. If only she had let him kiss her instead of being so stupidly cautious! Tara rubbed the lamp energetically. If only a genie would appear! The day seemed endless. She couldn't concentrate on what the *contessa* was saying. And Jorge would be leaving soon for Lisbon to meet with Mario Resende. Then she wouldn't see him at all! She would certainly be gone before he returned.

With the *contessa* peacefully dreaming away during her afternoon siesta, the day stretched even longer. Tara rubbed and polished, rubbed and polished, as though the action would banish the heavy ache in her heart. Suddenly she sprang up, unable to sit a moment longer. She would put fresh flowers in the *sala*.

She was in the middle of arranging red, pink and white roses in a bowl when Ashta came in, muttering something about visitors coming before she tottered off down the hall. When she returned her mouth was compressed into a thin disapproving line. Behind her frail bent fingers was Dennis Moreston.

CHAPTER NINE

TARA DROPPED THE FLOWERS, which scattered on the carpet at her feet. Her lack of welcome didn't seem to bother Dennis, for he strode quickly over to her and slid his arms around her waist.

The expression on Ashta's wrinkled face turned to one of dismay. She glared at Dennis's back as though she would burn holes right through him, then left, closing the *sala* door with a loud decisive bang.

"What on earth are you doing here?" Tara asked, staring up at him vacantly. After a moment of stunned passivity she tried fiercely to push him away. "Let me go!"

"I came to see you, darling! What other reason would bring me to this godforsaken place? By the way, however did you manage to end up here?" He smiled with complacent bonhomie, finally releasing her when her struggles made it awkward to go on holding her.

"But how did you find me?" She still couldn't quite believe he was really standing in front of her, his large feet crushing her roses.

"Oh, mother told me," he answered carelessly. "I suppose you heard I broke my engagement to Penny?" His hard brown eyes flicked intently over her pale face. "Say, is this what you call hospitality? How's about a drink? It's devilishly hot!"

Tara recovered some of her composure. "I'll have Ashta bring you a small glass of iced tea," she said pointedly.

"Something stronger?"

"A small Scotch, then." She looked at him as though he were an insect on one of her beloved roses. She called to Ashta, but at the same time Ernesta's voice came floating in off the terrace, demanding a cup of tea. For the first time Tara heard the old housekeeper grumbling.

Tara turned abruptly back to Dennis. She didn't want him here long enough to drink that Scotch. "What do you want?"

"Why, darling!" Dennis appealed. "I finished with Penny because I found I was still in love with you! Can you forgive me...for everything?" The smooth sincerity in his voice floated like oil on water. "As you can see, I came all this way.... Which reminds me, what are you doing here? It's not exactly the place for a society miss."

"Something tells me you came all this way for my inheritance, not for me," she said coolly.

"How ridiculous! I have plenty of money!" he protested.

"I know what happened in Edinburgh." Her tone was quietly scornful. "I know you were in financial trouble even before then. It always was the money, wasn't it? And now that you're in over your head you're hoping I'll bail you out. Forget it, Dennis!"

He looked like he'd received a solid blow in the

face. His features crumbled, then slowly twisted. Several taut seconds passed. "Yes! It was always the money! Do you really think you're attractive enough without it?" he added vindictively.

"I think it's time you left," Tara heard her own voice say. It was cool and steady, though a little high-pitched.

He laughed spitefully, and Tara, suddenly frightened of him, put the expanse of the table between them. "Every time I kissed you I was kissing two hundred and fifty thousand pounds!" he declared. "That's the only way I could bring myself to do it!"

He was showing his true colors at last. Not one vestige of his charming facade remained. "And you would really marry me, feeling that way?" she asked curiously.

"Money is the only thing that matters in this world, and you know that as well as I do! Nobody's going to get the better of me, least of all you! You'll be sorry—"

"Perhaps you didn't hear me, but I said, 'I think it's time you left!'"

"Ha! You would have married me if you weren't such a prig about the other women in my life. There were plenty, Tara, plenty! And I would never have given them up. It's the accepted thing these days!" The words spilled out of his mouth in a confused rush. "I made just one mistake. That was kissing Penny at your damn party! But I'm not making any more mistakes. I'll get what I want. I always do!" Suddenly he circled the table, and catching one of her arms, jerked her roughly against him.

"What an idiot you are!" she spat. "In case you aren't already aware of it, I don't go in for cavemen tactics!" Her loathing showed plainly, and her full lips curled with disdain as she looked up into his face.

Ashta's head came around the door, the rest of her following shortly. In one hand was a broom, in the other a tumbler of Scotch.

"You'll never have me or my money," Tara continued, saying each word slowly and distinctly, shaking her arm free. "Go away!"

"As cold a fish as ever!" Dennis hissed in her face. Whirling around, he almost knocked the tiny peasant woman off her feet. The glass of Scotch dropped to the floor and shattered as the door to the *sala* swung shut behind him.

Very slowly Tara subsided into a chair. Ashta puttered anxiously, patting her shoulder and peering into her expressive face.

Then wave after wave of hot anger poured over Tara. Her hands doubled into fists. Kissing her inheritance, was he? She had been right all along about his greed for money—any money, hers included. But how insulting of him to come here expecting her to fall into his arms after all that had happened. What enormous effrontery! She felt outraged; hadn't she made herself clear enough back home?

Rousing herself, she heard Ashta mumbling Portuguese insults under her breath as she swept up the glass fragments and the crushed roses. Tara started to gather up the undamaged flowers. She still felt a certain numbness in her limbs, and her primary reaction was relief that Jorge hadn't been present.

Her legs still felt a little weak as she walked into the kitchen. In the doorway leading onto the terrace she stopped short. There was Dennis holding the *contessa*'s hand. Obviously he was at his most charming and winsome, chatting away as though he were a welcome guest invited for a lengthy stay. The moment he saw Tara he started guiltily. With a casual wave of his hand, but as quickly as he could without appearing to run, he strode across the terrace and around the corner.

Tara followed him, feeling a niggling suspicion. What was he up to? Why didn't he use the front door? She caught sight of him running past the high ballroom windows, and then he vanished around the south side of the villa. She broke into a run as well, her suspicion intensifying. The terrace continued along the south wall, ending at the corner with a short drop to the ground. Tara leaned over the banister rail, craning her neck to see around the bulging wall of the turret. But Dennis was already out of sight. In hot pursuit, she swung herself over the stone banister and dropped lightly to the ground. Hopping over small shrubs, she rushed headlong into a veritable thicket of mimosa; a shower of the tiny white and pink flowers drifted down to cling to her. She reached the outer courtyard wall too late, however, and was just in time to see Dennis scramble into a red rental car and shoot down the avenue of evergreen oaks.

And then the estate jeep came jumping over a small incline in the road. For a heart-stopping second it looked like the two vehicles would crash. Dennis was driving much too fast. But the jeep swerved in the nick of time, and the red rental car screeched over the rise, to disappear down the dark green tunnel of trees. Tara expelled her breath. She drew a shaky hand across her forehead and sagged against the whitewashed wall. She was convinced now that Dennis was out of his mind.

One look at Jorge's face as he stopped the jeep a few feet from her told her that his mood hadn't changed for the better. She sighed again, not feeling strong enough to withstand his anger after what had just happened.

"Who the hell was that? Obviously some kind of an idiot, to take the road at that speed!"

Tara could only agree with him. She was feeling weaker by the moment. Unconsciously her eyes clung to him, loving the tumbled waves of blue black hair, the straight fierce line of black brows. He hadn't bothered to shave that morning, and his chin was slightly shadowed.

"Well?" he asked impatiently. "What are you staring at?" He looked more closely at her. "Don't you feel well? Have you been climbing through the bushes? *Tara!*" He uttered an explosive exclamation as she sagged farther down the wall. Grasping her by the shoulders he pulled her against him with a kind of rough tenderness.

"What am I to do with you?" he asked, brushing some of the flowers from her hair. "Why can't you behave like ordinary people?"

Her dark eyes slowly filled, and one large tear spilled over to slide disgracefully down her cheek.

"Oh, God!" he groaned. Gathering her into his arms he strode through the courtyard into the villa, calling for Emilio to bring brandy, to bring something, to bring anything, immediately. Tara turned her face into Jorge's cotton shirt, making large wet splotches where her tears touched the material. She stirred like a kitten in his arms, taking advantage of the situation, and again he shouted urgently for Emilio.

This time the butler's immobile face looked as though he was exerting a real effort to keep it that way. Jorge placed Tara none too gently on the couch and then paced to the windows, where he stood with his fingers drumming on the sill. Emilio put a warmed snifter of brandy into Tara's hands. She sipped it, feeling rather off-balance. Warily she watched the rigid line of Jorge's back.

He turned abruptly, to lean on the sill and fix her with an intent gaze. "Now will you explain who that man was? Why he nearly killed me? And why you were climbing through the mimosa? I know the flowers look very attractive scattered through your hair like that, but I hardly think that's why you did it. Other women might conceivably but not you. Oh, no, not you!"

After that remark, where was she to begin? Tara searched her mind, then gave up. "That man is Dennis Moreston. He was angry, I suppose. And I was trying to catch up with him. That's why I was climbing through the bushes."

"You couldn't use the front door?"

Tara flushed. Now that she thought about it, the

chase through the bushes did seem pointless. "He. . .
I. . . ." How could she explain her inchoate suspicions? They would sound even sillier.

"Who is Dennis Moreston? Perhaps we'll clear
that up first."

Tara took a deep breath. "We, uh, were once engaged. He, uh. . . ."

"Came to make up?" Jorge prompted. His eyes
glittered strangely. From across the room he looked
very foreign and very large.

"Not exactly. . . ." Penny's words came ringing
through her head: "You'll never know whether a
man wants you or your money!" And how could she
tell Jorge that Dennis wanted only her money?

"A man either does, or does not want to marry
you, Tara! Now did he or didn't he?"

"Well, yes. But not for the right reasons."

"So you refused him. That might explain his
anger, but not your flight through the mimosa. Did
you have a change of heart? Were you trying to call
him back?"

"I, uh. . . don't think I want to go into why. . . ."

"Hmm!" The simple sound held a wealth of
meaning. "So here's another suitor in the shadows!"

"I've had a few in my time." She was beginning to
feel a hot release of the tension culminating from the
past few days, and had to struggle to hold the lid
down on her temper.

"Funny you never mentioned him in your life
story!"

"There didn't seem to be any point!" she said
through gritted teeth.

"You were once engaged to him but you never even gave him passing reference? How many other men have you been engaged to but didn't bother to mention? How many men do you have on a string at any one time—or is that too personal a question to ask?"

"I'd say that's getting pretty personal, yes! But if that's the way you want it I'll tell you!" she practically yelled.

"Don't bother! I can't spare the next hour!" He gave her a black unfathomable glance and left the *sala*.

Tara looked despairingly at Emilio. He stared back at her, and then eloquently shrugged his shoulders. The helpless gesture brought a faint smile to her lips. Emilio wasn't half bad.... She slouched against the back of the couch, while Emilio discreetly left her in peace. Rolling the brandy snifter between her hands, she gave a great sigh. Well, Jorge was back. If she weren't feeling so terribly frustrated she would be on top of the world!

Action seemed the wisest course to take, so eventually she set down the last of the fine old brandy and went in search of the *contessa*, whom she found still drinking her afternoon tea. She sat down and casually asked what Dennis had talked to her about. But Ernesta, looking secretive, would only say that she found Dennis charming, and rather like her son-in-law, Mario Resende. Further delicate probing only locked the old woman's lips. Tara almost groaned in frustration. She should have stayed in bed that morning, with the covers pulled up over her head!

Jorge did not appear for dinner that evening. *Creme de camarão*, the delicious shrimp soup that Ashta made so well, went back to the kitchen untasted by Tara. Then she pulled apart her pastry pie of chicken, beef, olives and mushrooms and pushed it from one side of her plate to the other until Emilio rescued it from her relentless fork. The *contessa* made poor company, for Tara was thoroughly vexed with her, and her own unease had doubled with the woman's secretiveness.

The second Ernesta was finished eating Tara excused herself and ran through to the kitchen, hovering for a moment in the doorway that led onto the terrace. Ashta was banging her pots around and muttering under her breath. The whole day seemed to have gone wrong for everyone, and rightly or not, Tara felt she was to blame.

With the red rock solidly underfoot Tara gazed out over the Atlantic Ocean. The wind curled her skirt around her legs and tossed her hair around her shoulders. It whipped up little whitecaps on the incoming waves, etching each rolling crest clearly against the midnight-blue waters. Coming steadily on in regular procession, as if propelled by some giant heartbeat, the waves crashed against the rocks below her bare feet and reared up to splinter into a million teardrops high in the air. Gradually Tara relaxed into the soothing rhythm, the eternal mesmerizing song of water and rock.

Several hours later Tara and Ricco entered the villa through the kitchen. All was quiet and dark. The mother cat stirred in her wicker basket, and the two of them heard the plaintive mewing of the kittens as they tiptoed out into the hall. Emilio had left one of the lamps on, and by its feeble glow they could just make out the near dimensions of the cavernous hallway.

"I won't forfeit the hope that one day we shall be more than friends!" Ricco insisted, coming to a halt.

"Don't hold your breath," replied Tara with a smile.

"Hold my breath? What do you mean? Is that an...an...."

"Idiom? Yes. If you hold your breath until that day you will asphyxiate in the meantime. That's what it means."

"Asphyxiate! Turn blue and choke and...?" He turned his hands thumbs down.

Tara nodded, her smile a little wider.

"You can be cruel sometimes!" Ricco reproached her, and she laughed out loud.

Something in his face stopped her laugh, and she followed his startled glance down the long hall. Jorge stood in the open doorway, the courtyard behind him a bare shade lighter than the surrounding blackness.

"Good evening, Dom Valente!" Ricco said pleasantly. "I was just this minute taking my leave of Tara."

"There's no need to rush off," Jorge replied courteously from the nether reaches of the hall. Behind him the massive door swung slowly shut.

"Ah, but there is! I'm escorting a party of Americans through the caves, and thereafter to a midnight supper at one of our tavernas."

"Through caves?" asked Tara. "In the dark?"

"They're floodlit, *bela*," Ricco chuckled, "and lovely to see. But not half as lovely as you. What man in his right mind would go to look at caves when he could hold you in his eyes!"

"Not many, I'm sure," Jorge commented dryly from out of the deep shadows.

After Ricco had taken his departure Tara made it to the stairs without tripping over anything. The carpet had been tacked down again during the cleanup. The stairs wound gloomily out of sight. On the bottom step, her hand on the banister post, she hesitated for a split second.

"Have you...been out for a walk?" Jorge asked. He was only a few paces away.

"Yes," she whispered back, her eyes enormous in the dim light. Was he extending the olive branch? "It's been ...a beautiful day."

"I spent most of it in an office." His quiet voice sounded rueful.

"At your hotel in Sagres?"

"Uh-huh. And at the one in Vila do Bispa. You had a pleasant evening, did you?"

She noticed how finely tailored his cream suit was, how well it fit him. Shrugging slightly, she returned, "It was nice, considering.... I'd like to see the hotel in Sagres. What's it called?"

"The Caravela. And I'd take you if you had some shoes to wear." An edge ran through his last sentence. It made Tara remember that she'd refused his offer to provide her with a few necessities. Now she wondered why she'd done it.

"What do you suppose can have happened to my trunk? Mother told me she would send it that very day! And it's been six days already!"

He brushed one hand through his hair. "Little mix-ups always happen. Are you getting impatient to leave? Is time hanging heavily on your hands?"

"Heavens! There's not enough time to—to get everything done," she finished hurriedly.

"The place is looking magnificent, Tara. I can't imagine how you've managed to get so much done in so little time. You have my wholehearted thanks. Emilio says you never stop for a moment, no matter how many times he tries to coax you into simply relaxing—as you're supposed to be doing!"

"Now that I would find boring." A hint of a smile shaped her mouth. Standing on the bottom stair as she was, they were right at eye level.

"Still, there's no need to clean lamps until midnight."

Tara caught her breath. "It wasn't midnight! And Emilio really does keep an eye on things, doesn't he?"

Jorge smiled a little, too, at the annoyance in her tone. "He feels he should keep me informed of the general goings-on. I've no doubt that evening didn't seem at all unusual to you, but for Emilio it was quite something to see a *contessa* and a servant woman at the same table cleaning lamps together." His mouth eased into a bigger smile.

"Oh. I never thought of it that way."

"My point is taken." By this time the smile was wide. "I wish I could have been there."

"You'd have had your share of lamps to clean."

"No doubt." His eyes hung on to hers. "It seems there's no one who can resist you...when you set your mind to something," he qualified after a rather suggestive pause. Then, abruptly, "I'm going to Lisbon tomorrow to see Resende."

"Oh," she said, swallowing her almost insurmountable disappointment. "Things are coming to a head? Will it...take long to sign all the papers and...and close the deal for the *quinta*?"

"Not more than a couple of days at the most."

"My clothes will probably arrive tomorrow." There was a mournful note to her voice that she didn't notice.

"I shouldn't worry about your clothes. They'll turn up sooner or later."

"Yes." She swallowed again, then smiled at him quite brilliantly. "It will be wonderful when the *quinta* really belongs to you. You have no idea how excited everyone is. Santa, Lianna and Rosa get close to tears just talking about it. And apparently their menfolk and the other workers have decided that it is, indeed, going to be a better world tomorrow. Ricco said it was sure to make a big difference to the young people. More of them would be willing to stay on, you see...with you here."

His eyes ran over her shadowy slender figure, balanced between the first step and the second; over the softly rounded swell of her breast rising and falling under the thin white blouse, up to the dusky-rose mouth and the great, smoky-black eyes shimmering into his.

"Jorge?"

"Oh...yes, I'm happy, too." He held her gaze and smiled faintly.

"H-have you had a chance to talk to Ricco yet?"

"No. I tried the other day, but he and Ashta had just another go-around, and he was in no mood to listen to anyone. Don't worry about him, Tara. I'll see that he comes to no harm." He grinned widely. "I've been sending him families and parties from the hotels, and he's so busy with them...." Jorge spread his hands eloquently.

Tara laughed delightedly at his subterfuge.

"And you're right about his making a good tourist guide. I can cheerfully entrust my most difficult patrons into his care. Every female from three to ninety-three is eating out of his hand. And he knows enough about the area to make any tour interesting for the men. Ashta did a fine job raising him. She's wasted as a housekeeper; she should be a nanny! I've noticed she's not too keen on housework."

"But she's a very good cook," Tara pointed out. "So are you, for that matter."

"You think so? Well, that's something, isn't it?" Although his tone was quite serious, his eyes were smiling. "What about you?"

"I can't cook worth a damn. All I'm allowed to do in Arthur's kitchen is lick the bowls."

"Arthur?"

"The family butler. I think he and Emilio would see eye to eye on a great many things."

"You speak of him as though he's an institution."

"You'd think so too. Just wait till—" She had

been about to say, "Just wait till you meet him," but he wasn't going to.

"Yes? Until what?"

"Uh, until Emilio is a few years older. He'll be one, too. The signs are in full force."

"You're probably right." A lingering smile touched his mouth as he stood surveying her, one hand in his pocket, the other on the banister post beside hers. He was silent for so long that Tara wondered, a little confused, if she should say good-night. The longer he looked at her the higher her heart climbed up her throat. She made a slight movement of withdrawal.

"Do you still plan on going to Las Palmas to write?" he asked.

"Actually, I thought I might as well stay here. In Portugal, I mean," she added hastily. "The—the *contessa* has been kind enough to invite me to stay with her in Albufeira for as long as I please. She says her villa is much too large for her alone and she'd be glad of my company."

"It's unpleasant rattling around a big house all on one's own; I can see that. Well. . . good night, Tara. I'll be out for most of the day tomorrow. As soon as I can get away I'll be off to Lisbon, so I might not see you until I get back." He hesitated, then ended by saying good-night to her again.

UP IN HER BEDROOM, Tara straightened her pillows for what seemed like the hundredth time and rolled over once again. She turned first to one side, then to the other. Ashta's nightgown, which had always been very comfortable before, now felt itchy and kept tangling around her body. . . .

She was in Brackenhill. The windows were locked, the doors barred and an eerie gloom filled the house. The ominous clink, clink, clink of coins followed her in her desperate flight from room to room. The coins were everywhere. They sank when she tried to walk over them and they poured around her legs, holding her fast. More and more rolled toward her; like quicksand they sucked her down. The more she pushed the coins away the faster they closed in on her, until sheer terror overwhelmed her. She cried again and again for help, for Jorge, her young voice intense and brittle in the night air.

Then strong hands closed around her shoulders, shaking her roughly. Whimpering, half-awake, her own hands reached out. Her arms instinctively wrapped themselves around the masculine form that held her, sliding under his robe to feel his warmth, to know that he really was there.

Lights flared and there were voices, questioning, answering. But she heard none of them. She listened only to the steady beat of his heart beneath her cheek, letting it calm her. She was breathing quickly, erratically. Physical contact with him was shattering, yet it saved her. The room tilted back into focus. Dennis vanished into the shadows on the wall.

She felt Jorge take a deep breath and release it slowly, a little at a time. Was he fed up with her? She expected a storm of ridicule to break around her ears, but she didn't loosen her hold. He shook her again, his hands biting into the soft flesh of her upper arms.

"Sit up, Tara!" His voice was brutally alive and vital. It cut through her quivering state.

With a quick fluid movement she pulled her arms free and fell back onto the pillows. Wildly disheveled, her hair made a cloud about her flushed face. Her eyes, unnaturally large and bright, gazed at him as her only help in a dark world.

He appeared anything but. His shadowed, self-contained features were formidable. A muscle jerked beside the curve of his imperious mouth.

"I knew you would come," she said softly, surprised that she could find her voice at all. Her eyes traveled around the room. The lamp on the dresser shed a softly glowing circle of light in an otherwise dark room. Curiously, Emilio and Ashta seemed to be having quite an argument about something by the door. "I woke everyone up," she remarked, feeling dazed and unsure, as though she were on the brink of some great discovery. "It w-was a nightmare," she said, trying to defend herself before Jorge's searchlight gaze. Her eyes widened as she appealed to him, all the while struggling with the bedclothes to sit up, and not accomplishing that goal. The memory sent an icy shudder through her frame. She gave up her struggle and lay back. "I know you've had enough, but. . . ." Her voice trailed away into a whisper.

With a blinding flash of realization she knew what it was she was struggling with. She loved him! Heavens! Why had it taken such a long time for her to understand? Suddenly everything was clear: her crazy emotional flights; Anthony and Cleopatra; the desire she felt flaming through her when he took her in his arms; the constant battles she had with him; the way she loved to look at him, to feel him close by. It had been right in front of her nose the whole time. . . .

"Tara!"

She couldn't look at him now; she just couldn't! He would see—she knew he would. A small sob tore at her throat.

"Tara!" His exasperation was evident. He reached out to grasp her wrists, jolting her up. "Stop it!"

"And you can stop shouting at me!" Rebelliously she freed her wrists. "Just because I haven't your marvelous control is no reason to rant and rave! I don't suppose you are ever frightened of anything! No! You wouldn't be!"

"And what was it that frightened you half to death?" He leaned over her, dangerously close, one hand on either side of her effectively closing off an escape route. The situation was perilous. Why did she always have to be in bed when a really dangerous argument cropped up? And were they really arguing? Again? Tara shook her head. She yearned to touch his bare brown torso, to feel the warmth, the reassurance, the strength, the boundless vitality encased within. To absorb some of it through her fingertips.

"Ah!" he said knowingly. "The ship. . . ."

She gasped, looking up quickly into his blazing eyes and just as quickly away.

"But that's not all."

It was a bald statement. Damn the man! Was he a mind reader? One of his hands curved around her chin, forcing her head up. "Look at me, you perverse little wretch, and tell me what it was!"

His mouth was mere inches from hers.... Tara's gaze was irresistibly drawn to the strong white teeth and the sculptured masculine lips.

"I'll bite you if you continue to harass me!" she spat out, rather breathless.

"That would be the day!" he laughed grimly. "Shall I go?"

It was a threat of sorts. Distress reflected immediately in her eyes. "I won't sleep! I can't!"

"Will you sleep with me here?" he taunted.

"I'll never sleep again," she moaned tragically, believing it.

He made no reply to this, but looked down at her, engrossed by the refusal in her eyes and by the inviting, willing, slightly parted lips so close to his.

There was a certain urgency to his quick command. "Emilio? Where in the devil has he gone!"

The butler appeared magically, as though he'd been awaiting summons just outside the door. "Bring hot milk and those tablets Doutor Couto left!"

"Never!" Tara yelped.

Her vehemence brought a sudden full smile to his lips. His hand slipped around her throat to gently, persuasively caress her nape. "You'll sleep like a baby. Now don't be stubborn. It's not even two o'clock. No point in being an early bird. The worms don't crawl out of bed until five." The soft deceptive purr held a note of command. His authority exerted itself effortlessly. Tara didn't mind, though. She couldn't, for his hand on her neck was having a hypnotic effect, and it blotted out everything except the immense fact that she loved him.

Emilio had laced her milk with brandy and honey, which made it much easier to swallow. The pill that came with it was probably large enough to make three people sleep for a month, Tara thought, eyeing it in resignation, but leaving it on the night table. She lay in an attitude of defeat, avoiding Jorge's gaze, trying to reerect some quick defenses. Her whole world was tilted upside down by Jorge Valente. How was she ever going to right it again?

"Yes, that's all, Emilio. You can go now—and tell Ashta to get back to bed, as well. I'll take care of Tara."

The door closed quietly behind the gloomy-faced butler.

"Oh, Jorge, you don't have to take care of me!" she protested mournfully.

"I know I don't have to; I want to! And that's an entirely different thing. Come along now, take this pill."

Did he have to sound so maddeningly rational? "I don't want to sleep," she pouted, forced into accepting the tablet when his fingers on her chin made it imperative. He handed her the milk to wash the medicine down, and satisfied that she'd swallowed it, prepared to go.

She clutched at his robe. "Oh, don't leave me, Jorge!"

He sank back onto the edge of her canopied bed, the line of his jaw hardening, and said crisply, "You want me to hold your hand until you fall asleep?"

"No, no. . . ."

"Then just exactly what do you want?"

"Would a. . . a good-night kiss be asking too much?"

He stared at her, incredulous. "You must be out of your mind!" he said. Then, as startled tears sprang to her eyes he grasped her shoulders and bent over her. "Tara, *querida*, don't cry. Oh, darling, don't cry!" He kissed her carefully on one cheek, on the other, then over the wet trail her tears had made. "Is that better?"

"No, no!" she whispered, her arms going around his neck. For a brief moment her lips clung to his, warm and infinitely sweet, their erotic impact instantaneous. He pulled slightly away, and she laid her head back down on the pillows, looking into his startled eyes and taking a deep trembling breath.

A frown hovered between the black brows. "*Querida*. . . I'm a little confused," he murmured, his eyes holding hers forcibly. "Didn't you tell me not to push? How can you kiss me like that and expect me not to do anything about it?"

"But I didn't mean you were pushy. We got all mixed up somehow. And then you looked so angry. . . ."

"Couldn't you explain?"

"Jorge, look in the mirror the next time you're in a temper. I doubt if you'd want to talk to yourself. I. . . thought I'd wait until you cooled down a bit. And you really haven't given me a chance until tonight."

"You certainly choose the time and the place...."

"And you haven't kissed me yet."

He smiled. "You do possess a one-track mind," he said, and lowered his head.

There was a hairsbreadth between their lips. "Father calls it my monomania."

"As long as it's directed toward me...." His mouth covered hers, his hard arms slid around her, his weight bore her down against the down-filled mattress.

His second kiss slowed, lengthened, deepened in languorous, ever growing desire. As her hands tangled in his black curls, his lips left hers to hungrily trace the line of her jaw. She turned her head so that he could kiss and nibble at her earlobe. This delight sent slow shivers coursing through her, and a low moan of pleasure caught in her throat. His mouth returned, devouring hers, and he shifted his weight slightly so that one hand could gently caress her while the other held her to him. Passion quickened between them, overflowed and enveloped them both in a rushing sensuous fire. Tara kissed him back with a sweet burning abandonment she had never dreamed possible. Ashta's thick and woolly nightgown was far too bulky.... With his fingers wedged between them he undid the old-fashioned mother-of-pearl buttons. A long slow sweep of his hand brushed the nightgown away and off one shoulder. Tenderly urgent, his touch against her bare skin was a delicious shock to her senses. Her body moved against his seductively. Her arms went around his torso underneath the robe, holding him to her....

"*Minha querida*, listen to me for a second." His low voice was husky and muffled against her throat. "If we go any further we're both going to get our fingers burned." He shifted a little more, bringing her up beside him and almost on top of him, his long hands around her waist, holding her close to his warmth.

Tara's fingers slid through the drift of black curls on his chest. "Yes, let's," she whispered back.

Her hair spilled around him in a curtain of silk as he abruptly pulled her to him and kissed her on the mouth. Then he started laughing. She could feel his chest shaking beneath her hands.

"Did I say you chose a good time? Your timing's awful, Tara!"

"What do you mean?" she asked, perplexed and a little unsure of his wide white grin.

"Don't you remember? You took that pill. You'll be asleep in...oh, ten minutes. Probably sooner."

"Oh, hell."

Her soft expletive started him laughing again; the glow in his eyes gave her a blush that could be seen in the dim half-light from the lamp, so far away. A smile trembled on her mouth as his hands roamed possessively over the curve of her buttocks all the way up to her shoulders, the one clad, the other bare and enticingly beautiful in the scant light. Against his dark skin the swell of her one exposed breast gleamed pearly white.

"I've never wanted to go back on my word as much as I want to tonight, and now it appears I won't have to, after all. It seems fate has stepped in,'' he told her softly, his throaty voice a caress, his smile tender and slightly crooked. "If this whole situation weren't so farfetched, I might think you'd arranged it.''

"Oh, but I didn't, Jorge!" Tara hastened to say, then added thoughtfully, "Had I thought of it before I would have tried it some time ago.''

"You are a little cat, aren't you?" Amusement filled his low tones. "If the *contessa* weren't here I'd sleep with you, my love. I'd hold you in my arms all night long.''

"Couldn't you anyway?" she questioned with soft yearning. A filmy layer of cotton wool was insulating her mind.

"The *contessa*, while not very effective as a chaperon, does take her duty seriously. And she's a light sleeper. I've found her checking up on you a couple of times late at night. The least suspicion that we'd spent a night in the same bed—no matter what we'd done there—would have her sending off the details in telegrams to both our parents—and, incidentally, to anyone else who cared to read them along the way.''

"Oh, Jorge, that would be ghastly!" Even though Tara was quite serious a giggle rippled up her throat. "Mother would hit the roof! She'd be out for your blood after receiving that telegram. I wonder how Ernesta would word it?" She chuckled richly and rather sleepily.

"You can be sure, no matter how flowery, that the message would be explicit.'' His hand ran through the thick cascade of her long black hair. "I'm almost tempted to try it. Tara, *minha querida*, are you still awake?'' Her head, lying on his chest, nodded drowsily. ''We could even drag a red herring across the *contessa*'s path. . . .''

He held her in his arms until she was fast asleep. Before he left her he buttoned the nightgown all the way to the top and drew the blankets up to her chin. Hesitating there, one hand reached out to smooth a few straying tendrils away from her forehead.

CHAPTER TEN

TARA SLEPT VERY LATE the next morning, and when she did get up she wasn't very wide awake. The after-effects of the sleeping pill made her feel as though she were floating a few feet off the ground. Lianna, Santa and Rosa were already at work in the bedrooms; Ashta had sent them there, for she hadn't known of Tara's plans for the library.

Tara felt too sleepy to rearrange anything. Jorge and Emilio were gone, she found out, to parley with the fishermen.

Tara breakfasted with the *contessa* on the terrace. Ernesta's gown this morning was of violet blue silk with froths of Chantilly lace at the neck and wrists. Tara tried again to find out the content of her conversation with Dennis, but to no avail. Eventually, thoroughly annoyed by the woman's secretiveness, Tara left the terrace to wander around, not knowing exactly what to do with herself. If she sat down she would go to sleep, and if she didn't get busy at something she would think of nothing but Jorge, and of what had almost happened last night.... She went upstairs to see how the women were doing, and finding everything in order and her assistance not needed, sneaked up the turret stairs to finish cleaning the little

round room. It didn't take her long. An hour later
she was downstairs, feeling, if anything, a little more
befuddled as the day grew hotter.

Finally realizing she could no longer push Jorge to
the back of her mind, and wanting to be alone, Tara
sat down in the dusty courtyard, away from the bus-
tle going on indoors. She leaned her head against a
high-backed marble bench and closed her eyes
against the sun. Her head slowly tilted to one
side.... She jerked upright. Hopefully she would see
Jorge before he left for Lisbon, just to make sure last
night hadn't been a dream. Hopefully he would want
to see her... at least to kiss her again before he left.

The memory of last night's lovemaking, the warm
marble at her back, the sun overhead and the potent
effects of the knockout drug all proved to be too
much for Tara, and she drifted off into a fast sleep.

A hand was dragging at her shoulder, almost pulling her arm from its socket. She seemed to be propelled through space, then landed against something
hard and unyielding. As she cried out, drugged with
sleep, a rough hand clamped over her mouth, forcing
her lips into her teeth in sharp pain. She struggled
against her unknown assailant, but her efforts were
weak and puny compared to his. Tears of pain shimmered in her eyes and down her cheeks. It was a
nightmare, another nightmare—but much too real
this time! She was being pulled toward the outer door
of the courtyard, and vainly she struggled through
her sleepy haze. There was a resounding rip as her
skirt tore. And then she saw it—the red rental car.
Her blood turned cold. Her dream should have fore-

warned her: Dennis was back and he had said she would be sorry. . . .

The passenger door was yanked open, and she was tossed onto the seat. It was all happening too fast. With a crashing of gears the car jerked forward several times before it plunged down the bumpy road. Tara struggled upright, wide awake now, but the horror was still too new to comprehend. Turning her head slowly, as though she didn't want to believe he was really there, she stared at him. Revulsion widened her dusky eyes and shot purple sparks through the irises. Fear wound its icy fingers around her. Her heart was a sledgehammer against her ribs.

They hurtled down the leafy green tunnel and shot over the rise, to crash down again in contact with the road. Tara braced herself against the dashboard. Dennis *was* out of his mind!

It was then that she noticed the metal cylinder in his lap. It was about four inches long and not quite as wide. Grease covered it and wires curled out of both ends.

"What's that?" she gasped. It hardly seemed of importance, considering her situation, but there was something ominous about it. And Tara meant to take her suspicions more seriously from here on in.

"Just a little detail that will take care of His Royal Highness, Jorge Emmanuel Valente de Silves!" Dennis laughed, gloating in triumph. The harsh sound grated on her nerves and sent trembles coursing through her body. "His little ol' helicopter just isn't gonna fly nohow! He won't be able to track us without it—not until it's too late!"

Tara found her teeth were chattering and clamped them tightly together. He would *not* reduce her to helpless terror.

"It was so easy!" Dennis's voice rose to a gleeful pitch.

The orchards whizzed by on either side. Tara swallowed to keep her stomach down.

"You played right into my hands! Sleeping in the courtyard with no one in sight!" he chortled. Then, seeing her eyes on the metal cylinder, he twisted open the glove compartment and threw it in, locking the small door.

He laughed again, thumping his hands against the steering wheel to emphasize his words. "Didn't I say I would get what I want? Didn't I? And now I've got you! Thought you were going to hook yourself a bigger fish than me, eh? I'm every bit as good a catch as that Valente fellow!"

"Oh, for heaven's sake!" Tara groaned. "What drivel!" She shook her head, not quite believing he could be so stupid, so misguided. "Let me out—at once!"

"Kidnappings don't work that way, darling!" he retaliated cheerfully.

"Kidnappings? Dennis! You can't be serious! You won't get away with this. You—"

"I've already got away with it!" he interrupted her. A trickle of perspiration ran down his cheek. It was terribly hot in the small car. "And once it's over it'll be too late for anyone to do anything about it, including you!"

"Once what is over?" Her mouth took on a peculiar dry papery feeling.

"Our wedding, of course!"

Tara felt her face blanch. "You're mad!"

"Not at all."

"I won't do it."

"You don't have any choice," he answered smugly. "Ever heard of a shotgun wedding? The traditional role will be reversed this time, because the gun will be in the bride's back. It's a kind of justice."

"Justice?" her voice squeaked. "It won't work!"

"It will, and extremely well, too. No one here will be surprised if you marry me. After all, we were once engaged. And no one in Hampstead will know until it's done! And darling, who will believe a ridiculous story about a kidnapping?" he sneered. "You'll be branded as a neurotic bride! Frightened by the marriage bed!"

"And you would go through all this just to get my inheritance?" Tara spoke quietly, her fright almost under control. She shifted her position so that the tear in her skirt didn't show and her legs were covered. She would think of something in time to save her. She'd really rather die than become his wife.

"Well, yes. You see, darling, your inheritance is the only money available to me at this moment. I need money—a lot of it—fast. I came across an absolutely marvelous opportunity, so naturally I had to take steps. I mean, I couldn't pass it up."

"Naturally," Tara murmured wryly. It was another case of the ends justifying the means. She would have to wait for him to slip up...and then escape. He was right in one sense, for who would believe a kidnapping story? Or a shotgun wedding?

"What happens if I don't choose to sign my inheritance over to you?" Tara was thrown against the door as the car lurched down the rutted road and out of the orchards.

"Ice maidens usually put their virginity before all else. You'll pay up!" To her horror his eyes left the road to travel slowly down her body. With satisfaction he noted the tangled disorder of her long hair, the soft curves under the peasant blouse, the narrow waist enclosed in the embroidered waistband. The rip in her skirt showed one gold-tanned, shapely thigh. He laughed as she hastily tucked the skirt tighter around her legs.

"I thought that would rile you! Actually, darling, my plan's a little more down-to-earth than that! It's well known that you're an heiress; just the fact that I'm married to you will quiet my creditors. All I really need is a small sum to go to each—to keep them content until I'm on my feet again. And you'll be happy to shell out, for if you don't you'll have any number of goons—strong-arm men," he explained for her benefit, "trailing around after you like a clutch of chicks behind a hen. And I don't have to tell you that that would be a little frightening, not to mention downright embarrassing! Then, of course, there's my little Edinburgh scheme that backfired." He sighed. "I may have to go to court over that, and I can't take the risk of your blabbing out what you know about the bribe. A wife can't testify against her husband. You see? I've considered it from all angles. I have to marry you. But don't look so shattered, darling. We can always get a divorce in several months' time."

Tara slowly assimilated his speech. "But...but didn't you say you needed a lot of money fast? For some marvelous opportunity! What's that all about?"

"Darling," he remonstrated, "do you really think I'm going to make the same mistake twice? Oh, no, I'm not telling you one single solitary detail of this venture! I will need a big chunk of your money to handle the down payment, but don't fret. I'll pay you back!"

Dennis hadn't been paying enough attention to the road. The car teetered on the verge of a ditch, and with a curse he swung the wheel sharply to the left. He overestimated, however, and the little red car charged nose down into the other ditch. Tara closed her eyes, gripping the edge of the seat. Their breakneck speed, the unbearable heat in the car, Dennis's reckless driving and her fright were all combining to make her feel nauseous. She hung on mutely as Dennis righted the car and steered it back into the deep ruts of the road.

Vividly she remembered the last time she'd driven down this same road...with Jorge. Would he try to rescue her? If no one had seen Dennis take her from the villa, what would the master think when she was found missing? And so far she hadn't seen a soul who could identify the car or point out the direction they had taken.

She pondered her situation. The judge, or justice of the peace, or whoever Dennis had lined up to perform the wedding ceremony, would be handsomely rewarded, and so would turn a deaf ear to her pleading. Dennis had probably chosen a route and a place where there were few people, so no help could be expected from that quarter. The car was going much to fast for her to jump out, and she would have to unlock the door first. So *that* seemed an unlikely method of escape. Reluctantly Tara had to admit that her situation was desperate. She could expect no help from anyone; this time she was really on her own.

She proved to be right about their route. They left the vineyards behind and climbed swiftly up into the *charnecas*. Barren sunburned slopes gently undulated on either side. Craggy, twisted olive trees, like lone witches, stood sentinel over the wastes. She tried to keep track of the turns they made, but soon lost all sense of direction. There were no landmarks, nothing unusual to pinpoint their route. Only sandy red earth and scrubgrass, wattle and sagebrush could be seen for mile upon mile. Tara didn't even know if they were still on the Valente estate.

The sun blistered down on the red roof of the car, turning it into an oven inside. They drove on and on and on, and could have been going around in circles for all the change in countryside. Dennis chuckled and gloated over his triumph, while the perspiration ran into his eyes and down his neck. He unbuttoned the collar of his shirt and loosened his tie. He swore a little under his breath as he drove with one hand and held a road map with the other. He wouldn't even let Tara open the window in case she should scream bloody murder at some passerby. And when she pointed out that they would scarcely see someone on this deserted stretch of road, he threatened to tie her hands if she didn't shut up. She resigned herself to waiting patiently. Every time they topped a rise or rounded a corner the same view stretched out before her.

Eventually he would have to slow down, Tara reflected, closing her eyes and leaning her head wearily against the headrest. Dizzy spells swept down on her like whirlwinds. Somewhere, sometime, he would have to slow down or stop, even if it was just before they met the judge. Her hand crept up toward the lock button on her door. Her fingers tightened on it. She coughed to cover the sound of it popping up, then settled in the corner of her seat to hide it from his eyes. At the right moment she would yank the door open and run for dear life.

She screamed as a small brown rabbit bounded into the road and disappeared under the car. Grabbing Dennis's arm she shook it violently, crying for him to stop. "It might be hit! Y-you've got to stop!" she sputtered.

He shook her off with a loud oath, glaring furiously at her. "What are you trying to do? Push us off the road?" His eyes went past her to the door. He saw the button in the unlocked position and cursed her roundly as he lunged past her to lock the door again. Then he stepped on the brakes. The sharp acrid smell of rubber filled her nostrils. She grabbed for the button, momentarily losing her head. With his fingers painfully biting into her flesh he pulled her back from it. A wild struggle ensued. He won by brute force. Five minutes later Tara's hands were tightly bound behind her back. He had used his tie.

From the frying pan into the fire, Tara thought disconsolately, leaning her aching head back against the seat. It was impossible to find a comfortable position with her hands tied. How silly of her to lose her head like that! She should have pretended he'd forgotten to lock her door. A sob caught in her throat and she choked it down. She would not give Dennis Moreston the satisfaction of seeing her cry! And despite appearances she was not beaten yet. If there was a way to get out of this mess she would find it!

"You're quite crazy, you know," she stated sweetly, some time later.

His mouth curled. The pale brown eyes, once so familiar, shot her a malevolent glance. "Nope. Just smart." A small smile never left his thin lips.

"Oh?" She would unnerve him if she could. "Really? You call losing that deal in Edinburgh smart? Your resort business is ruined, and it's all your fault." She kept her tone at a low sugary level. "It's too bad. Your father worked so hard. He spent over forty years building his business, and you managed to destroy it in a mere three years. Do you call that smart? And not only that. You've ruined your credit and you've lost your good name. Think of what you've put your mother through. Think how embarrassing it must be for her! How will she ever be able to hold up her head in society?"

"Shut up!"

"For a smart man you sure make one hell of a lot of mistakes," she continued relentlessly. The smile had disappeared from his lips. And if she wasn't mistaken he was about to explode. She'd said enough for now. Knowing the way his mind worked, she suspected her words would eat away at him and make him careless. She sighed, pleased with herself. For all his deviousness, he was really quite simple. She tried to relax, to conserve her energy.

Her blouse clung uncomfortably in the sticky heat. The pain in her wrists spread down to her fingertips and up her arms. Her throat was dry and parched and it hurt to swallow. She ran her tongue over her lips to try to moisten them. There was a cut under her lower lip where Dennis's hand had pushed it into her teeth. How long ago had she left Hampstead in search of adventure? It seemed years, when in fact it had been only a little longer than a month. Nothing had happened to her for two years; now everything was happening at once.

Her thoughts whirled in circles, and inevitably settled on Valente. She had always thought love would be comfortable and complacent, like companionship. But that idea had been shattered like the waves against the rocks at Minha Casa. Her love was the searing aching pain of wanting him, the wild transcending heights of joy, eclipsing all else. It was a force, a power that ran through her like a rushing current. It was a complete giving of herself. She hadn't asked to fall in love with him. She'd fought her natural feelings all along and had still lost to him. So what was to be done now?

Nothing, she answered herself resolutely. He obviously felt desire for her. Whether he felt anything more remained to be seen. When she'd mentioned that her trunk might arrive while he was away in Lisbon he hadn't made a move to invite her to stay on at the *quinta*. He hadn't even dropped a hint, and yet...and yet....

She could only go on with her original plan—find herself a new home and get down seriously to her writing. Then she would see what happened. If she stayed in Albufeira she wouldn't be that far away. He could come calling if he wanted to. And considering last night, it was very likely that he would.

A faint dreamy smile curved her lips. She shut her mind against the possibility of a future without Jorge Valente, forced herself to think practical thoughts, to keep a clear head. She concentrated on the restoration work still to be done by her women at Minha Casa.

But thoughts of the villa brought with them an intense longing to be back in its cool dim halls and its sunny rooms. How pleasant Ashta's voice would be now, and Emilio.... She would hug him when she got back home. *Home.* She shouldn't be thinking of it that way. And what if she never did get back?

Their route was a tortuous one and it made absolutely no sense to her. Looking for her would be like looking for a needle in a haystack. Would Jorge even bother to find out where she'd gone? Tara stopped her train of thought abruptly. She could depend only on herself, and she wouldn't even be able to do that if she put herself into a depressed state by mulling over what Jorge would or would not do.

Dennis picked up the road map from the floor under his feet, where he had flung it in a fit of anger.

While twisting the paper around and snapping it to smooth out the buckles, it tore. He cursed more vehemently than the situation warranted, and Tara wondered if he was already crumbling. Hope inched up inside her.

They drove on and on, climbing higher and higher into the *serras*. The sun sank slowly behind them toward the western horizon. Dennis's mood did not improve. He shoved his foot down on the accelerator, but the car would not do more than ninety. It shuddered and rattled alarmingly when pushed beyond that point. Suddenly they bounced over a bump, and the car swerved as pebbles caught under the tires. He uttered a string of oaths, reminding Tara of Captain Baker's imprecations, and a tight smile etched her lips. Grudgingly Dennis slowed down. It did not make him happy. Tara sat quietly and didn't risk saying a word. He picked up the road map again, but could barely see the small print in the slowly gathering twilight. Disgusted, he threw it away.

Dennis was lost! She could have crowed for pure joy. No wonder the landscape seemed so similar, even though they'd been driving steadily all afternoon. They had been going around in circles! Tara felt absurdly like giggling but was afraid to start, for she sensed her laughter would be more than tinged with hysteria. Soon she might have her chance to escape, and she had to keep herself together.

As they rattled down the gravel road the sun dipped past the horizon. A purplish blue light spread quickly across the empty land, dark in the shallows, lighter on the crests of the low hills. The last golden glow disappeared from the sky as olive trees and sagebrush turned into black lacy silhouettes. Silence lay like a heavy cloak over the land. Nothing could be heard except the chug and occasional sputter from the car's overheated engine and the crunch of flying gravel beneath the tires.

The car sputtered, and then sputtered a few more times. Surreptitiously glancing at the fuel gauge, Tara saw it was down past the empty mark. Her spirits rose higher, but plummeted when Dennis stopped the car to haul a large jerrican out of the trunk. Refueled, they drove on again. Tara shook her head wearily.

About half an hour later she spied a feeble light winking over the scrubgrass and wattle. She peered at it intently, and as they drew closer, decided it was some sort of human habitation. As if in answer to her prayers the car sputtered once more. It coughed and shuddered and then stopped completely.

Tara sat up, smiling in the darkness. "Dennis?"

"Oh, shut up, will you?"

"Does this mean we won't be getting married, after all?" There was a high lilt in her voice.

"No, damn you! There's no chance of your getting away! My man isn't expecting us until tomorrow. I didn't think it would be quite so easy to get you away, so I gave myself extra time."

"But has it been easy?" She was teasing him again. "Aren't we lost? And out of gas? My, my, my!"

He stomped out of the car and around to her door. Tara was feeling giggly again, and for a moment wondered if she really was dreaming. His rough hands pulling her out of the car convinced her otherwise. He pushed her ahead of him in the dark. Now she could make out the lines of a ramshackle cottage wedged between clumps of rock. "It's better than nothing," she heard Dennis muttering behind her.

"Don't you think you'd better untie me? After all, where can I run to? We're in the middle of nowhere, and I'm as lost as you. Obviously I can't use the car. My hands look rather suspicious this way, don't you think?" She couldn't resist the little taunt. He muttered some more, but did untie her hands. As blood flowed freely once more into her fingers the pain made her gasp. Then she bit down hard on her bottom lip, sore as it was.

As they walked closer to the cottage a curious muffled whimper came from inside. Then a high mournful wail split the night air. Tara's skin crawled, and she stopped. Immediately Dennis's hand was at her back, shoving her on.

It was a very old woman who opened the rickety door to Dennis's thumping. Tears were running unchecked down her withered cheeks. At once she grasped Dennis's upraised hand and began to kiss it fervently, crying on the Almighty, who, she said, had brought him to her.

Tara stared at her with wide shocked eyes, but Dennis, with a sweep of his arm, pushed the old woman aside and stepped past her into a small low room. Tara peered in warily. By the dim light of the one candle in the window she saw a young woman lying on a cot in the corner. Her eyes were glazed and fretful, and she lay immobile as though with great fever. From beside the hearth came another whimper, and Tara stared in further surprise at a newborn baby. The whimper turned into a widemouthed cry.

"Damn! Are we going to have to put up with this all night?" Dennis snapped.

Tara turned on him. "Sit down somewhere and be quiet!"

He scowled and threw himself into a wobbly chair opposite the baby on the hearth. The old woman, bewildered now, broke into such a storm of Portuguese that Tara didn't understand any of it. She sat her down and carefully wiped the tears from the wrinkled cheeks with the hem of her homespun skirt. With gentle coaxing, she learned that the woman's name was Maria Duarte, and that it was her daughter who lay on the cot. Josefa had given birth earlier than expected, and due to complications she had turned feverish. For three days the fever had grown worse, and today she hadn't been able to breast-feed her baby at all. Maria couldn't possibly leave Josefa and the baby alone while she went for help, since it would take her almost a day to walk to the village.

Tara quite forgot her own plight when she heard that no one was expected through here for at least a week. She cast about for some quick solutions. Senhora Duarte obviously expected her to help. Yet how could she? Dennis had no food in the car, let alone milk. She could walk for help; it didn't matter how long it took. But would Dennis let her go?

The baby began crying again, and Josefa, hearing it, sobbed piteously. She struggled to sit up, but fell back among the threadbare blankets before either Tara or Maria could help her. Tara was now almost beside herself with a totally new set of worries. In the background Dennis muttered an oath, cursing her, cursing Maria and Josefa, the baby, and then the whole world beyond the mean little cottage.

Through all this confusion Maria managed to convey to Tara that she possessed a cow, and that luckily it had recently calved so that the milk was thick and rich and nourishing. The milk would save the baby, but although Maria had desperately tried to milk the cow her hands were so knotted with rheumatism that she couldn't manage to get any out. And Josefa was in no condition to do anything. That was why the old woman had been weeping: her helplessness might have meant the death of both her daughter and her grandson. But now that they were here in answer to her prayers, Maria nodded confidently. Everything would be all right. The gentleman would surely milk the cow, no?

Tara's relief at this point was so great that she hugged the peasant woman. "Dennis, listen! Will you milk the cow? The baby hasn't eaten and might—"

"If you think I'm going to touch a filthy cow, think again!" He slouched back into his chair, ignoring them both. Fishing about in his jacket pockets he pulled out a flask, from which he took a long swallow.

"I'll milk the cow!" Tara told a perplexed Maria, even though her stomach tied itself into knots at the thought. She placed an arm around the woman's stooped shoulders, putting on a brave front. "Just show me where the. . .the cow is." One more look at the baby's pinched face gave her all the courage needed to tackle the job. She'd never milked a cow before, but there was a first time for everything!

The formidable beast was tethered to an olive tree behind the cottage. A young calf, all curly and clean from its mother's tongue, blinked at the shielded candle Maria was holding. Tara saw the milking stool hanging from one of the tree's branches and placed it firmly beside the cow where Maria pointed. She swallowed as she saw the cow's pointed, wicked-looking hooves. Under Maria's direction she inched the stool closer until her cheek was almost touching the brown aromatic flank. She put the pail between her legs and gripped the teats; nothing came out. She squeezed harder. Nothing happened except that the cow's smelly damp tail swished around and fell over her face. She looked up at Maria.

With sign language the woman showed her how to move her hands rhythmically, closing first the thumb and forefinger, then her other fingers in sequence. A drop of milk hit the bucket, and a grin lighted Tara's face.

The cow shifted and looked around at her. Tara smiled back and continued squeezing, squeezing, squeezing. It was actually quite pleasant milking in the moonlight. The foaming, creamy-yellow milk crept up in the pail. When it was two-thirds full she stopped and showed Maria the contents.

Feeding the baby was a joy. Tara watched over Maria's shoulder as the little pink mouth eagerly sucked at the milk. She couldn't wait to tell Jorge she'd milked a cow.... Thinking of him and of the cow at the same time triggered a memory. Jorge had aided a cow in giving birth, and the calf outside didn't look very old. Could it possibly be the same one? She asked Maria, speaking slowly so the woman would understand her halting Portuguese, and was answered by Maria's emphatic nod. That meant they were still on the estate!

She filled a tin beaker with milk and helped Josefa drink it. The feverish eyes were brimming with so much thankfulness that Tara felt quite embarrassed. She straightened out the girl's blankets and plumped her pillows. Dipping a rag into a pail of cold water, she used it as a compress for Josefa's burning forehead. Tara wished there was something more she could do for her. She saw the slim band of gold on Josefa's left hand and wondered where her husband was and why he would leave her alone at a time like this.

A few more black marks went up against Mario Resende; if Maria Duarte and her daughter hadn't been so poor this pitiful situation might never have developed. From Maria she then learned that both their husbands were in Lisbon, looking for work. They were *vaqueiros*, but with all the cattle sold what work had they here? They could no longer feed their families, and so had gone to the big city. But things were bad there, too, for who needed cowboys in the city?

Tara's dislike for Mario Resende was growing by leaps and bounds. He was solely responsible for this state of affairs. But why hadn't Jorge left the women more food? Or firewood?

He had not known that Josefa was about to bear a child, Maria answered simply. She hadn't told him because he had already done so much for them.

Tara could only stare at her in wonder. The staunch pride of this old woman, of all the peasants, amazed her.

Staunch pride or not, Maria Duarte seemed completely exhausted, and it was apparent that a great many household chores were overdue. A fire was needed first, Tara decided, as the night chill was definitely upon them. She checked with Maria and was dismayed to learn that twigs had to be scrounged piece by piece from the *serras*. She glanced at Dennis, but he had sunk into a gloomy reverie by the fireplace and took no notice of what was going on around him.

A twig here, a twig there. . . . It was slow painstaking work in the dark. Tara carried the precious burden home, knowing all too well that it would last only a short time, for they needed hot water and hot food. There was nothing else for her to do but pull some boards off the shed at the back of the cottage. They came away easily. She had to prop them against the olive tree and then jump on them to break them in half—Maria's ax was minus its haft—and got several splinters in her feet for her efforts. The cow blinked at these antics but kept on chewing her cud, while the calf thought it was some sort of game and followed on her heels, frequently getting in the way. But with a proper fire inside the drab whitewashed walls didn't look quite so dismal and forlorn.

Tara sat a kettle on to boil for tea and added the few vegetables she could find to the stew pot sitting on the hearth. As the pot swung from its big black hook over the flames, she poured some of the heating water into a pail and washed out the baby's diapers. These she hung on the olive tree to dry, patting the cow as she passed it. On her way back in she refilled the pail with cold water from the outside pump. The kettle was boiling by this time, and she made tea for them all. Theirs was such a meager supper that Tara felt guilty eating her tiny share, but she had to out of politeness to Maria. Dennis ate his few mouthfuls with a poor show of spirit.

Tara found it impossible to sit still, and although Maria protested she washed the supper dishes and then swept the dirt floor with a twig-and-straw broom. She tidied the cottage further, and when that was for the most part accomplished the baby required another feeding.

From time to time she noticed Dennis's head dropping on his chest. She puttered around attending to one thing after another, biding her time. She even got around to washing the three small windows that the cottage boasted. More boards came off the shed to keep the fire alive. The baby needed changing, and that meant more diapers to wash. Tara worked herself right out of things to do, while Josefa drifted off into fitful slumber and Maria, cuddling the baby, nodded by the fire.

A brooding silence lay over the cottage. The soft regular breathing of sleep was the only sound. Tara hunched her shoulders and rested her elbows on her knees. Unfortunately Dennis had finished the contents of his flask; she would have enjoyed a few sips. The one greasy candle flickered in a pool of liquid wax in its dish by the window.

She began to pace restlessly, her bare feet making no sound on the packed earth floor. How lonely it was, and how quiet. Dennis's head dropped farther down on his chest. She would have to wait until he was in a deep sleep before making a move. A shower of sparks flew up the chimney. The few remaining twigs and boards crackled and glowed. With a last weak flicker the candle in the window died. . . .

Dennis was snoring! She wheeled around to give him a closer look. With a grim smile Tara picked up his tie from where it lay crumpled at his feet. She found a long piece of rope coiled on the door. Her fingers shaking with suppressed nervousness, she looped the tie around his crossed ankles. Very carefully she tightened and then tied the silk material. She drew a deep breath and held it, frightened in case she made a sound and woke him. His gentle snores went steadily on.

Tying up his hands, though, was a bigger problem, for they rested on either side of the armchair. Frowning in concentration, she started winding the rope around him, his upper arms and the back of the chair, looping the ends down around the armrests and his wrists. It couldn't be too tight or he'd wake up. Yet it had to be tight enough to hold him securely. She stood back to survey her effort and wasn't entirely satisfied. He could still wriggle out. She untied the long rope ends, rewound them around the chair's back legs, then up around his neck. Very, very carefully she inched the rope under his chin, and that done, tied the ends together at the back of his neck. By the time she was finished her heart was beating so loudly she thought its thumping alone would wake him. But he snored on. As a final precaution she put the large iron frying pan close by, in case he woke and the ties weren't tight enough. One little tap on the head would take care of that contingency.

Once more he had been too sure of himself! Tara almost wanted to wake him up to see his reaction. Instead she contented herself with a short but gleeful dance of triumph in the center of the dirt floor. Now let Valente say she couldn't take care of herself!

She fell to pacing again. One big problem was now under control. When morning came she would tie Dennis more securely, so that he would have no chance to escape. Then what could she do but go out on the road to wait for a car, a donkey, a goat—anything that came along. Could one ride a goat? Yes, she would just have to wait until someone came, then either go with them to the nearest telephone or have them take a message for her. Or she would have to walk to reach help. This whole nightmare could be over with one phone call to Jorge. Luckily they were still on the estate.

She chewed on her lip, deep in thought. Of course Dennis belonged in jail for his treachery. But she had absolutely no proof that he'd kidnapped her! No one had seen her hands tied, no one had seen him take her, and he had no need to send a ransom note because the inheritance came with the mere fact of having her. Very likely the police here would think she was a neurotic foreigner if she started regaling them with her story. Shotgun wedding, indeed!

It was chilly in the crystal light of early morning. Tara took the bucket and milked the cow. Left, right, left, right, left. . . . It wasn't that difficult once she'd got the knack of it, but she had trouble with the calf who kept trying to butt her out of the way. She tiptoed back inside and set the half-full bucket beside the hearth to keep the milk warm. The baby wailed once, and somewhat clumsily she fed him, after which he went contentedly back to sleep. Everyone else was still asleep.

She walked out into the middle of the gravel road and looked around. Stones jabbed the tender soles of her feet. The crystal light turned a flaming pink and gold over the eastern *serras*, and a soft mist rose from the ground and hung in the still air. Sailing up over the horizon, the sun was a hot golden ball flooding full power over the pink-hued landscape. The mist vanished. The sagebrush and wattle were tipped in gold. The last shadows disappeared. Tara shivered with weariness. Would Jorge come from her? Would he?

In sudden despair she recalled that he would be in Lisbon by now, and all her hopes were crushed. Sadly she realized just how much she had been depending on his coming.

Josefa needed a doctor right away. There wasn't enough food left for another meal. As for Dennis, she would have to untie him if only to let him go to the bathroom. And Maria had said she wasn't expecting anyone to come by. A tear trickled disconsolately down Tara's cheek. She knew now that she would have to walk for help, but at the moment she was too tired to lift a finger. Another tear followed the first one. She sat down where she was, right in the middle of the road, to rest before she started the trip. Maria was depending on her, and it would never do to cry where she could see her. Tara sobbed into the hem of her skirt. Everything was bearable except the fact that Jorge was not coming to find her.

Trying to control the misery that swamped her, she wrapped her arms around herself. It would take her the better part of the day to walk to Carrapateira, the nearest village, which Maria had told her was eighteen kilometers away. And it would be a rugged journey over the *serras*, over the rocks and through the gullies in her bare feet, without even a road to guide her. For the shortest route to Carrapateira lay directly cross-country. She estimated she would arrive there by late afternoon, if she was lucky and didn't get lost. From the village she could send food and a doctor to the cottage and then go back to Minha Casa. Her clothes had most likely come from Hampstead in the meantime. Without an invitation and without an excuse to stay longer she should then leave the estate.

But if Jorge hadn't returned from Lisbon she might never see him again. What if he didn't want to see *her* again? What if the other night was just one of those things that happen on the spur of the moment, without rhyme or reason? What if—

Angry with herself, she wiped the trickling tears

away with the back of her hand. She looked up and down the road, narrowing her eyes against the glare. The chill was beginning to fade from the morning air as the sun crept higher in the sky. It was about 7:00 A.M., she judged by the sun's position. She would have to set out soon. . . .

Her ears, straining for the least little sound, picked up a humming noise. A car? A plane? Her imagination? She jumped up, held her breath and listened.

She began to tremble from head to foot as she recognized the estate jeep bearing down the gravel road toward her. With a wildly exultant cry she ran toward it, quite unmindful of the sharp stones underfoot.

Jorge caught her in midflight, his hands settling around her waist as he lifted her up in the air. Looking down into his darkly tanned face, Tara laughed with pure happiness. Her arms circled his neck, and she pressed herself against his long hard frame. After the slightest hesitation his arms enfolded her, crushing the breath from her body in the sweetest sort of pain.

"My God, woman, is there no end to your caprice?" he muttered into her hair, his voice quite thick.

Tara clasped him tighter. In her overwrought state of mind her love for him couldn't be denied. The feel of him against her, the strength of his hard arms around her and his bare chest beneath her cheek where his denim shirt opened gave her a shattering dizzy delight.

"Tara. . . ." He tried to disentangle her. His hands curved around her shoulders and gently forced her back a little, so that he could see her face.

She looked radiantly up at him, a small secret smile playing over her red lips.

He caught his breath. His eyes slid intently over her wide eyes, shimmering with emotion. "Tara," he began again, patiently, "what the devil have you been up to this time?"

"Oh." She began to laugh joyously. "You won't believe it! I even milked a cow!"

"Tara!" Jorge groaned.

"And I fed the baby and changed his diapers," she went on, ignoring his exasperated unbelieving expression.

"What have you been doing?" he repeated, grasping her hands and turning the palms up. Dark bruises showed where Dennis's tie had cut into her wrists. There were scratches from when she'd gathered firewood, a sliver and several broken nails earned in a struggle with Dennis.

"Oh, hello, Emilio!" Tara cried.

Her glad voice made the butler start. His straight long face crinkled a little around the mouth; it was obvious he wasn't used to smiling. His eyes, however, were dancing and blatantly curious.

"Good morning, *senhorinha*," he said politely, as though they found her every morning stranded on the *serras*.

She caught the grim determined gleam in Jorge's fierce black eyes, and was hastening to explain that this excursion wasn't her idea when a clamor rose from inside the cottage. Jorge and Emilio turned to stare, as though they expected its crumbling tile roof to blow right off. The baby was screaming, Dennis was bellowing, there was crashing and banging—a hopeless cacophony of sound bursting out of the small place.

The scene inside was priceless, at least in Tara's opinion. The baby had been unceremoniously shifted to the center of the floor, where he lay screaming and beating the air with tiny fists. A further look explained all: Dennis had knocked over his chair and he lay on his back, feet in the air, shouting at the old woman. The pail of milk, which Tara had so carefully acquired, had tipped over, and the rich liquid was seeping through Dennis's shirt and creaming his hair. His face was quite red. Maria Duarte stood over him with the frying pan, threatening to let it fall, her scratchy voice rising and falling in excited vehemence. But it was the look on Jorge's face that made Tara hold her sides with helpless and sudden laughter. She was feeling a little light-headed.

"I should have known it would be something totally out of the ordinary!" Jorge stated. He looked at Tara with a mixture of exasperation and amazement.

She lifted her hands in a helpless gesture.

Jorge took the frying pan from Maria, then righted Dennis—chair, rope and all. The cream made a plunking noise as it dripped off him.

"You can't be left alone for a minute!" Jorge continued to scold her as he began to untie the slippery rope. "I'm surprised you're not in Africa riding a rhinoceros!"

Tara could only giggle. Control over herself had simply slipped away. She bit into her knuckles, but that didn't help. Her shoulders shook, a pain started up in her stomach and the sweet innocence of her laughter spilled over the room. It made Jorge angrier.

"If ever anyone deserved a—a—" Fitting words to express himself were not available. "Do you have any idea of the chase you've led me on? I could shake you till your teeth rattle!" His very white teeth snapped with emphasis. He looked rather ferocious. Taking an upward glance at him, Dennis hunched his shoulders and tried to make himself smaller. His fingers fumbled at the tie around his ankles, then he started to head for the door.

"Just where do you think you're going?" Jorge grabbed him by the back of his collar and lifted him right off the ground. Dennis sagged back into his chair, the picture of misery.

"It was all his fault!" Tara managed at last. "He kidnapped me!" She explained quickly what had happened.

Dennis cowered even further down in his wobbly chair, as between erupting giggles Tara told the whole story. Even her inheritance was finally out in the open. Jorge, Emilio and Maria all listened in utter silence, Maria bent forward in an effort to understand Tara's far from perfect Portuguese.

"It could only happen to you, I'm sure!" Jorge exclaimed when she was finished. "So that was why he came before and asked you to marry him?" His black eyes turned toward Dennis, who paled visibly.

"Y-yes," she stammered.

Without more ado Jorge pulled the sticky perspiring Dennis roughly out of his chair. Emilio followed them outside. About half an hour later Jorge and the butler reappeared, but Dennis wasn't with them. Jorge was holding the greasy metal cylinder in his hand.

Curiosity about what had happened out there—apprehension, too—made Tara look searchingly at Jorge's rather stern face. Without a word she handed him some tea in a chipped cup. She had torn more boards off the shed to make it.

The taut lines around Jorge's mouth relaxed as he drank the hot liquid. He held the baby in the crook of his arm, where it soon fell asleep. Josefa lay exhausted on her bed, but a weak smile curved her lips as she gazed with shining eyes at her son. The sunlight poured into the cottage in solid bars of gold while Maria and Jorge discussed the situation and what had to be done about it.

Tara, curled up on the now cleaned hearth, looked eminently pleased with herself. Her eyes kept returning to Jorge's autocratic profile. With passionate abandon she let her love show, but dropped her eyes every time he glanced her way. A remaining measure of shyness stained her cheekbones a wild rose as she remembered in vivid detail the way he had kissed her and held her the night before Dennis had kidnapped her. Bemused, she gazed out the window and did not see Jorge's intent look, nor the muscle jerk beside his lips. It was enough for her that he had come.

"Oh, Jorge!" she gasped suddenly, sitting upright. "What about Lisbon? Aren't you supposed to be there today?"

He shrugged, and a faint smile tugged at the corners of his mouth. "Lisbon will still be there tomorrow."

"How did you find me?"

"I wondered when you'd get around to that! Ashta saw the back of Moreston's car just before it disappeared over the rise in the road. She went looking for you but found you gone. She was in a panic by the time Emilio and I arrived. She told me then about the first time he came—the argument you'd had. I made a few telephone calls, discreet inquiries in Sagres and Lagos and Aljezur, but they turned up nothing. I wasn't absolutely positive you were with him, you see. I know you like to go for walks, but I remembered the strength of the sleeping pill you'd taken and that ruled out the walk. Then I thought you might have gone regardless and fallen asleep out in the woods again. When the helicopter wouldn't start and I found the fuel-control unit missing, I knew something decidedly unpleasant was afoot." He glanced at the metal cylinder.

"He was in worse shape than Ashta was," Emilio finished dryly.

Jorge shot him a withering look, but Emilio gave a barely perceptible shrug. His face was wonderfully bland.

"Naturally I was upset...." Jorge was looking at his butler as if daring him to say more. Tara, her interest quickening, glanced from one to the other.

"You frightened Ashta out of her mind with your shouting," Emilio injected calmly.

"Perhaps you should continue from here?" Jorge struggled to keep the wrath from his tone.

"Oh, not at all, sir. It wouldn't be my place."

"Well? What happened then?" Tara interrupted tactfully.

"I gathered the peasants together and asked them if anyone had seen you, Moreston or his car. It took a while, but we finally came up with a clue. Lianna's son had seen a red car take the northbound turnoff, just past the vineyards. I then made more inquiries in Alfambras and Bordeira to see if you'd gone through there, but as no one sighted you or the car I guessed you were still on the estates. So the search began. There are about forty people turning the country upside down looking for you, Tara—with Ricco at their head. And here we are!"

He turned to Maria. "We must go, Senhora Duarte. Thank you for your hospitality. I shall send a doctor out today, and also someone to take care of things until Josefa is well again. Come along, mermaid. You look as though you've had just about all you can take!"

He swung her up in his arms before she had a chance to properly stand up. And once in the jeep he placed her firmly on his lap. The red rental car was hitched to the back of the estate vehicle, and in it sat Dennis, tied up. Tara avoided even looking in that direction.

"Right, Emilio, let's go!" Jorge ordered, folding his arms loosely around her.

"Really, this isn't necessary, Jorge," Tara said, flustered.

"Who are you trying to kid? I prefer to have you where I can see you! Now just sit still and try to behave. I know it goes against the grain—'' a wry smile tugged at the corners of his mouth "—but *do* make an effort!''

She lay against his arm, wishing he would let her sit in the back of the jeep. What did it matter if it was full of grain, chicken and cattle feed? In some ways it would be more comfortable than sitting where she was. Queer little tremors raced up and down her spine. He was torturing her, for he knew she loved him and— Oh, she was being silly! He was autocratic, entirely self-contained and self-assured, and in his opinion she was a troublesome schoolgirl, as he had once said. Or more precisely, he probably thought her a pain in the neck. He had had to cancel his trip to Lisbon on her behalf, and he had spent the whole night looking for her. So it was no wonder that he was treating her like a child with his aggravating blend of patience, exasperation and tolerant amusement.

The road slipped by under Emilio's sure hands. The wind on Tara's face felt soothing. She subsided against Jorge's wide hard chest, a ruffled flower tired beyond knowing, and as ever, oblivious to her fragile femininity. She only knew that Jorge Emmanuel Valente de Silves was a tower of strength, and she wished desperately that he was hers. She loved every line of his darkly tanned face, every last hair on his proud head. She loved his strong body with its broad shoulders and narrow hips. She loved every one of his moods, even the most difficult. He was magic to her, a dark sorcerer who could play on her emotions, her thoughts. She would never be rid of his spell... never.

"Tara—" his voice was low so that only she could hear "—mermaid, listen. I'm sorry I screamed at you back there. I didn't mean to start shouting the moment I saw you but...I died a million deaths while you were gone...."

There was no need to answer him. His words circled round and round in her head, and one of her hands went up to lie beside her face on his chest. It was an odd movement of almost childlike trust, only it meant a lot more than that alone. Some of the rigidity went out of Jorge's shoulders. One long brown hand moved slowly up her back, in a gesture very much like a caress, to settle on her nape. His fingers gently flexed her soft skin, and Tara gave herself up to the exquisite warmth of his touch.

And that was when she noticed the change in him; a minute change, definitely, but it was there. The hand on her nape felt very possessive, and the chin just above her head was ever so slightly more determined than it usually was. Her tired nerves leaped and quivered in an agony of uncertainty. She moved closer to him, and suddenly, although she had had no previous thought of doing so or even wanting to do so, she planted her lips in the hollow where the brown column of his throat met his shoulder. It was not a "thank you" kind of kiss; it was a soft statement of sensuous desire and brimming love.

His reaction was immediate and electric. The hand at her nape wrapped itself around her hair and with a soft tug pulled her head back. His other hand tightened around her waist, drawing her firmly against him. Her torn skirt slipped open from where she'd carefully tucked it, and she heard the deep intake of his breath before his mouth took hers with magical precision—a definite statement of aroused male passion. It was over almost before it began. She was left staring a little wildly up at him. His black eyes glittered back into her own.

"I'll deal with you later!" he muttered under his breath. Wings of excitement fluttered up and beat against her slender rib cage. "But for the moment... enjoy the view."

That broke the tension, and Tara laughed with him. The rest of the ride home was accomplished in a most companionable way. Dennis and his car were left with the police in Sagres; Jorge would be satisfied with nothing less.

CHAPTER ELEVEN

ERNESTA COULD BARELY CONTAIN HER EXCITEMENT over Tara's kidnapping and subsequent rescue. She thought it a marvelous romantic adventure, and inquired whether Jorge would duel with Dennis Moreston. That dueling was a hundred years out-of-date didn't make any difference, she insisted. It was foolish to have taken him to the police, for this was a personal affair and should be dealt with accordingly!

Lunch was a very festive occasion. Ashta laid a generous table, inviting Santa, Lianna and Rosa to celebrate with them. The effusive welcome surprised Tara. She was flushed and a little overwhelmed by everyone's happiness at having her back, Ricco included. And every time Jorge's black eyes rested on her she experienced tremors of suspended excitement, a quickening heart and a terrific shortness of breath. What had he meant by "I'll deal with you later?"

Toward the end of the luncheon Ashta hurried into the *sala* bearing a small brown paper package, which she explained as she handed it to Tara, Emilio had brought from the Sagres post office yesterday. Tara took it eagerly, reading the Hampstead return address. It turned out to contain copies of her published books, enclosed with a letter from her parents.

She scanned her mother's writing quickly. She had sent her books separately, Mrs. Lownes said, because she had forgotten to pack them in the steamer trunk with her other things. Everything was as usual in Hampstead. Penny had gone home to Edinburgh in a huff, and Mrs. Moreston was entangled in an ongoing battle with Dennis's many creditors. Not surprisingly, her mother had a large party planned the moment she returned home. And, oh, yes, Tara was not to forget to thank Mr. de Silves in whatever way she thought most suitable, for fishing her out of the sea. Her father, of course, would thank him formally at a later date.

Tara folded the letter with a wry smile. What would her mother think if she knew exactly how her daughter wanted to thank Mr. de Silves?

Tara looked into the envelope again to make sure her parents hadn't sent a check or money order. To her secret relief there was none. They must have packed it in the steamer trunk. And it could stay wherever it was, she thought, at least for another week or two, maybe even three. She should inquire about it, however; she should at least sound anxious about her things.

"There was nothing else?" She hoped her voice sounded more eager than it did to her own ears.

Jorge looked away from her and stared out of the window for a moment. "No. No, nothing else. I'm sure your clothes will arrive shortly. Not to worry." He turned back to her and smiled brilliantly. There was some devil at play in his eyes. Nonchalantly he took *Toodles, the Bear with a Bad Case of Big Nose* away from Ricco.

Tara tensed and unconsciously held her breath as he studied the cover. He opened the book and flipped rapidly through the pages, stopping now and then for a closer look while Tara fidgeted in her chair.

"Did you do the artwork? On the cover and inside?"

"Yes. I—I did. My publisher thought the drawings suited the story, so. . . ."

"They're lovely!" He looked again at a bright dreamy watercolor of *Toodles* looking sadly down his nose. "I shall read it tonight before I go to bed."

He chuckled at Tara's surprised glance, then eyed the flush that spread over her cheeks at his praise.

Ernesta and Ricco were poring over *A Witch's Pleasure*. The *contessa* looked up when Jorge asked, "Did you do the paintings for this book also?"

"No, my publisher found that artist."

"Yes," Ernesta commented, picking up *Toodles*. "I can see the difference in style. You should do your own artwork from now on, Tara. I'm sure it suits your writing style, although this witch illustration is good."

"And is this yours, too?" Ricco asked. "*Where the White Goes When the Snow Melts*?"

Tara nodded.

"Lovely!" exclaimed the *contessa*. "I shall take them all out on the terrace if I may. With all the excitement I did not get enough sleep last night, and I think I shall start my siesta early." With a chirpy smile directed at the three of them, she left the *sala*, her gold brocade morning gown rustling elegantly.

The peasant women had been sent home early with full pay. Emilio had vanished somewhere, and Ashta could be heard moving about in the kitchen, banging the occasional pan.

Jorge sat across from Tara, his long legs spread under the table, his eyes half-closed as they watched her. A lazy smile indented his finely cut lips.

Tara sipped her *vinho verde* somewhat nervously and wished Ricco would shut up. His grandiloquence was a little too heavily laced with outrageous compliments, with hints that there was more to their relationship than met the eye. In fact, if Jorge was doing any reading between the lines he might even suppose there was a torrid love affair in full swing. She usually ignored most of Ricco's nonsense when he slipped into one of his amorous moods. But did Jorge know Ricco well enough to ignore it, as well?

Emilio came into the *sala* with another bottle of wine. Tara felt grateful for the interruption. But she almost choked over her topped-up glass when the butler, after filling Jorge's glass, went to fill Ricco's and while doing so slyly kicked the young man in the shins.

She never would have believed it if she hadn't seen it. As she took a sip of her wine Tara pretended not to have noticed either the kick or Ricco's pained expression. Her curiosity aroused—Emilio's action was totally uncharacteristic—she covertly eyed the butler, who was informing Ricco of a telephone call that needed an immediate reply. Grumbling, Ricco rose from the table. Tara watched the two of them leave, sensing that in the near future, at least, Ricco would not return. She would have to corner Ricco later to try to find out what the little episode had meant. Not for a moment did she believe Emilio merely wanted to ensure some privacy for her and Jorge!

"Tara?"

"Y-yes?" She turned back, facing Jorge once more.

His eyes ran intently over her face, throat and breasts while beneath, unseen, her heart started a slow ponderous beating.

"Are you in love with Ricco?"

With a quick intake of breath her eyes widened. "No, of course not!" She almost laughed at the idea. "I like him very much, but that's all. One has to... know when to take him seriously and when to...." She waved an expressive hand.

"Then this... romance with you is all in his head?"

"Entirely."

"Then he hasn't, er, made love to you? At all?"

"Not except for the odd small kiss—"

"Just how small is small?" he interrupted.

"Peck on the cheek variety, if you must know exactly!" replied Tara, her eyes dancing at his sober expression. There could only be one reason for his asking all these in-depth questions, and she felt a singing elation coursing through her blood.

"Ahh!" he said, meaningfully, staring at her. "Now I want to know if you're in love with Mr. Moreston."

"*No!* Oh, no!" she finished a little less vehemently. "I never was. Our engagement was a—a mistake, an idiotic mistake right from the start!"

"Why didn't you tell me Dennis wanted to marry you for your inheritance?"

"I—I— Well, it's an embarrassing thing to have to confess!" Tara stated.

"And you didn't want me to know you were an heiress," he persisted in his slow soft drawl. He took a cheroot from the lacquer box on the table and lighted it with calm deliberate fingers.

"I wanted to forget that I was! I wanted to depend only on myself and on the money I earned from my books. It isn't much as yet, but I was sure I could manage and—"

"That was why you didn't tell me?" His eyes surveyed her from under half-closed lids. He was like a great slumbering tiger—deceptively quiescent, for at any moment he might spring.

She felt trapped, backed into a corner. She wasn't yet prepared to tell him the real reason, and Penny's words floated through her mind. But how could she keep her motives from him? He was terribly difficult to lie to. She searched for something to say.

"Why, Tara? Was it because you thought I might be interested in the inheritance also?" He laughed in his throat, uncoiling his long length from the chair. Tara gazed at him in mute alarm as he sauntered around the table to her chair and pulled her gently to her feet.

"No!" The delicious curve of her full bottom lip trembled.

"No?" His hands slid from her shoulders down to her waist. His thumbs moved along the line of her hips, and she shivered at the feelings his sensuous touch evoked.

"For heaven's sake, Jorge! How did you expect me to introduce myself? 'Hello, I'm Tara Cybelle Lownes, the virgin heiress'? Oh, dear!" Shaken by her slip of the tongue, she took a few rapid steps backward, so embarrassed that she wished the ground would swallow her.

"Come back here!" His astonished order made her whirl around, heading for the *sala* door.

A long arm stopped her before she could escape. While he turned her around in his arms she muttered, "Oh, no, no, no!" Holding her pinned against him, he pried up her chin. Tara kept her eyes tightly shut, refusing to look at him.

"You'll have to open your eyes sooner or later," Jorge teased her gently. They opened instantly when his warm kiss flooded through her.

He smiled faintly. "I thought you were, the first time I kissed you. When I was washing your hair, remember?"

How could she ever forget? Tara's furious color heightened.

"But further...amorous encounters with you persuaded me otherwise." His smile increased by a fraction. "What I'm surprised about is that you were engaged to Moreston for two years and.... How did he manage to keep his hands off you for so long?"

"I—I don't believe I ever...gave him any...encouragement. And then he had his...amours on the side.''

"My lord! It really was a mistake, wasn't it!''

"I think I mentioned that before!'' Tara snapped.

He laughed at her ill temper, his hands sliding silkily up her back. "I can tell you one thing for certain, mermaid. Were you engaged to me it would *not* be for two years; two weeks would definitely be long enough! But then...you *have* encouraged me, haven't you?'' His sly crooked smile and the dancing sparkle in his eyes robbed her of some of her peevishness, although his words sent another tide of color through her cheeks.

"Well, one has to start sometime,'' she returned glibly, knowing the flip statement would irritate him.

It did. His fingers tightened on her shoulders, digging into her flesh. His voice, however, was his habitual easy drawl. "Is that what you were doing with me, Tara? Experimenting?''

"It did cross my mind,'' she replied offhandedly, then flashed him a quick grin. "Although I decided against it after a bit of serious thought.'' Looking up at him through her lashes she could see he didn't appear pleased.

"Your claws are getting longer and sharper, *minha querida*.'' His gaze traveled from the top of her head down to her rather dirty feet, taking in her white blouse the worse for wear and the long rip in the black homespun skirt. His hands moved back to her waist, curving her body toward him. "No doubt you'd look equally as enchanting in a potato sack, or in a gown by Givenchy. You really live in your clothes, don't you?'' Laughter again edged his deep tones. Languidly he surveyed her averted face. "Perhaps I'll try some experimenting of my own!''

"Oh, no, you don't!''

He held her fast. "Stop squirming, Tara. I'm trying to kiss you.''

"No!''

"Yes!''

"Why?''

He threw his head back, laughing aloud. "If you need that explained you're younger than I thought! I want some answers, fast, and I figure it's the best way to get them!''

"What is it you want to know?''

"If I asked you, you'd never tell me. You'd pussyfoot around and around, and in the end I'd be no wiser than at the beginning. You can be uncommonly perverse, you know. I think this other method will be much more satisfactory!''

"Jorge, no!'' she whispered, pushing her hands against his chest in panic. At that moment he looked very much like his pirate ancestors, a hard dark conquistador about to take what he wanted with full confidence and a startling hint of panache. "I'll tell you whatever you want to know! Really I will. . . .''

Relentlessly she was pulled closer. His arms enfolded her, crushing her against the hard length of his body. He was an erotic whirlwind on her senses, but here there was also strength and safety, a strange security she'd never known before.

His warm mouth touched the corner of hers softly, slowly, as though he would entice her into surrender.

Then he took her lips as his perfect right, persuading her into response with an exquisite subtlety and sensuous technique that she could not match. Without conscious volition her body turned to liquid and melted into him like warm summer rain. Her lips parted of their own accord, and she made a small murmur of conciliation.

His embrace then changed. Fiercely possessive, he held her to him, and she was unprepared for the strength of the male passion that flared through him. In total surrender to his touch she had to at last openly admit her love for him, her need of him. A flame seared through her. The hot blood pounded in her veins as she answered his mounting desire. . . .

He raised his head at last. His black eyes devoured the pallor of her creamy skin, the brimming intensity of emotion in her eyes.

"Well, that takes care of that nicely!" he muttered deeply. One finger touched her swollen just kissed mouth tenderly, and he kissed her again. "Mmm. . . I'm crazy about the way you answer questions!" His hands roamed over her slender back and hips as though she already belonged to him.

"Is there anything else you'd like to know?" she asked, and there was nothing innocent about her this time.

He chuckled softly. "That was just the beginning, my love. But I'm afraid if I keep you on your feet much longer you'll faint in my arms—and Doutor Couto will have my head if you're not a bouncing picture of health when he comes back. I'd say you've done enough, er, new things in the past twenty-four hours to last you till I get back from Lisbon!'' The devilry returned to glitter in his eyes. ''Shall I tuck you in?''

''When will you be back?''

''If I leave first thing in the morning I'll be back in time for supper the day after tomorrow.''

''I'll be waiting here for you.''

''You'd better be here! You can take that as a warning. No getting into trouble while I'm gone, and no experimenting of any sort! We've got several things to settle when I get back.''

''My, aren't we the lord and master!'' she declared with a smile.

''Mmm. And don't you forget it!'' His teeth flashed white and compelling.

Impulsively she slipped her arms around him and sighed, a catch in her breath. She didn't want to talk. She laid her cheek against his chest, moving to the opening of his denim shirt and nuzzling the bare brown skin, the dark mat of hair. She felt the muscles across his chest grow taut, and his arms tightened almost ruthlessly around her slim form.

''Stop that, *querida*,'' he muttered into her tousled hair. ''How much do you think I can take? God knows I don't need encouragement where you're concerned!'' His hands moved up to her shoulders and gently pushed her away. Dryly he added, ''At the moment I'm trying very hard to resume the role of benevolent uncle.''

''I've already got an uncle.''

''You won't have two for long!'' His kiss was hard and quick and very real. ''Come on. Bath and bed for you. I'll have Ashta bring you supper on a tray, and Emilio will stave Ricco off long enough for you to get some sleep." His voice carried an almost impersonal concern, as though he really was trying very hard to assume the role of uncle. Then his lips twitched with an irresistible thought. "I would have loved to see you milking that cow!"

Slipping an arm around her waist he guided her out of the *sala* and down the long hall. They had started up the stairs when they were precipitately stopped by an authoritative voice.

"Just where do you think you're taking her, young man?"

They both turned to stare at the *contessa*.

"Up to bed," Jorge replied gravely.

"Certainly not. No, indeed you're not!"

"But you let Ricco take her off for hours!" Jorge protested in an aggravated tone.

"Pooh! Ricco is a boy! You, you are a man!"

Jorge muttered something under his breath, then smiled charmingly down at the old woman in gold brocade. "I'll be back downstairs in half an hour," he promised.

"Worlds have been lost in half an hour!"

"Fifteen minutes?"

"Ten minutes. In ten minutes I will send Ashta up to help Tara prepare for bed. And I shall watch the clock! Sleep well, my dear. You deserve your rest." She fluttered a hand at Tara.

"Here we are," Jorge murmured, opening Tara's bedroom door, his black eyes glinting. "In your bedroom—with only ten minutes—again! Since we've only got ten minutes, what do you think we ought to do?''

"I remember once when I was sick my uncle came up to play checkers...." Her laughter spilled out at his expression. "Suddenly you don't look much like an uncle to me!" She slipped away to the bed and sat down on the edge of it, smiling at him.

"I'm not very convincing, am I?" He came over to sit beside her. "Maybe that's because I feel only one way about you. Damn! We haven't even enough time to talk! And I'm not risking Ernesta taking you off to Albufeira while I'm gone, so we'd better tow the line. Was it my stupid idea to have a chaperon?"

"What are all these things we have to talk about?" she asked.

"First and foremost is an arrangement whereby we can be alone without fear of interruption!" He grinned, tipping her backward onto the bed with him. As his mouth closed over hers his hand found the rip in her skirt and slid through it, running up the length of her bare thigh.

Tara's fingers curled in his hair at his tactile lovemaking, awed by how sensitive her skin was, how soft and seductive the touch of his hand was... and how much she loved him. His flaring demanding passion took her breath away as she sweetly snuggled closer to him.

His hand left her thigh and he wrapped both his arms around her, holding her tightly to him. "*Minha querida*, do you think ten minutes would be long enough for you to list all my... foibles, I believe was how you put it?" His eyes laughed into hers.

An imperious pounding on the door brought them both upright. Tara remained sitting, while Jorge leaped to his feet in exasperation. "Who the hell is it?" he demanded, striding for the door.

Ashta came through it with her hands on her hips in a righteous stance, her wrinkled face set adamantly.

"Our ten minutes aren't up!" he told her furiously.

Pointing a gnarled finger at the door she cried, "Out! Out!" and a great deal more that Tara roughly interpreted as what was the world coming to and what an impertinence it was for him to be in a young girl's bedroom. Had he lost all sense of propriety, she added, and what would Tara's parents say when they found out! The old woman put herself between them, folded her arms over her skinny bosom and glared at Jorge.

He literally towered over her, and was looking down his aristocratic nose at her when she unleashed a new spate of words. Whatever he had to say to Tara could be said downstairs in the company of others, and if not, then he shouldn't be saying it at all. The *contessa* was much too modern in her outlook, and he had better get out before Ashta herself took a broom to him!

Tara couldn't help her hilarious giggles. At that Jorge threw up his hands. Saying to Ashta that she was lucky he tolerated her, he swiveled around, and just before he closed the door behind him, blew Tara a kiss.

Tara received thoroughly pampered treatment

from Ashta before she finally fell into bed. Once there she stretched out with only the sheet to cover her, intending to sleep until suppertime. Her head was buried comfortably in her pillow, which in her imaginings turned into Jorge's shoulder. How she would love to fall asleep in his arms.... She drifted off with a dreamy smile curving her lips and slept right through dinner.

Later, still fast asleep, she never noticed that Jorge came quietly into her bedroom just before going to bed himself. Her three books were under his arm. He stood beside the large carved bed looking down at her for a long moment. Then he stooped and drew a light blanket over her slight form. He turned to go, but then, as though he couldn't help himself, he bent over the large bed once more and brushed her mouth with a gentle kiss.

Tara slept right through until the next morning, and didn't wake up until Jorge was already an hour away on his flight to Lisbon. He had taken the *contessa* with him so that she could have a short visit with her daughter.

While Tara ate her breakfast with enormous appetite she made plans for Santa, Lianna and Rosa to begin work on the library, for by lunch they would be finished with the last bedroom upstairs. The nursery, the adjacent schoolroom and the nanny's bedroom could wait until later, she thought absentmindedly. There was scarcely any need for them now.

With her mouth full of scrambled eggs she suddenly remembered Ernesta's secretive conversation with Dennis. That still hadn't been explained, she thought, frowning. Even if he had decided by then to kidnap her there was no reason for him to talk to Ernesta, nor to flee when Tara came into sight. But she could think of no suitable explanation to the riddle, and so had to give it up.

The day moved pleasantly into the afternoon and evening. The women had never seen Tara's face so wreathed in smiles, nor heard her clear laughter ring so often through the rooms. They whispered among themselves about what they suspected had brought about the change. Ashta beamed continuously the whole day, and even Emilio's long face seemed a little less glum.

The kittens Lianna had brought were now venturing out of their basket, and when they weren't under Ashta's feet they were under Tara's or Emilio's. Without the customary visit from Ricco and without having to humor the *contessa*, Tara had plenty of free time. To keep from thinking about Jorge all day long she armed herself with paper and pencil and started rewriting the pages of *Toodles* book two that had gone down with the *Adventure Star*.

Amazingly, the whole library was finished when the women left for the day. Toward the end of the afternoon they'd exerted a burst of energy that had left Tara gaping. When she tried to tell them to slow down, Lianna had shrugged and laughed and winked at her, but would not explain why they were in such a hurry. Tara made a mental note to tell Emilio that the women had earned their wages several times over, so that he could pay them accordingly.

Unexpectedly, the *contessa* arrived shortly before

Tara was about to sit down to her solitary dinner. She arrived in a taxi, to Tara's even greater surprise—Ernesta had an aversion to taxis—and appeared rather flustered.

"Why, *contessa*! I thought you went to Lisbon!" she exclaimed, helping her out of her velvet coat.

"I was on my way, dear," Ernesta answered, adjusting the many rings on her fingers so that all the gems were arranged to her satisfaction. "But when we were flying over Vila Nova de Milfontes I remembered I had left my diamond tiara behind in Albufeira. And I never go to Lisbon without it! Dom Valente simply could not understand the importance of having my tiara with me, and he refused to fly back for it!" she added indignantly.

Tara murmured in sympathy and swallowed her smile, handing the *contessa* a glass of sherry.

"When he left me in Vila Nova de Milfontes I told him I was on my way to Albufeira to collect it. But then it seemed too much trouble to continue with any original plan. I do not really feel like going to Lisbon at this time of year. And Angelica does not approve when I visit without invitation. So here I am. That taxicab was dreadful! I have never had such an uncomfortable journey!" Her many necklaces shook. "I am certain that driver never received a proper license to drive that vehicle. Why, most of the time we had only two wheels upon the road!"

Anything above thirty miles an hour was too fast for Ernesta. Tara smothered another grin by sipping her sherry, managing to look sympathetic.

THE NEXT MORNING Tara was up at her usual early hour. When she came downstairs Emilio was already at his typewriter, working on another formidable list of figures. She stopped on her way past him.

"Emilio, what did Jorge do before he decided to buy the *quinta*? I mean, besides his hotels?"

"Why, *senhorinha*, they kept him busy! They still do. He'll be stopping in at the one in Lisbon before he returns here today. Thirteen hotels require plenty of work! And they're all large, extremely luxurious hotels."

"Thirteen?" Tara exclaimed weakly.

"Yes, *senhorinha*. Dom Valente is not a superstitious man."

"I never for a moment supposed he was," she murmured, wandering to the table to lift the lid of the silver chafing dish. She did not notice his long look after her, nor the small frown that nicked his brows before he returned to his work.

A little later she let herself into the massive dining room, which was situated across the hall from the *sala*. Its one end opened onto the terrace beside the kitchen; the other had French doors leading into the salon. The room was gloomy and dark, covered in dust. She would start the women in here today, she decided, throwing open the window blinds. But maybe one of them should be detailed to clean the den. Jorge could probably make good use of it.

Her heart missed a few beats. He would be back today, and the *quinta* would be his! She must tell Ashta to prepare something special for dinner. And they would eat on the terrace tonight. She would cut fresh flowers and—and probably be in a complete nervous dither by the time he arrived!

Tara bit her bottom lip to keep from smiling such a wide ridiculous smile. Was it really possible to be so happy? To feel so warm, as though the sun were shining from inside her instead of from the blue, blue sky? It wasn't at all possible to contain what she was feeling. He had said— Well, he hadn't actually said anything, but he had implied. . . .

The three peasant women arriving for work took one look at her and nodded among themselves. The young and beautiful *senhorinha* was even more radiant today than she had been yesterday, and that could mean only one thing: Dom Valente would be home before the sun set.

At midmorning Emilio started moving his stacks of papers and ledgers into the fresh and spotless library. When Tara told him that she and the other women would be glad to help him move the enormous ornate desk he murmured polite thanks but declined the offer.

She hung around the *sala*, curious to see how he would accomplish the feat by himself. When every last paper had been moved he went calmly to a hall closet, wheeled out a dolly, tipped the desk over onto its side onto the dolly and wheeled it into the library without getting one speck of dust on his immaculate clothes. She'd known he was efficient, but not to what extent!

A little later, when she was between tasks, Tara slipped upstairs to the turret room and settled for a moment on the settee. She plumped the cushions for her back and then gazed out of the curving windows. But she didn't see the brightly painted fishing ketches bobbing on African-blue waves; she saw nothing of the garden wilderness or the jagged shoreline. Instead a tall lean figure shimmered before her, with laughing black eyes and white teeth that flashed when he smiled. Brows that frowned so fiercely and a strong, determined chin. . . .

Like a dark cloud on the horizon Dennis drifted into her mind. Had he secured his release from the local prison yet? He had boasted that his lawyer would have him free in twenty-four hours. . . . What was he up to now? What new devious plot was he hatching to embezzle money from someone else? She almost felt sorry for the misguided man; his priorities were all wrong. He caused his own problems, but he caused them so regularly and bungled them so supremely that he appeared in a pitiful light. It must have been a terrible blow, losing all his money in Edinburgh, being penniless when he'd always had plenty of money to spend. Tara stood up abruptly. She was annoyed with herself, wanting to shake off the uncomfortable feeling that she hadn't seen the last of him.

RICCO FINALLY SHOWED UP in the afternoon. It didn't take Tara long to see that he wasn't in his usual jubilant mood. In fact, he appeared rather distraught. He wouldn't sit down for a cup of coffee and wouldn't sample Ashta's freshly made lemon tarts. Tara was to drop everything and come for a walk, he instructed. Intrigued, she agreed.

"I did not come to visit you yesterday," he stated once they were seated on the red rocks overlooking the ocean.

"No, I noticed," Tara replied, wishing he would hurry up with what was on his mind, but knowing it was wiser not to push him.

"I wanted to!" He turned on her intensely. "But I couldn't! I couldn't. I couldn't bring myself to come, but today I couldn't *not* come. Do you understand?"

"I'm sure I will," she said, looking at him with an encouraging smile.

"I have a confession to make," he went on with great solemnity. "A dreadful confession. You may not like me afterward."

Tara's eyebrows rose a little. "Is it that bad?"

"You will think so when you hear."

She sat waiting, her attention fully caught, and after a minute Ricco blurted, "Emilio paid me to... to... make overtures to you. To make Dom Valente think we... we...." He twined two fingers together and held them up for her to see. "Were like this." Every line of his body was rigid while he waited for her reaction.

He couldn't have unleashed a more effective bomb. "He *what*?" Tara cried, her voice rising to a disbelieving squeak.

"He paid me a lot of money." Ricco shook his head sorrowfully. "I'm so ashamed! This is a... a—"

"An ignominious situation?" Tara supplied wrathfully. "Oh, Ricco, how could you!"

He hung his head. "I took the money only because I wasn't doing anything I didn't want to do in the first place, don't you see? And you gave me to understand that Dom Valente meant nothing to you, nor you to him. So I thought, what harm would it do? As I saw it I was getting a lot of money without really having to work for it. It seemed silly to me, but I needed the money, Tara!''

"That rotten so-and-so!" she exclaimed through her teeth.

"Who? Me?"

"Emilio! That was a dirty, rotten, filthy thing for him to do! That sneaky devil! I was right; he doesn't care for me at all! It was his way of getting me out of the way, I suppose. Wouldn't I just love to say a few things to him!" She sprang to her feet.

"No!" Ricco gasped, clambering to his feet beside her. He clutched at her hands. "No, you must not say anything to him! He swore me to secrecy, and already I've broken my vow. But I—I just couldn't talk and laugh with you and—and.... And then after what Dom Valente said to me!"

"What did he say to you?"

"Don't you know? He said you did. About finding a tutor and a school, and how you were concerned for me. And several other, er, more personal matters. It was after lunch, after you had gone to bed. The way he talked about you made me realize—what a fool I was—that he must have an affection for you! Oh, Tara, I was so ashamed of myself and what I'd done I could scarcely look him in the eye!"

Tara's brow was puckered in concentration. "Why did Emilio kick you under the table at lunch that day? And then call you out to the phone?"

"Oh, that. He said our agreement had come to an end and that I need no longer try to seduce you."

"He did, did he?"

"And that I could keep the money anyway. I did offer to return it. It has given me no pleasure, Tara," he added mournfully.

"Oh, Ricco! I can believe you didn't mean to do any harm, and that you didn't think you were. But Emilio knew exactly what he was doing! And just when I was beginning to like him!" she sighed.

"What are you going to do?" Ricco asked her cautiously.

"Do? About what?" Tara smiled a little grimly.

He stood quietly for a long moment while Tara stared at the running waves. He glanced sideways at her several times.

"Could we—do you think it's possible that...we can remain friends?" he asked humbly, not looking at her.

"Yes. And thanks, Ricco."

"For what?"

"For telling me. For making a clean breast of things. Gosh. You know, sometimes I think you're even more naive than I am!" With a laugh at his suddenly indignant expression she skipped down the rock and started back for the villa, calling over her shoulder, "How about a lemon tart?"

The table on the terrace had been laid with a white damask cloth. A big bowl of large red and yellow roses glowed in the center, and four beeswax candles flanked them. Paper-thin china with the Valente crest was accompanied by shining silverware and tall fluted wineglasses. Tara sighed and smiled at the same time. Emilio did know how to set a table.

She went to dress for dinner, or more precisely, to help the *contessa* dress for dinner. For the first time she did mind that her clothes hadn't yet arrived. It would have been nice to put on one of her more attractive outfits, to have eye shadow and lipstick and perfume.

It took a long time before the *contessa* was arrayed to her own satisfaction. She was going to sign the deed for the *quinta* over to Dom Valente tonight, she pointed out, and she had to be properly turned out for such an occasion.

When at the end of the intensive session Jorge still hadn't arrived home, Tara began to worry just a little. She pushed her anxiety aside as pure nerves. Why should anything go wrong? It was just that she'd been so happy and excited over his return that she expected a flaw.

Finally Tara went downstairs, letting the *contessa* make her final decision about which rings to wear by herself. Tara was ready for a soothing glass of sherry and a chance to sit down. In the hall she stopped before the large gilt mirror and arranged the black lace mantilla that the *contessa* had loaned her for the evening. It was very lovely, and draped around her shoulders it made her peasant clothes look like fashionable evening wear. She could be starting a new trend, she thought, dimpling. Plucking two small red roses from the bowl on the table, she twisted them into her hair.

She heard the helicopter then: the soft whirr of its

engine as it approached in; the louder roar as it circled and landed. Her mouth went dry; her throat tightened with anticipation. She stood quite still until the massive oak door swung open and Jorge appeared. Then she started running toward him.

But the expression on his face held an icy blast of scorn, and it stopped her in her tracks halfway down the hall. Her face was all eyes as she stared at him in utter consternation. His gaze stabbed through her, cutting her to pieces before he had said a word. And then he lost his carefully controlled temper.

"Damn you! How could you do this? Cheating, lying.... There aren't words to fit you! And what a damn blind fool I've been not to see you were playing us off one against the other! What were you saving me for? A consolation prize? In case Moreston didn't get what he wanted? I could—" He stopped, shaking with rage. Then he swung on his heel and disappeared into the courtyard, banging the huge door violently behind him with such force that the noise reverberated throughout the villa.

The next second he was calling for Emilio. The butler came out of the kitchen at a run, and with a startled glance at Tara, rushed after his master.

She stood where she was, staring blindly at the door, stunned out of all feeling. It seemed that even her heart had stopped beating. Her trembling hands reached for a little side table to hold her up, to give her some support in a world that was tilting crazily at an angle. Dizzy and sick, she turned unknowingly to face another of the mirrors and saw herself in it: her eyes like great black pools; the bitter irony of the two rosebuds in her hair. Slowly she reached up to pull them out, crushing them in her palms without realizing what she was doing.

From outside she heard the helicopter start up. It set her feet in motion. "Wait! Jorge, wait for me!" she cried, running down the hall.

The roar increased; he couldn't possibly hear her! Louder and louder the engine drummed, and then faded away into the distance. When she could hear it no more a shudder ripped through her slender frame. She was still standing on the same spot when Emilio came in.

"Will you be having dinner now, *senhorinha*?"

"What?" Her voice was no more than a whisper. "Oh, no! No!"

"You won't be having anything to eat, *senhorinha*?" he repeated.

How could he sound as though nothing had happened? For whatever reason Jorge now despised her. Emilio must know why and must himself dislike her more than ever. What could she have done?

"No, thank you. I couldn't possibly." She turned slowly away from the glum-faced butler. In a daze she walked toward the *sala*. The mantilla slipped off her shoulders, falling in a ripple of lace on the floor. She didn't notice. The door closed behind her and she leaned against it, for her legs had turned to water.

The *sala* was dark. There was only one lamp on; that and the small fire in the grate barely lighted the room. She was glad of the shadows, which echoed the gloomy feeling inside her. She wanted to stay in the soft gentle darkness forever and hide away.

A thorn from the roses pricked her palm, and she opened her hand to look down at the crushed petals. As their sweet essence wafted to her nostrils she took no delight in it, but dropped the petals into the fire and watched as they curled and burned.

What had Jorge said to her? The words seemed remote, as though he'd said them in another time and place. Gradually they came back. "Lying and cheating. . . ." When, where, how? Why?

Her mind leaped to Dennis. Dennis had conjured up some new evil. Or perhaps Emilio. . . ?

"Oh, there you are, dear! Why are you sitting in the dark? Hasn't Dom Valente arrived yet? Why, I thought I heard his helicopter!" Ernesta, resplendent in pink and mauve, tapped on her shoulder with a mother-of-pearl fan.

"He's come and gone," Tara answered in dull lifeless tones. "Something went wrong in Lisbon, and no, I don't know what. I. . .guess our celebration is. . .is off."

"Oh, what a shame! I was so looking forward to a party! Aren't you coming to dinner? Emilio tells me it is ready to be served."

"No. I couldn't possibly eat now." The thought of food made her cringe.

"Oh, dear, oh, dear! He has upset you, hasn't he? Take my advice, Tara, and don't worry. Men have their moods. Why, I remember my late husband Antonio—"

"Tell me about it in the morning, *contessa*." Tara managed a faint smile. "I'm sure your dinner must be getting cold."

"Oh, of course! I had forgotten about dinner. Thank you, dear."

Tara lay back in her chair and closed her eyes. The *sala* was dark and peaceful once more. A tear forced its way out from under her tightly closed lids and was joined by another and another. At the moment it was impossible for her to think clearly, but she knew Dennis was mixed up in this somehow. Only she couldn't fathom what he had done to turn Jorge against her. How could Valente believe Dennis and not her? How could he! His opinion of her must be dreadfully low, his affection for her little and his trust in her nonexistent if he took to heart some wicked insinuation Dennis had made. And what else could Dennis have done but insinuate? Why hadn't Jorge asked her instead of accusing her?

CHAPTER TWELVE

THE NEXT MORNING Tara couldn't bear to face Emilio or the three peasant women when they arrived punctually for work. Ashta, who tried to coax her into eating breakfast, took messages down to them. The women were to finish their work in the den and the dining room but were to leave the rococo chairs alone, since the needlepoint covers had to be professionally cleaned and mended. Outwardly Tara was functioning almost normally, but inwardly she wasn't functioning at all.

She'd slept fitfully the night before. The morning sun was filtering through the filigree woodwork that separated her from the courtyard, and its warm rays mocked her cruelly. She paced nervously around her room, trying to formulate plans that kept dissolving before she got through the initial stages. One thing was obvious: she would have to leave Minha Casa before Jorge returned. There didn't seem any point in staying. Not now. If he wanted to ask questions later he could find her, but she wasn't going to stay to be insulted again. Somehow or other, without clothes, shoes, money or identification, she had to get to Sagres. . . .

Where would she go? Where *could* she go? Before

when she had contemplated her departure she had
considered Albufeira as good a spot as any. It wasn't
as touristy as Sagres was. What she remembered of
the steep, narrow little streets, the whitewashed
houses, the churches with their Moorish cupolas and
the wide sandy beach broken by jagged cliffs was all
very attractive and very Portuguese. Albufeira was
flavored with the mystery of the Orient, with a dash
of North Africa thrown in.

She'd thought to stay with the *contessa* while she
looked for lodgings of her own, for Ernesta had said
she would be glad of her company. But now Albufeira itself was out of the question. A bare sixty miles
separated the town from the *quinta*. It was much too
close for any peace of mind should Jorge *not* come
asking questions. She would have to go farther away,
to make it an effort for him to come to her. Faro,
perhaps, with its mud flats and marshes and huge
eucalyptus forests. Or past Faro to Olhão, where
dazzling white houses had narrow stairways climbing
steeply to flat terraced roofs. It was called the cubist
city, the hangout of artists.... But it had become a
main fish-canning center, and factories had sprung
up around the outskirts. No, Olhão was still too
close.

Aljezur, Alfambras, Vilo do Bispa. Silves, former-
ly called Xelb by the Arabs, with its Moorish castle
that dominated the town.... No, it, too, was too
close. And the same with Lagos, Praia da Rocha and
even Loulé, with its roughcast white houses topped
by typical Algarve chimneys pierced with filigree, its
terraces smothered in camellias and its thick forest,

where she had walked so blissfully two years earlier. Perhaps it would be better to get right out of Portugal altogether. Go to Spain....

Spain! She couldn't even get to Sagres, since she didn't have even one *escudo* to her name.

By lunchtime Tara was downstairs talking on the telephone to a bank manager in Sagres. When she explained that she wanted to wire to Hampstead, England, for money, he sounded suspicious and would promise her nothing until she came into the bank personally to see him. She was about to dial a taxi company to ask them if they would give her credit when she heard Ashta's voice outside the *sala* door. She was obviously arguing with someone.

With the receiver in one hand Tara turned as the peasant woman came stomping in. Behind her was Dennis Moreston, looking as much like a cat full of cream as was humanly possible. Tara dropped the receiver and it hit the floor with a crash.

"No much good he come!" Ashta stormed. "Emilio, I no find!" She turned on Dennis, shaking her knotted fist in his face. "You take *senhorinha* it go bad! Much bad! You see!" She left the room reluctantly after casting a worried look at Tara's pale composed face.

The young woman just stood silently, watching the new arrival. She didn't really feel all that surprised; she had almost expected to see him again. She noticed he was wearing a rather flashy new suit, a white gabardine with a tan shirt and tie. His brown eyes were watching her while a smile played around his lips.

"Good afternoon, darling," he said smoothly, as though they'd parted the best of friends. "I thought I'd drop by, seeing as the master of the house isn't in."

"What do you want?" she asked coldly.

"Why, your hand in marriage, my sweet. What else? I'm addicted to your charms!"

She permitted herself a thin smile. "I thought I made it clear I have no interest in you."

The air in the room became suddenly still. Tara felt it was the calm before the storm.

"Now, now, darling, don't ruffle your feathers. After all, you didn't get hurt on our overnight jaunt, did you?" His eyebrows shot upward and he spread his hands. "Surely you can forgive a harmless kiss in a garden! And I don't blame you for refusing to marry me when I was after your inheritance. But this time, believe me, that's not the case. Not now!" Triumph edged his hard voice. "My marvelous opportunity panned out without your money! I'm a rich man now, Tara, and you'd be a lucky girl to marry me!"

"You really are amazing," she answered in a light calm voice. "You ought to be put in a museum as a specimen of persistence! The sign on the plate glass could read: Here Sits the Man with the World's Thickest Skull!"

"Tut, tut! But, darling, I *am* glad you've kept your sense of humor. I like that!" He smiled placatingly, "I know we're a good match, darling, so don't play hard to get. You'll make a charming wife! You're pretty enough for any man, and although I don't like to admit it you even have some brains! And if you insist, I'll let you write your silly—your books. You know, I think you'll be good for me! Yes, indeed! Your terrible honesty and respectability might make a decent man of me yet! Being that close, some of it would have to rub off...." He chuckled, his eyes openly appreciating her feminine curves.

"You should go to a doctor to get your ears cleaned."

"But you don't understand, darling! I'm not after your two hundred and fifty thousand pounds! I'm wealthy! Fabulously so!"

"I wouldn't marry you if you were plated in gold," she exclaimed.

"I see I have to cross the t's and dot the i's. So just once more, I'll tell you about my business affairs. The first time I came to this godforsaken place I had a little chat with the *contessa*, and she obligingly told me about all this land being for sale. It's a steal at any price. Oceanfront property! With resorts and hotels popping up everywhere, this land, developed, would be like having a license to print money! Well, as you can imagine I went immediately to Lisbon to contact her son-in-law, Mario Resende. I offered him more than Valente was willing to pay—not much more, but enough to swing Resende in my favor. That's where you came in. I needed a down payment, and just a slice of your inheritance would have taken care of that nicely. But that plan misfired, unfortunately, so I went back to Resende and agreed to get a carte blanche for him at every one of the hotels built on this land. As you can see that's a sizable bribe, and he's a man who likes his luxuries. A carte blanche would save him a fortune in entertaining and whatnot. He accepted without much persuasion and waived the necessity of a down payment as a return favor. I've already contacted some of the larger contractors—''

"Wait a minute!" Tara interrupted, her face ashen although her tone was still steady. "Isn't there a clause that forces Resende to sell the *quinta* back to the original owners? He can't sell to you!"

"Nonsense! The clause is out-of-date—not much more than a gentleman's agreement, really. That's easily overcome!" Dennis enthusiastically replied. "Mario just sells to me, and then it's up to Valente to drag this thing through the courts. In the meantime I quickly parcel off the land and sell to the highest bidders. The money goes in my pocket, Resende gets paid and poor Valente, who doesn't really have much of a legal leg to stand on, gets stuck holding the bill for trying to get an injunction. Slick, eh? So you see, darling—and I can't make it any plainer—this entire estate is mine, lock, stock and barrel! All I need is the *contessa*'s sweet little signature on the deed—and she'll do whatever Mario tells her!" He spread his hands again and smiled. "It was child's play, and I must say I enjoyed every minute of it!"

It was now quite clear what Jorge had been talking about. The meeting between him and Resende must have been terrible. Perhaps Dennis had even been in the office with them. But how could Jorge think she had helped her ex-fiancé to get the property? How could he think such a horrible thing of her? A fierce pain burned in her chest; a mist momentarily blinded her eyes. She blinked rapidly. Now was not the time to go to pieces. She had to keep her head. Ernesta still hadn't signed the deed.

"That's very unscrupulous business, Dennis," she said smoothly, gritting her teeth to control herself, to push down the searing mixture of anger and pain.

"Most business is, my sweet," he said, grinning.

"I don't suppose you've thought for one moment about the peasants? What's going to happen to them?"

"They'll be evicted." He shrugged his shoulders. "Heavens! Who cares about a few peasants? They'll be better off in the city anyway."

She walked over to him and put her hands firmly on her hips. "I'll do whatever I can to stop you!" she hissed in dead earnest. Dennis took an involuntary step backward. "Ernesta still has to sign that deed, and if I can manage it she won't! Not to you! Now get out! Get out!"

Dennis just stood there, an expression of belligerent amazement on his face. It was obvious he had never considered that she might try to ruin his scheme.

Tara went to the *sala* door and opened it. "Emilio!" she called. The butler materialized as if by magic. "Show this man out!"

"Immediately, *senhorinha*!" Emilio's tone was, as usual, most polite, but there was a wicked gleam of pleasure in his eye. He walked calmly over to Dennis. "This way, Mr. Moreston."

Dennis came to life. "If you think you can make

me leave before I'm good and ready you're wrong. I could stomp you into the ground!'' Dennis leaned over the smaller man, red in the face. Rage made the vein in his temple throb.

In a flash Emilio grasped one of Dennis's arms and twisted it behind his back. It all happened so quickly that Tara gasped, sagging against the table in surprise.

''Ready now, Mr. Moreston?'' the butler asked in his even tones. He propelled a shouting Dennis firmly toward the door and out to his car. Tara shuddered at the sight of the familiar vehicle. If she ever had to rent a car it would *not* be red!

''Thank you, Emilio!'' she said distantly when he returned.

''Not at all, *senhorinha*.'' The butler gave her a short bow and disappeared into the library. Moments later she heard the steady tapping of typewriter keys.

Now...Ernesta! Tara headed up the stairs. She knew the *contessa* was having her siesta in her bedroom instead of on the terrace. Somehow she had to convince the frivolous woman that Resende was not the charming man she thought he was, and that the fate of the peasants—which was her responsibility— had to be taken seriously. They could not be thrown out of their homes after so many long years of loyal labor! And Jorge would not be done out of his rightful property!

''Ernesta...Ernesta, wake up!'' she said urgently. ''I have something very important we must talk about. No, it can't wait!'' Gently but firmly she woke the *contessa* from her afternoon siesta.

"Oh, dear me, what is it?" The old woman blinked sleepily, looking irritable. "I have no head for serious matters. Mario handles all my serious matters."

"That's part of the problem! It's time you took an interest in your affairs! Have you had a look at the *quinta* in recent years? Have you seen the condition the peasants live in? They're poor, terribly poor! Many of them don't even have enough food! Think of their children, growing up without the proper nutrition. Think of—"

"Nonsense, my dear. Mario sees that they are cared for!"

"Mario hasn't seen to anything, Ernesta! I realize you don't believe me. Well, there's just one thing to do, in that case!" She bundled the protesting woman out of her bed and down the stairs, calling again for Emilio.

"Would you take us for a drive?" she asked him. "The *contessa* wishes to visit her peasants!"

"But of course, *senhorinha*. We will take the jeep."

"Oh, please! Not the jeep!" Ernesta wailed.

"It will have to be the jeep, because the roads have been neglected for so long that many of them are unpassable with anything else!" Tara stated matter-of-factly. The *contessa*'s visit was long overdue.

The miserable journey started. They were only a few yards from Minha Casa when Ernesta developed a migraine. By the time they reached the orange and almond orchards she professed to having a strained back. Tara turned a deaf ear and adjusted the *contessa*'s big straw hat on her head.

They took the south bend in the road when they reached the vineyards, then followed the fields of vines until they ended about five hundred yards from the sea. There tall sheer cliffs etched with brine and sea foam were hollowed out to hold a handful of small stucco cottages roofed in terra-cotta tiles. But the whitewash that Algarvians loved so well was faded and chipped into gray, and many of the clay tiles were broken, so that the roofs were patched with pieces of board. Flowers and trees were in abundance, providing the only happy note in the tiny fishing village. Wild geraniums blossomed from small inner courtyards. Mimosa and prickly pear and spiky Indian figs clustered around the houses, digging their hardy roots almost straight into the rock. Oleander and rose laurel, juniper bushes and yellow and white asphodels grew in wild profusion along the winding rocky path, spreading out on either side and carpeting the land with color.

Tara took a firm grip on the *contessa*'s elbow and steered the complaining woman ahead of her. Lean hungry dogs bayed at their arrival. Tanned children with big black eyes stopped their play in the dust to stare in mute wonder. The penetrating odor of salt brine and dried cod, herring, spindrift and tar from scaly nets assailed their nostrils. Down by the water's edge lay a tumbled heap of boats, or rather skeletal boats, for their bottoms were rotted away and the usable planking had long since been pried loose. More boats, ones still in fishing order, lay overturned on the sand, their hulls bleached and bare of paint. Great black streaks marked the places where they'd been repaired with scavenged boards and tar. A team of oxen, used to tow the boats in on their return from the sea, was tethered nearby. Tara pointed out their ribs, showing through as bumpy ridges on the rough brown hides. Other children looked up from their chore of mending nets—nets that seemed to be more holes than anything. Eyes appeared at cottage windows, but at first no one approached or spoke to them. The only other animal in sight, besides the oxen and the dogs, was an ancient scruffy donkey that was pushing with obvious weariness against the waterwheel on the village well. The other three harnesses on the wheel were empty. An elderly woman with a deeply lined face and bowed shoulders walked behind the one remaining donkey, prodding the poor animal on with a stick.

The village should have been teeming with life. There should have been donkeys and goats and milk cows, chickens and geese, several more teams of oxen.... Tara grasped the *contessa* by the shoulder and pointed this out to her.

And where was the bright paint on the boats, she queried. They had arrived in time to watch a ketch coming in from the sea. Something seemed to be wrong as the fishermen jumped out of the boat to pull it up on the sand. One of the men was dispatched to fetch the oxen. After several minutes it became apparent that the ketch needed extensive repairs, for a gaping hole showed in the hull as the oxen strained to pull it farther up the sand, out of the crashing waves.

Tara pointed out the absence of drying and cleaning sheds; a bleached jungle of decaying logs showed where they had stood once. Some of the logs had been moved to form a rough platform. Spread on this was a meager day's catch.

They talked mostly to the children. The *contessa* seemed reluctant to say much to the adults, but at Tara's insistence she stepped into one of the cottages, which lacked some of the bare necessities. The peasants' state could not have been plainer. When they were once more in the jeep Ernesta seemed a little more subdued and less inclined to protest.

After that they went to the farm and visited the peasants who worked in fields, as well as those responsible for the orchards, vineyards and vegetable gardens. This village was larger than the one they'd just visited and was situated in a small picturesque valley in the middle of the undulating *charnecas*. Great swaths in the hills were bare, showing dark patches of sunburned vegetation among the rippling waves of green gold grain. Emilio explained to the *contessa* that new piping was needed to replace eighty percent of the irrigation system; that explained the burned patches. The market gardens had failed entirely this year, he added, since the piping was worn beyond repair and the generator was completely broken down. He himself had checked it.

After that there was still the more dismal sight of the cattle, bull and dairy farms. There was really nothing left of them, and the *campinos*, the cattlemen, were perhaps the worst off of the lot. Maria Duarte and her family were in that group.

The last straw, the one that broke the *contessa*'s resistance, was a child with a dreadful skin rash. She was a beautiful little girl, and the large disfiguring sores were painful to look at. The mother hesitantly told Ernesta there was no money for a doctor, but that she had been trying to soothe the rash with a mixture of steeped herbs.

"Now do you understand what I mean?" Tara asked as she led Ernesta back to the jeep. "Home, please, Emilio. We'll try to finish this there," she added wearily.

"So you see," Tara continued when they were once more seated on the terrace with glasses of iced tea, "Mario isn't at all kind and thoughtful! These people are without hope! What will it be like when Dennis gets possession of the land and they're evicted? They've worked faithfully all these years for *you*. Are they to get nothing in return but gross unkindness? Mario wants to sell the estate to Dennis regardless of the clause, and you know what manner of man Dennis is. He'll stop at nothing for money! He bribed Mario—yes he did!" Tara affirmed when the *contessa* shook her head in disbelief. "He told me so himself." She explained what the bribe was and how Dennis and Mario planned to get around the clause that stated the land had to be sold to a Valente. That seemed to sway Ernesta slightly. Tara pushed on and on. She was close to her wit's end when the *contessa* finally wavered.

"Yes, yes, you may be right. I would never have believed it if I had not seen the evidence with my own eyes." As she talked she convinced herself. "Mario needs a stern reprimand! I shall not have anyone in *my* family accepting bribes and flaunting the law! And he is acting on my behalf! The disgrace! The estate will go to Dom Valente without question, and at the price we agreed on. It is a very fair price when one considers the dreadful condition the *quinta* is in—very fair! And it belongs to him, after all.''

Tara let out a long sigh of relief. ''Why don't you telephone Mario and tell him your decision?'' she suggested. She wanted it done while Ernesta was still feeling brave. Her fervor might die down, and Mario was probably a very smooth talker.

The call was put through, but with disappointing results. Mr. Resende was out of town, his secretary said, and she couldn't say where he had gone. All she knew was that he had left in a rather big hurry shortly after lunch.

Ernesta looked faintly relieved, but Tara felt frustrated. To have got so far and to be thwarted!

She thought hard for a few minutes. Mario had the deed. Ernesta, who had to sign it, was at Minha Casa, and Dennis had left here shortly after lunch. Mario, too, had left his office shortly after lunch.... It tallied, of course. No doubt Dennis had immediately called Resende and told him what had happened. Resende's big hurry was probably in this direction!

So what on earth was Jorge doing, Tara wondered. Why wasn't he here making sure things went as they should? And how long would it be before Mario arrived at Minha Casa? Today? Tomorrow? Jorge might be back by then, and Tara wanted to be gone.

She couldn't bear to see him again. His latest insult was his last one. He could go to hell, she thought, but there were tears in her eyes as she did so.

"Ernesta?" Tara hesitated. "You won't change your mind?"

"Certainly not!"

"Good. Because I have to leave. In fact, I'm going tonight, and—"

"Leave? But you must not leave! I am ashamed to admit it, but I am rather...rather afraid of Mario. He will be coming here to get my signature, and when I tell him my decision he will be angry with me. I cannot face him alone!"

"But Ernesta—"

"You must stay!" the *contessa* stated. Tara sensed that she was really frightened. "I have never disagreed with him before, and he will not like it. He will force me to sign if you are not here with me—I know he will! He has done it before— Oh, just talked and talked until I did not know what was up or down, and signed just to be finished with him!"

There was no other way out, Tara realized with a sinking heart. "I'll stay until he comes." Jorge had better stay wherever he was for that length of time, too, or they would have one final crashing argument to end all arguments....

"Oh, thank you, dear. I knew I could depend on you!"

Tara's answer was a bleak smile.

They were having dinner that evening on the terrace when Mario arrived. Tara looked up to see a large florid man standing over them, a hearty smile superimposed on his face. He could have come from Hollywood.

"Mother! How wonderful to see you looking so well!" He had kissed Ernesta before she fully realized he was there.

"Why, Mario! What a pleasant surprise! We have been calling you in Lisbon. Oh, do sit down." The *contessa* graciously made the introductions.

Mario's knowing eyes traveled appreciatively over Tara's slender shape, and she tucked her long, sun-gold legs farther under the table.

"Pleased to meet you, Miss Lownes. I've heard so much about you." His voice was as smooth as oil. "It's very kind of you to have Ernesta here for a visit. You love visiting, don't you, mother, dear?"

The air was charged with tension. Obviously Mario already knew that Ernesta wasn't going to be as pliant as he usually found her. He rambled on, talking as though he hadn't a care in the world and had come all the way from Lisbon to see that his mother-in-law was as happy as he wished her to be. But his eyes were crafty, Tara noted. She felt herself being sized up as a possible enemy. Now she fully understood Ernesta's fear of him. He was, if anything, meaner than Dennis; he had had more experience at it. A shiver tickled up her spine, although outwardly she was composed and as carefree as he.

He started innocently enough by drawing a box of costly chocolates out of his briefcase; naturally they were Ernesta's favorite variety. Then came a large bottle of expensive French perfume from Angelica, and after that, while the *contessa* was still in raptures, came a thin stack of official-looking papers.

"Now, mother, dear, I just need your signature on these. There's nothing really important. You don't even have to read them. I've already done that for you."

"Thank you, Mario—" the *contessa* caught Tara's eyes "—but I shall read them myself all the same. What are they about?"

"Just a few details about selling this wretched estate. I've decided to sell it to a Mr. D. Moreston." He glanced at Tara. "I believe you are acquainted with him?"

"We are all acquainted with him here, and not for the better, I might add!" Ernesta suddenly snapped. "I do not like him! He is a nasty, nasty man!"

"But mother, what we like or don't like doesn't come into a business agreement," Mario went on smoothly.

"What *I* like or do not like *does*!" Ernesta insisted staunchly, glancing at Tara for support. "I made a business agreement following the deed's special clause, and I will sell to Dom Jorge Emmanuel Valente de Silves!"

"Yes, mother, I realize that." Resende was keeping his voice friendly with an effort. "But since I'm in charge of all your finances, I found Mr. Moreston's offer to be a better proposition. The clause is really out-of-date."

"It appears to me that you have overstepped yourself," the old woman retorted. "You are not 'in charge' of my business interests. You merely handle them for me. It is *my* wishes that matter here, not yours. I own this *quinta*, not you! I shall ultimately decide what I want to do with it, and I do not want to sell to Mr. Moreston. Furthermore, I *will* not! And the clause is not out-of-date!''

"All right, mother, I'll make sure I see about that. Now if you'll just sign here—"

"I want to read it first."

"There really isn't time, mother!" Obviously Mario was holding his impatience in check.

"Why is there no time? I will take the time!" The *contessa* spoke with all the authority of her imperious background, looking down her nose at Mario. "I do not see why I should be refused. I shall read every word! Perhaps Emilio will provide my magnifying glass."

The butler had been hovering just inside the kitchen, and in seconds Ernesta had her magnifying glass. Then Emilio poured more wine for them all, his face as bland as ever.

"I'm sure you won't understand half the words, mother. Some are quite technical." Resende shot a venomous glance at Tara, and she was glad that she'd stayed to help the *contessa*. Without her presence she was sure Mario wouldn't have been quite so charming. She gave him a sweet innocent smile.

"Tara has a good head for words. She writes books, you know. And we have a dictionary."

"It will take all night!" Mario put his wineglass down with a clink. "Why must you read every line all of a sudden? You trusted me in the past. Why all this suspicion? Have I ever failed you?"

"I think you have, Mario," Ernesta replied calmly, although her hands were trembling. "I am not pleased with the way you have handled my *quinta*. The peasants are dreadfully, tragically poor. The land is barren from neglect. It seems I trusted you too much. And why, dear boy, are you in such a hurry to have my signature? Is there something in these papers that you do not wish me to see?"

"Don't be silly!" Mario snapped, his thick brows gathering in a frown. "Just sign the damn things!"

"You will watch your tongue, young man! Think again before you call me silly! Oh, I am well aware that I have bowed to your wishes in the past. I have done so too often, I see now."

"I'm sorry, mother." Mario smiled with some difficulty. "I've been under a lot of strain these past few days. Of course I didn't mean a word of disrespect. You know how much Angelica and I care for you—"

"It is becoming more and more evident to me! I may be an old woman but I am not blind. Now you will sit there quietly while I read!"

Mario Resende sank back into his chair. While Ernesta began reading the first of the papers he glowered at Tara. She smiled airily in return.

"I'm sure you will find this very tedious, Miss Lownes," he suggested smoothly. "Don't let us keep you. I'm sure you have many more...important things to do."

"Not at all," she answered sweetly. "I don't have a thing to do, and I enjoy business so much! My father brought me up to understand some of the finer points."

"How enlightening." He couldn't have sounded

more insincere. "And what *is* your business here, Miss Lownes?"

Tara recognized his tactics. If he could make her feel foolish or uncertain he'd have won half the battle. "I'm recuperating from an accident at sea— under doctor's orders, of course," she replied smoothly. "It's the air and the sun here that are so very beneficial."

"Very."

"I'm curious, Mr. Resende." It was her turn to attack. "Why do you want to sell to Mr. Moreston? Is it that he can give you a few fringe benefits you wouldn't get from Dom Valente?"

"No, of course not! Why, that's nonsense," he blustered.

"But it must be so. I know Mr. Moreston personally and I know that he can't even afford to give you a down payment. Yet Dom Valente has the entire purchase price, in cash, ready for your—excuse me— for the *contessa*'s disposal."

Ernesta looked up at him curiously. "Yes, an excellent point, Tara. What is your answer, Mario? Why are you so eager to sell to Mr. Moreston? After all, you have nothing to gain either way, do you? The land belongs to me, and therefore the profit from the sale does also. Whether I wish to give the money to you still remains to be seen. And if I remember correctly, I have left much money with you in the past. Where has it gone? Have you invested it for me? Or have you used it for your own personal gain?"

"I won't talk about this in front of strangers!" Mario declared. "You have no right—"

"I have every right!" the old woman snapped regally. "I realize fully now what I never wanted to believe. You have pulled the wool over my eyes long enough. I shall arrange for my business affairs to be handled by a more capable trustworthy person. From now on, Mario, you shall have to support my daughter with your own hands!"

"No! You can't—"

"Be quiet, Mario! I know about Mr. Moreston's bribe and your despicable plan to flaunt the law. I am embarrassed I know you! You shall have to tell Mr. Moreston that your unsavory deal is off!"

"Very well," Mario said, shifting his eyes from one woman to the other. "Have it your way. I'll take these papers after you've signed them, and then I'll explain to Moreston that you've changed your mind."

"I have not changed anything! You are a cunning fox, Mario, hiding the deed to Mr. Moreston in the middle, thinking I would not notice. But it was an amateur ploy!" The *contessa* drew several sheets of paper from the stack, and the rest she placed before Mario. "These papers I shall keep. I need them to transfer the ownership to Dom Valente. My lawyer shall be contacting you in regard to my other affairs. You may go now, Mario. My greetings to Angelica."

"You're not getting rid of me that easily!" Resende cried, knocking over his chair as he stood up. All his charm was gone, and his heavy handsome features were distorted. "You won't throw me out— not after I've worked for you all these years!"

"Worked for *me*?" Ernesta stood up also, her

small frame, clothed in lilac taffeta, insignificant beside Resende's bulk. The fighting spirit in her eye matched his, however. "You have done nothing for me! You have been sponging from my income and that is all! It is time Angelica had an honest husband doing honest work. You ought to be ashamed of yourself!"

"It's all your fault!" Mario turned on Tara. "You interfering—"

"You will leave immediately!" Ernesta ordered, and the blaze in her eyes could have shriveled a bigger man than Resende. "Angelica may visit me whenever she likes. However you will not be welcome in my home. I shall have no further dealings with you. Goodbye, Mr. Resende. I pity my daughter!"

She sat down gracefully, and Tara felt a burst of admiration for the older woman. She could still hold her own when it was necessary!

"Goodbye, Mr. Resende. I won't embarrass you by saying it's been a pleasure." Tara looked him straight in the eye.

"You'll sign the deed before I leave here!" Mario said grimly. "And you'll not be transferring any of your business from me, either. In fact, one of these papers deals precisely with that subject! You'll turn everything over to me!"

"I can see now why you and Dennis get along so well," Tara replied in a cool voice. "Both of you have a penchant for expecting other people to pay your way. But you can't force Ernesta to sign anything."

"Just watch me!" He jumped forward to grab the *contessa*'s arm.

At the same moment Emilio shot out of the kitchen with Ashta hard on his heels, broom in hand. The butler handled the man twice his size with remarkable ease. One karate chop to the shoulder, a kick in the stomach from a well-aimed foot, and Mario Resende was a quivering heap on the terrace floor.

Really, Tara thought, shaking her head, Emilio was priceless!

Moments later Resende was escorted to his car by the butler, Ashta at his back, brandishing her broom handle. The scene was so comic that Tara couldn't resist the laughter bubbling up inside her, largely caused by nervous relief. Ernesta gazed indignantly at her, then smiled herself.

"Oh, goodness! All that hard work has made me hungry!" Tara gasped at last.

"Yes, I daresay it has!" the *contessa* agreed. "I am so glad it is over with! I have been wanting to talk to Mario for years, but never had the courage. Getting things done gives one a marvelous appetite!"

"We must celebrate!" Tara decided. "There's no shortage of reasons, and to top it off Jorge has his *quinta*, whether he's aware of it or not. Emilio, do you think he would mind if we drank a bottle of his champagne?"

"No, *senhorinha*," the butler replied immediately. "He would be delighted to lend it to such a joyous occasion!"

Tara looked at him in surprise. Was Emilio really

softening up? He was seldom so cheerful! She put her theory to the test and gave him a quick smile of thankfulness. He smiled back, although not so widely as she. Nevertheless it was a bona fide attempt. Tara flushed with pleasure. It was too bad, she thought, that just when they had almost become friends she had to leave. There was still that other matter, too....

"Oh, lovely!" the *contessa* interrupted Tara's thoughts. "We'll have a party! Why, I have not felt so young in years!"

It was not long after that four champagne glasses clinked together over the table. The celebrants had already toasted the *quinta*, the peasants, and before that Ernesta herself.

"It's your turn, Emilio," Tara said. It was marvelous how one could cover up one's inner pain, she thought, smiling quite radiantly at the three people before her.

"Then I propose a toast to you, *senhorinha*, for without you we would not be celebrating now."

"Excellently spoken!" Ernesta raised her glass.

"*Senhorinha* much...fun!" Ashta beamed at everyone.

"Oh, no!" Tara protested, laughing at the same time. She shouldn't have had so much champagne, she thought, feeling tears starting up again in her eyes.

"Oh, one more thing, Emilio. You won't let either Dennis or Mario on the property again?"

"No, *senhorinha*. Most certainly not," he answered gravely.

"And Ernesta, I'm sorry it had to turn out this way."

"Nonsense, child. I warned Angelica against him when she first introduced him to me. I have been led down the garden path since, but no more. And Angelica shall always have a home with me if she ever decides to leave that scoundrel. Let us drink another toast! Ashta, where is Ricco? He has not been by all day!"

Over the champagne glasses Tara met the butler's eyes. Emilio looked away.

By the time their impromptu party was over it was much too late for Tara to go into Sagres to make financial arrangements for her departure. The banks had long since closed. There was nothing to do except wait until the next morning.

Tara was on her way up to her room when Emilio stopped her on the stairs.

"*Senhorinha*, if you please, may I discuss a matter of some privacy with you?"

She stared at the butler for several seconds before she agreed with a nod. He led the way into the *sala*, where he closed the door with a precise little click.

"Will you please sit down, *senhorinha*?"

"I don't care to sit down, Emilio."

His eyes slid away from hers and he cleared his throat. Then he began.

"Several days ago, before Mr. Moreston's first visit here, I was approached by him in the Caravela Hotel in Sagres. I had noticed him there the day before, lounging around, but did not pay him any mind. This day, however, he started a...casual conversation with me, and then, after he had my interest, drew me aside to where our conversation could not be overheard. He then proceeded to lay bare his heart—or what I took to be his heart at the time,'' Emilio amended at Tara's raised eyebrows. ''As I was not privy to your exact association with him I believed him to be telling the truth. He appeared most sincere.''

''He's good at that,'' she interjected dryly.

''Yes. He told me of your broken engagement and how much he wished to heal the breach. He said he knew Dom Valente and considered it. . . unfortunate that you were sharing his residence, as he understood Dom Valente to be an attractive man and feared that he would. . . I believe he said 'catch you on the rebound.' He asked me if there was a way to ensure this wouldn't happen while he awaited a new engagement ring to be made for you. I, er, suggested that Ricco would no doubt be happy to divert your mind from Dom Valente.''

''I see.'' Tara eyed Emilio, and something in his uncomfortable expression caused her to ask, ''And that was your sole reason for inveigling Ricco into your scheme?''

''Not. . . quite. I, er, had some other personal reasons for, uh, inveigling Ricco, as you call it. I have since regretted my action. However, at that time I thought it wise to. . . put a stick into the works, as it were.''

''I see! Carry on.''

He cleared his throat again. ''I was also trying to divert Dom Valente's mind from you.''

"Oh? Is this a customary practice for you to indulge in? Interfering with Jorge's relationships?"

"No, no, *senhorinha*! Never before have I done such a thing! Only this time it appeared he was serious—in so short a time—and...and...."

"You didn't consider me appropriate for your master, is that it?"

"Well, *senhorinha*, you did not seem to be an ideal match. I have since had time to understand you better and I realize now—I realized several days ago—that I had misconstrued your...your joie de vivre for flightiness, for a certain...empty-headedness—"

"Indeed!" Tara interrupted.

"Much to my present chagrin, yes. I have never misjudged a person more completely than I misjudged you. After what you have done here—" he waved his hand to indicate the state of the house "—after what you did to help Senhora Duarte, after what you did today for the *contessa* and for Dom Valente.... Suffice it to say I stand most thoroughly reproved. I did what I did to be of assistance to Dom Valente—through no meanness, I assure you. However, that alone will not vindicate me." Emilio contemplated his hands. "I would also like to say at this time that despite my...disapproval I have nevertheless come to find you most agreeable, even apart from your accomplishments."

"Well, well!" Tara exclaimed, half laughing at the glum-faced butler. "Am I right in thinking you no longer...disapprove of me?"

"Yes, *senhorinha*. Dom Valente would do well to make you his mate."

She looked up in surprise at his choice of words, then quickly recovered herself. "Thank you, I'm sure. Perhaps we'll say no more of this," she added quietly. "The whole thing is resolved after all." She was surprised to see Emilio shaking his head morosely. "No?"

"I'm afraid, *senhorinha*, Dom Valente will no longer desire me in his employ once he hears what I have done. I mean no disrespect, you understand, but he does have a temper to match his size."

"I've noticed that. But you can be sure I won't mention it."

"It is an unpleasant task I shall have to undertake myself. Besides the temper he is...undeniably touchy where you are concerned."

Tara chewed her bottom lip. "Well, Emilio, I doubt that he'll fire you, but if the worse comes to the worst you can always come and work for me."

It was the very first time she had ever seen him look surprised. "I'm not exactly penniless and I daresay I could keep you busy. And then, you're so efficient," she explained, spreading her hands wide. "You can even type, and that's one thing I've never been good at."

"You don't think that you shall make this your home? Excuse me, *senhorinha*. I did not mean to pry."

"No, Emilio, I don't think this will be my home." The heaviness around her heart suddenly seemed to be crushing her.

His low eloquent bow was answer enough to her offer. Tara climbed the stairs to her bedroom with heavy steps.

The next morning it seemed that telephoning the bank and the cab office was still not going to be easy. Tara wanted to do it in secret so that she could avoid lengthy explanations, but she wasn't left alone for a moment the entire morning.

The *contessa* rose from her bed early with a new gleam of purpose in her eye and set about cleaning out her voluminous handbag. She wanted Tara's opinion on a number of things, and pointed out that since she was setting out on a new phase in her life, she might not need many of the things she carried around with her. Her headache tablets, for example, were thrown into the wastebasket. She was determined not to have any more headaches, and confessed that most of the time she had made them up. An address book followed the tablets, for it had long been out-of-date. A theater ticket from the last time she'd been to Lisbon joined the heap; it was more than a year old.

Santa, Lianna and Rosa wanted to know whether they should use lemon oil or a furniture polish on the dining room's baroque woodwork. The heavy furniture had been pushed to one end of the room when the cleaning began, so they also wanted to consult her about where the rococo buffet, sideboard and china cabinet belonged—a matter of inches one way or another. Finally the women wanted to be told what to do next.

Ashta wanted to know if Tara would prefer *chouriço*, a hot spicy sausage liberally seasoned with red peppers, for lunch, or grilled octopus and mussels with new potatoes. And the two larger kittens were beating up the smallest one; what could be done about that? Tara solved the matter by carrying the kitten around with her until she could think of a permanent solution. Ashta mentioned, too, that no mouse had been seen since the cats' arrival. Then she wanted to know where Tara had found the new parsley patch, for she had looked and looked out there in the garden but hadn't found it anywhere.

But when Emilio asked her whether to move Jorge's private collection of books into the library or into the den she gaped at him. How should she know, she wondered. She hadn't been serving him for years and years as Emilio had! She looked at the butler in consternation; perhaps he wasn't feeling well. Had yesterday been a strain on him, after all? Was he really worried that Jorge would dismiss him? He looked his usual phlegmatic self, however, and just stood there, waiting in a dignified manner for her answer. She finally told him that she supposed the den was the best spot, as it was designed to be a masculine sanctuary and no doubt Jorge would want to use it as such.

It was almost as if there was a conspiracy against her using the phone, Tara thought vexedly, when the *contessa* interrupted her in the *sala* with yet another question. But finally she was talking to the bank manager, trying to explain enough of her situation so that he would take her seriously. After a great deal of cajoling in both English and Portuguese she managed to get an appointment with him. He even gave her his home address in case she arrived during siesta hours. She called the taxi company and had to go through several uninterested dispatchers before she got to speak to the manager, to explain her lack of funds and her need for a taxi. He seemed as reluctant to believe her as the bank manager had. But when she offered her ruby earrings as collateral against the cab fare he relented and said a cab would come for her as soon as they had one free. With that she had to be content. Then she telephoned a small inexpensive hotel in Sagres and made reservations for that evening.

Packing presented no problem. Her personal possessions consisted of a toothbrush, a tube of toothpaste, a comb, a nail file, her three books and the letter from her parents. It all fit neatly into a paper bag. The clothes she wore she would return once she bought more.

She sat down in her bedroom to wait, for the windows looked out on the avenue of evergreen oaks, and she would be able to see anyone coming. She didn't want to go downstairs and pretend everything was fine, either. It took so much energy, covering up and smiling! She'd done it all morning and needed a reprieve.

At lunch on the terrace she chewed and swallowed diligently, although she had no appetite for Ashta's crisply grilled octopus and mussels. She kept sneaking looks at the kitchen door and across the terrace in case Jorge should suddenly appear. She much preferred waiting in the privacy of her bedroom, and disappeared there as soon as she was able to without arousing suspicion.

The brown paper bag was waiting on the bed. She

placed the brass key ring that Emilio had given her on
the vanity where it would be easily spotted, then
combed her hair vigorously for something to do.
Eventually she sat down by the windows again to
wait for the taxi.

CHAPTER THIRTEEN

TARA WAS A BUNDLE OF NERVOUS TENSION and anxiety. Leaving Minha Casa was the hardest thing she'd ever done in her life. Her future looked uncompromisingly bleak and lifeless, for living without Jorge meant living without laughter, meant having nothing to look forward to, meant spending endless empty days with nothing to do but write lighthearted children's stories when she was miserable. Common sense told her that she'd been happy before she met him, so perhaps she could be happy again someday. But for once common sense didn't seem applicable.

He didn't want her; he never had, really. And a few kisses meant nothing in the twentieth century, no matter what Ashta had to say about it. But how could Tara ever love another man after loving him so completely? She would forever be comparing every one she met to him. Spain wasn't even far enough away from him, she thought a little wildly. South America seemed properly remote. In fact, if the moon was habitable she would go there.

She felt as crushed as the roses she'd pulled out of her hair and thrown into the fire. Her heart held a fierce aching burn. She caught her reflection in the vanity mirror and quickly looked away. When she wasn't hiding her feelings the agony in her eyes was there for all to see. One of the first things she would buy would be a pair of sunglasses—dark ones that she could hide behind. What was keeping that taxi?

Tara went up to the turret room for one last look. It seemed unfair that the Atlantic looked even more beautiful today, gently ruffled with whitecaps curling on the waves closest to the shore. She longed to walk along the white gold beach, to sink her toes into the warm soft sand and climb among the cliffs with the seabirds circling overhead.

Resolutely she turned her back on the scene. There was no point in torturing herself further by wishing for what might have been. Jorge had not the slightest bit of trust in her, so how could she expect anything from him? And besides, although he had never talked about the other women in his life there had to be some. Despite what Emilio had said to her last night, for all she knew he could be with some woman now!

Once more in her bedroom, she paced up and down, quite unable to sit still. It had been two-and-a-half hours since she'd called the taxi. Could it have come and gone without her? Emilio might have told the driver there had been some mistake and a cab wasn't needed.... She rushed downstairs, heading for the library. Although she didn't want anyone to know she was leaving until the point of her departure, it couldn't be helped.

"Emilio, has a taxi come?"

"No, *senhorinha*." He looked up from his paperwork. "Are you expecting someone?"

"No. I . . . I'm leaving now."

"Surely not."

"Yes, I am."

"But Dom Valente won't be pleased. There is no reason for you to go now!" He stood up, pushing his paperwork aside. "And where will you go, *senhorinha*? You don't even have shoes!"

"I must go. Don't ask me why. And I'll manage. I've already made reservations in a hotel in Sagres— oh, but you mustn't tell Jorge that! Even if he asks, which I doubt, you must promise me not to tell him!"

"I'll promise nothing of the sort! You're in a strange country with no shoes! Young women here do not travel by themselves; it is frowned upon. Why, I'm certain even in England young women don't travel around barefoot!"

"Damn the shoes! They don't matter!"

"I shouldn't advise you to leave, *senhorinha*. Dom Valente will be very angry."

"He already is! A bit more won't make much difference. Oh, this is all nonsense. Where is that damn taxi!" Her voice wavered suspiciously toward the end. She whirled away from him and sped up the stairs to avoid Ashta and the other women. Spending another nerve-racking forty-five minutes in her bedroom glued to the windows, checking the clock every few minutes, did nothing to restore her peace of mind. Finally Tara went back downstairs to telephone the taxi office, taking her brown paper bag with her.

She shut the *sala* door firmly behind her to try to

prevent interruptions. She was just talking to a frustrated employee when the door behind her opened. She turned around quickly, expecting to see Ashta or Emilio.

It was Jorge who stood in the doorway observing her.

The receiver slipped from her hand. She caught it just before it hit the floor. "Hello?... Hello?... It left half an hour ago, Miss Lownes. It should be there any minute," the disembodied voice insisted.

"Thank you," she replied weakly, hanging up the phone.

She turned slowly to face him, looking at a point just below his chin. Distractedly she noticed his suit jacket was missing and that his vest was crumpled. The sleeves of his viridian silk shirt were rolled up to his elbows, the buttons were undone almost to his waist and a dark stain covered half his shirtfront. She couldn't bear to look at his face, for her first glance had shown her stormy black eyes and frowning brows. Just the sight of him was like a physical blow to a million of her nerve endings. It wasn't at all fair that he should be so virilely handsome, or that he should affect her so profoundly.

A horn blasted outside, jolting Tara from her trance, and without a word she grabbed her paper bag and rushed past him down the hall and through the courtyard.

She had almost reached the taxi when he caught up with her. He grabbed for her arm but caught the bag instead, ripping it open so that her few possessions fell into the dust.

"Now look what you've done!" she cried, on the very edge of hysteria. "It was the only paper bag I could find!"

He just shook his head, as if to say "God help me!" and this time caught her arm.

"You can go!" he said peremptorily to the driver.

"You'll stay right where you are!" she contradicted. "Don't you dare go without me! Let go! Can't you see I'm leaving?"

"You can't go anywhere without shoes!" Jorge said patiently, although his teeth snapped somewhat over the words.

"Why this massive concern over shoes? For goodness' sake, leave shoes out of it!" She snatched up her things, glaring at the dusty toothbrush.

The taxi driver watched curiously. Obviously he wanted to chuckle but didn't know whether it would be wise. One look at Dom Valente's face convinced him not to, and he revved his engine.

Tara darted to the door of the car and Jorge pulled her back again, this time with his long brown hands firmly around her waist. He slammed the door shut and pushed some bills into the cabbie's outstretched hand.

"Go, will you!"

"Stay! Wait for me...." Tara cried, picking up her books again. By this time she was in a fine fury.

"Listen, *senhorinha*," the driver said, leaning out of his window, "I'm taking *his* advice. He's bigger and meaner-looking than you!" He stepped on the gas and bumped down the leafy tunnel of evergreen oaks.

"You *are* mean!" Tara sputtered furiously, blinking through her tears and hugging her books to her breast as though her life depended on them.

He looked at her and gave a long-drawn-out sigh. Then he simply picked her up, as he always seemed to be doing, and carried her through the courtyard, making little of her struggles to escape. Defeated by his unrelenting strength, her rigidly held body softened against him. She turned her face into his shirt, which smelled strongly of gasoline and car grease. Immediately his hold on her became gentle, and he muttered something that sounded very much like a throaty growl. She felt the touch of his eyes on her in an almost physical sense, and yet refused to look at him, burying her head in his shoulder.

"One thing is absolutely certain, sir," Emilio said calmly as he closed the door behind them, "it will never be dull here! We haven't had a dull moment since the day the *senhorinha* arrived!"

Tara blushed into Jorge's shirt, but Valente merely grunted and carried Tara into the *sala*, kicking the door shut behind him. He dumped her unceremoniously onto the couch, and there she exploded.

"Just because my father seems to have taken an unwarranted liking to you does not mean you can order me around! What right do you have to keep me here when I want to go? It took that taxi over three hours to get here and you, you just wave it away! I'll get to Sagres today if I have to walk the entire distance in my bare feet!"

"Don't be a little fool, Tara. You'll stay right here!" He bit the end of a cheroot and then lighted it.

"How would you manage in Sagres? You haven't a penny!"

"I would manage very well, thank you! I'm good at managing, despite what you may think! I milked the damn cow, didn't I?"

He threw the cheroot into the hearth and strode over to her. In one swift movement he had her standing in front of him. He appeared to be holding his volatile temper in check. Tara could see that, but she was too angry to let him speak. And she had to stay angry, for otherwise she would disgrace herself by begging to be kissed and held and damn the consequences!

"And who are you calling a fool?" she continued breathlessly. "I do what *I* please, and that gives you no right to call me anything!" She had to stop for air.

Her eyes were now focused on his chin. He'd forgotten to shave again and and it was rather stubbly. She could control her mind to some extent, but not her wayward traitorous body. It ached for his touch; his very nearness was sending quick hot shivers all over her.

"You great bully!" she went on. "You've been treating me like a child since the first moment you found me, and I think it's insulting! I'm twenty-two and far past the thumbsucking stage! Oh, dammit, just when I had it all arranged. You don't know how long I spent getting that cab to come out here in the first place! And how did you manage to sneak up on me like this? I didn't hear the helicopter!

"Oh, forget the blasted helicopter!" she raced on.

"I'm so mad I could cry. I don't want to stay here, don't you understand? I couldn't bear to stay here after what you said to me! If you think you can call me a liar and a cheat and God knows what else and expect me to take that lying down, then you've got rocks in your head! You just automatically assume I'm guilty of—of whatever it is. Oh, yes, helping Dennis, that was it. Well, I'm not! And you must think *I've* got rocks in my head, too, if you think I'd help Dennis to do anything! How dare you accuse me without even giving me the benefit of the doubt! You pompous—"

"Shut up, Tara!" he interrupted.

"I'm going to clear out, and if you so much as try to stop me you'll regret—"

"Will you let me get a word in edgewise?" he cried. "You little cat, why should I give you the benefit of the doubt when I heard you, with my own ears, talking to Moreston in that hotel room!"

She gaped at him. "What hotel room? When? What are you talking about?"

"Don't give me that! You were in Lisbon that night—"

"I was in Lisbon what night? I haven't been in Lisbon for two years! You've lost your mind, too!"

"Tara! I heard you! There was no mistaking your voice—or your laugh!" he ground out. "I'd recognize your laugh anywhere!"

"When was this?" Tara was doing some fast thinking.

"When!" It was almost a snarl. "The day I went to Lisbon to finalize the sale with Resende. Moreston just happened to be in the office, as well. You can imagine, I'm sure, how that meeting went! Moreston wasn't above dropping a few hints that whoever ended up with the *quinta* would end up getting you as well—and that he had things pretty much wrapped up—''

"And you believed him? Oh, Jorge!''

"Will you please let me finish! I went around to his hotel room that night...and that's when... when.... I was just outside the door, ready to knock, and I heard you as clear as can be, laughing. I'll tell you, I wanted to rip that door down and wring your pretty neck! Instead I stood outside the door like a fool and heard what sounded to me very much like verbal foreplay. Need I make myself any clearer? Neither of you was bothering to keep your voice down! And on top of everything else you had the nerve to tell me you were a virgin!''

"But it wasn't me. It wasn't—''

"You expect me to believe it was merely coincidence that Moreston picked up some girl in Lisbon who just happens to have an English accent and who just happens to have *your* voice and *your* laugh! I may be crazy about you, but that crazy I'm not!''

"But are you absolutely certain? I mean, through a hotel door—''

"Tara! Do you think I enjoy torturing myself? Do you think if there was the least doubt in my mind...?''

Tara's anger vanished. Abruptly she sat back down on the couch, as though she needed something to hold her up. "Good heavens. Penny didn't go back to Edinburgh, after all," she said to herself. "Or else Dennis sent for her. She'd come running, of course.... Gosh, he's a worm, to fool around with her and then come crawling back here, wanting me to marry him!"

"Penny?" Jorge snapped. "Who's Penny? What are you mumbling about?"

"It had to be Penny there with him, don't you see? Don't you remember I took my cousin's place on the cruise? Well, two weeks after I broke off Dennis's and my engagement, he and Penny became engaged. They were supposed to get married on the first of June, but Dennis never showed up at the church. But that's beside the point. She sounds just like me; she always has! When we were kids we used to play tricks on our parents because of that. So it must have been her in there with him! And you thought it was me!" She threw herself back against the couch. "I wish you had broken that door down!" she told him, perfectly sincere.

Jorge's mouth snapped shut. "Are you trying to tell me that you and your cousin sound exactly the same?"

"That's right. On the telephone no one can tell us apart, and I would imagine a hotel-room door would have the same effect."

"You mean you were here all the time?"

"Ask the *contessa*, or Emilio, or Ashta. Ask anyone!"

"I never thought of that." Jorge looked nonplussed, as though he didn't know quite what to say next. "You were really here all the time," he finally muttered, bewildered.

"Yes! And to think he actually came back here asking me to marry him! That man never ceases to amaze me!"

"What did you say?"

"What do you think I said?" Tara sat bolt upright in her vehemence. "Of course I turned him down! And that was when I found out about his plans for the *quinta*!"

"And that's what prompted your jaunt around the estate with the *contessa*? I've already seen her, but she was so excited that I couldn't make much sense out of what she was saying."

"I had to make her understand— Oh, the meeting with Mario last night was quite something. You should have been there. By the way, where were you?"

"Well—" he ran a hand through his hair and sighed "—when I left Lisbon the following day, after not being able to come to an agreement with Resende I, er, decided to stop in here to talk to you, as you know. But when I opened the door and saw you standing there with those roses in your hair. . . . Well, all I wanted to do was wrap my arms around you. So I'm afraid I lost my temper instead. I set out for Albufeira—"

"Albufeira! Why?"

"Because that was where Ernesta told me she was going. To get her diamond tiara, of all things! Of course, when I got there her villa was shut down tighter than a clam, and I had to phone all over the place trying to locate her. Talk about a wild-goose chase! On my way back here the copter decided to act up and I had to land in Portinão. Moreston must have damaged the fuel control when he tampered with it. There I tried to rent a car, but with the festival in Loulé.... Well, I did finally manage to get a ramshackle thing that ran like a bucket on wheels. Not only did I have two flat tires, but the muffler fell off and the police stopped me because of the racket." He dropped his hands in disgust.

"Oh, Jorge!"

"I said the same thing a few times! I could have been home yesterday—even the day before had I been using my head—but I'm afraid I was rather distracted by visions of...lovemaking behind a hotel-room door!" He stood staring at her as if he would commit every line of her face, every curve of her body forever into his memory. "So here I am at last. And I find everything's been done for me! The *contessa* has the deed ready to hand over. Moreston and Resende have both been booted off the place.... I don't mind telling you I feel a bit redundant!"

His disconcerted expression caused a smile to tremble on Tara's mouth. "It happens to the best of us occasionally," she said mildly. Her deepening smile was outrageously provocative.

"Tara, darling, I'm sorry. You...you won't go, will you? If I ask you very nicely will you promise you'll stay?"

"Well...."

"Please?"

"Well, I suppose I could stay, at least until my clothes come. There's quite a lot yet to be done here...."

Jorge was shaking his head. "I've got something to show you. Come with me."

"Where to?" Hesitantly she stood up. He was holding out his hand.

"Just come."

"What have you got to show me?" she asked curiously, putting her hand in his.

"You'll see."

With her interest thoroughly aroused she went without a murmur out of the *sala*, down the hall and through the kitchen. There Jorge opened the stout cellar door, and picking up a coal oil lamp, began to head down the stairs, still holding firmly on to her hand.

"Jorge," her voice wavered, "this isn't going to be one of your jokes, is it? It's creepy down here!"

"Yes, but I'm with you. And the cats have scared all the mice away, so there's no need to worry." Unperturbed, he continued down the many stairs that wound away into darkness.

"There are cobwebs and all sorts of nasty—"

"Just a little farther."

At last they were standing together on the cold stone floor. Tara inched closer to his protective warmth, and he let go of her hand to slide his arm around her waist. "Look over there—" he held the lamp high "—in the corner."

The weak glow of light revealed a rectangular object. It was a shiny, bright blue metal steamer trunk with crisscrossed brass bindings and leather handles at either end. Tara stared at it, and then up at the face above hers.

"But—but...."

"That's your trunk, and it's been down here for over a week and a half now. Tara, sweetheart, I was determined to keep you here one way or the other. Do you begin to understand? I'm in love with you. I'm so in love with you that I was going to keep you here until you fell in love with me, too. I, er, was very optimistic and refused to believe you wouldn't! And I thought things were going well, too, despite Ricco and Moreston. Then I found out that Emilio put Ricco up to it—"

"You're in love with me?"

"Dear God, yes! Didn't you know? Why do you think I brought you here? Emilio even had the audacity to say I was behaving like a lovesick puppy! I wanted to tell you before I left for Lisbon, but Ashta made mincemeat of that attempt. On my way back here in that awful car I decided to try to persuade you to marry me instead of Moreston—as long as you promised never to see him again."

"M-m-marry me?"

"Yes, Tara! I don't want you to stay here to clean the damn place! I want you to marry me and stay forever!" He put the lamp down on a stair and took her by the shoulders. "Didn't I say we had to make some arrangements? What other arrangement could there possibly be? What did you think I meant?"

"Well," she began, feeling dazed, "I—I wasn't sure what you meant and I was hoping— But then I thought, well, maybe you meant something like... like an affair, or—"

"You were hoping?"

"Oh, yes, Jorge. I was hoping you would want to marry me!"

"Then you will?"

"Oh, yes!"

"Then. . . you are in love with me?"

"Yes. Completely. Absolutely. Entirely!"

They smiled at each other in the semidarkness. Cobwebs overhead, the trunk, everything else was forgotten.

"I've never been so happy!" His hands tightened on her shoulders.

"Neither have I."

"Soon?"

"In two weeks!" she laughed up at him.

He put his hands on either side of her face and kissed her so that she was deliciously warm in the damp chilliness of the cellar. When her arms wound around his muscular back he folded her closer, holding her as though she was infinitely precious, as though he would never let her out of his arms again. His mouth captured hers with all the fierce possessiveness of a pirate staking a claim. Her lips parted under his assault on her senses, and their bodies molded together, seemingly designed by a master hand for that express purpose. Intense passion, the white fire of love, flared uninhibited and all consuming between them.

Eventually they made it to the upstairs hall, where they were found by the *contessa*, Ricco, Ashta and Emilio.

"Where have you been?" Ricco demanded.

"We have all been looking high and low for you!" exclaimed Ernesta.

"Not low enough," Jorge grinned, his arm around Tara's waist. "We were in the cellar."

"Ahh!" said Emilio, a glimmer of a smile in his eyes. "Whatever were you doing in the cellar?"

"As a matter of fact, I was proposing!"

"In the cellar?" the *contessa* repeated, aghast. "Good gracious, dear boy, I cannot think you did a proper job of it in the cellar!"

"If you mean did I go down on my knees, no, I didn't. It was a little dirty for that."

"Whatever have you done to Tara, Jorge? Just look at her blouse!" Ernesta waved the papers she was holding toward Tara's offending blouse, which was now sporting a greasy stain much the same as the one on Jorge's shirt.

Jorge looked down at Tara's blouse, and the rise and fall of her breast beneath it with a faint smile on his lips. "We, er, believe in sharing everything, even axle grease," Jorge explained gravely. "But it's allowed. We're engaged!"

"If you think that surprises me, it does *not*! I knew it would happen given a little time. I did not think you invited me to chaperon on a whim!" Ernesta's sternness melted and she cried gaily, "Congratulations!"

"You are a lucky man, Dom Valente, to become betrothed to Tara!" Ricco enthused, "and to gain possession of the *quinta* all in one day! My heart rejoices for you both!" A mixture of happiness and relief shone from his handsome dark eyes.

"Oh, yes, the *quinta*!" Ernesta exclaimed. "You were in such a hurry to get to Tara, Jorge, that you forgot to sign the papers. Here they are! Shall we go into the *sala* and do this properly?"

"Oh, yes, let's!" agreed Tara. "Do hurry and sign them, Jorge, before anything else happens!"

"An excellent idea!" He chuckled with her.

Everyone converged on the *sala* door at once. Ashta pulled Ricco back so that the *contessa* could sail ahead. Once the deed was spread out on the table and Emilio had procured a pen, Tara leaned over Jorge's shoulder to watch, holding her breath to steady herself, trying in vain to control her happiness. Ashta beamed from across the table. After Jorge had added his final flowing signature there was a concerted sigh of relief.

"I recommend a bottle of champagne, sir." Emilio was the first to speak. "I believe dual celebrations are in order? I took it upon myself to order in a supply of Dom Pérignon, and it's a very good year!"

"By all means, bring in the champagne!" Jorge looked up at Tara and smiled into her smoky shimmering eyes. Then he added in an undertone, "He told me if I fired him he'd go to work for you. And as we'll shortly be old married folk there's really no point in shuffling him around, is there?"

Tara's laugh rang out, and Ashta, as though she'd understood every word of his low murmur, laughed with her.

"Did I miss something?" Ernesta asked.

"I believe you were meant to miss it, *contessa*." Ricco put in.

Emilio had no sooner popped the cork on the first bottle then suddenly there came a tremendous commotion from the hall. Everyone turned and stared at the *sala* door, but no one took a step to find out what it was, not even Emilio. They all remained rooted to the spot. It sounded as though a hundred people, at the very least, had invaded Minha Casa!

"Ahh!" Jorge stood up with a knowing look on his face. He took Tara once more in his arms. "I believe I hear the sainted voice of my mother," he said dryly. Listening again, he added, "And, it would appear, my father also! And, good Lord, Juana and José! My sister and brother," he explained, as a look of horror swept across Tara's face. "Don't worry, *querida minha*. . . . But who are all the others?"

A rising tide of excited babble seeped through the *sala* door.

"Oh, no! My mom and dad are out there, too! What possessed them? Will we have enough bedrooms for everyone? There's someone else out there, too. Oh, Jorge, my blouse! I don't have any shoes! How can I meet your parents without shoes?" she cried. The Duque de Silves's formidable visage swam before her eyes. Then she recognized the high-pitched mystery voice. "It's Mr. Pillaring!" she added in a shocked whisper.

"Who?" Jorge's arms tightened almost painfully. "If it's another suitor, Tara, he's out on his ear!"

"M-my publisher!" She looked up at him, aghast.

A tide of laughter swept through Jorge, and he threw back his head to roar most unsympathetically.

"Oh, Jorge! How can you laugh at a time like this?"

He bent his head down so that only she could hear. "Because I love you, mermaid, and because you look so beautifully disheveled, and because Emilio was more than right when he said never a dull moment! Kiss me quickly, *querida*. It's the last chance we will have for quite some time!''

Tara looked speechlessly up at him. One moment she was distraught, the next breathless, for the look in his glittering black eyes sent stars shooting through her bloodstream, blotting out all else.

Midnight magic. His spell was complete. His hands, very sure and strong, lifted her right off the ground as he bent his curly black head to kiss her. They neither saw nor heard the door of the *sala* burst open. They were completely oblivious to the whole row of popping eyes and gaping mouths.

''My w-word!'' William Pillaring stuttered.

''I knew we should come!'' Nona Valente and Lillian Lownes cried in unison, then looked at each other and laughed.

''I had a *feeling*!'' added Mrs. Lownes.

''So did I!'' exclaimed the *duquesa*.

''My son, let the dear girl breathe!'' expostulated the Duque de Valente de Silves.

''What the devil?'' came from Matthew Lownes.

''They are to be married,'' the *contessa* announced, smiling graciously at everyone. ''And you are all just in time for champagne!''

What readers say about SUPERROMANCE

SUPERROMANCE

Longer, exciting, sensuous and dramatic!

Fascinating love stories that will hold
you in their magical spell till the last page
is turned!

Now's your chance to discover the earlier
books in this exciting series. Choose from
the great selection on the following page!